A New

Betty Firth grew up in rural West Yorkshire in the UK, right in the heart of Brontë country... and she's still there. After graduating from Durham University with a degree in English Literature, she dallied with living in cities including London, Nottingham and Cambridge, but eventually came back with her own romantic hero in tow to her beloved Dales. Betty Firth also writes romantic comedies under the pen name Mary Jayne Baker and Lisa Swift, and wrote *Edie's Home for Strays* as Gracie Taylor.

Betty Firth

A New Home in the Dales

hera

First published in the United Kingdom in 2023 by

Hera Books
Unit 9 (Canelo), 5th Floor
Cargo Works, 1–2 Hatfields
London SE1 9PG
United Kingdom

A CIP catalogue record for this book is available from the British Library.

Print ISBN 978 1 80436 190 0
Ebook ISBN 978 1 80436 189 4

This book is a work of fiction. Names, characters, businesses, organizations, places and events are either the product of the author's imagination or are used fictitiously. Any resemblance to actual persons, living or dead, events or locales is entirely coincidental.

Look for more great books at www.herabooks.com

Printed and bound in Great Britain by Clays Ltd, Elcograf S.p.A.

1

This book is dedicated to two former editors of The Yorkshire Dalesman *magazine: Adrian Braddy, who first suggested to me the premise of this book, and the late WR 'Bill' Mitchell, whose wonderful memories of his early days as a cub reporter and interviews with Dalesfolk of the past provided much of the inspiration for this story.*

Dialect glossary

Afore = before
Allus = always
Any road = anyhow
Aye = yes
Badly = ill
Bairn = child
Beck = stream
Bonny = pretty
A brew = pot/cup of tea
Canny = sensible
Capped = pleased
Clout = a slap (or a cloth/item of clothing)
Dale = valley
Favver = father
Fell = hill or mountain
Fettle = to fix or put in order
Flayed = afraid
Flit = move house
Frame thissen = get to work; get on with it
Gang = go
Grand = excellent
Gruver = old term for a lead miner
Lad = boy/man
Happen = perhaps; possibly
Herssen = herself
Hissen = himself
Laiking = playing

Lass = girl/woman
Lish = nimble, strong
Mam = mother
Mardy = grumpy
Missen = myself
Mourngy = sulky or miserable
Mun = must
Nay = no
Nithered = feeling the cold
Nobbut = nothing but; only
Nowt = nothing
Oss = horse
Owd = old
Owt = anything
Shippon = cattle shed
Sin = since
Sithee = goodbye/look here
Snicket = a small path or alley between buildings
Summat = something
Swadi = Swaledale sheep
T' = the
Tha/thee = you
Thi/thy = your
Thine = yours
Think on = watch what you're doing; be careful
Thissen = yourself
Thrang = busy
Tup = stud ram
Tyke = someone from Yorkshire
Us = our
Yon = yonder/over there
Yow = ewe

Chapter 1

October 1940

Bobby Bancroft tried to shut out the sound of Billy Ternent and his dance orchestra playing *Music While You Work* as she concentrated on the story she was typing.

Don would insist on having the wireless on. After all, he said, you never knew when there might be an important announcement. If Tony or Jem, the younger reporters, tried to object to the noise – which they did, several times a day – he pulled rank on them as deputy editor. If the war ended this afternoon, did the editorial staff of the *Bradford Courier* really want to be the last to know? They were reporters, weren't they? They were supposed to have their fingers on the pulse of the nation – or as much of the nation as existed within the boundaries of the newspaper's circulation area.

But the war wasn't going to end this afternoon, and it vexed Bobby no end to have the chirpy fairground jingle of 'Don't Dilly Dally On The Way' or 'Sweet Georgia Brown' getting into her head and messing with the clack-clack rhythm of her fingers hitting the keys of her Remington typewriter. She didn't dare to complain though, lest Don tell tales on her to Mr Clarke, the *Courier*'s grumpy editor. Old Clarky, as they liked to call him when there was no chance of him hearing them, had no idea that Tony sometimes let her write his copy for him while he was out 'chasing down a story' (which seemed to be code for taking his girl to the pictures on the newspaper's time). All right, it was only the occasional report on a WVS cake sale or

I

something else Tony would describe in a derisive tone as 'girl stuff', and yes, it carried Tony's byline and not hers, but it was real reporting work. When Bobby held the printed newspaper in her hands and saw her words, right there in black and white for all the world to see – or a sizeable portion of Bradford, at any rate – she felt a surge of pride unmatched by anything she'd achieved so far in her twenty-three years on the planet.

Tony wasn't at the pictures today. He was idling back in his chair with his feet up on his desk, sucking on a Capstan with his eyes blissfully closed. There was no joy like the joy of knowing other people were doing the work you were being paid to do.

Eventually, he finished his cigarette, sighed deeply, and opened his eyes.

'Do we have to have this racket on?' he asked Don for the umpteenth time that morning, jerking his head towards the wireless.

Bobby tried to ignore them, focusing her attention on the page of Pitman's shorthand she was referring to as she typed her notes up into a story.

'It helps me think,' Don said, not looking up from the galley proofs he was checking.

'Well it doesn't help me think,' Tony said. 'It gets right on my nerves.'

'You don't need to think, you lazy loafer. You never do any work. Why don't you write that piece for tomorrow's edition instead of making Bobby do it?'

'It's all right, Don,' she chimed in quickly. 'I like doing it.'

'That's as may be, but it's not your job. It's his,' Don said, jerking a thumb at Tony. 'You're paid to type, not to write.'

'I can do both. I do a good job, don't I?'

'Aye, not bad,' Don agreed grudgingly. 'Better than Tony. Doesn't change the fact he's drawing a salary he doesn't earn. He'll be for it if Clarky gets wise.'

'I let Bobby give me a helping hand out of patriotic duty, if you must know,' Tony said loftily.

Don sighed and put down his blue pencil. 'All right, go on. What's the gag, Tony?'

'You know I can only write longhand. I get through twice as much paper as you and Jem.' He adopted a superior expression. 'Is that sort of waste any way to win a war, I ask you? I'm merely preserving our precious paper rations – and, by the way, probably saving this place a fortune into the bargain. I should get a pay rise for being so public-spirited.'

Bobby couldn't help laughing. Tony relied far too much on his cheeky chappy demeanour to get him out of trouble, but it was rather fun. Don, however, didn't join in.

'Oh, war, war, war,' he said, giving the proofs he was checking a disgusted look. 'Tell you what, I remember the days when we got proper stories at this place. Murders and sex crimes and things; really juicy stuff. Now what's the old rag full of? Church whist drives to buy comforts for the troops. Girl Guide tableaux in aid of our men who are prisoners overseas. Mothers' Union bazaars for the Red Cross. "Patriotic" stuff to "boost morale", whatever that means. Nothing but propaganda and mindless, tedious drivel, as if there isn't enough of that in the damn cinemas.'

'We still report on other issues,' Bobby said. 'There are two murders and a housebreaking in this week.'

'In the old days we'd have twice that many. Not to mention that Clarky's banned me from giving anything negative front page space, unless it's war news.' He leafed through the pages. 'Look at all this nonsense. Blackout times, lists of Spitfire Fund subscribers, food shortages... We can't even tell people if the sun's going to shine this weekend in case Hitler happens to be ambling down Ivegate and stops to pick up a copy of the *Courier* to see if it'll be good weather for his bombers. I nearly fell asleep checking the proofs for this week's edition.'

'Come on, it's not all that bad.'

'"A Bingley merchant has been fined for selling eggs at above the legal maximum"; Don read from his proof. '"William

R. Longbottom was reported to the Ministry of Food for selling eggs at two shillings sevenpence a dozen, instead of the maximum of two shillings sixpence. Mr Longbottom has been ordered to pay a fine of two pounds." How utterly, utterly thrilling. Hollywood'll probably want to make a film of it. Roy Rogers plays William R. Longbottom in *The Great Egg-scapade*, with Trigger as his cockerel.'

'There's no need to be sarcastic, Don,' Bobby said. 'I wrote that bit.'

'Well. We've a nerve calling this sort of thing news and charging people a penny a go to read it, that's what I think.'

Tony shrugged. 'It'll be over by Christmas. Then things can go back to how they were before.'

'Oh Lord, I hope you're right,' Bobby said fervently, reaching up to smooth the red-chestnut hair she'd pushed hastily into a crocheted snood before work that morning. 'I look a complete fright from washing my hair with soap flakes and castor oil. They dry it out like nobody's business. I'm dying to get my hands on a proper bottle of shampoo, but there's been none in the shops for ages.'

Tony shook his head. 'Women. Always thinking about your looks. Why can't you ever think of anything important?'

'Such as what?'

'Such as onions.' His eyes took on a faraway expression. 'I never did appreciate onions when I had them. You know, if I could get one now – if you put it right in front of me and said, "there you go, Tony, it's all yours" – I'd bite straight into it. No word of a lie, I'd eat it raw and cry onion-flavoured tears of joy while I did it.'

Bobby laughed. 'I'm glad it isn't me who has to kiss you then.'

'Chance'd be a fine thing, eh?' Tony said with a grin, winking at her.

Don was ignoring them, still staring glumly at his proofs.

'Just one bomb, that's all I want,' he said, clasping his hands in earnest supplication. 'A nice, meaty blitz to go on the front page: is that really too much to ask? You know, they told us it'd be raining bombs around here at the start of the war. We had one night back in the summer, then the Luftwaffe decided we weren't worth the trouble. I'm sure Göring did it just to spite me.'

Don made a joke of it, but there'd been nothing funny about that night in late August when German bombs had destroyed Lingard's department store and wreaked havoc in the centre of town. It was the first time Bobby had felt the war was a real thing that was actually happening; a thing that could hurt them here in their homes, be they ever so far away from the fighting.

She gave up on trying to write the piece Tony had assigned her about a vegetable-growing competition in Shipley and shook her head at Don.

'You don't mean that,' she said. 'You wouldn't wish more raids on Bradford just for a front page.'

'Wouldn't I though?'

'We wouldn't be allowed to put it on the front page anyhow,' Tony said. 'When our lot bomb theirs, it goes on the front page. When they bomb us, it's two lines on page six – that's unless we can say we shot down a few of their bombers so we can claim it as a victory. I suppose the Jerries are getting the same sort of treatment at their side. Do we even know who's winning?'

'We are, aren't we?' Bobby said.

Don laughed. 'You of all people should know not to believe everything you read in the papers, love.'

She smiled. 'I know you're not as cynical about the war as you like to pretend, Don. You gave ten bob to the WVS lady who came round collecting for the Spitfire Fund last week. Don't try to deny it; I saw you.'

Tony raised an eyebrow. 'Is that right, Donald?'

Bobby nodded. 'He told her he didn't have any change, but I was looking out of the window and I saw him slip her a note after he followed her out.'

'Shameless slander. I've never had ten bob to spare in my life. I didn't get into the newspaper business to make money.' Don rubbed his eyes and picked his pencil up again. 'Put the kettle on, can you, sweetness? I'm gasping here.'

Don only ever called her 'sweetness' when he wanted a cup of tea. Bobby wasn't sure why he bothered being nice to her. As typist, secretary and general office factotum, it was part of her job to make the tea, as well as light the fire, fill the inkwells, fetch copy paper, wash up cups, open the post, and anything else her male colleagues thought was beneath them. She did it all uncomplainingly, in the hope of better things to come.

'There's a good girl,' Don said absently as she stood up to stoke the fire.

After she'd filled the kettle at the dirty old sink and put it on to boil, Bobby went to stand at the window, looking out at the grey-brown city wearing its customary weekday coat of smog.

Tony had started complaining about the wireless again.

'At least let's have the Forces Programme,' he said to Don pleadingly. 'There might actually be something on that worth listening to.'

'I like the Home Service,' Don muttered as he made a mark on the proofs with his pencil. 'Anyhow, it'll be the same at this time of day. It's *Music While You Work* on both.'

'Then turn it off so we can hear ourselves think.'

Don opened his mouth to deliver a retort, and Bobby jumped in to change the subject before the hourly argument started up again.

'Where's Jem today?' she asked. Their seventeen-year-old cub reporter hadn't been in the office when she'd arrived at work that morning.

'Out covering a council meeting or something,' Don said vaguely. 'I told him to fetch us some pie and peas on his way back. Save you a trip.' Fetching the reporters' lunches was another of Bobby's many jobs around the office.

The yellow smog outside looked suffocating. The silhouettes of huge mill chimneys dotted the skyline, belching the evil stuff out in spades.

Bobby's mind wandered back to before the war, when every morning the mill buzzers would sound, summoning people to work. Each mill had its own distinct sound – they could still be heard every once in a while, although now they were used only to alert people to the presence of enemy aircraft. Bobby's mother, father and both her brothers had been slaves to those buzzers, rising every day with unquestioning obedience to work long days for low pay. But it wouldn't happen to her. She'd sworn that many years ago when she was still a child. She was going to be a journalist, like her hero Dorothy Lawrence, who'd posed as a soldier in the last war and actually served in the trenches before her true identity was discovered. Bobby Bancroft was going to make the news.

That hadn't happened yet, but still, she was here, even if she was only the typist. And she had made some news, even if it was WI jumble sales rather than daring exposés of life on the front lines. Even if it had Tony's name on it, it was still her news. She just needed to keep her focus, wait for her chance, and one day Fate would surely make it happen for her.

Bobby breathed in deeply, relishing that wonderful aroma of the newsroom: the perfume of the printer's ink; the flaking yellow paper of the archives; the comforting smell of over-brewed tea leaves mingling with smoky, smouldering coal and the fug of Don's favourite Tom Long pipe tobacco.

'I wish I was out there with Jem,' she said.

Tony frowned. 'With the boy? What for?'

'I wish I was out getting stories, I mean. Being a newspaperman.'

Don was stuffing his pipe. He gave a hoarse laugh.

'I hate to tell you this, Bobby, but you're missing one vital ingredient.'

Bobby had been embarrassed by this sort of ribald barrack room humour when she'd first started working here, but she was used to it now. You quickly grew accustomed to how men spoke in their own spaces when you were the only girl.

'You know what I mean,' she said, turning to him. 'Doing what you two do. That's what I want.'

'You want to spend your life writing up council meetings and nodding off during diabolical amateur dramatics perform-ances?' Tony shook his head. 'You're dafter than you look, Bobby. Stick to making the tea, if you know what's good for you, and wait for the day some poor deluded fool decides to make an honest woman of you. You're not a bad-looking girl, even if you are getting on a bit. Some man's bound to be mug enough to take you on.'

Usually Bobby responded in kind to Tony's teasing, but she didn't have the heart for it today. She turned away and started spooning the last of their Althams Tea – 'the tea that gives more cups to the ration!' – into the chipped yellow teapot. She was sure it gave exactly the same number of cups to the ration as any other brand, but Althams was one of their advertisers, so Mr Clarke insisted they use it.

Her colleagues never could understand why the jobs they took for granted would be a dream for her. Tony's attitude, in particular, irked her. After three of his predecessors had gone off in quick succession to army, navy and merchant navy respect-ively, Tony had got his job on the paper primarily because he had asthma and couldn't be called up. Tony Scott was a bad speller, a mediocre writer, he refused to learn shorthand, and he had absolutely no nose for a story – not to mention that he spent half of his working day playing truant so he could spend time with Flo, the ATS girl he was in love with. He had no idea how lucky he was, and Bobby knew she'd never be able to make him see it from her point of view.

It wasn't only Tony who couldn't understand her ambition to make the news – friends and family were equally puzzled. Most of the girls she'd been friends with at school were married and settled now, content in homes of their own as they tended to husbands and babies. Those whose husbands earned a good wage devoted themselves entirely to their duties as wives, while those in more straitened circumstances worked shifts in the textile mills or took in washing, as Bobby's sister-in-law Sarah did. All, however, felt that they had succeeded in life. They had gained the status afforded to married women and mothers, and it was incomprehensible to them that Bobby would rather have a career than a husband. Men aspired to have careers. Women aspired to have homes, husbands, children. But while her old friends might look askance at her for her determination to remain single and make something of herself in the world of newspapers, Bobby knew, as surely as she knew her own name, that she wanted more than society had dictated was appropriate to her sex.

Chapter 2

Bobby made the tea, then sat back down to concentrate on her – or really, Tony's – story. But she'd no sooner put fingers to keys when someone banged the door knocker outside.

'Jem's back early,' Tony observed.

'Jem would just walk in. It must be someone else.' Bobby got up to let whoever it was inside.

On the doorstep, she found a large brown mackintosh with a trilby perched on top. She presumed the mackintosh contained a human being somewhere among its tweed folds, although very little of them was actually visible.

'Reg Atherton,' it said, in a voice that sounded more like a growl.

'Excuse me?'

'Reg Atherton. Here to see Pete Clarke.' The folds of the haunted mackintosh parted slightly, revealing a nut-brown, weather-beaten face. 'It's all right, lass. He knows me of old.'

'Oh.' Bobby hovered uncertainly. The editor generally kept to his office, and any visitors were dealt with by the staff. Mr Clarke didn't like to be bothered by trivialities while he was working – in fact, he didn't like to be bothered by anything. He could get very cross if he was disturbed for something he deemed unworthy of the interruption.

'Look, we're old friends,' the mackintosh said, sounding impatient. 'Let us in, can you? I'm hoarser than a toad in this damned fog.'

'I suppose that will be all right,' she said cautiously. 'Um, follow me.'

Reg followed her inside. Once he was in the newsroom, he shed his voluminous mackintosh and hung it on a coat peg with his hat and gas mask box. Bobby noticed that he walked with a stick, leaning his weight heavily on it. His lame left leg trailed uselessly after his right whenever he took a step.

Who was he? And more importantly, *what* was he? He didn't look like one of their readers. He didn't look like a resident of the city at all, in fact. If Bobby had to guess at the man's job, she would assume he was perhaps a farmer, or some other country profession – except manual labour was surely impossible, since the man was a cripple. His woollen trousers were worn, patched and none too clean, his waistcoat shabby and ill-fitting, and there was a distinct smell of dog about him. She couldn't imagine what he wanted with the newspaper, or why he had to speak to Mr Clarke – or indeed, how her boss would ever have come to be friends with such a person. Yet Bobby couldn't help feeling intrigued by this new individual, so unlike their usual visitors, and so incongruous here in the office beside Don and Tony in their smart suits – if rather rumpled from a morning's loafing, in Tony's case.

Don looked up from his proofs and took his pipe from his mouth. 'Morning, Reg.'

So the man wasn't a stranger to Don either. Bobby resolved to wheedle some information from him as soon as Reg Atherton was out of earshot.

'Good to see you, Don,' Reg said, shaking the younger man's hand. 'The old feller in, is he?'

'Aye, he's in his office. Bobby can show you up.'

Bobby hesitated. 'Do you think that's all right?' she asked. 'He told me he didn't want to be disturbed for anything that wasn't urgent.'

'Oh, he'll want to see old Reg,' Don said, waving a hand breezily. Bobby felt this casual attitude was all very well when Don wasn't the one showing Reg up. Mr Clarke was known for his blazing rages, and Don was as afraid of him as any of them when he was the one likely to be in the line of fire.

She beckoned Reg to follow her and led him up the stairs to the second floor, where Mr Clarke's office was located. It took a little while for Reg to navigate the bare stone steps with his stick, but Bobby could sense he'd be offended if she offered help.

'What?' a clipped, irritated voice snapped in response to her knock. She opened the door a fraction.

Her boss's face was dark as he regarded her. He had a page of copy in front of him, over which hovered his dreaded black pencil. No schoolmaster's scrawl could evoke more terror in his young charges than the marks made by Peter Clarke's subbing pencil.

'You'd better not be interrupting me for anything less than Adolf Hitler's personal surrender,' he growled.

'Um, no.' Bobby forced herself not to take a step back, where she'd be out of range of his glare. 'I've got someone to see you, Mr Clarke. A Reg Atherton. He seemed to think… that is, Don said it would be all right.'

Mr Clarke's face cleared. For the first time ever, she saw him actually smile.

'Oh, it's Reg, is it?' he said, almost brightly. 'In that case, show him in.'

She turned to Reg and waved him into the office. He approached Mr Clarke and pumped his hand heartily.

'Well, old lad, it's been too long,' Reg said.

'It certainly has. What brings you all the way out here from the sticks? I thought Mary must've stopped letting you out.'

'Business.' Reg looked glum. 'I need a favour, Nobby.'

Mr Clarke glanced at Bobby, who was still hovering by the door. 'You can go, Miss Bancroft. I'm sure you must have typing to do.'

'Yes. Sorry.'

She went back downstairs, disappointed not to have found out more about their mysterious visitor. She could feel her story nose twitching. Whatever the boys said about it being no work for a woman, she knew she had a journalist's soul, and Reg Atherton had got it all stirred up.

'What did he want?' Tony asked her.

'I don't know. He mentioned a favour, but Clarky sent me away before I could find out any more.'

'Do you know who he is, Don?'

'Army pal of Clarky's,' Don told him without looking up. 'You know, the last lot. They were in France together.'

'It's a crime how people exploit these old army friendships,' Tony said, a sanctimonious expression worthy of a choirboy appearing on his face.

Don finished marking up his proofs, adding a flourish to his last correction by way of celebration. 'There we are, ready to go back to the comp room. Eight pages of sheer rubbish. I wouldn't wrap my chips in this edition, let alone read it.'

'Ah, now there's an idea. I could do with some grub.' Tony picked up a pile of unsold copies of last week's *Bradford Courier* and tucked them under his arm. 'I'm going down the chip hole with this lot. That ought to be worth a penn'orth of chips and scraps to them.'

Don shook his head. 'Clarky says he wants all unsold copies to be given to the Wolf Cubs for salvage when they come collecting. He'll go spare if he knows you've been swapping them for chips on the sly.'

'Well he doesn't know, Donald, and what he doesn't know won't hurt him,' Tony said, tapping the side of his nose. 'Besides, I'm starving. It'll be two hours before the lad gets back with our pie and peas.'

'You're a greedy, lazy, good-for-nothing young libertine, Anthony Scott, and I for one hope you choke to death on a fishbone.'

'Just for that, you can't have a chip,' Tony announced with mock hauteur. 'I'll share them with Bobby instead. See you both in a little while.'

He left the office with his newspapers, whistling.

'He's destined to die on the gallows, that boy, you mark my words,' Don said when they were alone.

'Don, who is Reg?' Bobby asked. 'He doesn't look like he's from the city.'

'He's not, although he did live in town for a while. He lives out in some country hellhole now – Silverdale. You can imagine the sort of place: more sheep than people, rains three hundred and sixty-four days a year and the local pub stinks of manure.'

'You sound like you know it.'

'I do a little. That's the place our Sal was evacuated to last month: out in the Dales, round Settle way. But Reg used to be a journalist, back before he abandoned civilisation.'

Bobby raised an eyebrow. 'Him a journalist?'

Don smiled. 'If you really want to be one of us, love, you need to start by learning not to judge from appearances. Reg Atherton might not look the type, but he was a hell of a good reporter. Used to work for the *Leeds Mercury*.'

'He looks more like a farmer. Is he retired then?'

'Last time I saw him, he'd just launched some rag of his own. Rural affairs, that type of thing. Not a bad little magazine for what it is, but no future in it.' Don sucked the end of his blue pencil thoughtfully. 'He'll have lost his shirt on it, I suppose, and be touching up old Clarky for a loan. Pete Clarke talks tough, but Tony's right: he'll do anything for an old army buddy. Not surprising, really. Those chaps went through hell together for king and country.'

'Reg and Clarky did?'

Don looked at her over his glasses. 'I mean all of them. The men who were out there in the last war – and the boys. No more than bairns, a lot of them.' He shook his head slowly. 'Poor buggers. Drowning in mud and blood and brains, for death and bloody glory. Glory, pah! All that "Charge of the Light Brigade" flannel we lapped up in the nursery while we played at toy soldiers. There's no glory in death, Bobby; only oblivion. And now here we are at war again – different uniforms, same enemy.'

With a sudden movement, he slapped the desk with the flat of his hand. 'What a *waste* it all was! What a shameful, pointless waste.'

Bobby knew this mood of Don's. At thirty-seven, he was a few years shy of the age to have fought in the 1914–18 war, but he'd lost two older brothers – one who'd lied about his age, gunned down by the Germans months after his sixteenth birthday. Bobby, too, had lost an uncle – one of the Bradford Pals who'd been slaughtered in the massacre at the Somme – and had a father come back who'd never been right in his mind afterwards. There was a moment of sombre silence between them.

'What happened to Reg's leg?' she asked when it seemed appropriate to speak again. 'Was that a war wound?'

'That's right. He caught some shrapnel in the trenches. Rotten luck. Still, he came home. More than some did.'

They were interrupted by the sound of Reg's stick on the stairs, followed shortly by Reg himself as he came into the office with Mr Clarke. He took his mackintosh and hat from their peg and bundled himself up again, then turned to shake his old comrade's hand.

'Thanks, Nobby. You've been a great help.'

'Now don't get your hopes up too high,' Mr Clarke said. 'For that wage, it's unlikely you'll get much interest. There're so few lads around now that the ones there are can have their choice of jobs. Then no sooner have you got them trained up, they get their call-up and flit.'

'I know, I know. I can't afford to pay more until things pick up. I've not got a penny to scratch my arse with at the moment, Nobby, and that's a fact.' Reg gave him a hopeful look. 'You don't know of anyone yourself, do you? Some keen young lad straight out of school? I don't need owt special. If he can type and he's got a good nose for it, he'll do for me.'

Mr Clarke shook his head. 'Sorry, Reggie. I've had enough staffing problems of my own. But if I hear of anyone suitable, I'll let you know.'

'All right,' Reg said morosely. 'Sithee then, old lad. I'll stand you a pint when I'm next in town.'

Reg stomped out of the office on his good leg.

'Here.' Mr Clarke approached Bobby's desk and slapped a scribbled note down on it. 'Type this up and drop the copy off with the lino lads, can you? It's to go in the situations vacant for the next edition. No charge for it, if Edna asks.' Edna was the advertising manager, who had her own office in a little room above the chip shop.

Mr Clarke went back upstairs to his office after further grim instructions to disturb him for nothing less than an air raid or German invasion, and Bobby glanced at the advertisement copy on her desk.

> Junior reporter wanted for rural magazine. Non-negotiable salary of 12s. 6d. a week, bed and board included. Would suit youth not eligible for military service. TYPEWRITING EXPERIENCE AN ADVANTAGE. Write with experience, typing speed and age to The Editor, The Tyke Magazine, Moorside, Silverdale, Yorks.

She started typing it out, smiling to herself. It seemed that Fate had played her hand at last.

Chapter 3

The day was creeping to the edge of the dark as Bobby walked home from work that evening. Heavy black curtains or rect-angles of beaver board were starting to appear in windows as the hour of the blackout approached.

She'd finished Tony's vegetable competition story for him after typing up the small advertisement for Reg Atherton, then she'd taken the copy for both to the basement-dwelling linotype men to be typeset. But she'd held on to the scrawled note Mr Clarke had placed on her desk earlier, which she'd put carefully away in her purse.

The sun was sinking behind the rows of soot-blackened terraced houses when she arrived at the family home on Southampton Street, which she shared with her father and two of her three siblings. Her middle brother Raymond, who'd married young, lived a few streets away with his wife and two daughters – although he was currently off doing basic training after getting his army call-up three months ago.

Jake, the nineteen-year-old baby of the family, was in the yard in his overalls, crouching beside his pride and joy: his Triumph 6/1 motorcycle. It was a 1934 model that had sold badly, so Jake had been able to pick one up for a song – or so he said. Since her brother was notoriously naive about money matters, Bobby suspected that in reality he'd been overcharged.

Still, whatever the price, it made the boy happy. As soon as Jake came home from the mill, he'd don his overalls and spend whatever daylight hours remained tinkering with the thing. Bobby was never quite sure what he did to it, since it seemed to be exactly the same clattering, sputtering pile of tin as it always had been, but every night she found him out here under the dimmed streetlights, oil-stained and happy with a spanner in his hand, refusing to leave the machine until darkness finally forced him back into the house.

'Heyup, our Jake,' she greeted him genially, ruffling his hair. It was nice to feel she could take off her work manners and use her at-home voice again. Her mam, when she'd been alive, had advised Bobby the day she'd started her secretarial training at Pitman's College in Leeds that it did a girl from a mill family no harm to 'act a bit posh' – whether that was for the benefit of potential employers or potential husbands. The then fifteen-year-old Bobby had taken her mother's advice to heart, developing her workplace persona as a quiet, obedient, well-spoken young lady who ought to be taken seriously. But when she came home, her native Bradford accent was given free rein once again.

'Bob, geroff.' Jake shook his head impatiently to dislodge her hand, then smoothed his Brylcreemed hair back into its side parting. 'What're you messing my hair up for? I've got a date with Nessie Tate in an hour.'

'Then you'd better get inside and clean yourself up a bit, hadn't you? You look a right state, you greasy beggar.' She wiped her hand on his overalls, so the Brylcreem deposit he'd left there could join the rest of his grease stains.

'I'm doing it! I was just about to do it.' He brushed down his overalls and stood up. 'Why're you in a good mood? Did you get a pay rise or something?'

'What would it matter if I had? It'd only go down Dad's throat, same as the rest of our money.'

'Well, what are you happy for then?'

Bobby rested a finger on one side of her nose. 'Wouldn't you like to know? I just am, that's all.'

Humming to herself, she went inside the house.

Her dad was in the living room in his shirtsleeves, poking moodily at the plate of sausage and mash her twin sister Lilian

18

had made for his tea. The wireless set in its brown bakelite cabinet was switched on but it wasn't tuned, filling the room with an uncomfortable hiss.

'Nobbut breadcrumbs,' her dad muttered, jabbing one of the sausages. 'I thought I told your mother to stop buying this rubbish, Bobby.'

She winced at the reference to her mam, who'd been dead now these seven years. She knew Dad must be having one of his bad days when he forgot that.

His voice was already slurred. Bobby glanced at the glass of whisky on the table by his old horsehair chair, wondering what number it was. He could only have been home from the mill for an hour. He didn't seem able to hold it like he used to these days.

'It's all there is, Dad,' she said, not bothering to correct the slip about her mam. It would only upset him. 'It's the war. Butchers have to make the meat go further, so they mix the pork with more breadcrumbs. We're lucky to get sausages at all these days so you should really enjoy them while you can.'

She approached to plant a kiss on his balding crown, which he neither welcomed nor rebuffed.

'Huh. Enjoy them. They've a nerve calling 'em sausages. Bread in a skin is what they are.' He sawed the end off one and took a grudging bite. 'Hand it over then, lass.'

'Hand what over?'

'It's payday, isn't it?'

Of course; *that* he remembered. She sighed and took her wage packet from her handbag.

'I'm keeping twenty bob back for the housekeeping,' she told him.

'Don't talk daft. You don't need twenty bob for house-keeping. You can have fifteen.'

'It's my money.'

'And it's my house you're living in – don't you forget that. I can just about manage to keep a roof over all our heads, even if I can't do a right lot else these days.'

He sounded stern and sad, his tongue tripping over the words and his glassy eyes fighting a battle to stay in the present.

'Honestly, I need it, Dad,' Bobby said, in a gentler voice. 'For all of us. Things cost more now, because of the war.'

'Oh, sod the bloody war!' her dad roared, throwing his fork across the room. It bounced off the fender and came to rest on the hearth rug. 'I fought in the war to end all wars, did you know that? That's what those old buggers called it – *the war to end all wars*. They lied to us all, the bastards. And then… then they took our sausages away.'

It sounded like a joke, but Bobby knew her father was deadly serious. A little sob bubbled in his throat. He looked so pathetic, sitting there; so small and defeated and broken. She wished she knew of a way to comfort him that didn't come out of a bottle.

Her sister Lilian appeared from the kitchen. She shot a look at Bobby, who nodded towards the fork in front of the fireplace. Silently Lilian picked it up and took it to exchange for a clean one while Bobby counted out twelve shillings from her purse.

'Here you go,' she said, giving it to her father. 'Twelve for you, and I'll keep eighteen back for the housekeeping: you can't say fairer than that. I'm sorry about the sausages, Dad. I'll try to get better, but it's not easy at the moment.'

He'd withdrawn back into himself now. Lilian brought a clean fork from the kitchen, and she wrapped his fingers around it for him. Meek as a child, he started cutting up his food, his eyes fogging as they stared into the distance and into the past.

'I'll talk to you upstairs,' Bobby murmured to Lilian. Her sister nodded and left the room. Bobby tuned the wireless to the Forces Programme before she left her father to his meal, although she wasn't sure why. He was in his own world now. Whatever was playing, he'd never hear it.

In the bedroom she shared with her sister, Bobby found Lilian sitting in front of the mirror. She'd taken her hair down and was running glossy auburn curls through her fingers.

'I'm going to wear it in pinned ringlets for the dance on Friday, like Mrs de Winter has hers when she wears Rebecca's ballgown,' she announced. *Rebecca* – and how to look more like Joan Fontaine – was Lilian's current obsession. 'What do you think, Bobby? Will it suit me?'

Bobby smiled. 'Of course it will. Everything suits you.'

It was an undeniable fact that when the two sisters went out on the town with their increasingly smaller number of single girlfriends, it was Lil who drew every male gaze. The Bancroft girls weren't identical, but they were alike – in looks, at least. Both had the delicate features and subtle auburn colouring of their late mother. Yet Lilian had something her twin would never possess: an instinctive sense of style. While Bobby favoured fashions that were practical, even boyish, with her hair frequently pushed into a snood or up into a bun where it couldn't bother her while she worked, Lilian's pin curls, clothes and make-up were always immaculate. A combination of healthy natural curves and tightly laced corsets meant that when Lil moved, she didn't walk so much as shimmy. One thing they did have in common was that like Bobby, Lilian was committed to remaining single – for a little while, at least. In Lilian's case, however, this was motivated by her desire to have as much fun as possible before she settled rather than any commitment to a career.

'I need to talk to you about something.' Bobby sat cross-legged on the bed and took Reg's scribbled advertisement from her purse. 'Lil, you'll never guess what.'

'What?'

'Go on, try to guess.'

'Oh, I don't know. Gary Cooper walked into your office today and announced a deep, unquenchable *grande passion* for you.' Lilian worked as an usherette at The Majestic cinema, and consequently spent more of her time in Hollywood than she did in the real world.

'No, but nearly as good,' Bobby said. 'Here, look at this.'

She handed over Reg's advertisement copy. Lilian read it, her smooth white brow puckering as she pondered the words.

'I don't understand, Bobby,' she said at last. 'You don't mean you want to send in an application?'

'Of course I do. Why not? You know this is what I've always dreamed of. It has to be fate, that it landed in my lap like this.'

'I know you've always wanted to be a reporter, but they're after a boy, aren't they?'

'They don't say they are. It just says they want someone who can type. Well, sixty-five words per minute isn't to be sniffed at, is it? And I've got shorthand, too.'

'But this is… what even is this thing? A country magazine? I'll bet a million pounds it's nothing but photographs of cows' bottoms and lists of… oh, I don't know. The price of corn or something.'

'It isn't. I know what it is. Don at work had a copy of their first number that he gave me to keep.'

Lilian frowned. 'You didn't tell him you were going to apply, did you? If he tells that mardy editor of your yours, he might give you your cards for looking elsewhere.'

'I didn't tell him – not yet. I said I was interested in what sort of magazine it was and he gave it me. He wouldn't tell anyhow; we're friends.' Bobby took her copy of *The Tyke* from her handbag and put it down on the bed between them. It was a little thing, about six by eight inches in size and printed on thin paper, with twenty-eight pages of pictures and articles inside the covers. 'Here, take a look for yourself.'

'It's for farmers,' Lilian said dismissively as she turned the pages. 'What do you know about farming, our Bobby? Most of the grass you've seen in your life was poking out between cobblestones.'

'I can learn about it. How hard can it be? Anyhow, it's not all about farming. There are loads of articles, about folklore and history and nature and interesting Dales characters and… and all sorts. There's a lot of humour, too. Some of the articles are really quite witty, written sort of tongue-in-cheek. It'll be a challenge for me.'

'Twelve and six a week though! We barely get by on the thirty bob you get at the *Courier*. No one can live on twelve and six. It's a child's wage.'

'Yes, but it's bed and board included, and it'll mean training and experience. It's a step on the ladder, Lil, that's all. I can send half my wage packet home every week. There ought to be enough when you're not having to pay for my food and clothes and things.'

Lilian lowered her eyes. 'Whisky doesn't come cheap these days, Bobby. Not when he's having to go to the black market for it.'

'I know.' Bobby was silent for a moment. 'Is there no chance of getting him off the stuff?'

'After what he's seen, it doesn't seem fair to try.'

'I suppose not. I wouldn't want to be the one to tell him we've got nothing stronger than cocoa for him when he wakes up in the night screaming.'

'It's the only medicine that seems to work. He's not a cruel drunk, is he? A lot of men who went through what he went through... but he's never raised a hand to us, or to Mam when she was here. He's just... in his own world.'

'I know, Lil. But... I'm sorry, but I can't fix that.'

'I don't suppose anyone can, now,' Lilian said soberly. 'He'll miss you if you go, Bob.'

Bobby sighed. 'He'll not even notice. Not until payday.'

'All right, then I'll miss you.'

'Well, let's not put the cart before the horse. No sense fretting when I might not get the job. Anyhow, you'll be leaving too if you get accepted into the Wrens.' Bobby cast a wistful glance around the room they'd shared since childhood. 'It feels strange to grow up, doesn't it?'

Lilian was silent, examining the pattern on the threadbare olive carpet.

'What's going to happen to Dad, Bobby?' she said. 'I might be leaving to start training soon, and now you could be moving to the middle of nowhere. We have to worry about it, don't we? Our Jake can't take care of him. Besides, he'll be off too as soon as he's had his medical.'

'Alice next door will look in, I'm sure. Sarah will cook for him.' Sarah was their brother Raymond's wife. 'And I'll come home whenever I can, I promise. He's not so bad, most of the time. Not every day is like today.'

'But sometimes he is bad. I can't help feeling we're abandoning him.'

'What can we do? We have to live our own lives too. I can't stay here and stagnate when a chance like this lands in my lap, otherwise I'll spend the whole rest of my life regretting it.' Bobby seized her sister's hands. 'I've been waiting so long for my life to begin, Lil. This is my chance to get out there! To be hunting stories and making the news, like I always wanted.'

'Are these really the stories you want to be hunting?' Lilian freed her hands so she could flick through a few pages of *The Tyke*. 'A day in the life of a country parson. An essay on the habits of the moorhen. In praise of Yorkshire dialect. The history of some village's whittling tree, whatever that is. It's not exactly hard-hitting journalism, is it?'

'At this point, I'll take any stories I can get,' Bobby said fervently. 'All right, it's not exactly my dream job, but it's a foot on the ladder. My own byline. Everyone has to start somewhere.'

Lilian looked again at Reg's advertisement copy. 'But twelve and six a week! Who can live on that? It's hard not to feel it's a step backwards when you'd be cutting your wage by more than half.'

However, Bobby refused to let anything dampen her optimism. It had to be fate, didn't it, that the advertisement which held the key to her future had landed right on her desk? Reg Atherton may look like a gruff Yorkshire farmer, but he was really a ministering angel disguised in a shabby mackintosh.

'Twelve and six is only the beginning, Lil,' she said. 'If I can earn my stripes as a reporter, who knows where it might lead? This could be the first step towards a job on a national newspaper one day in the future.'

'Aren't you better off staying where you are if it's a paper you want to write for?' Lilian cast another scathing look at the magazine. 'This isn't news.'

'There are more opportunities for me at *The Tyke* than at the *Courier*. Clarky wouldn't let me write for the paper if I worked there for a hundred years. At least, not unless I can magically transform myself into a man.'

Lilian smiled. 'Like your hero – what's she called, the lady journalist who disguised herself as a soldier?'

Bobby smiled too. 'Dorothy Lawrence. Now there's an idea. I should have thought of trying drag sooner.'

Lilian leaned forward to hug her. 'If this is really what you want, then I'm behind you. Which isn't to say I think it's a good idea, but it's your life, little sister.'

'You know, you're only ten minutes older than me.'

'But oh so many, many years wiser.'

Bobby laughed. 'Thanks for listening, Lil. I knew you'd see it from my point of view eventually.'

'Do you really think you've got a chance of getting it though? They're obviously after a lad.'

'I don't know. But I have to try, don't I? I have to try *something*.'

Chapter 4

Jem dumped that morning's pile of post on Bobby's desk. 'Here you go.'

'Thanks, kid.' As their youngest reporter, Jem was always 'lad', 'kid' or 'the boy' and would probably remain 'lad', 'kid' or 'the boy' until someone younger joined the newspaper to inherit the title.

Dealing with the paper's correspondence was another of the many jobs Bobby was assigned because Don, Jem and Tony didn't want it, and usually she found it a tedious business. Most of the post they received for the readers' letters page these days was on the same general theme: the hardships of the war or nostalgic reflections on the happy days of plenty. No fewer than four of the letters she'd opened yesterday had contained a variation on 'An Ode to the Onion' as the scarcity of that once common vegetable continued. Bobby was sure Tony might be secretly responsible for one of them. Any letters that weren't complaining about food shortages seemed to take pains to point out every single spelling mistake and printing error that had slipped past Don's blue pencil. His proofreading had become increasingly sloppy in his bitterness about 'bloody war stuff' filling what he saw as his newspaper.

But this week, Bobby had scanned the post eagerly when it landed on her desk in the morning. Starting from the day after she'd sent her application to Reg Atherton for the junior reporter position at *The Tyke*, she'd sifted through the letters and packets hoping to see an envelope with her name on it. She had given her address as 'care of the *Bradford Courier*' so there'd be no chance of her father intercepting the letter. She could cross that bridge when she came to it.

Jem had picked up the top envelope and was squinting at it.

'R. Bancroft,' he said. 'Who's R. Bancroft?'

'I am, you barmpot.' She held out her hand for it.

'No you're not. You're called Bobby.' Jem was a nice boy, but he wasn't the brightest.

'Only for short. I'm called Roberta, if you really want to know, after my dad. Give it here, Jem.'

He handed it over, and she waited until he'd wandered back to the desk he shared with Tony before tearing it open.

> *Many thanks for sending your letter of application and a sample of your writing. Mr Reginald Atherton (editor, The Tyke) would like to hereby invite you to attend an interview at the magazine offices at Moorside, Silverdale, Tuesday week at three p.m....*

She only barely suppressed a squeal, covering her mouth with the letter. Don looked up from the story he was working on.

'What the hell was that noise?' he said in an irritated tone. 'You're not going hysterical, are you? The thing I always liked about you, Bobby, was that you weren't one of those squealing, squawking women. Bloody annoying to have them whimpering all over the place when you're trying to work.'

'I'm not going hysterical. It's... someone's sent in a good joke for the paper.'

'All right. Care to share it with the class, since it's such a source of hilarity?'

'It's, um, a bit blue for mixed company,' she said, indicating Jem with a sideways movement of her eyes. 'Don?'

'Hmm?' His attention had wandered back to his story.

'Are we playing darts this afternoon?'

'Tuesday, isn't it? Course we are.' He looked up. 'Why, what's it to you?'

'I wondered if I could have a word with you about something. Later, in the pub.'

'Have a word now, if you must. I don't like anything breaking my concentration when I'm trying to play darts.'

'No. Not here. I'd rather do it at the Swan, after—'

She bit her tongue. After he'd had a few pints, she'd been going to say. Don became much more sociable when he was half-cut, and, for all that he liked to play the part of a grumpy, cynical misanthrope in the office, she knew he secretly harboured a sort of brotherly fondness for her. It was for her sake and not Tony's, she suspected, that he'd never told tales about her secret contributions to the paper to Clarky. Of all her colleagues, Don was the only one she trusted enough to confide her secret in and ask for some advice.

'I'd just rather do it later,' she said.

'All right.' He looked surprised. 'You're not going to tell me this oh-so-hilarious blue joke, are you?'

'No. This is about… something else.'

–

Tuesday was the day the weekly newspaper was finished and ready for printing. Before the war, it had been put to bed on Wednesdays, ready to go on sale on Thursday morning, but now there was the additional step of sending a set of galley proofs to the Ministry of Information censor in Leeds, so sensitive stories could be redacted before printing. Bobby, whose job it was to package up the proofs and send them to the censor by express delivery, couldn't help reflecting with a wry smile on what the enemy would make of the *Courier* if they did get their hands on it, and if they'd be impressed by Mrs Olthwaite taking first prize in the Eccleshill Women's Institute's jam-making competition Thursday last.

Once the pages had been posted off to the censor, to be returned the following day with an official stamp and any changes marked in blue pencil, the editorial staff enjoyed the luxury of an unofficial few hours off. It had become a tradition that they would leave the office an hour earlier than usual and head to the White Swan pub across the road for a celebratory pint or three and a darts match against a handful of Local Defence Volunteers – or Home Guard, as they'd been rechristened by Mr Churchill over the summer – who congregated there before parade. Clarky, as strict as he generally was, turned a blind eye to this practice, presumably in the belief it helped keep up staff morale.

In the early days of her employment at the *Courier* – back in early spring before the invasion of France, when the war had still seemed so very far away – Bobby hadn't been invited to join the boys at the pub. She'd kept herself to herself in those days, quietly getting on with her work, but alert and observant to what was happening around her as she endeavoured to learn what made a newspaper office tick. Her colleagues, for their part, had regarded the woman in their midst with a wary detachment at first. They'd treated Bobby politely and watched their language for a short while until, after a couple of weeks, she'd become invisible enough for them to behave as they normally would around others of their own sex – almost as if she wasn't there.

It had been Tony who'd made the observation, one Tuesday in the office, that Bobby had a good arm when he'd noticed how she always got her crumpled waste paper into the basket on the first throw. He'd asked her to join them for darts that afternoon, and after acquitting herself well – for a girl, as Tony felt obliged to remind her in case she got ideas above her station – she'd been officially invited to join the *Courier*'s darts team. Now, nearly eight months later, the men at work accepted her if not quite as one of the boys then at least as one of them – a part of the place. Playing darts with the lads from the office made Tuesday Bobby's favourite day of the week.

It wasn't until after they'd given the old men in their ill-fitting khaki uniforms a good thrashing that evening and the staff of the *Courier* were sitting around their usual table with a pint of beer each — or a half, in Bobby's case — that she got a chance to speak to Don about what was on her mind.

Tony, in the seat next to her, was a little drunk, which tended to make him flirtatious. He slipped an arm around her shoulders.

'When are you going to find yourself a young man, Bobby?' he asked, in a slightly slurred voice that was louder than he probably realised.

'When young men stop getting on my nerves,' she said, shrugging the arm off her shoulders.

'The clock's ticking for you, you know. What are you now, twenty-three? Twenty-four?'

'You're not married and you're nearly thirty.'

'It's different for men. For a girl, twenty-three's practically an old maid. You're letting your prime slip away, love.'

'And with so many charming young bachelors in my circle too.' She let out a convincingly heartfelt sigh. 'Oh well, I suppose I'll just have to learn to cope.'

The arm appeared around her shoulders again. 'I'm only concerned for you, as a friend. You're a good, obliging girl, and not too upsetting to look at, but girls don't keep their looks forever. Shame to waste your sweetness on the desert air, that's what I say.' He gave her a slightly droopy wink. 'Get yourself wed, Bobby. Tell you what, if you like I'll even give you away.'

Bobby knew how to deal with this kind of thing. She'd won the liking and respect of her male colleagues by always giving as good as she got in exchanges like this. She smiled with false sweetness at Tony.

'Who did you have in mind for me, Tony?' she asked. 'You? Or perhaps Don? There's quite an age difference and his wife might be a little put out, but I'm sure we can come to an arrangement.'

Tony nodded to shy, solid Jem, quietly supping his pint opposite them. 'What about the kid? He hasn't got a girl yet. Have you, Jem?'

Jem spluttered on his pint, blushing red to the roots of his blond hair.

Bobby gave Tony a nudge. 'Oh, don't tease him. He's too young for that sort of thing.'

'Well, you ought to find yourself someone. It isn't right, a girl your age still single. A woman's place is in a good man's bed.'

Don tapped the arm that had snaked around Bobby's shoulders. 'All right, don't get lewd. Leave her alone now, Tony. You've had too much to drink.'

'Rubbish. I've only had four pints. The beer in this place is half water these days anyhow.' He gave Bobby a squeeze. 'You forgive me, don't you, Bob? You know it's all in fun.'

'I forgive you, Tony. In fact, I might even decide not to tell your Flo that you had your arm around me.'

This sobered him up a little. He glanced around the pub as if suddenly remembering his fiancée could have spies anywhere, withdrawing his arm from Bobby's shoulders.

'Go get us a round in if you want to make it up to her,' Don said. 'Take the kid with you.'

'I will. But only because I was going to anyhow, not because you told me to,' Tony said, moving from the first stage of drunkenness – loud and lecherous Tony – to the second stage: belligerent, sulky Tony. 'You're only my boss when we're at work, Don, not in the pub. Come on, Jem.'

'Thanks, Don,' Bobby said when they'd been left alone. 'I know he doesn't mean anything by it, but once he gets going, he won't let it lie.'

'When he's had a few drinks he can never tell when he's crossed the line with a girl. He's a dirty old man in the making, that lad.'

'I can look after myself though, you know.'

Don smiled. 'I believe you. Now come on, while they're gone: what was this mysterious thing you wanted to talk to me about?'

Bobby glanced at the bar, where Tony and Jem were queueing. There were quite a lot of Home Guard men waiting to be served as well, so they had a little while to talk about what she wanted to get off her chest.

'You can't tell the others, all right?'

'I never do. Well, what is it?'

'Don, I could really do with some advice. And some help, if you're willing.' She took the letter she'd received that morning and passed it to him to read.

He raised an eyebrow. 'This was addressed to you?'

'Yes. I sent in an application last week for that job Reg Atherton advertised.'

Don frowned at the letter for a moment. 'You bloody fool, Bobby.'

'Well, what can I do? There's never going to be a chance for me to write at the *Courier* – under my own byline and not Tony's, at any rate.' She met his eyes. 'I want to do this, Don. To do what you do. You know I'm capable of it.'

He was silent.

'You're a bright kid, and a damn good writer,' he said at last.

She smiled. 'For a girl. Go ahead, say it.'

'For anyone. But there's more to being a reporter than that, Bobby. A country reporter especially.'

'Like what?'

'The people you'll have to deal with if you get this job… You haven't spent much time in the country, have you?'

Like most city folk, Bobby occasionally went for walks around the rural areas that surrounded the city: Shipley Glen and the moors at Baildon. That was certainly the countryside, but it was close enough that it felt in many ways like an extension of her home town – a kind of urban park. It brought a sense of freedom, being out there in the wide open spaces where you weren't hemmed in by the dark, clustering buildings of Bradford, but there was also the reassuring sight of the mills in the distance to remind you that home was no more than a hop and a skip away. Bobby sensed these day trips to local pleasure grounds weren't what Don had in mind when he referred to 'the country'.

'Not really, no,' she said.

'My stepfather was a Wensleydale man. The Dalesfolk aren't like us, Bobby. They've got Norseman in their blood. For hundreds of years, they've had to work that isolated land in all weathers, in prosperity and poverty, until they became all but part of it. They're Chapel folk mostly, hard, solitary and austere, and they don't take to outsiders even to the third and fourth generation.' He paused as he let the picture he'd painted sink in. 'I wouldn't take Reg's reporter job for a hundred guineas a week, let alone twelve and six.'

'Are you saying the people there won't like me?'

'I'm saying they won't accept you. You're not one of them, and you're a woman into the bargain. A woman journalist is rare enough in the city, but you'd be a sideshow out there. You'll never get them to take you seriously.'

'Then why would Reg Atherton want to interview me at all?'

Don laughed. 'Have you not read this letter?'

'Of course I've read it. I read it at my desk this morning when you started accusing me of being hysterical.'

'Obviously not very carefully.' He pointed to the greeting at the top.

Dear Mr Bancroft…

Bobby stared at it. She had been so excited to get the letter, she'd skimmed over that part to the message below inviting her to come for an interview.

'They're expecting a man?' she said. 'But… I put my name on the letter I sent. My Sunday name, not Bobby.'

'Type it on your Remington, did you? With the weak A key?'

'Well, yes, I—' She stopped. 'Oh.'

'So Reg, whose eyes are probably none too sharp these days, has had an application from a Mr Robert Bancroft. He's going to get the surprise of his life when you walk in.'

'Oh,' she said again, in a quieter voice.

'I'm sorry, Bobby,' Don said gently. 'For what it's worth, I think you deserve a chance. I'll speak to Clarky if you want, see if he'd consider letting you handle some of the women's interest stuff for us. The *Post*'s got a couple of girls now, dealing with the sewing patterns and the Kitchen Front pages. I don't see why he shouldn't consider it when he knows what a good little worker you are.' Don pushed the letter back to her. 'But this… it's not for you.'

'No.' She frowned with determination. 'No. I won't be put off. I'm still going to go.'

'What? Bobby, don't be mad.'

'I can convince him, Don. If I show Reg what I can do, he has to consider it. He's desperate, isn't he? I'm a fast, precise typist, I know shorthand, and I'm a bloody good writer too. I don't see what being a man has got to do with anything.'

'It's got plenty to do with it when you're dealing with Dales farmers. They'll never take Reg's magazine seriously if he sends a girl out to talk to them – not just any girl; a townie as well.'

'I don't care. I'm going to do it.' She looked over at the bar, where Tony and Jem were finally being served, and lowered her voice. 'They'll be back in a moment. Look, will you help me? Please, Don.'

'You're really determined to do this? Throw your career at the *Courier* away for a pathetic twelve and six a week?'

'I have to do something.'

He sighed. 'All right. Because I've got a soft spot for you, Lord knows why… I'll cover for you to Clarky if you want to pretend you've got a headache or something and leave early next Tuesday. And I suppose I can write you a letter of recommendation, so Reg knows it was your work and not Tony's on all those pieces you wrote for the paper. Reg is a good bloke and I don't think he'd tell tales to Clarky – not that Tony isn't due a comeuppance, but it'd mean all of our necks for covering for him.'

She squeezed his arm. 'Thanks, Don. You're a pal.'

'Just don't go blubbering if you don't get it. And don't let Reg intimidate you either, or he'll lose respect for you.' He finished the last of his beer. 'Look him in the eye and remember what you're worth, girl or not. A damn sight more than twelve and six.'

'I will. I'll try.'

'I hope I don't end up regretting this,' he said in a low voice as Tony and Jem made their way back to the table with drinks. 'Good luck, Bobby. You're going to need it.'

Chapter 5

The following Tuesday, a little after noon, Bobby alighted from her train in Skipton and went to wait for the bus that would take her from there to Silverdale.

She hadn't liked lying to her workmates and felt uncomfortable about the excuse she'd given to Clarky on the telephone as to why she couldn't come to work that morning. Pleading an unspecified 'woman's problem' gave exactly the impression she was anxious to avoid: that her sex made her fundamentally less capable than her male colleagues. But she also knew the embarrassment it would cause the old man would guarantee her the time off that she needed with no questions asked. Don, as promised, had backed up her complaint, telling the editor she'd seemed off colour all the previous afternoon, and he'd also written her a letter of recommendation that was now stowed carefully away in her handbag.

She was really very fond of Don, who'd started to feel almost like an older brother in the eight months she'd been working at the *Courier*. He never tried to flirt with her in the way that Tony sometimes did when he was in his cups – in fact, Don was rather a sweetheart to women generally, despite his pretended cynicism. Of all her colleagues, he was the one who treated Bobby most like an equal – as long as she still made his tea, at any rate. Still, she felt he respected her as far as the differences in their sex and positions would allow him to. He was the only one she'd really miss if by some chance she actually managed to convince Reg Atherton she was what he and *The Tyke* needed.

Don's dire warnings still rang in her ear, reminding her of the far from warm welcome she might expect from the Dalesfolk, but she ignored it. She ignored everything except the feeling in her gut that told her this was her one chance to achieve her dream and she needed to seize it with both hands, twelve and six a week or not.

She smoothed down the checked tweed suit that Lilian had bought second-hand at the market on her behalf a couple of days earlier. Paired with her mam's pearls – which the girls kept carefully hidden from their father, who was liable to pawn anything of value he could get his hands on to buy more black-market Scotch – the costume made her look more like a middle-aged country schoolmistress than a reporter. However, it was smart and clean, and Bobby felt as close to confident as she could in it.

The orange-and-black-liveried Pennine bus she was waiting for chuntered to a stop in front of her. When the doors opened, Bobby mounted the step.

'One to Silverdale, please,' she said to the elderly driver.

'Nay, can't take thee there.'

She frowned. 'This is the Settle bus, isn't it? I understood I needed to catch this for Silverdale.'

'Aye, close as tha'll get,' the man muttered, not turning to face her. 'But I can't take thee there.'

She waited, but apparently that was all the information he was willing to volunteer.

'How close do you go?' she asked.

'Bull and Heifer pub. Some two mile from t' village.'

'Two miles! How will I get the rest of the way?'

'Most folk use their feet.' He finally looked at her, curling his lip at her smart tweed suit, pearls and brown leather court shoes. 'Or if tha's too fine to walk, happen the coal man'll take thee rest o' t' way for a consideration.'

'All right.' Bobby was starting to feel extremely nettled by the man's unhelpful attitude. 'In that case, what's the fare to the Bull and Heifer?'

'Ninepence.'

'Here you are.' Bobby paid the ninepence, took her ticket and went to sit beside a solid middle-aged lady in a headscarf with a poodle swaddled in a blanket on her lap. Bobby really hoped the bus driver's surly attitude wasn't a flavour of things to come.

She had been nervous when she'd set off from Bradford that morning, but excited too; even confident. It had felt as though she was vibrating with anticipation as she had carefully dressed herself in her new suit, pinned back her hair, tucked Don's letter of recommendation and the letter from Reg Atherton into her handbag, along with some samples of her work on the newspaper, and hopped on a tram bound for the railway station. But now, as she looked out at the gloomy autumn drizzle with the old dalesman's unfriendly demeanour still rankling, she felt her spirits becoming depressed.

She'd invested everything – all her future hopes, her dreams of becoming a journalist – in this single opportunity, convincing herself it must be Fate, finally stepping in to help her place her foot on that first rung of the ladder. But what if she was deceiving herself? She knew it was someone male Reg wanted, and his letter had made it clear he was expecting a man to arrive at his offices at three o'clock today. He might well slam the door in her face when he realised he'd been made a fool of. And worse, he might tell his old friend Peter Clarke of the fib Bobby had told that morning at work, which could, in turn, cost her the newspaper job. For all its frustrations it had a lot of good points, and the wage wasn't bad compared to what she could earn in the mills. She liked all of her colleagues, most of the time – she'd even grown attached to Tony, with his laziness and doomed get-rich-quick schemes. If there was a chance she could be throwing that away for a job she had no hope of getting…

After half an hour, the rickety bus creaked to a stop again and up climbed a man in a cloth cap and gaiters who must surely be a farmer.

'Now then, Fred,' he greeted one of his fellow travellers, who had shuffled up to make room for him. 'How do?'

'Aye, fair. Or fair to middling, any road.'

'How's yow I sold thee getting on? Did tha get her served wi' Mick Northrop's prize tup?'

'Aye, by Gaw. Come t' spring she'll be bellying like yon brokken wall o' thine,' said the other man, and they both laughed.

This might as well have been Greek for all that Bobby could understand of it. Suddenly she felt very far from home.

Strange new country flashed by outside the window. It was beautiful, yes, but it was a terrible kind of beauty. The heather-clad fells clustered dark and forbidding above them, garlanded with the ubiquitous drystone walls to prove that despite appearances, man and beast both had a presence here. Only the barest trace of civilisation could be detected in the form of an occasional isolated farmhouse and sometimes, rarely, a cluster of hardy stone buildings that formed a hamlet or small village. When Bobby thought of the noisy, bustling town she'd left only hours ago, with its tightly packed terraced houses and black mills spreading out as far as the eye could see, the Dales felt like another world. Even the dialect here made little sense to her, although she'd travelled barely twenty miles from her native turf.

Was she making a terrible mistake? Should she alight at the next stop, wait for a bus that could take her back to Skipton and forget all about her absurd attempt to become a country reporter?

Bobby felt something rough and wet against her fingers and glanced down. The little poodle had wriggled out of its blanket and decided to give her hand a bath.

'Oh!' she said when she took a closer look at the animal.

The woman who owned it turned to frown at her. 'What's matter wi' thee?'

'Sorry. I hadn't realised... I thought it was a little dog you had.' Now that she looked more closely, Bobby could see that what she'd thought was a poodle was actually a young sheep. It blinked big brown eyes at her, more fearless than Bobby had been led to believe its kind generally were. She'd seen plenty of untreated wool piled up outside the mills of her home town, but this was the first time she'd encountered some still attached to the animal. She'd never met a live sheep before. It seemed so... clean. So clean, and so alive.

'Nay, he's a Swadi-Cheviot hogg,' the woman said in a scathing tone, as if this should be obvious just from looking at the beast. Bobby had no idea what a Swadi-Cheviot hogg was. Some sort of pig, she would have assumed, but while her knowledge of farming was admittedly slim, she was certain this was definitely a sheep.

'Does he often go around by bus?' she asked.

'Aye, well, I've to get him to t' vet some road, haven't I? He's been badly wi' his legs these last two days,' the woman said. She spoke with that same resentful belligerence the bus driver had displayed. Were all Dales people like this? Don had described them as austere and unwelcoming to strangers, but Bobby hadn't expected them to be quite so unreasonably hostile as this.

'I didn't mean any offence,' Bobby said in a conciliatory tone. 'I was just a little surprised. I haven't travelled much in the country.' She gave the lamb's ears a tickle by way of an apology, which the little chap seemed to like, letting out a low bleat of appreciation. This seemed to appease the woman somewhat and she drew her lips back over a gummy mouth in what might have been an attempt at a smile, although it more closely resembled a grimace. This, Bobby assumed, was the friendliest treatment she was likely to receive today, so she smiled uncertainly back.

The journey to the Bull and Heifer pub from Skipton took close to an hour, the bus groaning and clattering down narrow, tortuous roads until Bobby felt quite sick. When she stood up to get off, the woman with the lamb stood also, cradling the little thing in her arms.

Bobby had grown rather attached to that lamb during the long and uncomfortable journey, taking comfort from the warm tongue that occasionally flicked out to embrace her fingers. On a bus full of strangers who felt entirely alien to her, the little licks had seemed like a friendly gesture, and Bobby had felt her subdued spirits start to rise slightly. She'd almost asked the farmer's wife – she assumed that's what the woman must be, with her hard, weather-lined face framed by a simple worsted headscarf – if the lamb had a name, but had stopped herself, thinking this was probably a foolish question. Farmers were unlikely to name their lambs, she assumed; they were only stock to them, after all. Instead, she gave him a name in her head – Donald, after her friend – and sent up a silent prayer that the vet, whoever he should be, would be able to heal the lamb of what ailed him.

Bobby stepped down from the bus at a crossroads, closely followed by the woman and lamb, and the driver clattered off.

She had no idea which way it was to the village. There were no signposts any more; not since they'd all been removed the previous summer to bamboozle any marauding Germans who might find their way to British shores.

Bobby glanced at the pub, wondering if this was where the mysterious coal man could be found. The Bull and Heifer wasn't much like Bobby's idea of a pub, appearing to be a stark, forbidding sort of place with little of warmth or welcome about it. It made her long for the cosy snug of the White Swan, where later on, her colleagues would gather without her for the weekly darts match against the Home Guard boys. Storm clouds rolled across the glowering sky and Bobby wished herself with Don, Jem and Tony, safe back at home.

'Excuse me for asking, but do you know which road leads to Silverdale?' she asked the woman with the lamb.

The woman turned to scrutinise her. 'What's tha wanting to go thear for?' she asked in a surprised tone – at least, Bobby thought there was a slight inflection that could denote surprise.

The Dales people seemed to betray little emotion in either their voices or expressions. It made them very hard to read.

Bobby wondered how big *The Tyke*'s offices were, and what sort of building they might be located in. It didn't seem to have occurred to this person that the magazine must be her destination, although there was surely no other reason for her to be visiting a village so removed from civilisation that it was two miles from the nearest bus stop.

Hunger was starting to gnaw now as well. She hadn't had any dinner. It was only then that Bobby realised she'd left the packet of luncheon meat sandwiches Lilian had made for her on the bus.

'I've got an appointment to keep with a man there,' Bobby said. 'I mean, a business appointment,' she clarified hastily, seeing how the woman's brow knit with disapproval.

'I never heared o' no business appointments going on in Silverdale,' the farmer's wife said, radiating suspicion. Bobby was sure the stolid daleswoman must have decided she was some sort of debauched good-time girl, here to bring depravity to the God-fearing folk of Silverdale – although she was certain such women were very rarely dressed in tweed suits and pearls.

Nevertheless, the farmer's wife pointed out the dirt road that ran alongside the pub, winding through the fields and away to the distant fells. A cluster of houses was visible some miles in the distance. 'That's village yon. If tha bides a spell, coal man'll be by. He'll allus take folk down for a consideration.'

'What is his consideration?'

'A pint o' mild in the Golden Hart is his usual fee.'

The woman fell silent again, scowling into the distance with Donald the lamb bleating softly in her arms. From this, Bobby assumed she, too, was waiting for the enigmatic coal man and waited in silence likewise.

The time was now a quarter past two, and Bobby was in danger of being late for her appointment with Reg Atherton. Had she realised how difficult the journey was going to be, she'd have set off earlier in the morning – but it was of no use regretting that now. She was starting to wonder if this whole plan had been cursed from the very beginning.

Chapter 6

It was no more than a quarter of an hour later when what appeared to be a very elderly horse plodded into view, pulling a soot-blackened wagon. The horse was being driven by an equally soot-blackened man, who halted beside them, grinning with pearly white teeth.

'Where're ye two bound?' he asked jovially.

'I'm to see Charlie Atherton in t' village,' the woman said, climbing into the back of the wagon.

Bobby's ears pricked up at the mention of the name. This must be the vet the woman had told her she was going to see. Was he some relation of Reg's? A son, perhaps?

'This young lady's going same way,' the woman told the coal man. 'She's to go to a "business appointment".' Her tone dripped with disdain.

'Aye, I'll take you for a consideration,' the coal man told Bobby.

'A pint of mild in the Golden Hart pub. I know,' Bobby said.

'Or t' value thereof. That's eightpence in these parts.'

'I'll make it a shilling if you can hurry. I'm rather late.'

The man stared as if he wouldn't know what to do with such unimagined riches.

'Climb up, then,' he said. 'I'll go quick as I can, but you must mind t' oss can only go so fast. He's on his last legs, poor owd lad.'

Bobby eyed the coal wagon with distaste. The woman with the lamb in her arms had settled herself comfortably on a pile of coal, seemingly unperturbed by the dust that got into Bobby's lungs and eyes, making her cough. After hesitating a moment, Bobby climbed on to the wagon but opted to remain standing. Her tweed suit, so neat when she'd donned it that morning, was crumpled now from the long journey, and there was mud on the heels of her court shoes. Bobby was also aware that, thanks to Donald, she now smelt faintly of sheep. If possible, she wanted to avoid arriving at *The Tyke*'s offices in an even more dishevelled state than she was in already. If she snuggled down in the coal wagon as the farmer's wife was doing, she was liable to look like a chimney sweep by the time she arrived in Silverdale.

Bobby stumbled as the rickety wagon set off, half crouching to steady herself by clutching the side. The woman's lips twitched with amusement.

'Sit thissen down, lass,' she said. 'Tha can't be stood all t' way thear.'

'I need to keep my clothes clean for my appointment.'

'Clothes made to keep clean aren't clothes for out here.'

'I'm starting to realise that.' Bobby looked over her shoulder at the coal man as the wagon jolted along the stony track at a leisurely pace. 'Is it not possible to go any faster?'

'Nay. I told you, t' oss can't do it. Not at his age. Got the rheumatism.'

'Tha needs to get a bit o' black pepper and willow bark on him,' the woman said with authority. 'Mix some in a bread poultice and get it on his joints every night after tha's rubbed him down. Worked wonders for our old dray, and my Alf too.'

There followed a long conversation about home remedies for various aches, pains and ailments that was only half intelligible to Bobby. She concentrated on trying to stay semi-upright and as free of black smudges as was possible when travelling by coal wagon, all the while with her eyes fixed on the little cluster of dots in the distance that gradually grew larger and larger until it became a village.

The coal man's rheumatic old horse had a top speed, it seemed, of about four miles per hour. It was some half an hour later that the wagon finally crossed an old carthorse bridge over a rocky, chattering beck and entered the village. It slowed to a halt in front of a whitewashed coaching inn that looked like it must date from at least the time of the Tudor kings and queens.

There was an old stone well outside the pub, with an empty pram beside it. A well-built young man with dark curls and a rather languid air was idling against the well in his shirtsleeves, amusing himself by throwing in small pebbles over his shoulder to make a splash at the bottom. He straightened up when he saw the wagon approach, smiling warmly.

'Well, and is this my patient?' he asked when the woman with the lamb alighted.

For the first time in their brief acquaintance, Bobby saw the woman's face light up with a full, warm smile.

'It is,' she said. 'I only wanted him to see thee, Charlie Atherton. My Alf wouldn't have another vet touch our beasts and nor will I. If any soul can fettle him, it's thee. It's his back legs, see.'

Bobby settled her debt with the coal man while this conversation went on, handing over the promised shilling in spite of the slow journey, then she climbed out of the wagon and waited. Whatever relation this Charlie was to Reg, she was sure he could help her find *The Tyke* offices. And he didn't speak in a dialect so thick she'd need a translator to understand him, which was also a benefit of getting to know him.

'Back legs, is it? I have an idea of what that might be,' Charlie said to the woman. 'Hand him over and go get yourself and Bert here a drink. You must've had an uncomfortable journey. I'll take this lad back to the surgery and have a look at him, and then I'll bring him back to you in a trice.'

The woman regarded the inviting open door of the Golden Hart with longing in her eyes. 'I wouldn't say no to a pint of milk stout, now tha mentions it.'

She handed Donald over and departed with the coal man for the badly needed drink, while Charlie tucked his charge

46

into the pram. Donald looked rather comical, swaddled up like a baby with his little sheep's face blinking up at them. Anyone who leaned over the pram to coo at the infant within was going to get the shock of their life.

When he was done, the young vet straightened up and turned to look at Bobby for the first time. He frowned now that he examined her properly.

'You can't possibly belong here,' he said. 'Are you lost?'

'I am a little,' she said, smiling awkwardly. 'I'm also rather late. Can you point me in the direction of Moorside – *The Tyke* offices?'

He laughed. 'The what?'

'*The Tyke* offices. You know, the little magazine?' A sudden worry shot through her. She hadn't come to the wrong Silverdale, surely? 'They are in this village, aren't they?'

'Yes, they're here: about a mile's walk. Come with me. My surgery's not far from there; I can show you to them personally.'

'Oh. Thank you.' Had she had time to spare, Bobby would have far preferred seeking the place out by herself. She didn't like to be beholden to anyone, especially not to men – and to strange men most of all, no matter how jolly and friendly they might seem on the surface. Who knew what isolated roads this Charlie might take her down, or what unwanted attentions he might press on her once he had her alone? But it was now after three, the time that had been set for her interview. And after all, how much could she have to fear from a man wheeling a sheep in a pram?

'Will you be able to do anything for Donald?' Bobby asked as she walked beside him past the tumbledown stone cottages that huddled around the village green.

Charlie frowned. 'Donald?'

She flushed, mentally berating herself for the slip. 'I mean the lamb. I... decided to give him a name. He was the only friend I had on the bus here from Skipton.'

'Ah, I see.'

47

'He's a Swadi-Cheviot hogg,' Bobby said, anxious to demonstrate her newly gained farming knowledge.

Charlie smiled. 'And what is a Swadi-Cheviot hogg?'

'Don't you know?'

'I know. I only wondered if you did.'

'It's… a sheep.'

'That's right, a young one. A hogg is a lamb between weaning and its first clipping. This little one's a cross between two breeds, Swaledale and North Country Cheviot.' He leaned over his pram to tickle Donald between the ears. 'Well, don't worry. I need to give Donald here a full examination, but from old Mrs Allison's report, I suspect there's nothing more serious ailing him than early stage selenium deficiency. One injection and your little friend will soon be grand again.' He glanced at her. 'Do I detect that you're not from these parts?'

'No, I'm from Bradford.'

'What brings you to see old Reggie?'

'A job. At least, I hope so. He advertised in the *Bradford Courier* for a junior reporter.'

Charlie's eyebrows lifted. 'Are you serious?'

Bobby smiled awkwardly. 'I know, I'm not what he was expecting. But he invited me for an interview, which means he must think I've got the skills to do the job. And he wouldn't have to worry about me being called up, so I've got that in my favour.'

'I think you'd give him plenty of other things to worry about.' Charlie skimmed her figure before his gaze darted to her ringless wedding finger, then quickly away again. 'You'd really be willing to work for that salary? Reggie had in mind a lad just out of school.'

'I want to be a journalist, and if that's what it takes to become one, so be it. I'm trying to think of it less as a job and more a sort of apprenticeship.'

Charlie cast her a sideways glance. 'Did you really travel all the way from Bradford by yourself?'

She smiled. 'It's not such an impressive feat, is it?'

'It's rather unsafe. You'll be making your way home in the blackout. And I don't know many city girls willing to travel by coal wagon.'

'What choice did I have? I needed to get here. Besides, I'm a big girl. I can take care of myself, Mr Atherton.'

'It's just Charlie. Reggie's all the Mr Athertons our family can hold. What do they call you?'

'Bobby. Bobby Bancroft.'

He nodded his approval. 'It suits you. Better than that suit does, at any rate.'

Bobby smiled, enjoying the good-natured teasing. It reminded her of the boys at work, putting her instantly at ease around this stranger in a way no attempt at charm or chivalry would have been able to do.

'This suit is my ticket to gainful employment, I'll have you know,' she told him with mock indignation.

'Oh, I'm sure Reggie will be impressed. He can't resist a woman in tweed.'

Bobby looked at him as they walked, trying to trace any similarity to the man she'd met at the *Courier* offices that day. She would never have identified Reg and Charlie as relatives, although, now she examined Charlie carefully, there was a certain resemblance around the eyes. They were a similar creamy brown, except Charlie's didn't hold that hard, haunted look the older man's had. Instead, she saw in them an expression of lazy, slightly wicked fun that looked as though it could be either endearing or infuriating, depending on the mood of its owner.

What was their relationship? Reg was probably just old enough to be Charlie's father – or an uncle, perhaps. Or if not, that would make him...

'The devilishly handsome, charmingly irresponsible younger brother,' Charlie said with a smile, reading the question in her face. He nodded to a group of buildings up ahead, at the top of a long, rough track. 'This is the place. Moorside Farm.'

49

Bobby stared at the ramshackle farm buildings. There was a large farmhouse with a couple of outhouses, a stable and a yard at the back where a few chickens pecked at their grain. Some little distance away was a smaller building that must once have been a barn but seemed now to have been converted into a sort of cottage, with bare briars curling tragically around the arched door. The main farmhouse looked rather sorry for itself, with some of the slate missing from the roof and the whitewash chipped and peeling. A battered black car was parked at the bottom of the track.

'This place is a magazine office?' Bobby said in disbelief.

'Certainly. And my surgery. And the Atherton family homestead for four generations. Reggie and his wife Mary live in the main farmhouse, and the old cow house' – Charlie pointed to the converted barn – 'is where I work, sleep and entertain. Cow House Cottage, I like to call it. It's not much, but it's all right for a bachelor. Come on and I'll take you up.'

Feeling rather dazed, Bobby followed him to the house. This, she supposed, was where she would be living if she got the job, since it had been advertised as bed and board included. This unpromising little farmhouse was where she would make her mark as a reporter, earn her first byline, and finally discover what her future held. It couldn't have been more different from the cramped terrace she shared with her father and siblings back at home.

'I'll leave you here,' Charlie said when they reached the front door. 'Now listen. Don't let Reggie frighten you, and get Mary on your side if you can. My brother likes to think he rules the roost, but everyone in Silverdale knows who's really in charge. Here.'

He produced a handkerchief and held it out to her.

'For your face,' he said as she stared at it. 'I'm afraid the coal wagon's been a little rough on you.'

'Oh.' Bobby flushed and took a compact from her handbag so she could examine herself in the mirror. There was indeed a large black smudge on one cheek. She accepted the handkerchief and rubbed it off. 'Thank you.'

'Keep it. Maybe it'll bring you luck,' Charlie said as she offered him the handkerchief back. 'I'd better get young Donald here on the mend. I hope you get the job, Bobby Bancroft. I'd like to see some more of you.'

He walked off in the direction of the barn-cottage that was apparently both his home and his veterinary practice, pushing the lamb snuggled contentedly in its pram.

Bobby took a deep breath and knocked on the farmhouse door. It was answered a moment later by a plump, motherly sort of woman, although there was a sparkle of keen intelligence in her blue eyes that told Bobby it wouldn't do to underestimate her.

'Good afternoon.' Bobby smiled uncertainly. 'Sorry I'm late. Mr Atherton is expecting me, I think.'

'I'm not sure he is, love. He's got an appointment this afternoon.'

'Yes, I know. Um, it's me. I'm the appointment, I mean.' She opened her handbag and presented Mrs Atherton with the letter inviting her for an interview. 'There's been rather a muddle. I didn't realise it at first, but I believe Mr Atherton might have mistaken me for a man. I'm Roberta Bancroft.'

'Oh,' the woman said, looking somewhat bewildered by this turn of events. 'Well, in that case, I suppose you ought to come in. Reg is in the parlour on that infernal clattering machine of his.'

It became clear to Bobby as she followed Mary Atherton through the farmhouse that *The Tyke* was very much a cottage industry. Piles of magazines filled every spare corner. The lady of the house had attempted, not very successfully, to make them blend into their surroundings with the addition of crocheted doilies and vases of flowers placed on top. Bobby could sense the frustration that came of being a housewife forced to share your home with your husband's pet project, and Mary seemed to have channelled all of it into flower arrangements.

Mary gave the door of the parlour a cursory tap, then beckoned Bobby to follow her. Reg was in there sitting at his typewriter, his stick leaning against the desk next to him. A couple of very large grey dogs – wolfhounds or something – lay at his feet. One lifted its head lazily to blink at Bobby as she entered, but it didn't look particularly interested in who this new person might be.

'So he's here at last, is he?' Reg said in his gruff voice, not looking up from his typewriter. 'I hope this isn't a typical example of his timekeeping.'

'I'm afraid there's been something of a muddle, Reg,' Mary said.

Reg looked up and frowned when he saw Bobby. It seemed to take him a moment to place her.

'You're that girl of Nobby Clarke's,' he said at last. 'The one as does his typing for him.'

'Yes, that's right,' Bobby said. 'We met a few weeks ago when you came into the office.'

'You look like you've been dragged through a hedge by your hair, lass. What brings you out here?'

'Um, you advertised a job with us. For a junior reporter.' Reg continued staring blankly, and Bobby flashed him a weak smile. 'I'm Roberta Bancroft. You invited me to come for an interview.'

He laughed. '*I* invited you? Is this some kind of joke?'

'It's not a joke. Look.' She presented him with the letter he'd sent her.

'I can do the work, Mr Atherton,' she said as he stared blankly at the letter. 'I know I'm not what you were expecting. I didn't mean to lie to you – the A on my typewriter sometimes doesn't make a proper impression, but it was an accident, I assure you.' Bobby's mouth now seemed to be operating completely independently of her brain, spewing out words as if powered by a motor. 'But I've got experience of a newsroom, and I've done some writing for the paper that I can show you, and there's a letter from Don to prove it's mine and not Tony's, and I was trained at Pitman's College, so...'

She trailed off as Reg's face seemed to catch up with what was happening, and his expression turned hard.

'A girl?' he said in a harsh voice. 'A girl out here?'

'There are lots of girl reporters now in the cities,' Bobby said, realising she sounded rather desperate. 'Or at least, there are some.'

'Young lady, I might as well drive you out to Blackpool Zoo and throw you into the wolves' enclosure as send you out there among these folk. I'm sorry, but I'm afraid you've had a wasted trip.'

He turned back to his typewriter as if that ended the matter.

Bobby couldn't help herself. It had been such a long, uncomfortable, dirty journey, with hardly a friendly face to be seen, and she was so tired and so disappointed that it had all been for nothing after all. She hid her face in her hands and wept.

Chapter 7

'Oh now, Reg. What did you have to go and do that for?' Mary Atherton bustled forward to put her arm around Bobby. 'There, there, my love, don't take on so. It'll be all right.'

'It's for her own good,' Reg muttered, although he looked rather uncomfortable about this unforeseen turn of events and the sobbing woman now standing in the middle of his parlour. 'Sorry, love, but reporting is man's work out here, whatever goes on these days in the towns. It has to be.'

'At the wage you're offering, you're lucky it's anyone's work,' Mary said sternly. 'The butcher's boy is earning as much, and him nobbut fifteen.' Gently she guided Bobby to a wicker chair and pushed her into it. 'Now then, lass. You have a sit down until you feel better, and in a minute, when you're calmer, I'll make us all a brew.'

'I'm so… sorry,' Bobby gasped through her sobs. 'It's just… been such a long, awful journey to get here. I should never have come. I should have written to you about the mistake.'

She took out Charlie's handkerchief and dried her eyes, no doubt adding a generous smear of coal dust to her face. By now she was far too miserable to care. What did it matter anyhow? She didn't need to try to keep herself nice any more. There was nothing to be gained from it. It had all been for nothing.

'Why didn't you write?' Mary asked her.

'I hoped I could convince you to give me a chance,' Bobby said, glancing at Reg. 'Or at least, to listen to what I had to say. I did so want the opportunity.'

'And why not? That's what I'd like to know,' Mary said, glaring at her husband. 'She's as lish as any lad, and she must have a brain in her head for you to ask to see her, Reg.'

'I asked to see her because I thought she were a man,' Reg grumbled, with the air of a petulant child who's had his hand slapped by his mother. 'Look at her. I can't be having crying women around the place when I'm trying to work.'

'Is it any wonder she's crying when she's travelled here all the way from Bradford only for you to refuse her the time of day? You'd be enough to make a grown man cry, you would, Reg Atherton. Half an hour is all she's asking from you, just to hear what she's got to say, and you throwing her out without so much as a "good afternoon".' Mary turned to Bobby again. 'And I suppose you've had nothing to eat since breakfast, have you?'

Bobby shook her head. 'I left my sandwiches on the bus.'

'Then we can put that right to begin with. It's the belly as hods the back up; that's what we say around here. We'll have a little early tea together before you go back home.' Mary glanced at Reg. 'And since I've no intention of sending this young lady back to Bradford in the blackout with an empty belly, and it's going to take me at least half an hour to make the tea, I think you might as well hear what she's got to say as not, don't you?'

'Hmph,' Reg said as his wife left the room. But he turned from the typewriter to examine Bobby.

'Auditioning for a minstrel show, are you?'

Flushing, Bobby took out her compact to examine her face. She looked an utter fright. She was white and drawn, her eyes bloodshot from tears and coal dust, and black smudges had appeared under her eyes. She rubbed them off with the only remaining clean corner of Charlie's handkerchief.

'I came down from the Bull and Heifer on the coal wagon,' she told Reg by way of an explanation. 'I'd have walked, but I didn't know the way.'

'Come all the way from Bradford by yourself?'

'That's right.'

Reg was silent, not giving anything away. The fact she'd travelled here alone had seemed to impress Charlie, who Bobby was sure had given her credit for more nous than she really possessed. Was Reg impressed likewise?

'Well, go ahead then,' he said at last. 'You may as well say what you came to say, since my missus insists on feeding you before you go home.'

Bobby beamed at him. 'Thank you. You won't regret it, I promise.'

'Never mind that. How long have you been typing for Nobby?'

'Eight months. I did shorthand typing and secretarial work for a wool merchant before that.'

'Got good shorthand, have you?'

'A hundred words per minute. I was the fastest in my class at Pitman's. I can type up to sixty-five words a minute too and hardly ever make a mistake,' Bobby told him eagerly. 'I've done some writing as well, for the *Courier*.'

He raised an eyebrow. 'Nobby lets you write for him?'

'Well, no, not exactly. That is, he doesn't know.' She took the letter from Don from her handbag, along with a scrapbook where she'd glued cuttings of every piece of copy she'd written for the newspaper. 'These are all mine though.'

She handed the scrapbook and letter to him.

'Byline on these says Anthony Scott,' he said, glancing at the cuttings. 'Tony Scott… he's the young layabout Nobby was complaining to me about. Always laiking when he should be working.'

'I know, but it's my work. The letter explains.'

Reg opened Don's letter and read it in silence while Bobby twisted her handkerchief nervously. He didn't say a word after finishing it but turned his attention back to her scrapbook.

'Surprised Nobby never noticed these were someone else's,' he said at last. 'Your copy's a damn sight cleaner than Scott's.'

She beamed at him. 'Thank you. You won't tell Clarky – Mr Clarke, will you? Only I don't want Tony to get into trouble.'

'I won't. I should, but I won't.' He looked again at the items in her scrapbook. 'I'm sorry to break it to you, Miss Bancroft, but there's more to reporting out in the country than clean copy, no matter how well-written it may be.'

'I know. But I'm very keen, and I'm willing to learn.'

The house had started to fill with the delicious aroma of frying bacon and home-baked bread. Bobby tried to stop her mouth from watering as she focused on winning Reg over.

'There's more to country reporting than being keen as well,' Reg said. 'The people here can be close; uncommon close. If you make a friend of them you've a friend for life, but they're careful who they give that friendship to. They're used to solitude and hard graft – survivors from another age, you might call them. If I send some slip of a city girl out to talk to them about farm life, well, I'll be a laughing stock. Me and my magazine.'

'I can earn their respect with time. I know I can.' Bobby took a deep breath as she prepared to make her final plea. 'Mr Atherton, I know I'm not what you want, but what other choice do you have? Perhaps I will have to work harder to impress the people I'll need to deal with here, but will it really be worse than sending out a lad of sixteen or so? Because that's all you'll be able to get for twelve and six. As your wife said, it's barely an errand boy's wage.'

'Hmm.'

'I know you must be desperate. Men and boys are getting called up every day. Well, I won't be. I'm keen, I'm dedicated, and I've got skills and experience you won't find in any male reporter willing to work for the wage you're offering.'

'You might not get called up to the army, but that doesn't mean I won't be wasting my time training you,' Reg said.

'What do you mean?'

'Women have their own sort of call-up. All of 'em are keen to marry. Have bairns. They work a while, then they want a family and off they go with some likely lad to set up home.'

Bobby flushed. 'I've got no interest in marriage.'

'Are you not courting? Most girls your age are already wed.'

'No, I'm not courting. I'd rather work than gad.'

Reg took his stick from where it was leaning against his leather-topped desk and got slowly to his feet. 'What I need, Miss Bancroft, is someone with two young, strong legs who can get about when I can't. A fast, accurate typist who can spell, with a good eye and nose for a story.'

'I can do all of that.'

'I also need someone who can earn the respect of the people in this part of the world. That's no easy matter.'

'I can do that too,' Bobby said, trying to convey a confidence she didn't feel.

'Hmm.' Reg limped to the window on his stick and beckoned Bobby to him. 'Look out here and tell me what you see. Look with the eyes of a writer.'

Sensing this was a test of sorts, Bobby followed him to the window. It looked out over the chicken yard and then on to a neighbouring farm, with the village green in view to the far right. High above, the silhouettes of the fells walled them in.

'I see... isolation,' she said quietly. 'The hills that shaped the character of the people here. Stark and simple, but with an awesome beauty all of their own.'

'Aye, very poetic, but I didn't mean that sort of writer,' Reg said dryly. 'The fells are all well and good, but they're only dressing. Try looking further down.'

Bobby did so, looking across to the neighbouring farm where a young man was driving a tractor through a field. There was a cart filled with manure hitched to the back, which another man stood on top of and forked over the sides.

'I see a couple of farmhands going about their work,' she said simply. What was Reg expecting her to say? She couldn't see what wasn't there.

'I'll tell you what I see,' Reg said. 'I see Dennis and Eric Dixon, Ted Dixon's youngest boys – fifteen and sixteen year old, the last ones left at home after their brothers went to war – doing the muck-spreading all by themselves with that noisy contraption. Thirty year ago, I'd have looked out to watch their grandad doing the same with a team of four men and a couple of dray horses. These young farmers now, they're more mechanics than men of the land.' He looked at her. 'The Dales are at the end of an era, Miss Bancroft. Silverdale used to be its own little world until the wars came and changed things. Same for all the Dales villages. If you'd said before the last war that you wanted to marry a girl from the next village, folk'd look at you like you'd grown a second head. Right clannish, these Dales communities were. But now there's the wireless bringing the whole world into your parlour every day, and there's the war taking folk out into the world. The old ways are fast disappearing – so fast that if you blinked, you might miss them.'

'Is that entirely a bad thing?' Bobby said. 'Not the war, obviously, but people experiencing the world outside their own community.'

'It's neither bad nor good. It just is.' Reg watched the little grey tractor pensively as its pungent load was deposited across the field. 'When I were a lad, it felt like life hadn't changed here for a hundred year. Now I reckon it's changing every day. Even the way folk speak is starting to change, with the talkies from America turning all our youngsters into Yanks. We're on the edge of a new age in the Dales, and I plan on being that age's chronicler.'

It struck Bobby that most local people would feel rather sad about this, yet Reg didn't seem so. Instead his eyes sparkled with passion for his subject, and Bobby started to understand, if only a little, what had driven Reg Atherton to start his magazine in the first place.

'Like Shakespeare,' she said. 'Jonson called him the soul of the age.'

'Aye, there's summat o' that about it. Glad to hear you know your books.' His gaze had drifted back to the tractor, but he turned to look at her now. 'There was a man lived in this village: Arthur Gregory. Died the other day at more than a hundred year old. Nobody knew how much older than that he might be. They didn't write such things down when he were born – not for poor folk, at any rate. Art had been a gruver in his youth, working in the old lead mines. By, but he must've had some memories! All of 'em lost now because he was never taught to read or to write so he could set them down.'

'And you want to preserve the memories of others like him.'

'I do. I want these people and their way of life to be recorded, and to be celebrated while it still exists, not to be forgotten when the ticking hand of time moves us on. You need to put people before things in journalism, Miss Bancroft, always. Not just important people: politicians and the like. People as might be called ordinary, although it's my experience that there's no such thing as an ordinary person.' Reg picked up a copy of *The Tyke* from one of the many piles around the room and handed it to her. 'In my first Editor's Journal, I wrote that I started this magazine to document the people, places and activities of the Dales, and to be of interest to all who love this countryside. But more than that, I started it because there are things that ought to be remembered – that need to be remembered. Every day we're witnessing history in the making, and despite what folk think, it isn't only happening across the sea in Europe. It's happening here on our doorsteps, and it's disguised as Dennis Dixon's tractor. Do you understand what I'm trying to say to you?'

'I understand,' Bobby said quietly. 'I can help you.'

'Hmm.'

They were interrupted by Mary Atherton, who entered to let them know tea was ready.

'We'll eat at the kitchen table,' she said. 'And mind, no work talk while we're eating, the pair of you.'

At home in Bradford, the evening meal they called 'tea' was usually very simple: often little more than a few slices of jam and bread, with perhaps some tinned pears for pudding. In the Dales, it seemed 'tea' had quite a different meaning. Bobby's eyes grew wide as she followed Mary and Reg to a scrubbed kitchen table in front of a roaring fire and saw the spread laid out there.

After months of shortages in the city, it looked like enough food to satisfy the entire British Army. There were hot buttered scones and plates piled high with bacon, oat cakes and freshly boiled eggs. Doorstep-sized sandwiches with thick slices of moist pink ham in between looked like they would fill you up for a week, and a pot of fresh tea filled the air with a delicious aroma.

'You didn't need to make all this for my benefit,' Bobby said, although her mouth was watering.

'Oh, nonsense. We can't send you back hungry.' Mary gestured for her to take a seat and handed her a plate so she could serve herself. 'We're lucky out here in the countryside. With our own beasts providing for us, we're not so affected by the shortages. Take some back for your family if you like.'

'It's weeks since I had an egg,' Bobby said, eyeing them hungrily. 'Thank you, Mrs Atherton. You've been very kind to me.'

'Well, we want you to come back to us.' She glanced at Reg. 'Don't we?'

'We'll see,' he said, keeping his expression blank.

Chapter 8

Despite the difficulties of navigating in the blackout, which began at half past six in the evening at this time of year, Bobby's journey home was a little easier than her trip to Silverdale. Mary Atherton's kindness to her had continued after their meal and she'd insisted that Reg drive Bobby back to her bus stop in his battered and mud-caked old Wolseley, which he did despite much grumbling about the waste of his petrol coupons. He maintained a sullen silence all the way to the Bull and Heifer, but it was still far more pleasant – and in spite of the maximum speed of thirty miles per hour imposed during blackout hours, significantly faster – than the dirty, uncomfortable coal wagon.

In Bobby's arms was a paper bag filled with food that had been left over from their huge tea, which Mary had given her to share with her family. Mary had optimistically packed up several copies of *The Tyke* too – as much to get rid of them as because she thought Bobby was likely to get the job, Bobby assumed. Reg was remaining tight-lipped about her chances, but she suspected that if he had an application through the door tomorrow from a boy or man, be he ever so inexperienced or poorly suited to the role, her hopes would be dashed.

She wasn't sure why the idea upset her so much. She'd had the most awful day, with Mary and Charlie the only two friendly faces she'd met other than Donald the lamb. The idea of living amongst these stern, inexpressive people in a world so different from her own, hemmed in by a landscape that both awed and scared her, was as daunting a prospect as any she'd faced in her life. It invoked a feeling of childlike helplessness that reminded her of the period after her mam had died, when her father had withdrawn so completely into his own head and Bobby had been forced to accept that as young as they then were, she and Lilian were now the adults of the family. And yet something in her soul spurred her on, hoping, praying, that Reg might be persuaded to give her a chance.

His speech as they'd looked out of the window together had touched something in her. Lilian had sneered at the sort of stories *The Tyke* liked to print, and no doubt many of Bobby's fellow townies would feel the content of the magazine – an assortment of articles on country crafts, long-forgotten traditions and folklore, sketches of country characters, jokes and dialect poems – was twee, foolish and frivolous. But Reg was right, no doubt: the life of the Dalesfolk, untouched for what felt like centuries, was now changing day by day. The world outside their borders was seeping in thanks to the war and new technology, and in a hundred years' time, the Yorkshire Dales of today would probably be as lost a world as Atlantis, the civilisation claimed by the sea. As small and unexciting as it seemed, this was history – as much so as the battles raging in Europe or the nightly blitzes on British cities. There was something important in what Reg was trying to do, and Bobby longed to be a part of it.

It was after eight o'clock when she finally stepped off the tram and walked the last quarter-mile home. Her father was in the living room in his carpet slippers, unshaven and bleary-eyed but relatively sober and seemingly lucid enough. The wireless was tuned and he appeared to be listening to it, which meant he was at least aware of his surroundings.

'Where's our Lilian?' Bobby asked him.

'Gone to some dance with a girlfriend.'

Knowing her sister, Bobby felt it more likely she'd gone out dancing with a boyfriend, but she kept quiet on that subject.

He turned to look at her. 'You're late today. Where've you been?'

'The pub,' Bobby lied. 'It's Tuesday. You know I always play darts after work on a Tuesday.'

'Huh. I don't like you doing that, Bobby. They'll say you're fast, always laiking about wi' lads in the pubs.'

Bobby smiled, pleased to find him inhabiting enough of the real world to be concerned about her reputation. She went to perch on the arm of his chair, as she used to do when a girl.

'Things aren't like they were in your day, Dad,' she said, kissing the top of his head. 'Lots of girls go to pubs. Besides, Don's there to chaperone and keep me respectable. He doesn't let me fraternise with the wrong sort of boy.'

She knew her dad approved of Don, who'd visited the house when she'd been unwell once with a gift of fruit and flowers. Bobby didn't remember Uncle Dick, but on the sideboard sat a photograph of him in the uniform of the West Yorkshire Regiment (16th Battalion) – the Bradford Pals, as they'd been known. He had a certain expression that reminded her of Don, and she wondered if the similarity to his lost younger brother was why Dad had taken a rare shine to her friend.

'Well, make sure you keep out of trouble,' her dad said, somewhat mollified.

'I will. Have you eaten this evening?'

'Some bread and butter, I think,' he recalled vaguely.

'Shall I make you something?'

'You can fetch me a drink if you want to make yourself useful.'

'Have something to eat first. It'll line your stomach.' She pointed to the bag she'd put down by his chair. 'I've got a suppertime treat for you tonight – hard-boiled eggs, and bacon too. The good sort we used to get before the war.'

This seemed to stir him a little. 'Eggs? Long time since I had an egg.'

'I know. Someone from the countryside gave them to me. Shortages aren't as bad out there as they are here.' She paused. 'Dad?'

'Hmm?'

'You know that… that when we all leave home, us kids, we'll make sure you're looked after, don't you?'

Her dad gave a humph of irritation. 'I'm not an old man yet, Bobby. I can look after myself.' He glanced up at her. 'Was there somewhere particular you were planning to go?'

'Well, Jake's had his call-up now so he could be leaving any day for the army, and our Lil might be going off to train as a Wren soon. It'll be a big change for you, not having us all at home.'

'You're not going anywhere, are you?'

'I… might be. I can't stay at home forever, can I? I'm twenty-three, Dad. Most girls my age are married with a bairn or two, as certain men of my acquaintance often take pains to remind me.'

'What's brought this talk on?' He narrowed his eyes. 'That spiv sort. The one you play darts with.'

Bobby had to think for a moment to work out who he might mean.

'Tony?' she said.

'Aye, that's him. I've heard about him. Sounds a right rum lad. Has he been trying it on with you?'

She laughed. 'No. At least, not in any serious way. You don't need to worry about Tony, Dad. He's engaged to an ATS girl; she keeps him well in line.'

'Well, who is it you've got in mind as husband material then?'

'No one. I was talking in general terms, that's all. I just wanted you to know that if I did have to leave home one day, I'd make sure you had everything you needed.'

His eye twitched at the corner. 'I've needed a drink this quarter of an hour and that hasn't appeared yet.'

Bobby sighed. 'All right, but have some food with it, for God's sake. I'll bring you a plate of sandwiches.'

'There's a good lass.'

He took her hand and gave it a hard squeeze, which was all the affection he was able to muster these days. Bobby squeezed it back before going to the kitchen to prepare his meal and whisky, thoughts of the past and of the future racing around her head.

–

Three weeks passed, carrying the year well into November, and no news, either welcome or unwelcome, arrived from Silverdale. Every morning Bobby rushed to the office to intercept the post before anyone else could, both hoping and fearing to see an envelope with her name on it, and every morning there was nothing. But still she didn't give up hope – until one day, when Mr Clarke came down to the office to speak to Don.

'Here,' he said, handing Don some copy he'd been subbing. 'Check that through, then get a clean typed copy from the girl to hand over to the lino lads. Oh, and while you're down there, that small advertisement of Reg's can come out. I've just had him on the phone and he's got it all sorted out. There's no need to run it again.'

Don glanced at Bobby. She tried not to show any emotion, hiding her face behind the sheet of copy she was typing.

'Got someone for the job, did he?' Don asked Clarky.

'Aye, a likely prospect, he says. Didn't tell me much about him. Some young lad, I suppose. He won't get much more than a bairn for that wage.' Clarky shook his head. 'It'll never thrive, that little mag. Nice concept but too niche. I told him that the day he came to me with the idea, wanting me to back the thing. But there's nothing harder to change than Reggie Atherton's mind when he's set out to do something.'

When he'd gone, Don approached Bobby's desk under the pretence of giving her the sheets of subbed copy Clarky had brought down.

'I'm sorry, Bobby,' he said in a low voice, so the other two wouldn't hear. 'It probably doesn't seem like it at the moment, but it'll work out for the best. A young thing like you isn't cut out for country living. It'd bore you stiff holed up out there with nothing to do at night.'

'That's up to me, isn't it?' Bobby said, her voice rather choked as she tried to keep her emotions from spilling out.

'Well, there's nothing to be done about it. Tell you what, I'll talk to Clarky about getting you some byline work like I promised. You never know, he might go for it. That'll cheer you up, eh?'

Bobby felt like the opportunity to get her name on a couple of Kitchen Front pieces about how to make the most of your cabbages was poor compensation for the loss of a job she'd been pinning all her future hopes on, but she summoned a weak smile for Don, who was sweet to want to make her feel better.

'That's the spirit.' He slapped her back. 'Stiff upper lip, old girl. It'll all work out.'

She couldn't stop a tear slipping out. 'I know. I'm sorry, Don. I just really thought… this could be it.'

'Something else'll come along for you. Something better than a junior reporter job working for a pittance at the back of beyond. Now why don't you go out and pick us all up some dinner?' He nodded to Jem and Tony, obliviously working away at their shared desk. 'If you fix your make-up and things before you get back, those two won't be any the wiser.'

'Yes. All right.' She dashed the tear away and flashed him another watery smile. 'I'll be back soon, make-up in place and upper lip stiffened. Sorry for blubbering at you when I promised I wouldn't.'

'Bloody over-emotional women. I always said they had no place in a newsroom.' But he was smiling.

—

As soon as she was out of the office, Bobby slipped down one of the ginnels that ran between the rows of terraces and gave in to her tears for a moment.

Of course she'd known there was almost no chance of her getting the reporter position. Mary Atherton had clearly been on her side, but what had Clarky said? There was nothing harder to change than Reg's mind when he'd made it up about something, and he'd made it up about her the instant she'd appeared in his parlour and revealed herself to be the wrong sex. And yet it still hurt, watching the castle in the air she'd built for herself come tumbling down.

Bobby took Charlie's handkerchief from her handbag, freshly laundered that morning, to dab her eyes – she'd been carrying it with her almost every day, after what he'd said about it bringing her luck. Bobby wasn't sure if there was any such thing as a lucky handkerchief, but somehow she took comfort from the little cotton square with its embroidered monogram, CA, in one corner. There was a horseshoe symbol embroidered above the initials – a horseshoe for a vet, of course – so she supposed that might bring luck.

Except it hadn't, had it? She hadn't got the job, and the people she'd met that day, Charlie and Reg and Mary and Donald the Swadi-Cheviot hogg, would disappear into her memory like dreams she'd once had. She must have been carrying the handkerchief upside down or something, and all the luck had fallen out.

It was so hard to stop the tears now they'd started. Bobby perched on a dustbin lid while she dabbed at her eyes. A child wearing a colander on his head ran along the cobbles waving a wooden sword, paying no mind to the strange lady crying her eyes out under a line of drying clothes that flapped like ghosts in the breeze.

Who had Reg got for the job, Bobby wondered? Some young lad, as Clarky supposed? The editor was right when he said no one else was likely to work for the schoolboy wage Reg was offering – at any rate, no one but her. Yes, it'd be a lad of fifteen or sixteen, with no skills in shorthand, no typewriting ability, no experience, no nose for a story; in fact, nothing to recommend him but a pair of good legs. And this was who Reg would rather have than her, simply because he'd been lucky enough to be born a member of the sex who apparently were entitled to have everything in life handed to them on a plate.

Suddenly, Bobby felt a surge of anger. Suddenly, her tears weren't tears of grief at the loss of what might have been but tears of rage at how unfair it all was. What did it even mean to be a man? Did they have better brains, greater abilities? They always seemed to think so, but she'd never seen any evidence for it. What they did possess in spades was the arrogance to fake what they lacked – and, of course, they weren't required to bear children, although they were generally happy enough to help make them. Apparently, these were the qualities the world valued over actual ability and intelligence. It was all so unfair; so painfully, miserably unfair.

What really galled her was that Reg hadn't even bothered to write and tell her she hadn't got the job. After she'd gone all that way on that rickety old bus and ruined her tweed suit – a suit that, even though second-hand, had cost her the best part of the sixty bob she'd managed to put by without her dad finding out – on the jolting, bouncing coal wagon; after all his wife's kindness to her. It was the rudeness of it that upset her as much as anything. After hesitating a moment, Bobby wiped her eyes with Charlie's handkerchief, took a couple of pennies from her purse and strode towards the nearest telephone box.

'Silverdale 85 please,' she said to the operator.

The operator connected her, and a moment later, a woman's voice was heard down the line.

'Hello?'

Bobby felt some of her anger dissipating, and with it, her confidence. She'd been hoping it would be Reg who'd pick up, so she could tell him exactly what she thought of his appalling manners.

'Hello, Mrs Atherton.' She fell silent, fumbling for the right words. 'Um, it's Roberta Bancroft. I came to see your husband about the reporter job three weeks ago.'

'Oh, Miss Bancroft!' Mary's voice was filled with warmth, sounding genuinely thrilled to hear from her. 'I am glad you've called. I was hoping you would. There are so many things I need to talk to you about.'

Bobby blinked. 'You need to talk to me?'

'Aye, now, what would you like to do about your food? I think it's best, if you're happy to, that you give your book to me and I can sort us all out together when I go to the shops in Settle. Of course, if you prefer not to then I'm sure we can arrange it another way, but it seems the simplest solution.'

'My book?' Bobby said, feeling dazed.

'Your ration book, my love. Is that all right?'

'Um, yes. No. I mean, I'm sorry, but why would you need my ration book?'

'Well, so I can feed you, naturally.' Mary Atherton paused. 'You're not calling to say you've changed your mind, I hope?'

'Changed my mind about what?'

'About the job, of course. You did get Reg's letter?'

'I don't think I can have.' Bobby leaned against the back of the box, feeling suddenly dizzy. 'Are you saying... you're not saying Mr Atherton wants to hire me for the reporter job after all?'

'Hire you? My dear, we're expecting you to start next week.'

Chapter 9

'And you're sure you've got enough flour to last you the week?' Bobby asked for about the fourth or fifth time as she lingered in her old bedroom the following Saturday afternoon, stretching out the last goodbye with her sister.

'We'll be absolutely fine, Nervous Nellie. I cross my heart.' Lilian kissed her on the cheek and pushed her suitcase into her hand. 'Now go on, go, before I burst out crying again.'

'Yes. OK.' Bobby started to go, then turned back again. 'And you know where I keep all the ration books, don't you? In the kitchen dresser in the—'

'—in the bottom cupboard, the one with the lock that Dad can't get into,' Lilian finished for her. 'Yes, Bobby. I know where the books are, I know which shops we're registered with, and I know that if you flirt with Will at the butcher's then he'll slip you some under-the-counter sausages. We'll be all right, I promise.'

'And you'll write to me?'

'Of course.'

'Every day?'

Lilian laughed. 'Definitely not. If I have to write to you every day, I'll have no social life at all. I'll write once a week, or more if anything happens. Which it won't.'

'Right,' Bobby said, somewhat reassured. 'I get paid on Fridays. I'll send a postal order for half to you straight away, at The Majestic so Dad can't get his hands on it.' She picked up her case, then hesitated. 'Look, do you absolutely promise you're happy about this?'

'Bobby, go! You'll miss your train if you keep dithering.'

'Because I meant it when I said I'd turn it down. I mean, I want it, more than anything, but if you really thought you couldn't make ends meet on what you and Dad and Jake were bringing in—'

'Bobby.' Lilian put her hands on her sister's shoulders. 'We've been over the money situation. Yes, things are going to be tight for a time, but we won't have your food to pay for, and when Jake leaves for training and if I get accepted to the Wrens, we'll both be on higher wages than in our current jobs. Perhaps Dad could take in lodgers for the empty rooms too.'

Bobby bowed her head. 'How could he have strangers in the house, with... well, you know. The nightmares.'

'There might be a way. We'll talk about it when the time comes.' Lilian mustered a smile. 'Anyhow, you'll be a high-flying reporter on *The Times* by then, won't you? Able to keep us all in the lap of luxury.'

Bobby smiled too. 'I hope I might be earning a little more before long, at least, once I've been able to prove myself. We just need to get along as best we can for a while.' She put down her case to give her twin another hug, pressing her eyes closed. 'I'm so sorry, Lil. I feel like I'm abandoning you all, leaving like this.'

'You're not abandoning us. We'll miss you being here, that's all.' Lilian sighed. 'I suppose one of us had to be the first to go.'

'Everything's changing, isn't it?'

'Life does that. I wish it didn't. On the other hand, I'm sort of glad it does from time to time.' Lilian held Bobby back to look into her face. 'I hope this job is everything you dream it'll be, little sister. I'm proud of you, do you know that? Mam would be too. She always said all she wanted was for us to be able to stay out of the mills and make something of ourselves.'

'I'm not sure earning twelve and six a week while lodging in a broken-down old farmhouse in the middle of nowhere is quite what she had in mind,' Bobby said, smiling. 'But I'm sure this will lead to better things for me. It has to.'

'I hope it does,' Lilian said, although her eyes still looked far from convinced the job in Silverdale was a good prospect. 'And mind, if it doesn't, you come straight back home to us, OK?'

Bobby lowered her gaze. 'It's unlikely there'll be anyone here to come back to by the spring, isn't it? Only Dad. Jake's off to war, and you might be following him before long. It's going to feel so empty here, Lil.'

'Dad won't notice. Not so long as there's enough to drink.'

'No. I don't suppose he will.' Bobby bent to pick up her suitcase. 'I'd better go and say goodbye to him.'

'He might not hear you. It's a bad day today.'

'I have to do it all the same. Goodbye, Lil. Take care of him. And yourself.'

'I will.'

Bobby gave her sister a kiss and went into the living room to speak to her father.

He was in his horsehair armchair, his body limp and sagging and an empty glass by his hand. If it hadn't been for the fact his eyes were open, Bobby would have assumed he was asleep.

'Dad?' she said softly.

There was no answer. She put down her case and went to perch on the chair arm.

'I came to say ta-ra. I'm going now. To start my new job, like I told you.'

No reply. Only a sort of rattle in the back of his throat indicated that her father was conscious. These were the worst days, when a combination of alcohol and the visions she knew tortured him constantly rendered him entirely out of reach of his children.

'I'll come home as often as I can,' she said, although she knew she was speaking for her own benefit rather than his. 'Lilian will be here to take care of you, and Sarah and the bairns will be around nearly every day.'

There was no answer, of course. Sighing, Bobby planted a kiss on his unresponsive scalp. She picked up her suitcase, threw her battered gas mask box over her shoulder and headed outside to say goodbye to her brother.

As usual, Jake was tinkering with his motorcycle. He barely looked up when she came out. At nineteen, there were more important things to worry about than big sisters leaving home; things like bikes and girls and what was on at the pictures that night.

'So long then, Trouble,' Bobby said, ruffling his slicked hair in that way she knew drove him barmy. 'You take care of yourself, and of Lil too. You know you're really the man of the house now that Dad's... the way he is.'

'He isn't talking today,' Jake said as he tightened a nut with his spanner.

'I know. He didn't even blink when I said goodbye. I'll telephone tomorrow if I can get permission to use the phone at the farmhouse. I might be able to make him understand then.'

Jake straightened up. 'What's the matter with Dad anyhow?'

Bobby sighed. They'd had this conversation before, and she never had been able to make her brother understand. She wished he hadn't chosen today, when she was leaving, to talk about this again.

'It's what they call battle fatigue. A lot of men who fought in the last war had it. I suppose men do in this war too, although no one talks about it. Bad for morale, probably.'

Jake snorted. 'Fatigue. It's twenty years since Dad was in battle. He can't still be tired.'

'Call it shell-shock then, or whatever you like. It isn't something he can help, Jake, whatever name you choose to give it.'

'Seems to me he should be better by now, instead of trying to drink it away.' Jake drew himself up. 'The way he screams about it at night, like a bairn having a bad dream. It's unmanly.'

Bobby knew how much it hurt her brother, feeling he had a father he couldn't respect. She knew he felt ashamed and avoided bringing friends or girls home because of it. But he was young, and the war was still little more than a game of toy soldiers in his boyish mind. Perhaps the army would help him to understand.

'It isn't that simple,' she said quietly. 'There are things that can't be forgotten. Things that, once seen, you can never stop seeing. That's why Dad drinks – why he screams in the night.'

'What things?'

Bobby flinched. She didn't like to think about that, but she had some idea. Her father's night terrors weren't always unintelligible. She'd heard him say things, when she'd gone into his room in the darkness to administer a sleeping draught and a shot of whisky to chase it down after another screaming fit. Sometimes he'd be speaking to her, but more often he addressed himself to men long dead, conjured again in his memories.

Death and fire and blood and smoke. Bodies, limbs, wherever you looked. Monstrous things that had once been the faces of friends and comrades, no longer recognisable – no longer human. This was why Bobby never begrudged her father his whisky – God knew she'd want something to make her forget if she had to live in that hellscape. She was glad her brother didn't know of such things and hoped he'd never be called upon to learn about them first-hand.

'Horrible things,' she said quietly to Jake. 'Things they don't show you in the war pictures.'

'It won't ever happen to me. I swear it won't. I'm no coward.'

She rested a hand on his arm. 'I really hope it won't, Jake. For your sake.'

He was silent for a moment, scowling.

'When are you coming back?' he asked at last.

'Soon. Before you leave for the army, I promise.' She kissed his forehead, and he grimaced in the way little brothers are obligated to do when overly demonstrative sisters insist on kissing them. But he did deign to tolerate a hug.

'I'll miss you, our Jake,' she said softly.

'Aye, well, you're all right,' he said, which in the language of a lad his age constituted the very highest praise. 'You're going to write, aren't you?'

'Not to you. You won't read it. I'll write to Lil, and she can read you the interesting parts.'

He grinned. 'That suits me. Ta-ra, Bob.'

His attention was once again consumed by the beloved Triumph, and Bobby departed to hop on a tram.

There was a surprise waiting for her at Forster Square Station. When she arrived on the platform, she found Jem, Don and Tony there, bearing a handmade banner on which the words 'We'll Meet Again' had been painted.

She laughed. 'You daft so-and-sos. You know I'm not off to war, don't you?'

Jem rubbed his neck awkwardly. 'It were Tony's idea. He reckoned we should see you off properly.'

'It wasn't my idea,' Tony said, looking pained at the suggestion. 'Don was the one who said we should see you off.'

'But you wanted to make a sign,' Don said.

'It wasn't me who said we should get her a present as well though, was it?'

'Maybe not, but you paid your seven bob for it, same as we all did.'

'It's really very sweet of all of you,' Bobby said, beaming at them. All three men were blushing now, casting embarrassed glances at the other people waiting for the train, some of whom had turned to watch the little tableau. It meant a lot to Bobby that they'd made the gesture – even Tony with his oh-so-fragile *amour propre* and Don with his determination to have everyone think he didn't give a damn about anyone or anything. She almost felt like hugging them all, except that she suspected their flushed cheeks might actually combust if she did.

'Um, we all chipped in for this,' Jem said, handing Bobby something vaguely spherical wrapped in old sheets of the *Bradford Courier*.

'You didn't need to do that.'

'We know, but we did anyhow.' Tony nudged her. 'Open it then. You're a lucky girl, Bobby.'

Intrigued, Bobby unwrapped the present, hoping it wouldn't be some off-colour wheeze of Tony's.

'Oh my goodness! I don't believe it!' She held the ripe brown onion to her nose, savouring the sweet, flavourful tang that had once been so familiar. 'Wherever did you find it? I can't remember the last time I saw one in the shops.'

'It wasn't easy.' Tony looked rather pleased with himself now, although moments earlier he'd been keen to disavow all responsibility for the farewell gift. 'Wasn't cheap either.'

'We bid for it at a charity auction, if you must know,' Don said. 'One onion in exchange for a guinea to the Shipley Spitfire Fund.'

If anyone had told Bobby a few short years ago that the humble onion would one day be so highly prized as to be auctioned for charity at a guinea a time, she'd have laughed at them. Now, all she could think of was beef and potatoes, Welsh rarebit, corned beef hash, and a hundred other delicious concoctions that just weren't the same without an onion.

'Thank you all,' she said softly. 'Especially you, Tony. I know what a wrench it must've been for you to give it up.'

Tony sighed. 'Can I please smell it? Just for a moment?'

'Of course.'

She handed it over, and Tony breathed its aroma deeply before reluctantly handing it back.

The Skipton train could be heard approaching, ready to take Bobby towards her new life in Silverdale. She wrapped the precious onion in newspaper again and put it away in her handbag before shaking hands with each of her former colleagues in turn.

'I never thought I'd say this, but I'm going to miss all of you to pieces,' she said. 'I know you're going to tell me that's the sort of silly emotional thing you'd expect a girl to say and I don't care a fig because it's true.'

Don nudged Tony. 'Not going to cry, are you?'

'If I do, it'll be from saying goodbye to that onion.'

Bobby laughed. 'Do you think you'll be able to brew your own tea all right when I'm gone?'

'If we must, we must,' Don said in a resigned tone. 'Mind, we'll probably never win another darts match. It won't be the same without you, Bobby.'

'You'll come to visit me, won't you?'

'Won't need to,' Tony announced confidently. 'You'll have had enough in a few weeks. I'd offer good odds you'll be back here before Christmas.' He probably meant it too. He was always running a book on something or other.

'You said the war would be over by Christmas too, and that's not looking likely,' Bobby pointed out.

'But I'm right about this. Maybe Clarky'll even offer you your old job back.'

'When he realises how much of your copy I was writing? I should think he might. I won't be coming back though.'

The train had pulled in now. Don clapped Bobby on the back.

'Fare thee well, young Bobby,' he said. 'I hope the reporter life brings everything you want it to.'

'Well, it's brought me an onion. That's more than I ever expected of it,' she said, trying to lighten an atmosphere that seemed to have become rather sombre as she prepared to depart. 'Bye, boys. I'll see you all again.'

Don took her case from her. 'Here, let me help you on with this.'

There wasn't much in it, and Don was able to lift it easily on to the overhead rack in her compartment. When Bobby had gone through her wardrobe, she'd discovered very little suitable for country living; nothing to withstand mud, cold, coal wagons, rampant beasts and rocky fells. In the end, all she'd packed had been a handful of blouses, sweaters and skirts that ought to be suitable for indoor work, her sturdiest shoes, a smart powder-blue crepe dress that she thought ought to suffice for her meagre social life out in the countryside, and an old, warm overcoat of her father's that she was planning to alter for her figure. Anything else she needed would have to be provided by her knitting needles, at least until she was able to put some money aside from her scant wages. The only other item she wanted to bring was her Remington typewriter, which had been parcelled up and sent on ahead, so at least one old friend would be there to greet her.

'Will you write to me?' Bobby asked Don. 'I want to know everything that's going on at the *Courier*.'

'When I can spare the time.' Don took a scuffed leather box from his pocket and handed it to her. 'Here. This is from me. Don't go into hysterics about it, and for God's sake, don't tell that lot.'

Bobby opened it. Inside was a handsome green onyx marble fountain pen.

'I thought you should have something longer-lasting that an onion to remember your time at the *Courier*,' Don said. 'Mind, it's not new. All I could afford. Might help you find the words you need in the new job.'

Bobby looked at him, touched.

'Thank you,' she said quietly, wishing she could hug him but knowing 'making a fuss' would only embarrass him. 'It's beautiful, Don. I've never owned anything so nice.'

'Aye, well. See you at Christmas then.'

He hopped off the train before the porter closed the doors, even redder now than he had been when he'd got on.

Bobby found herself a window seat where she could wave her old colleagues goodbye. The three of them followed her down the platform as the train set off, Tony mugging and making grotesque faces to try to make her laugh. As soon as they were out of sight, Bobby took out Charlie's handkerchief to mop up tears that had nothing to do with her onion.

'Goodbye,' she whispered as she watched the dark, tightly clustered buildings start to recede into the distance. 'Goodbye.'

Within minutes, even the mills with their towering chimneys seemed far away. Bobby watched as her old life became smaller and smaller, until eventually it disappeared completely into the smoke.

Chapter 10

Bobby's mood continued wistful and a little homesick throughout the train journey to Skipton, her mind filled with thoughts of those she'd left behind. The tangy scent of onion hung around her handbag, reminding her of friends and family. A woman with a small baby in her lap who had taken a seat opposite kept casting suspicious looks her way. No doubt she suspected Bobby of being some sort of black-market onion smuggler.

Bobby's mood improved when she was once again aboard the orange Pennine bus on her way to Silverdale, however. On her last journey, the countryside had been garbed in mist and fine drizzle, filling her with foreboding. Today it was suffused with bucolic charm, bathed in a golden late-autumn sunshine that lifted her spirits. The fells, which had seemed like malevolent monsters closing her in during her last journey into the Dales, now felt like warm and avuncular giants, protecting the homely little farming villages in the valleys from the darkness and smog of the cities.

For the first time, it occurred to Bobby that she'd actually done it. This was it – her dream achieved at last! She was a reporter – no less of a real journalist than Dorothy Lawrence, in spite of the humble magazine she was to be employed by – and come the new year, she might well be looking at her very first byline. Optimism filled her, and she beamed around the people on the bus. Although her fellow occupants regarded her with that suspicion they reserved for outsiders, just as those she'd travelled with before had done, these Dalesfolk no longer had the power to make her feel like a strange alien in a world where she didn't belong. She was one of them now, and she'd make them accept her no matter how long that was going to take.

Bobby hugged her handbag tightly, smiling to herself as she tried to picture Mary Atherton's face when she presented her with the onion. It would likely have been many months since she'd seen one last. That would go some way to paying her back for all her kindness on the day Bobby had come for an interview. Perhaps even the dour Reg might smile at her when he saw the pungent addition she'd brought for their evening meal.

After alighting once again at the Bull and Heifer crossroads, Bobby set off walking at a leisurely pace towards Silverdale, enjoying the unseasonal warmth of the November sunshine on her arms and neck. It was a Saturday afternoon, and apart from the occasional farmer going about his work and the low bleating of the sheep, all was calm and serene. It was hard to imagine that war was raging across the channel, where Göring was no doubt gathering his bombers for another assault on their cities. The countryside here felt entirely untouched by the war – as if she was walking back into another time.

Bobby had seen very little of the local countryside when she'd travelled this route by coal wagon, so focused had she been on trying to keep her suit free of sooty smudges. Now, she was able to appreciate it in all its glory.

This was limestone country – Bobby knew this from a book of walks she'd purchased to learn more about the place that was to be her new home. Such was her naivety about the countryside in this part of the world, she had imagined this as meaning that the rock must have a greenish tinge, like the fruit. Instead, the walls that segmented the rolling fields into a patchwork were a dazzling silver-blue, so smooth as to be shiny in places and dotted with patches of yellow and white lichen: a complete contrast with the rough, grey-black millstone grit of home. The walls glowed in the light of the sun, silver fading to pink as Bobby followed their crisscross threads with her eyes. When the sky had swelled and glowered on her last visit, she had thought of this landscape as being possessed of a beauty quite terrible in its scale and ruggedness. Today, walking alongside the rolling fields that stretched out to heaven, everything felt fresh and mellow. The countryside seemed to open up to her like a warm and welcoming friend.

Everything here seemed so… clean. The little houses in the distance shone like burnished gold in the sun. For centuries the thick, dirty smoke of the mills had been painting the sandy buildings of Bobby's home town black. By contrast, Silverdale looked like a vision of heaven.

'Afternoon,' she called to a farmer who was forking out hay for his sheep, and he touched his cap to her with a look of surprise.

After half an hour of walking, her suitcase swinging at her side while she whistled a jolly dance tune, Bobby reached the packhorse bridge that would allow her to cross the snaking silver beck.

She cast a glance at the well outside the pub as she passed it, remembering how it was here that she'd first encountered Charlie Atherton. Did he know that his brother had offered her the position, she wondered? She was looking forward to seeing him again – not for any romantic reason, she hastened to remind herself, but to find out what had become of Donald the Swadi-Cheviot hogg.

Nevertheless, she had been struck by Charlie's looks and manner on their first encounter. Still, if romance hadn't been on the cards with any of the boys she'd known back in Bradford then it certainly wouldn't be on the cards out here – not even with handsome vets who set out to charm with their deep eyes and unruly curls. If that was what Charlie had in mind, well, let him try if he liked. He would soon find out she was immune.

After growing up with two brothers, Bobby generally found the opposite sex easy to get along with. She enjoyed the teasing and jokes of the men she knew and the way they spoke their minds. She found their company suited her just as well as that of her own sex, and counted many of the male of the species among her friends. But unlike her twin, she very rarely went out on dates with them. She might dance with a boy if he asked, because it was polite and because she wasn't such a stuffy old spinster that she couldn't enjoy a polka or a waltz now and again, but she avoided anything that might lead to a serious entanglement.

There were plenty of good reasons for not wanting romance at this time in her life, in spite of Tony's jibes about becoming a veritable old maid if she wasted much more time. There was the war, of course. Marriage was a difficult and often expensive business at a time of international turmoil. There was also the fear of separation and ultimate loss if the object of her affection were to be called up and sent to serve overseas. But more than all of this, there was her career. All her life Bobby had dreamed of becoming a journalist, and perhaps ultimately finding herself a place on a national newspaper. Now, finally, she had taken the first step towards that. Reg had already expressed his fear that he might waste his time training her only for her to decide to marry and start a family. From his point of view, that would be worse than being called up. At least the boys who went off to war would eventually come home to their old employment – most of them. When a woman married, she was expected to settle down to a new career as a wife and mother. There was no way back.

That was why Bobby had sworn to herself that no man would ever come between her and her ambition to make the news, be he ever so handsome or charming. No, not even if it meant being an old maid. Love was a happy and glamorous fiction for the pictures, but she knew it was a fantasy that couldn't withstand real life. She'd seen it too many times in the marriages of old schoolmates. Even the grandest passions cooled when there were chores to be done, clothes to be washed and

84

bairns to be fed. Whereas her dream of being a journalist was something tangible, something she could actually hold in her hands.

Bobby hoped Charlie's thoughts tended the same way. It would be nice to make a friend out here, and she had enjoyed his company, but he needed to understand that he mustn't expect any more than friendship from her.

She had ascended the track up to Moorside Farm now, and put down her case so she could knock on the front door. It was answered a moment later by Mary, who immediately welcomed her with a hug. Bobby, who hadn't been expecting a welcome quite as warm as this, stood still for a moment before embracing her new landlady in return.

'You don't know how glad I am that you've come to us,' Mary said, sincerity ringing in every word. 'Now get yourself inside and I'll show you where you'll be sleeping.'

'Thank you.' Bobby followed her into the house. 'I brought something for you, Mrs Atherton.'

'I think it can be Mary now we're going to be living together, don't you?'

'I'd like that very much.' Bobby produced the newspaper-wrapped onion from her handbag and handed it to Mary. 'Um, this is for you.'

'Whatever is it?' Mary asked, eyeing it quizzically.

Bobby smiled. 'Open it and see.'

'Oh!' Mary said when she'd unwrapped it. She held it to her nose. 'Wherever did you find it? My Reg is devoted to onions. You'll have a friend in him for life when he sees this.'

'My friends at the newspaper gave it to me as a leaving gift. They bid for it in a charity auction,' Bobby said. 'It cost a whole guinea, apparently. I thought we might have it with our supper tonight.'

'Oh, yes. A nice Welsh rarebit with cheese and bacon and roast onion,' Mary said, beaming. 'Reg won't believe it when I put it in front of him. I don't think we've had an onion since the spring. You must be sent from heaven, Roberta.'

'My friends call me Bobby,' she said shyly.

'Do they indeed? Well, then I shall do so too. Come on upstairs, and you can get yourself all settled in.'

Chapter 11

Bobby followed Mary up a narrow flight of stairs, wondering how she and Reg had ever come to be married. They seemed to be complete opposites in their personalities: his wife so warm and merry while Reg hobbled around the house looking like a thunderstorm incarnate. And yet Bobby had no doubt that there was genuine love and affection between them. She'd noticed it the day she'd come for her interview when they'd all had tea together: Mary's tender care of her husband, the way they gently teased one another and sat so comfortably sharing the same space.

The room Mary showed Bobby to was small, but it looked comfortable. There was little in it other than a single bed, a wardrobe, a standard lamp and a chest of drawers, all old but serviceable and more than big enough to store the few things she'd brought from home. The wallpaper was faded and worn, but when Bobby looked closely, she noticed it had what must once have been a brightly coloured print: pictures of carousel horses. Had this been a child's room? A nursery, perhaps?

Bobby glanced at the single bed as she put her suitcase down. It was going to feel strange, sleeping alone.

'Is it all right for you?' Mary asked, looking worried. 'I know it's rather spartan, but everything is clean, and the mattress was bought new ready for you. The only other room is the attic, which is bigger but rather dark and musty. Reg has it filled with boxes of magazines at the moment.'

Bobby roused herself, summoning a smile. 'It's perfect, thank you, Mary. Sorry if I looked unhappy. I was thinking how odd it's going to be tonight, sleeping on my own. Ever since we were children, I've shared with my sister.'

'I know how you feel,' Mary said, a far-off expression in her eyes. 'I shared with my younger sister until the day I got wed. She's gone now. Tuberculosis. I still wake up sometimes and think she's there beside me.'

'I'm sorry.'

'Well, it was long ago. How many sisters do you have?'

'Just one, and two younger brothers,' Bobby said.

'Is your sister older or younger?'

Bobby laughed. 'She acts as though she's much older and more grown up than I could ever be, but there are only minutes between us. We're twins.'

Mary raised her eyebrows. 'Twins! You mean there's another one like you back in Bradford?'

'We're not the identical kind, but people say we look alike in spite of that. We both take after our mother in looks – our late mother. She passed away when we were sixteen.'

'I'm very sorry to hear that.' Mary's gaze was drawn to the pattern on the old wallpaper. 'Life contains so much of loss. It hardly seems fair. But I suppose the good Lord has a plan for us all.'

'I suppose He does,' Bobby said vaguely, more to be polite than anything else. She'd often wondered – even more so since the war began – if there was really any divine plan at work. Death so rarely seemed to make any sense.

For a moment, Bobby wondered whether to ask whose room this had once been and if Mary and Reg had grown-up children, but that felt rather forward for a new acquaintance. Instead, she nodded to an eye-catching watercolour on the wall showing a local scene: a deer, captured at twilight on the old stone packhorse bridge that Bobby had crossed to get to the village.

'This is beautiful,' she said. 'Is the artist local to Silverdale?'

Mary flushed. 'I suppose you might say that.'

Bobby glanced at her pink cheeks, then at the signature in the corner of the painting. 'You painted this?'

'It's something I like to do when I have the time. "You and your daubings", my Reg always teases me.'

'But Mary, this is really impressive!'

'Oh, it's nothing special. A little something I do to lift my spirits.'

'No, I mean it. That wasn't idle flattery. It's really well done.' Bobby looked at the painting again. '*The Tyke* includes art as well as photography, doesn't it?'

'Aye, when Reg thinks it's worth the paper. He's a lover of art, is Reg.'

'You should ask him to include some of yours.'

Mary laughed, although she looked rather pleased at the compliment. 'Now, if that isn't the daftest thing I've ever heard.'

'Well, why not? This is as good as anything I've seen in the magazine.'

'It's a hobby, that's all. I'd feel such a fraud being in there with all those professionals. Everyone would think Reg had gone soft, putting his wife's messes in with the proper artists.'

'They wouldn't at all. They'd be surprised and impressed, the same way I am. But I won't nag if the idea makes you uncomfortable.' Still, Bobby resolved privately that she'd speak to Reg about it when she knew him a little better. She'd known the first time she'd seen Mary and noticed the sparkling intelligence in her blue eyes that there was more to her than might be obvious from her motherly appearance. Bobby wasn't an art connoisseur by any means, yet she was sure the work in front of her was a match for any of the paintings she'd seen for sale in the art shops at home.

'Well, I'll leave you,' Mary said. 'Just step downstairs and say a word to Reg when you're feeling refreshed, then the afternoon's your own until we have our supper at six.'

Mary left her, and Bobby lay down on the bed for a moment. She wasn't tired, but she did feel that she needed a few minutes to process the events of the day.

Already, life felt so different. She'd woken up that morning in the same bed she'd shared with Lilian nearly all her life, in the same dingy room in the same squat terraced house: one among a thousand like it. Now, she was in a light, airy bedroom facing a window that presented a view of rolling green vistas as far as the eye could see. The autumn air, free of the unhealthy city smog, seemed sweet and fresh as she took in great deep lungfuls. When she pushed the window open a little wider, Bobby could hear the belly-laugh call of some moorland bird – a pheasant or red grouse, perhaps? – and the soft, low bleats of grazing sheep.

She glanced again at Mary's painting, captured so vividly in earthy tones and exuding a mellow warmth that seemed to belong to this place. The deer's eyes, in particular, were quite compelling: a deep, creamy brown that seemed to shine with innocence and wisdom combined. For some reason, it made her think of Charlie.

Her gaze drifted then to the pattern on the old wallpaper. The merry-go-round horses must have been very bright and jolly once, although they were so faded now that they were only barely visible. This would have been a child's room, Bobby was sure. She wondered where that child was now, and what age.

When she felt rested, Bobby made her way downstairs to the living room – or the parlour, as they seemed to call it out here. This, she assumed, was where she was likely to find Reg, since it seemed to serve as both living space and study to him. She knocked on the door and was summoned with a gruff 'Come!'.

She entered and discovered Reg wasn't alone. Charlie was with him, propped semi-reclining on the settee like a Victorian lady of leisure. One of the huge grey dogs sprawled across him. The other, meanwhile, sat at Reg's feet while he read the newspaper in an armchair. Charlie waved when Bobby entered.

'Hullo again, Bobby Bancroft,' he said. 'I was hanging around hoping you might turn up.'

'You two know each other, do you?' Reg asked, putting down his copy of the *Bradford Courier*. The sight of it sent a fresh wave of homesickness washing over Bobby, but she pushed it down.

'We met when I came for my interview,' Bobby told Reg. 'Your brother helped me to find you.'

'Did he indeed?' Reg shot Charlie a suspicious look.

'What happened to that lamb you were treating?' Bobby asked Charlie.

'Donald, you mean?'

'Donald?' Reg said. 'Damn silly name for a beast.'

'It sounds it, doesn't it? But he did have a very Donald-like face,' Charlie said, with a warm smile for Bobby. 'Don't worry, he's back at home and fighting fit again. Selenium deficiency, as I suspected.'

'So you actually managed to do a day's work recently, did you?' Reg remarked dryly to his brother.

'Oh, no. Not a whole day. I wouldn't want to exhaust myself.' Charlie dislodged the dog that was snuggled up to him so he could stand up. 'I'll leave you to enjoy your afternoons, now I've greeted the new member of the household. There's a pint of beer at the Golden Hart calling my name. Goodbye, Bobby. I hope to see you again soon.'

'Wait there,' Reg said to Bobby, pushing himself upright with his stick so he could follow his brother out. She did so, helping herself to the seat Charlie had vacated. She could hear low voices outside and wondered what the brothers were talking so secretively about. The big grey dog that had been at Reg's feet slunk off to the fire while the other one snuggled against Bobby, seemingly as happy with her company as he had been with Charlie's. She tickled him between the ears.

'I see you've made a friend of the dog, at any rate,' Reg said when he came back in.

'He's a placid old soul, isn't he?' The dog's tail thumped limply a couple of times, as if aware he was being talked about.

'Aye, more's the pity.' Reg settled himself back in his chair. 'I got the pair of them from the same litter ten year ago to act as guard dogs. The only danger a burglar's likely to be in from these two is if they lick him to death.'

'What are their names?'

'By you is Barney, and hogging the fire is his sister Winnie.' He had picked up his paper again, but Bobby could see him scrutinising her over the top of it. 'Ready to start work Monday, are you?'

'Ready, willing and able,' she said, sitting up straighter. This was what she really wanted to talk about.

'Hmm. I remember you once told me you'd rather work than gad. I hope you'll remember that when my brother makes it his mission to lead you astray – which he will. Charlie's the devil that finds work for idle hands you've probably heard tell about.'

'You've no need to worry about that. I've waited a long time for this opportunity, Mr Atherton, and I don't intend to let you down.'

'Glad to hear it,' Reg said. 'I took a big risk by employing you, young lady. I dread to think what folk are going to say when I start sending you out and about. I can see you've got the brains for it, but whether you've the guts is another matter.'

'Just give me the chance to prove myself,' Bobby said fervently. 'What will I be working on first?'

'I'll show you.' Reg heaved himself upright and limped to the desk occupied by his typewriter and an assortment of scrawled notes, newspaper cuttings and other miscellaneous papers. He picked up a thick volume and placed it in Bobby's hands.

She looked at it. 'The telephone directory?'

'Aye, that's right.'

'What do you expect me to do with it?' Bobby couldn't see how this would be a likely lead for a magazine story.

'I've a box of envelopes in the attic. Next week, I want you to start filling them with unsold magazines and posting them out to the people listed in that book.'

'Why?'

He tapped his temple. 'Use your brain, lass. Telephones don't come cheap, do they? If the folk in that book can afford a phone, they can afford four bob a year for a magazine subscription. We just need to show them what they're missing out on. If we send them a complimentary copy and a subscription form, some of them will hopefully come back to us with a postal order.'

Bobby had to acknowledge the wisdom in this, although filling envelopes hardly sounded like work for a junior reporter. That was the sort of thing she'd been expected to do in her previous position. She didn't dare to object though, lest Reg labelled her as uncooperative and decided to withdraw his offer of a job. Perhaps this was some sort of test, to prove she was willing to turn her hand to anything.

'How many subscribers do you have?' she asked.

'Our circulation's four thousand. That's subscribers plus what we sell at the newsstands.' Reg looked rather proud of this figure, and for his benefit Bobby endeavoured to seem impressed, although it sounded minuscule compared to the *Courier*. The small weekly newspaper had a modest circulation compared to a large daily like its rival, the *Bradford Post*, but it still sold an average of 60,000 copies per edition.

'I don't suppose it sounds much to you, but I've worked hard to build it up to that and keep it there, especially since they brought in paper rationing,' Reg said. 'It's been a bugger on us, the rationing. They based how much you were allowed on how much you'd used the year preceding, and since we'd only been running six months when they brought in the ration, we got six months' worth to last us the year. But with economy, reducing the weight and quality, I've kept each number at thruppence for twenty-eight pages, same as before the war.'

Bobby, sensing he was waiting for some word of compliment or congratulations, said, 'It must be heartening to know you have so many loyal readers.'

'Aye, but there are a lot more who would be loyal readers if they only knew we existed. I'm pleased with the start we've made, but we're in no danger of turning a profit yet.' He took the telephone directory from her. 'That's why this book is one of two things you're going to get to know very, very well in this job.'

'What's the other?'

'Tell me, Miss Bancroft – can you ride a bicycle?'

Chapter 12

Bobby could ride a bicycle, although she'd never ridden a bicycle quite like the old boneshaker Reg wheeled out for her the following day. After one week of riding it, the thing had turned her black and blue. Her foot frequently slipped off the broken left pedal, which then struck her on the back of her calf so that she developed a permanent purple bruise on the spot. The saddle was hard and solid, which meant that she was also sporting florid bruises in other, rather more intimate places.

As Reg had promised, Bobby got to know both the telephone directory and the old bike well over the weeks that followed. Every day she would painstakingly copy names and addresses from the directory on to envelopes before filling them with magazines and subscription forms, and every afternoon at the end of the working day she would load them into the basket of her bicycle and ride that juddering, wobbly pile of chipped black paint and rust a mile and a quarter to the post office in the village, often stopping a few times to reattach the bicycle chain when it came loose.

Thanks to these daily visits, Bobby got to know Silverdale well in the first three weeks of her job. It was a settlement of some hundred and fifty residents, she would have guessed, with around thirty or so little dwellings huddling around the beck at the heart of the village. Bobby started to recognise the local families as the days passed. She learned which cottage each occupied and what the head of the household did for a living.

Farming was the major employer locally, of course, just as the mills were back at home. Most of the men in the village worked on the farms that dotted the surrounding fells or ran little smallholdings of their own – mostly sheep, but there were some who went in for dairy. With the advent of war, a number had also turned over some of their land to crops, in spite of the fact the soil in this region didn't lend itself well to growing.

There was also the blacksmith, the cobbler, the butcher, the joiner – who was also the village undertaker – the pub landlady, the coal man, the postmistress, and half a dozen others Bobby learned to know by sight. Most regarded this interloper who'd appeared in their midst with wariness, if not outright hostility, although after the first fortnight, a few would greet her with a 'good morning' or a touch of their cap. Men were more likely to greet her than women, Bobby noticed. The young single women of the village seemed most distrustful of her, which gave Bobby little hope of making friends her own age in Silverdale.

The village was one of the few places she visited regularly, other than Settle and the surrounding area, when Reg sent her on the bus to collect advertisement copy from local businesses. In her new role as a country reporter, Bobby had filed corres- pondence, collected advertisements, typed letters and stories written by Reg and the handful of freelancers they worked with, and spent hours copying from the telephone directory, but she hadn't written a single word of copy. The only differ- ence between her new job and her old one was that she was no longer expected to make the tea, since Mary Atherton kept them well fed and watered throughout the day.

Bobby's early optimism had worn off now as disappointment in her new role set in and homesickness started to gnaw. Reg wasn't a bad boss – at least, he was more pleasant to work for than Clarky, whose sudden, white-hot rages were the stuff of *Courier* legend – but he rarely spoke to her while they worked, and she conducted her dreary tasks mostly in silence. She missed the camaraderie and bickering of the boys she'd worked with before; missed their teasing and the feeling that she was part of a gang. She missed the comforting smell of the newsroom and Don's Tom Long pipe tobacco. She missed her sister, feeling the absence of a bedfellow on the long, eerie country nights when tawny owls emitted their ghost-like cries outside her window. She missed the bustle of the city, where there was always something happening and somewhere to go, and she worried constantly about her father, although Lilian's letters assured her all was well at home. The only thing that had stopped Bobby throwing in the towel after a fortnight – apart from the unpleasant prospect of proving Tony right in his forecast that she'd never make it to Christmas in her new job – had been the continued kindness and companionship of Mary Atherton, who had taken to her almost as a daughter. After seven years of feeling like an orphan, robbed of her mother by death and her father by the horrors he'd seen in the last war, it felt good to have someone in her life who could stand in the stead of a parent to her.

Bobby's mundane routine was identical every single day. Each morning she woke to the sound of cattle being driven to the shippon for milking and wondered if today would be the day Reg would finally send her out to get a story. And each morning her spirits sank as she sat down at the little desk Reg had set up for her beside his own and found the now despised telephone directory waiting for her beside a stack of fresh envelopes. Her evenings were spent with Reg and Mary in the parlour, knitting and listening to the wireless, like the confirmed old spinster Tony had so often warned her she was at risk of becoming. There was no social life in the village to speak of, or at least none that she felt she'd be welcome to join – only the village pub, which she didn't dare to enter without company. Reg and Mary were very much homebodies, rarely leaving the house except on their once-a-week trip into Settle in Reg's Wolseley to buy groceries or to go to chapel on Sunday.

Knowing Bobby was Church rather than Chapel, Mary had offered to ask some friends among the village women if they would allow her to join them and their families at the village's Anglican church for the Sunday morning service. Bobby had politely declined, however, not wishing to inflict her company on any of those who regarded her with suspicion whenever she showed her face in the village. The Bancrofts weren't regular churchgoers at home – in fact, her father rarely left the house except to go to work. Instead, Bobby chose to spend her time off on Saturday afternoons and Sundays in her room with a book. She still hadn't summoned the courage to explore the rugged, weather-beaten countryside that surrounded Silverdale, although, in its wild way, it was rather enticing.

In short, she was rather bored with both her new job and her new life. She had almost exhausted the small supply of books she'd brought from home, and there was no library in the village. Mary had invited her to help herself to anything around the house that took her fancy, but Mary didn't read novels herself and exploring Reg's shelves hadn't yielded much of interest. They mostly contained books on farming or dry reference works on Yorkshire history and folklore that he used to research articles for *The Tyke*.

The only advantage to Bobby's new life was that she was starting to boast some actual curves, largely thanks to Mary's wholesome country cooking. She'd also developed a healthy glow in her cheeks from all the outdoor exercise on her bicycle. While Bobby didn't believe she had much in the way of vanity, she had always been envious of her sister's figure, so the change in her appearance was very welcome. Nevertheless, this felt like small compensation for the closeted and nun-like existence she was now living. What did it matter if her clothes hung well on her when there were no dance halls for her to show them off in? It didn't help that Lil's most recent letter, which had arrived that morning, had been full of dances she'd attended and films she'd seen. Bobby had never felt more homesick for her old life.

'How many have you done today?' Reg asked as Bobby gummed the flap on the envelope she'd just filled, as he always did once the clock chimed five.

She scanned the pile. 'About forty, I should say.'

'Grand. Better get them over to the post office, before they close for the day.'

'Right.' She started loading the envelopes into a satchel. 'Um, Mr Atherton?'

'Mmm?'

'I was wondering... I mean to say, don't you think it's time I wrote something?'

Reg wasn't paying attention. He was frowning at a page of copy she'd typed up for him the day before.

'There's three literals in this, Miss Bancroft. I hope you're not getting careless.'

Bobby flushed. 'Sorry. I must've let my mind wander.' Wander to home, family and friends: the life she'd left behind. It had been doing that more and more recently. 'It won't happen again.'

'Aye, well, think on in future. Off you go with that post.'

Bobby hesitated. 'But... shouldn't I write something? For the magazine, I mean. That is why you hired me.'

'All in good time, lass,' Reg said vaguely, his attention focused on the page of copy again as his pencil skimmed over it.

Bobby didn't know why she'd bothered to ask. It was the same answer he always gave. She didn't like to badger him too much, knowing this was only likely to make him more stubborn on the point, but she couldn't go on like this forever. She was doing exactly the same kind of work as she had been at the *Courier*, and for less than half the salary.

Perhaps she should confide in Mary about how she was feeling. She would surely have some influence over her husband, and she usually took Bobby's part. But Bobby hated to seem discontented with her lot when she knew – or at least, she strongly suspected – that it was her new landlady who had pleaded with Reg to give her the reporter job in the first place.

With low spirits and a deflated feeling inside her, Bobby dumped the heavy satchel of magazines into the basket of her horrible old bicycle and set off into the village.

On arrival at the post office, she was greeted by Gil Capstick, the sub-postmaster. He was a friendly young chap, just five foot tall, with bright red hair, copious freckles and a wide grin. Bobby liked it when she was served by Gil rather than the stern, staid old postmistress, Mrs Clough, who regarded her with the wary suspicion she'd become used to seeing on the faces of the villagers when 'yon lass from town' appeared in their midst. Gil liked everyone, and consequently, everyone liked Gil.

'Now then, Miss Bancroft,' he hailed her jovially. 'What've you got for me today?'

'I bet you'll never guess,' she said, pulling a face.

He laughed. 'T'owd man's still got you nose to grindstone filling up those envelopes, has he?'

'Hasn't he just? I wish I could throw that old telephone directory of his right out of the window.'

The little bell over the door jingled, and the familiar figure of Charlie Atherton strode in. He was clad in gaiters and splashed with mud up to his middle, which seemed to suggest he'd come direct from a job on one of the farms.

'Afternoon, Gil,' he said. 'And the charming Miss Bancroft too. My luck must be changing.'

Bobby ignored him, focusing on unloading the magazines from her leather satchel, but she smiled.

'Looks like tha's had a day of it, Charlie,' Gil observed, nodding to the mud that decorated the other man's costume.

'Been vaccinating that swine of a hog up at Tot Hector's place.' Charlie rubbed his thigh. 'She can kick like a mule, that pig. I've been wrestling with her these two hours.'

It was funny seeing Charlie fresh from work, Bobby reflected, glancing at him out of the corner of her eye. Somehow, his job as a vet always felt too... too grown up for him, she supposed. At any rate, it didn't suit him. She was sure nature had intended Charlie Atherton to be a wealthy young man of leisure, dressed in a top hat and tails, dancing with debutantes and smoking expensive cigarettes in a long holder. Either that or a gentleman jewel thief like Raffles, or perhaps a rogue adventurer cutting swathes through the jungles of South America. There was something about him that seemed to belong more to a *Boy's Own* story than a Yorkshire farmyard.

'Tha mun need a drink after that,' Gil said to Charlie.

'You read my mind. I'll be heading over to the Hart in a minute.' Charlie nodded to a sheet of stamps on the counter. 'How's the weather looking, Gil?'

Gil scrutinised the stamps closely.

'Rain,' he announced confidently. 'Curling to the left from bottom corner. Allus means a shower.'

Bobby laughed. She hadn't been in Silverdale very long, but already she knew that Gil Capstick's weather forecasts were the stuff of local legend. 'What's frightening is how often you get it right.'

'Never mock t' owd ways, Miss,' he told her soberly. 'That's how they get to be t' owd ways. Because they work.' He counted the pile of envelopes she'd placed in front of him, his lips moving silently as he calculated the postage. 'Six and eight for this lot.'

Bobby took out her purse and handed over the coins, then Gil gave her a receipt for Reg and disappeared into the back room to sort her letters.

'What brings you in here?' she asked, turning to Charlie.

'Nothing but the pleasure of your company.' He smiled at her expression. 'I saw that old velocipede of Reggie's outside. I didn't think you'd object to passing the time of day with me, even if my brother has forbidden me to speak to you.'

'Did he do that?'

'Yes, he told me the day you moved in that you're here to work and I wasn't to distract you.' He glanced at his wristwatch. 'But since I'm assuming you've now finished work for the day,

I think a little distraction won't do you any harm. Why don't you come to the Hart with me for a drink?'

It was certainly tempting, although Bobby suspected Reg would be angry if he knew she'd been fraternising with his brother. Charlie was well-liked in the village, but he did seem to have a reputation as something of a rogue when it came to women. No whiff of any real scandal, but still, mothers with pretty daughters drew them closer when Charlie Atherton walked by.

'I hope you're not asking me for a date,' she said. 'I've been given strict instructions by your brother that I'm not to let you lead me astray.'

'A date was the furthest thing from my mind,' Charlie said, his voice ringing with faux indignation at the very idea. 'I thought that a girl far from home in a new place might appreciate a little friendly companionship. That's the sort of thoughtful chap I am, you know.'

'Mmm. I've heard about the sort of chap you are.'

'Believe every word of it,' he said with a grin. 'You'll come then?'

She sighed. 'I can't, Charlie. Reg would have my guts for garters.'

Charlie dropped his usual teasing, flirtatious tone. 'Come on, Bobby. You look tired and worried, and it doesn't suit you a bit. I promise I'll be a perfect gentleman and walk you home afterwards so I can apologise to Mary personally for keeping you out. She likes me.'

Bobby hesitated. She knew she shouldn't. She knew Reg wouldn't like it, and Mary might well worry if she was late going back. But she was lonely and fed up, and the prospect of a little fun with someone young was too hard to say no to. Besides, what was the worst that could happen, really? After nearly a year of working alongside Tony Scott, she knew how to take care of herself when men seemed to grow extra hands after too much beer.

'Well, all right,' she said. 'One friendly drink, that's all.'

'That's what I wanted to hear.'

Bobby followed him to the pub, where she propped her old bike against the well outside. It ought to be safe enough. No one in their right mind would want to steal the thing, even for scrap. It was more than half rust.

Bobby had never been inside the Golden Hart before. The first thing that struck her as she entered was that this was a very different place from the White Swan, where the *Courier's* weekly darts matches against the Home Guard had taken place, or the Rose and Crown, which she and Lilian occasionally visited. It wasn't unusual to see women in those places: girls from the mills in their headscarves and overalls, having a glass of beer together after work, or sweethearts sharing a quiet drink in the snug. The Golden Hart, on the other hand, was clearly very much a man's domain. Apart from the barmaid and a solitary older woman sitting at one end of the bar, everyone here was male. Old farmers in broad cloth caps sat around tables playing dominoes, drinking from their own personal pint pots. The walls were exposed stone, and the floor, bare stone flags. Pipe and cigarette smoke hung heavy in the air, making Bobby cough.

Charlie seemed perfectly at home, however. He strode to the bar, leaving Bobby with no choice but to follow.

'Pint of the usual, Lizzie, and whatever this young lady's having,' he said to the barmaid.

'I'll have half of the same, please,' Bobby said.

Lizzie nodded wordlessly and took down one of the pewter pint pots that hung above the bar to pour Charlie a brown ale. When they'd both been served, Charlie took Bobby's arm and guided her to one of the high-backed settles that lined the walls.

'I feel a little conspicuous,' Bobby whispered when they were seated. 'There aren't many women in here, Charlie.'

'That's Silverdale for you. Always about one hundred years behind the times.' He noticed her look of concern and nudged her. 'Oh, don't worry. No one's looking at you, are they?'

'Well, no, but… I don't think your brother would like me being here much. I hadn't realised it wasn't the done thing for women to go to pubs out here.'

'Never mind what Reggie thinks. He's not your father.'

'No, but he's my employer.'

'Well, you've clocked off for the day. I'd say it's none of his business where you go – or who with, for that matter.'

'I don't think he'd agree, do you?' Bobby said, taking a sip of her beer. 'I would quite like to keep my job, even if it isn't what I hoped it would be.'

Charlie shuffled to look at her. 'Is that why you looked so miserable when I saw you in the post office?'

'Did I look miserable? I wasn't trying to.'

'But you did, all the same. What's the matter?'

Bobby wondered how much it was safe to confide in him. He was Reg's brother, after all. But she did feel like it would help her to talk to someone, and she felt better about sharing her feelings of discontent with Charlie than she would with Mary, her only other ally.

'I suppose… I'd built up such high hopes for this job, only to find it's really no different from the one I left,' she told him. 'I thought I'd be out getting stories, like…' She laughed softly at herself. '…like Dorothy Lawrence. Instead, I'm spending every day copying addresses from the telephone directory. That's hardly the work of a reporter.'

She waited, expecting Charlie to perhaps make a comment about whether the work of a reporter ought to be women's work at all, the way most of the men she knew would. But he just took a sip of his pint and said, 'Did you say Dorothy Lawrence?'

'Yes. She was a journalist in the last war.'

'I know who she is. I read her memoir. Very impressive lady. Did you tell Reggie that's how you feel about it?'

'I keep asking when I can do some writing. He always says, "all in good time, Miss Bancroft, all in good time".' She wobbled her head comically as she mimicked the dour old Dalesman's voice.

Charlie laughed. 'It's like he's here with us. You should write to Tommy Handley and ask to audition for *ITMA*, Bobby.' He took out a packet of Woodbines and offered one to her.

'No thanks, I don't.'

'Suit yourself.'

Charlie lit his cigarette, and Bobby watched him while he savoured it. She wasn't interested in romance, but that didn't mean she couldn't appreciate a good-looking man – especially when he laughed the way that Charlie did, his brown eyes sparkling with merriment. She wondered how old he was.

'There must be a big gap between you and your brother,' she observed, hoping he might volunteer his age in response.

He removed the cigarette from his mouth and nodded. 'Twenty years. He's my half-brother, actually; Reggie's mother died when he was seventeen, then our father married again. Although Reggie was more of a father to me growing up than our old man ever was.'

Bobby wondered why this might be the case, but she didn't ask. Charlie's expression had darkened, in a way that seemed to signal he didn't want to talk about it further.

'How old is Reg?' she asked.

'Not as old as he looks. The last war made an old man of him too early. He's forty-six, but you could be forgiven for thinking he was ten years older.'

Forty-six. So that made Charlie twenty-six, if there were twenty years between them.

Perhaps being raised by different mothers was why they had such a different mode of speaking. Both had a version of the local accent, but Charlie's was very light; more of a lilt than an accent. Reg's, on the other hand, was far broader, with a tendency to lapse into the dialect of his boyhood when he wasn't concentrating.

'Were your upbringings very different?' Bobby asked, as a roundabout way of trying to learn more.

'Reggie and Mary were responsible for most of my upbringing,' Charlie told her. 'My mother died when I was ten. Dad didn't want me around much after that, so Mary and Reggie took charge of me. I had a good brain, but neither parent had given me much encouragement to use it; my brother was the only one who ever told me I could make more of myself. After Mother died and Dad decided he wanted nothing more to do with me, Reggie insisted I was sent away to a decent school. Said he'd do it at his own expense if Dad wouldn't pay, although he wasn't earning much of a salary as a newspaperman – I suppose you know all about that. Anyhow, Dad was so keen to have me out of his sight that Reg didn't have to work too hard to talk him into it. In the end, they divided the cost between them.'

Bobby was dying to know why Charlie's father should be so anxious to be rid of him, but she didn't like to ask such a personal question so early on in their acquaintance.

'How did you like boarding?' she asked instead.

He shrugged. 'Not much. The other boys didn't think a lot of me, coming from some backwater farm with my thick Dales accent, and the boys I'd been pals with here didn't think a lot of me when I came back for the holidays with a new way of talking and some learning under my belt. But it made me, I suppose you might say. Forced me to buck up my ideas and make some use of my brain so I could go on to veterinary college – besides, it was better than being at home with Dad. I'll always be grateful to Reggie for making me go.'

Bobby smiled. 'You'll have to do me a favour sometime and help me out with the local dialect, since you're able to translate. I can only get about half of what anyone round here is saying to me.'

'Do we speak so very differently from in town?'

'The accent's a lot thicker. I suppose with the villages here being so isolated, it hasn't changed as much over the centuries as it has in the towns. And there are a lot of words we don't use at home. About sheep, mostly.'

He laughed. 'Well, sheep I can help you with.'

She sipped her beer thoughtfully. 'Funny, isn't it? All my family worked in the Bradford mills, and I've seen plenty of untreated wool piled up outside them, but I've hardly ever thought about it being attached to a sheep. The farmers here rely on the mills to buy their wool and the millworkers rely on the farmers to keep their industry going, one mouth feeding the other, yet we so rarely think about each other. I'm barely thirty miles from home, yet Silverdale feels like a whole other world.'

'I suppose you're right,' Charlie said. 'I've never really thought about it before.'

She roused herself. 'So it sounds like you and your brother are close.'

'In a way, we are.' Charlie tapped ash from his cigarette. 'He thinks I'm a bone-idle young wastrel, but I suspect he's secretly rather fond of me in spite of that. I always thought I'd quite like to prove him wrong one day, but I'd prefer to have a little fun first. Unless the war decides it has other plans for me, of course.'

'Not been called up yet?'

'Vets are reserved, but if they'll have me, I'll probably join up after Christmas. I've been putting it off, really. The Athertons are a Chapel family of the Quakerish persuasion so we've never gone in for that sort of thing. You know, war and all that.'

'I can see you're a strict Methodist,' Bobby said, laughing as she nodded to his beer.

'I admit we may have drifted from the narrow way a bit in recent years,' he said, swallowing down a mouthful. 'Anyhow, most of the lads I was at college with are in uniform now. They say the RAF are after men with strong maths, which I've got, so I don't think they'll turn me down. I'd rather fly than get shunted into the Veterinary Corps. I doubt I'm going to give old Schicklgruber too much to worry about, but it's probably past time I was doing my bit too.'

'How do you feel about that?'

Charlie paused to finish his cigarette, blowing smoke thoughtfully from the corners of his mouth.

'I'm not sure,' he said at last. 'It might be jolly to get out of Silverdale for a little while, but I don't much like the idea of having to kill. It's hard enough when I have to put an animal to sleep, and that's done in mercy. To kill another human being in malice isn't something I ever thought I'd be asked to do. Still, it isn't fair to expect other men to get their hands dirty on my behalf. I can't shirk my duty if that's where it lies.'

The subject was deadly serious, but Charlie spoke quite lightly, as if it was all somehow academic. As if the war was a story rather than something real. Bobby had felt that way too, until that night in the summer when the bombs had fallen on Bradford. Charlie might feel now that the war was something far away and unreal, but that wouldn't stop it harming him if he did choose to join up, just as the last one had cost his brother the use of his leg. Bobby felt a chill run down her spine at the thought. Would that be how Charlie would prove Reg's ideas about him wrong? Some foolhardy death-or-glory escapade? It was the sort of impulsive action she could well believe he'd be capable of.

He was looking at her now, a smile playing at the corner of his mouth as if there was something in her thoughtful expression that amused him.

'What is it?' she said.

'Nothing. I was just thinking it's nice to have something new and pretty to look at around here.'

She smiled, pushing away dark thoughts. 'You're not flirting with me, are you? Don't forget you promised to be the perfect gentleman. That was a condition of me coming out with you.'

'To be honest, I'm not sure. I spend so much of my time flirting with girls that I can't tell when I'm doing it any more.' Charlie scrutinised her face. 'It's good to have someone new to talk to though. You interest me, Bobby Bancroft.'

'Do I indeed? And now my line is "I bet you say that to all the girls".'

'I'm forced to confess that I say many things to all the girls, but that isn't one of them. You're not going to leave again, are you? You can't, you know. Not when I was counting on you to enliven our sleepy country society.'

She sighed. 'I honestly don't know. I'm starting to worry your brother might never give me a story to work on, and I've been terribly homesick since I came. Everyone in the village looks at me as if I'm a fifth columnist or some other type of ne'er-do-well. If this isn't going to be a real reporter job, I might as well go home.'

Charlie took a sip of his brown ale. 'What you need is to understand Reggie. I can tell you how to get what you want from him if you like.'

Bobby blinked. 'Can you?'

'Of course. No one knows him like I do, except Mary. Reggie's a stickler for the sort of nonsense they drum into you in the army. Showing initiative and all that rot.'

'You think I need to show initiative?'

He nodded. 'Don't wait for Reggie to send you out to a story. Go out and find one for yourself. Trust me, I know how my brother's mind works. Even if he doesn't print it, he'll be impressed you had the nous to do it.'

'But how can I, when he's got me addressing envelopes all the livelong day?'

'Use your own time. Then he'll be even more impressed.'

'I suppose I could do that,' Bobby said slowly. 'If I knew where to begin looking for the sort of stories we print in *The Tyke*. I don't know this area very well, and the people here don't trust me yet.'

He smiled. 'I might be able to help you with that. What are you doing tonight, Bobby?'

Chapter 13

'Will you be sitting in the parlour with us this evening?' Mary asked Bobby after they'd had their tea. 'I'm going to start a layette for young Elsie Farnell in the village. She's had a little girl this week. I wondered if you might help me by doing the bonnet.'

'I'll do the bonnet gladly, but I can't start it tonight. I'm… going out.'

Bobby glanced at Reg, whose attention was absorbed by his copy of the *Bradford Courier*. He always picked one up from the newsagent in Settle when he drove Mary in to buy her groceries, and it made Bobby feel extra homesick when she saw it, with the familiar bylines of her old friends. Even when visiting the outhouse she couldn't avoid it, since once Reg had finished with it, Mary cut it into squares to hang on the peg by the privy. Bobby had often thought while reading one of Tony's pieces by the light of the outhouse storm lantern how much better a job she could have made of it. She wondered when her turn would come.

Reg's head snapped up. 'Out?'

'Yes. To a social engagement.'

He looked suspicious. 'Who've you got to go to social engagements with?'

'No one yet, but it would be nice to get to know more people my age. I heard of a dance in the next village and I thought I might bicycle over there. I mean, if that's all right with you both.'

This wasn't quite an untruth, although Bobby, who never had become accomplished in the skill of the artful lie, felt her cheeks colour slightly all the same. She was indeed bound for the next village tonight, but it wasn't quite as she was choosing to represent it to her hosts.

'Hmm,' Reg said, still with that suspicious look on his face.

Mary nudged him. 'Oh, don't be such a mourngy old thing, Reg. She's young. She doesn't want to be sitting in every night with us two old miseries.' She smiled at Bobby. 'You go enjoy yourself, love. I wish I was coming with you myself.'

Bobby knew she could always count on Mary to take her side. She smiled at the older woman, feeling a needle of guilt stab her belly for lying – or at least half-lying – to that kindly soul.

'Do you want Reg to take you in the car?' Mary asked. 'I don't like you riding that old contraption in the dark.'

'There'll be no need for that,' Bobby assured her hastily. That would ruin the whole plan. 'You need to save your petrol coupons for more important things. Besides, Mr Atherton already drove to Settle and back today, and I know it hurts his leg to drive too much. I'll be very careful, Mary, I promise.'

–

Half an hour later, Bobby was mounted on her bike, pedalling as fast as she could towards the neighbouring village of Smeltham.

Mary was right about one thing: bicycling in the blackout with only the aid of a partially obscured lamp was no joke. Bobby spent as much time pushing the thing as she did pedalling, terrified of tumbling into the beck or going over the handlebars if she hit a rock. Once she reached the road, however, things became rather easier, and some half an hour later, she arrived at the Royal Oak pub in Smeltham. Charlie was lounging against the wall outside, waiting for her.

'Glad you could make it,' he said. 'I was worried Reggie might have locked you in your bedroom. I was all ready to stand outside your window calling, "Rapunzel, let down your hair!"'

Bobby laughed. 'He wasn't very happy about letting me out, but Mary stuck up for me.'

'She's a brick, isn't she? I never could understand how my grumpy brother got someone so sweet to marry him.'

'He looked suspicious though, Charlie. I'm sure he knows I'm out with you.'

'Probably. I imagine he thinks I'm trying to corrupt your innocent, girlish ideals with my lascivious bachelor lifestyle, which I must admit does sound like a lot of fun. But tomorrow you can show him your story and he'll know it was purely a business arrangement after all.' Charlie offered her his arm. 'Let's go in, shall we?'

Bobby ignored the proffered arm, instead delving into her handbag for her notebook and a pencil.

'Are you sure this is going to be worth a story?' she asked Charlie as she followed him into the pub. 'A country dance doesn't sound like anything all that special.'

'It isn't. It's only a dance. The same sort of dance as the people here have been holding for centuries.' The pub was virtually empty inside, but Charlie paid this no mind, taking her along a narrow stone passageway and through a door at the back of the building.

'Then why am I here?'

They were outside again now, in an enclosed field behind the pub. Nearby was a large barn, from which could be heard music and other sounds of merriment. Charlie turned to look at her.

'I suppose I could tell you it was the only way I could get you to come here with me, and you could accuse me of tricking you into coming on a date, and it would all be tremendous fun,' he said. 'But I'll tell you the truth instead. Just because a country dance isn't anything special doesn't mean it isn't worth a story, Bobby. I'm sure my brother's told you his theory that to make a good story, you need to focus on people and not things.'

'He has.'

'Village hops like this… they're dying out. A lot of young people prefer to go into the towns, to the modern dance halls where they can try out new steps and listen to jazz bands. Only a few of the more remote Dales villages still hold dances like this in barns and hay lofts, jigging to the old tunes, and I wouldn't be surprised if the war didn't see off the last of them.' He glanced wistfully at the barn door. 'I suppose change has to happen, but I'll be sorry to see them go. They were a part of my youth. It's sad to think my own children won't get to experience them.'

Bobby watched his face, which had a different expression on it than she'd seen there before.

'You sound like your brother.'

'Do I? Please don't tell him, for God's sake. I'll never hear the end of it.' He nudged her. 'Come on, or there'll be no supper left for us.'

Charlie rapped out a knock on the barn door that seemed to have a particular rhythm to it, and it opened a crack to reveal a woman's face. This reminded Bobby of a gangster film she'd once seen about the illicit American 'speakeasies' of the prohibition years. She half expected Charlie to have to give a password before they were allowed inside.

The woman's face beamed when she saw who it was. 'Charlie Atherton! Get yerssen inside, post haste. We're tragic for want of lads in here.'

'In that case, I'm going to have to apologise for bringing another girl with me. Sorry, Till.'

Till cast a suspicious look at Bobby, who had her notebook poised and ready. 'Who's this, Charlie?'

'This is Miss Bobby Bancroft. She's new to these parts. My brother's just given her a job.'

'You mean this is lass from t' paper?'

'Yes, that's me.' Bobby glanced at Charlie, then back at the woman. 'Um, is that all right?'

'S'pose it mun be since you're here. Come in then.'

The woman sounded put out, but she held the door open for them.

'Don't worry about her,' Charlie whispered to Bobby, taking her hand to lead her through the crowd. 'It's nothing personal, I promise you.'

'I'm starting to get used to it,' Bobby said. 'I was warned before I came that the people here don't take easily to outsiders.'

'It isn't that. Till's just nervous you're going to be libelling the natives in Reggie's next number. If there's one thing more worrying to people than townies, it's journalists.'

A girl of around eighteen ran up to them, very pretty, with a healthy pink complexion and stockings rolled down to her knees. She wore her chestnut hair loose around her shoulders and a short green dress that she looked to have outgrown years ago.

'Charlie!' She threw her arms around his neck and kissed him heartily in a way that would very likely earn her the description 'fast' in the dance halls of Bradford, but somehow seemed entirely natural out here. Charlie, laughing, picked the girl up and swung her around before depositing her back on the ground again.

'Charlie, come dance wi' me,' the girl said, tugging at his hand.

He nodded to Bobby. 'I'm here with someone, Mabs.'

The girl, Mabs, put out her bottom lip in a pet. 'But you mun dance. We've not enough lads to go round, Charlie. I've not had a dance tonight, I swear it.'

'Well, we can't have that, I suppose.' Charlie glanced at Bobby. 'Do you mind?'

Bobby, who was making a few notes in her book, shook her head. 'Do as you please. I've got enough here to keep me entertained.'

Mabs glanced at the notebook Bobby was scribbling in.

'Are you Chinese, Miss?'

Bobby blinked. 'Chinese?'

'That's Chinese writing, in't it?'

She laughed. 'Oh. No. It's called shorthand. It's a sort of code to help you write faster. I can write a hundred words in a minute by doing it this way.'

'And you can read that back? Like as you can read proper writing?'

'That's right. I take it home to my typewriter and turn it into real words.'

Mabs looked quite awestruck as she looked over the rows of symbols. 'I reckon you mun be right clever to learn to write like that.'

'Not at all,' Bobby said, although she was secretly rather pleased. 'Just willing to work hard at learning it.'

'And do you do it for brass, like?'

'It's part of my job, yes.' Bobby didn't mention how little brass she actually did it for to this new admirer, since that would be sure to take off the sparkle.

Charlie tapped Mabs's shoulder. 'Are we dancing or aren't we, lass?'

'Aye, all right,' Mabs said, her eyes still lingering on the symbols.

Bobby watched the pair of them as they were absorbed into the crowd of merry dancers who swung and twirled their partners around the room.

It was evident from the smell that the barn must be home to a number of cows during the day – Bobby assumed they were staying with friends for the evening to make space for the merrymakers. Old farm machinery and bags of harvested potatoes had been pushed into corners to create the dance floor. Yet despite their humble surroundings, nearly everyone was in their Sunday best – known out here in the Dales as 'setting-off clothes'. Most of the women wore long dresses and gloves, and the men were in their finest suits. The couples were of all ages, from young to old, dancing in a style that didn't at all match the finery of their attire. The music was fast and jolly, and the dancers threw each other around and swung each other by the hands in a way that made Bobby feel quite dizzy.

The music wasn't anything like the big-band tunes Bobby was used to hearing back at home in the Palais or the Ritz, the dance halls she sometimes visited with her sister and their friends. An accordion player with a gypsy-like appearance, clad in an old felt hat and a red neckerchief with a clay pipe poking from one corner of his mouth, regaled them with old-fashioned tunes like 'Yankee Doodle Dandy', 'My Girl's A Yorkshire Girl' and 'Grandfather's Clock' as he perched on a milking stool. He was accompanied by a man in similar garb on a fiddle, who stood at his side. The dancers didn't seem to care what the musicians were playing, as long as they could swing each other around to it.

There was a table at one side of the room on which had been laid out a great spread. Bobby thought that it would make Mary Atherton, who prided herself on keeping a good table, pop-eyed with envy. The table was large but was still inadequate for the amount of food, necessitating its extension by a couple of ironing boards on each side. A pig had been slaughtered and roasted for the occasion and was lying in state in the centre of the large table next to slab-like slices of home-baked bread and a bowl of pungent apple sauce. Anyone who found themselves hungry could carve a thick slice of pork and assemble a truly appetite-conquering sandwich before, with a polite belch behind a fresh-pressed handkerchief, they took their partner in their arms once again. Plates of cakes, tarts and biscuits; rosy Ribston Pippin apples; home-brewed beer; strong, sweet berry wine; a churn full of milk fresh from the cow. Coming from the meagre portions of the shortage-hit city, where their butter ration had to be spread so thin across the bread that it could barely be tasted, it made Bobby feel quite guilty to consider indulging in such a rural cornucopia.

Instead she satisfied the hunger of her eyes with notes rather than food, ready to report it all for the benefit of the eager readers of *The Tyke*. Many of their readers now lived in the towns, and increasingly, a number of their subscribers were serving in the forces. Bobby could understand the magazine's appeal to country men and women in exile who liked to think fondly of 'back home'.

She took care not to mention the pig in her description, the slaughter of which she felt may well get some local farmer into trouble with the Ministry of Food. Perhaps that was why Till had seemed worried at the arrival of 'lass from t' paper', fearing the appearance of a report on their contraband feast.

Bobby watched one of the younger couples spin past the table of food. The young man swept up a jam tart as he passed and popped it into his partner's mouth without even slowing down, for which his grateful partner repaid him with a kiss. Bobby smiled as she faithfully noted this down.

Charlie whirled back towards her with Mabs in his arms and dropped into a chair, panting. Mabs took the opportunity to perch on his knee, but Charlie swung her off again and deposited her in the empty chair at his side. Mabs didn't seem to mind this too much and reached over him for a scone from one of the ironing boards.

'I hope you're getting some good material for your story, Bobby,' Charlie said breathlessly.

'I think so.'

Mabs turned to regard her with wide eyes. 'You're not from t' paper?'

'Um, yes,' Bobby said, feeling a flush of pride that Mabs should seem impressed by this.

'That's how you know that special writing you showed me then?'

'That's right. I learned how to do it so I could make notes for my stories.'

'You're not going to write about us, are you?'

'I hope to, yes.'

'What for?'

'Well, because it's interesting. That is, I think our readers will be interested.'

'In our old dances?' Mabs glanced around the lively gathering. 'Don't see why. You can see better dancing all over the place. At pictures and that.'

Charlie pinched her cheek. 'You're young, sweet Mabs. You'll understand when you're older with bairns of your own.'

Mabs didn't understand the sentiment, but she understood the pinch on the cheek – and the reference to bairns.

'Dance wi' me again,' she said to Charlie: an order more than a request.

'Not now. I'm going to dance with Bobby.'

'Oh no, that's all right,' Bobby said, looking at the twirling, whirling couples with a feeling of alarm. 'I'm happy here, making my notes. Besides, I don't know the steps.'

'Never mind about that. I know them enough for both of us.' Charlie stood up, took her notebook away from her and pulled her into his arms. 'You can't write about it if you've never done it.'

As frightening as the fast-paced, wild dancing was, it did look a lot of fun. Surrendering, Bobby let Charlie spin her around to the old-time music.

'What do you think of old Heck?' he asked, nodding to the accordion player. 'Doesn't know a note of music. Plays it all by ear. He's been playing the hops around here since Methuselah was knee-high.'

'He's, um… very good,' Bobby said breathlessly, trying to keep her balance as the world spun around her.

'These folk'll be here until two or three in the morning, then straight to work in the fields. I've seen lads foddering their shorthorns in full evening dress many a time on my way to a job. I mean, the lads were in the evening dress. The cows were as naked as the day they were born, the hussies. Wine?'

Bobby felt rather dazed at the speed of both the dance and Charlie's conversation. 'I'm sorry?'

'Parsnip wine. Old Lizzie Bartle makes it to a secret recipe of parsnip, sugar and turpentine – that's my guess anyhow. Just uncorking a bottle can floor an elephant at ten paces.' Charlie swept up a couple of glasses from the table and pushed one into her hand, spinning her around all the while. Dizzily, Bobby took a sip.

The wine was indeed potent, and very sweet and tangy. As soon as they were within reach of the table again, Bobby put it down. She needed to keep a clear head if she was going to make a story out of this – and even more so now Charlie's arms were around her. They were firm and strong, with the sort of sinewy, tightly packed muscle gained by spending much of your day wrestling wayward farm animals. He smelt of tobacco and Lux soap flakes and soil and parsnip wine, and he was pressing against her as they danced in a way that might easily cause some girls – other girls – to lose their heads. Bobby noticed Mabs watching them sullenly from her chair and remembered the way she'd claimed Charlie when they first came in, throwing her arms around him for a kiss.

Bobby thought it unlikely that Mabs and Charlie were walking out together officially. Mabs was too young, and besides, Bobby suspected Charlie was on kissing-cousin terms with plenty of the village girls. Not quite a wolf, perhaps, but certainly a gadabout who thought of little but his own amusement.

Charlie was the sort to attract people, with an overgrown schoolboy charm that allowed him to find friends easily among men and women alike. In the short time they'd spent together, Bobby had come to enjoy his company, his conversation and his humour very much – in the way of common friendship, naturally. But she knew it would be a very, very foolish thing to allow herself to fall too far under the spell of Charlie Atherton's dubious charms.

119

Chapter 14

If it had been up to Charlie, Bobby would have stayed at the Smeltham hop until the early hours of the morning. She had enjoyed herself, finding the unrestrained freedom of the dance style rather addictive, but nevertheless, she kept her promise to herself to be home no later than midnight. After one more dance with Charlie, she had mounted her old bicycle and pedalled back to Moorside Farm, where she immediately got to work turning her pages of shorthand into what she hoped was engaging copy. She couldn't use her typewriter without waking the other members of the household, so she wrote as neatly as possible with the beautiful onyx fountain pen Don had given her, fully intending to present the story to Reg the next day as a fait accompli.

Remembering how Reg had praised her for her clean copy the day she'd come for her interview, she tried not to be tempted by a style too florid as she painted a prose picture of the village dance. That was something she had learned quickly at the *Courier* when she'd worked on Tony's pieces for him – Peter Clarke's subbing pencil never met with an adjective and let it live. Instead, Reg's mantra, *people before things*, swam around her brain as she described vividly the wild, joyous couples swinging each other lustily around the room until three a.m. before setting out to shear their sheep still in their Sunday clothes. She included details of the magnificent spread – although no mention of the pig, of course – and of Heck, the ancient, weather-beaten accordionist who played his old-fashioned tunes by ear. She talked of Charlie's belief that such dances were on the wane as the outside world encroached further and further on the Dales, and how the war might kill off the last of them. When she'd finished in the early hours of the morning, she signed it with a flourish then read it back.

Was it any good? Was it the sort of thing *The Tyke* might like to include? More importantly, would it earn her her first byline? She was too tired now to tell. Reg would have to be the judge. He'd be awake in a few hours. She ought to get what little sleep she could before the working day began.

Fully clothed, she lay down on the bed and drifted easily to sleep, to dream of dances and roast pigs and Charlie Atherton pressing against her as he swung her around in his strong arms.

–

'Young lady, you look like death warmed up,' Reg said the next morning as they ate breakfast.

Bobby flushed. 'Sorry. I had a late night.'

'Aye, and I know who with.'

So Reg had heard who she was out with last night. News travelled fast in these small country places.

'Charlie offered to introduce me to people,' she murmured, deciding there was no point now in attempting to dissemble to her hosts. 'It was good of him when he knew I wouldn't know anyone.'

Mary looked up from her toast, frowning. 'You aren't walking out with that young scamp, are you?'

'He's not so young as he likes to think he is,' Reg muttered. 'At any rate, he's old enough to know better. Still acting like a jack-the-lad when he ought to be well settled.'

'Not that we aren't fond of him, of course,' Mary said to Bobby. 'He's just rather… flighty, that one. You're such a sensible body. I'd hate to see you get dragged into Charlie's madcap world.'

'We aren't walking out,' Bobby said, focusing her attention on her boiled egg so she didn't have to meet the two sets of worried eyes now fixed on her. 'He spent most of his time dancing with a girl called Mabs. I had other reasons for wanting to be there.'

Reg raised an eyebrow. 'And what might they be?'

'I'll tell you after breakfast.'

'So it's a mystery, is it?'

'No. There's just something I have to show you first.'

After they'd eaten, Bobby went to her bedroom to fetch her piece, which she'd titled simply 'A Dance in the Dales', and took it down with her to the parlour.

Reg was already in there, seated at his desk. He nodded to the hated telephone directory next to her typewriter and a fresh pile of envelopes.

'Frame yourself then,' he said. 'I hope you can manage to stay awake today. If you must go out dancing with my brother – and on your own head be it if you do – then I'd appreciate it if you could do so on Saturday nights in future.'

'All right.' Hesitantly, Bobby approached his desk. 'Um, Mr Atherton? I wondered if you'd be able to read this.'

Reg glanced at it with little interest. 'What is it? A letter?'

'It's a story,' Bobby said, feeling her cheeks heat. 'About the dance last night. I thought… that is, I wondered if it might be good for the magazine.'

Reg laughed, batting it away. 'Nay, our readers don't want to hear about daft dances.'

'Please, Mr Atherton. This was why I went. Charlie said the last of those sorts of village dances are in danger of being swept away, and I thought, well, isn't that exactly what you told me when I came to be interviewed? That you want to chronicle a dying way of life?'

'Aye. I did say that,' Reg said slowly.

Bobby gestured to the window. 'When I came here that day, you asked me to look out there and tell you what I saw with the eye of a writer, and you were disappointed that I only saw the fells and not the man. Well, last night I made a real effort to see the people and what was important about them and to them. People before things, isn't that what you taught me?' She met his eye. 'At least read it before you decide. This is why I'm tired today. I wasn't up late gadding. I was up late writing this – because I felt like you were never going to give me a chance to write in working hours, and it was time I showed some initiative.'

'Initiative, eh?'

'Yes.'

Reg sighed. 'All right, hand it over then.'

He read it in silence. Bobby scanned his face, but he wasn't giving anything away.

'Well?' she asked eagerly when he put it down on his desk.

'Not bad' were all the words of praise he uttered. But he was a Yorkshireman, so Bobby knew this was high praise. She beamed at him.

'And you'll use it in the magazine?'

'I might find a space for it in one of the spring numbers. Dancing suits the season, and it does no harm to have something for the women. It doesn't do to forget them, since they're usually the ones paying the subscription bills.' He handed it back to her. 'But first, you'll cut two hundred words and type it up double-line-spaced to be subbed. Then it'll make a page. Needs a better first line as well – strong title and first line are as important as all the paragraphs after 'em put together.'

'That's fine. I'll do it now.' Bobby felt she could kiss him right at that moment. She didn't know which two hundred words she was going to be able to lose, but she'd trim them from somewhere.

'And then you'll fill at least fifteen of those envelopes and take them to the post office after dinner,' Reg said.

'All right.'

'And then…' He paused, looking at her as if sizing her up. 'I hope I'm not going to regret this. You can consider it payment for that onion.'

'What is it?' Bobby stood up straight. 'You aren't going to send me out to get a story?'

'God help you, I am.'

—

When Bobby had completed her morning's work to Reg's satisfaction and her stuffed envelopes were packed into the leather satchel, the editor briefed her about the story he wanted her to pursue that afternoon.

'I'm sending you out to talk to old Andy Jessop up at Newby Top,' he told her. 'I can't get up myself – not easily, at any rate. It's right over the tops. I've been putting it off, but you don't want to put it off too long with someone of Andy's years. He must be eighty if he's a day.'

'What's important about him?' Bobby asked. 'I mean, what's the story?'

'He's an old sheep farmer, no different than a dozen others around here. Long retired now, and his son and grandsons run his place. Farm's been in the family a couple of generations. I reckon he'll have some good memories about how it was growing up here when the old queen were alive.'

'So it's a nostalgia piece?'

'Aye, that's what it is, all right,' Reg said. 'Summat to remind the old folk of the old days when everything was better, the way they always like to be reminded, and the younger ones in the forces might find it a comfort while they're far from home. The Christmas number goes to print Tuesday week. It's not going to be a very merry one for a lot of folk this year and I want something in to cheer them up a bit. "Memories of an Old-time Farmer", we'll call it. Don't forget to ask Andy about Christmases when he were a bairn.'

That sounded like it would be an important addition to the Christmas number, not merely something to fill space or the trivial 'women's stuff' Tony used to get her to write for him at the *Courier*. Bobby felt rather pleased that Reg was willing to trust her with the interview. Charlie had been right, then, about taking the initiative to write the piece on the dance last night. She must remember to buy him a pint of beer the next time she saw him in return for the good advice.

'And, um…' She hesitated, not quite sure how to express herself. 'I mean, if you do put it in the Christmas magazine…'

For possibly the first time in their working relationship, Bobby saw Reg smile.

'Don't worry, lass, you'll get your byline,' he said. 'I always credit hard work where credit's due.'

She smiled too. 'Thanks, Mr Atherton.'

'Oh, make it Reg. You might as well now that you and my wife seem to be such bosom pals you're tossing Christian names around like confetti.' He handed her a piece of paper. 'Now then, you'll have to leave your bike in the village and walk from there. That old thing'll be no good for getting to Newby Top. I've written out the directions for you.'

'All right. And don't worry, I won't let you down.'

'See that you don't,' Reg said. 'Now be off with you, and don't come back until you've got me enough memories for two pages of good copy.'

'Yes, sir.' Bobby only just managed to restrain herself from saluting.

She must have broken a record bicycling into the village to drop off her stuffed envelopes with Gil. When this was done, Bobby propped the old bike against the wall of the post office – the uneven, pale grey stones clustered together in such a haphazard way that she was never quite sure how the buildings of Silverdale managed to remain standing – and took out the directions Reg had given her.

Reg always wrote like a man in a hurry, and it had taken Bobby a little while to learn to decipher his hand. However, after weeks of turning his copy into neat, double-spaced sheets of type, she had the knack and it didn't take her too long to work it out. It was typical of Reg: very terse, with the fewest words possible used to convey the necessary information.

*Path to left of pub. Over stile, cross field bearing left
(mind troy). Stile, left, stile, right along track to top of
hill. Head for stone cross in distance, then climb five-bar
gate and take track to farm. Knock side door.*

Bobby stared at the directions for a few minutes, trying to make
sense of them. How far was it? What was a troy – could this be
yet another dialect word specific to this part of the West Riding?
She'd expected she would have to work hard to earn her first
byline, but she hadn't predicted a literal quest.

Bobby glanced down at her clothes, feeling a wave of trep-
idation. She hadn't dressed that morning for a winter moortop
ramble. What she needed was a pair of good, sturdy boots and
some comfortable corduroy slacks, not her office wear of skirt,
stockings and court shoes.

But it was too late now, and besides, she didn't own any
hiking boots. Hopefully it wouldn't be too far and she could
keep herself smart enough to make a good impression on this
old farmer.

That was another thing. She presumed Reg had arranged
this interview with Andy Jessop some time ago. Did the farmer
know it was her who was coming to conduct it? Was he
expecting anyone this afternoon at all? Bobby doubted it was
common for these remote moorland farms to have telephones,
and she hadn't noticed Reg send out any sort of note that could
be carried up by one of the village lads.

She was wandering towards the pub, her gaze still fixed on
the directions as she puzzled over what the troy would be and
how she would know it, when a loud hiss sent her jumping
back with a yelp.

It was like a scene in a Western: the one where the baddie
and the goodie confront each other at high noon after one
or the other of them has refused to get out of town. The
only difference was that this baddie… was a goose. A huge
grey gander was standing in front of Bobby with the meanest

expression she'd ever seen on his face, blocking her access to the path her directions told her she needed to follow.

'Um. Hullo,' Bobby said. 'Sorry, Mr Goose, but I need to get by.'

The goose's beak opened again, and Bobby half expected him to tell her to go for her guns. But he just let out another loud hiss.

She tried to skirt around him to the left. He moved left. She moved right. He moved right.

A farmhand who was passing with a silver milk churn in his hand laughed. 'Are ye two dancing?'

Bobby turned to him helplessly. 'I need to go down there, but... there's this goose.'

She realised that sounded rather pathetic, but she wasn't sure what to do. The goose looked like the bitey, flappy type, and he was a large, muscular chap who came right up to Bobby's knee. Possibly he was enjoying his last chance to raise hell before he furnished someone's Christmas table in three weeks' time. He looked like he didn't have a single damn left to give in life. At the very least, Bobby wouldn't put it past him to see off her stockings before she managed to fight her way past – and this was her last good pair too.

'Ah, that's just Norman,' the man said dismissively. 'He's all beak and bluster, yon bird.'

'You mean he won't hurt me?'

'Oh aye, he'll peck you sore if you run at him. But he don't mean nowt by it. He's just showing off for t' lasses.'

The man jerked his head to where the beck chattered below them. A few prim geese were floating on its surface, ignoring the theatrical masculinity of Norman above.

'So, um, is there anything I can do?' Bobby asked.

'Mrs Hobbes'll be out soon as she's finished her dinnertime pint,' the man said, nodding to the Golden Hart. 'Best wait while she's done. She'll put yon gander in order.'

He disappeared with his churn, whistling.

Bobby wasn't quite sure what to do. She didn't know who Mrs Hobbes was, or how long she was likely to take over her dinnertime drink, or in what way she'd be able to neutralise Norman. But she also couldn't see any way to get by other than running at the bird and hoping he took off. The path she needed to take was a snicket between the pub and the butcher's shop on the other side. It was very narrow, barely wider than her hips, and Norman had now moved backwards in order to block it completely with his huge feathered frame.

She tried glaring at him, but that didn't work. He just glared back. Then she tried ignoring him, pretending that she was supremely uninterested in whether he chose to stand in that spot or not, but that didn't have any effect either. Eventually, she gave up and went to perch on the well outside the pub until either the mysterious Mrs Hobbes appeared or Norman got bored and went to start a fight with someone else. Norman remained steadfast, however, despite the lack of interest from his lady friends in the beck below.

Finally, the door to the pub opened and a middle-aged woman came out.

This was unusual enough in itself – as Bobby had noted on her one visit to the pub, it was very much a man's domain. But this woman… Bobby had never seen anything like her. She carried a bright red umbrella, although there was no sign of rain today, and wore a dress that had ceased to be fashionable some-time in the 1920s, with a fox fur stole around her shoulders. But what Bobby mainly noticed was her quite spectacular headgear.

Over her grey hair, Mrs Hobbes wore a close-fitting felt cloche hat decorated with so many colourful feathers that if a parrot ever caught sight of it, he would very likely try to make a date with it. There were shimmering green peacock feathers, feathers from exotic birds, feathers of blue and gold and red and purple, spread out as if to protect a fan dancer's modesty. It made Bobby think of the last Guy Fawkes' Night they'd been able to have before the war, when Butterfield's Mill, where her father and brothers worked, had invited workers and their families to a spectacular display of fireworks that had lit up the night sky in all the colours God had thought fit to create. This wasn't a hat. It was an explosion.

The purpose of Mrs Hobbes' unnecessary red umbrella soon became clear. Bobby watched as she surreptitiously checked from side to side. Then with a sudden movement, she drew out a pair of scissors from inside the umbrella and, with a speed Bobby would hardly have believed her capable of, leaned over someone's garden wall to snip off a bit of a plant there. Plant and scissors then disappeared inside the umbrella with the sleight of hand of a professional magician. Bobby wondered how many other stolen cuttings were currently residing in there.

Bobby waited a moment to give the old lady time to recover from her act of theft before standing up and approaching her.

'Are you Mrs Hobbes?' she asked.

'Yes, my girl. I answer to that name,' Mrs Hobbes said, looking her up and down.

For some reason, when Mrs Hobbes said this, it didn't sound like the innocent comment it might in someone else's mouth. It sounded like she answered to Mrs Hobbes only because she had a dozen other identities she was choosing not to answer to just at that moment.

'I was told you might know what to do about this goose,' Bobby said, pointing to Norman. 'He doesn't seem to want to move, and I really need to go that way.'

Mrs Hobbes smiled with her thin lips. 'Oh dear, is he causing trouble again?' She spoke in the tone of an indulgent mother who has been informed her cherished offspring was caught pulling the legs off spiders in the nursery. 'I told him Mummy would be very cross if he wasn't good while she was in the pub. He was supposed to wait for me in his basket. They're cruel not to let him inside any more, just because of one tiny little bite he gave to that old misery Seth Ogden. It was Seth's fault anyhow – he antagonises him deliberately.'

Mrs Hobbes didn't speak with the local accent. She sounded like she was from somewhere in Scotland, but was doing her best to disguise her natural tones. Her speech was refined, very carefully so, in such a way that it didn't entirely ring true. Bobby wondered what her story was.

'Do you think you could get him to move?' Bobby asked.

'Oh yes, I should think he's had enough fun for one day. It's time he went home for his din-dins now.'

To Bobby's surprise, the tiny, slight woman marched forward and easily hefted her huge pet into her arms. She crooned over him while the formerly ferocious Norman fawned against her fur stole with his long neck, as docile as a lamb. Bobby wondered what his girlfriends on the beck would make of such unmanly – or she should say, un-ganderly – behaviour.

'Now then, you little mischief-maker, it's time Mummy took you home,' Mrs Hobbes crooned to the spoilt bird. 'Come along, Norman, and we can let this young lady go about her business.'

Mrs Hobbes carried her pet – who looked to be nearly half as big as she was – to a bicycle that was leaning against the wall of the pub and placed him in the fur-lined front basket, where he settled down immediately. She hoisted her skirts above her knees so she could mount and off rode goose and woman, Norman's neck swivelling round so he could give Bobby one last meaningful dirty look from his basket as they disappeared.

Chapter 15

After the encounter with Norman, Bobby's journey to Newby Top Farm had started to feel less like a quest and more like an odyssey. As she walked quickly down the snicket between the pub and the butcher's shop that would take her out into open countryside, well aware that she could expect only a few more hours of daylight before the sun went down, she wondered what she might encounter next. A seven-headed hydra, perhaps, or even a cyclops?

The next thing, in fact, became apparent when Bobby reached the field at the end of the stony track and climbed the stile over the drystone wall that enclosed it. This was where she discovered what the 'mind troy' part of her directions meant, when she caught sight of the field's other occupant: a huge brown bull.

'Hello Troy,' she said weakly.

If Norman had been alarming, then Troy was a true monster: about two hundred stone of solid, meaty muscle topped with a pair of disturbing curved horns that looked like they'd stretch the length of her wrist to her elbow. He towered over Bobby's five-foot-five frame, glaring at her over the golden ring in his nose through narrow, red-rimmed eyes. This, Bobby reflected as terror froze her to the spot, must be how the Spanish bull-fighters felt.

However, she soon learnt a lesson about not judging from appearances. While Troy was a monster almost mythological in his proportions, it turned out he was nowhere near as cantankerous in nature as Norman the goose. After sizing her up, he let out a dismissive 'hrumph' and went back to chewing the cud. Bobby hesitated for a moment, then decided it was safe to continue her journey.

Troy, having satisfied himself that this human was too puny to be worth his attention, ignored Bobby completely now as she made her way through his field. However, the fright of encountering him made her hasty, which made her clumsy. She slid and stumbled through the field towards the stile at the other side, splattering her stockings and skirt with mud and cow dung. Her feet, when she examined them, were now more muck than shoe, and she'd lost one of her gloves when she'd dropped it into the centre of a fresh, soft cowpat and decided she didn't have the stomach to retrieve it. It was a chilly day, and the fingers of Bobby's ungloved hand tingled with encroaching numbness as she gripped the stile at the other side of the field with relief.

So this was real reporting, Bobby thought as she clambered quickly over the stile before Troy changed his mind about her and decided she might make a tasty addition to his dinner. Today, she was Dorothy Lawrence. The intrepid lady reporter, firm and steadfast in the pursuit of her story, deterred by neither rain nor snow nor goose nor bull. And what a story she was on her way to get, Bobby thought wryly. Not a daring report on life in the trenches, but the memories of an octogenarian farmer about such things, she imagined, as long-lost childhood games and archaic techniques for shearing sheep. She knew the sort of thing Reg wanted: an idyllic, rose-tinted picture of life in the countryside in days gone by, heavy on the nostalgia and light on the hardships. The sort of thing even a girl could write.

But that didn't matter. This was her story – her first byline. Once Bobby had that, who knew where it could lead? It was going to take a lot more than missing gloves and belligerent farm animals to make her turn back.

As she climbed yet another stile into yet another field – this one, thankfully, containing nothing but a few nervous rabbits that skittered away as she approached – Bobby thought about her last letter from Lilian, which had arrived in the post the day before.

There had been nothing in it to worry her, really, or at least nothing imminent. Lil had been accepted into the Wrens and would be leaving for Greenwich in February to start her training, which she was thrilled about. Jake, too, had been given a date for beginning his army basic training. He'd be leaving home in mid-January. Lil was full of plans for a last, big family Christmas together in three weeks' time, and had sent a list of things for Bobby to try and get hold of in the countryside for their Christmas dinner.

However, between the lines, Bobby could sense a note of concern. It wasn't only the shortages that were worrying her sister: it was money too. Lilian wasn't Bobby's only correspondent. She'd had a couple of letters from Don, who wrote less like a sister and more like a journalist, keeping her abreast of how life was changing for the inhabitants of her home town. She knew spirits were scarcer than they had been, and that consequently the black market stuff had increased in price. Every time she received her wage packet and went to the post office to make out a postal order, Bobby felt a stab of guilt about the paltry six and thruppence she was contributing to the family coffers – especially when she thought of her father waking in the night, screaming for the blessed relief of drunkenness to drown out the horrors in his mind.

But what could she do? She couldn't bear to leave her job here – not now Reg was finally giving her the chance to do what he'd hired her to do. And it seemed absurd to consider asking for a pay rise after a mere three weeks of work, before she'd had a chance to prove her worth with a story or two.

She was on open heath now, the sharp wind pinching at her cheeks as she picked her way through sandy scrub and flattened, silvery slabs of limestone pavement. There was no real path here – or perhaps it was more true to say that there were a dozen paths here, trodden by man and by beast, most of which joined each other or petered out or led to nowhere much at all. However, Bobby could see the squat stone cross Reg had described silhouetted in the distance and kept her steps bent towards it.

She must have been walking for about an hour in total, although it seemed much longer, when she finally arrived at the locked five-bar gate set in a drystone wall behind which was the rough track leading down to the farm. After a moment's hesitation, looking around her to make sure no one was watching – although she hadn't seen a soul except a pair of elderly hikers and a few semi-feral horses since she'd left the village – Bobby hoisted up her skirt and slip and swung herself over the gate.

At the bottom of the track was the farmhouse. Bobby ignored the front door, which she'd learned most Dalesfolk would only ever consider using on the occasion of either a marriage or a death, and instead located one at the side as described in Reg's instructions.

What a place to live! Wild, the wind clattering the slate on the roof of the farmhouse, but the view... you could see forever. The settlement of Silverdale was little more than a cluster of dots from the vantage point of Newby Top.

The farmhouse seemed very welcoming after her long and unpleasant walk to reach it: snug and warm, with the smell of baking bread emanating from somewhere in its depths. Bobby only hoped the people would be welcoming likewise.

There was a boot scraper by the door and Bobby cleaned the soles of her mud-caked shoes as thoroughly as she could before knocking, not wanting to alienate the inhabitants of the house by trailing mud and cow muck all over their scrubbed floors.

'Hello. Oh,' she said when the door opened, registering a familiar face. It was Mabs, the young girl who had shown such an interest in Charlie at the dance the previous night.

Bobby had been yawning all day, but Mabs, who had still been happily twirling around the room when Bobby had left at half past eleven, looked as fresh as she had the night before.

She'd changed out of her short green dress, however, and was instead wearing a simple stuff frock with an apron over the top. Her hands were covered in flour.

'Is it you?' Mabs said, frowning.

'The lass from the paper. Yes, it's me.'

Bobby was starting to get used to being the 'lass from t' paper' to all and sundry – 'magazine' didn't seem to be a word in the vocabulary of the local folk. In fact, she rather liked it.

'Hello again, Mabs,' she said. 'I didn't know you lived here. Can I come in?'

'What for then?' The girl radiated a hostility that Bobby suspected had nothing to do with the general suspicion of outsiders in these parts and everything to do with Charlie Atherton.

'I'm here to see your…' She paused, doing a quick calculation regarding relative ages. 'Your grandfather, I presume. Andy Jessop? I've been sent to talk to him. For the paper.'

Mabs looked rather awed by this.

'You're to interview Grandad?' she said in disbelief. 'Why, what's he done?'

'I'm sure he did lots of things that are interesting, when he was a young man. That's what I want to talk to him about.'

'And you'll write about it in Chinese, like our dance?'

Bobby laughed. 'I promise that when it goes into the paper, it'll be written in English.'

'You'd best come in then.'

Reluctantly, Mabs stood aside to let her into the house. The walls were bare stone and the floor uncarpeted flags, but it was still significantly warmer than the outside: a welcome relief after the chill wind of the moor. Bobby flexed the fingers of her ungloved hand, feeling the blood start to flow again.

'This way,' Mabs said, beckoning to her.

'Did you and Charlie stay out very late last night?' Bobby asked, hoping she might be able to thaw the girl's manners with some conversation. She'd detected a certain admiration behind

Mabs's jealousy the evening before, and believed she might be able to make a friend of her with a little effort.

'Nay, Charlie left not long after you.' Mabs shot her a look, as if she suspected this had been deliberately arranged as part of some illicit rendezvous. 'I hardly had a dance after that. Not enough lads, see. Not since half of 'em went off to war.'

'I'm sorry about that.'

'You and Charlie aren't walking out,' the girl said. She didn't phrase it as a question, as if it would pain her too much to do so, but Bobby could sense she expected an answer all the same.

'No,' Bobby said. 'We're just acquaintances. Charlie's brother Reg is my boss at the paper. That's how we know one another.'

This seemed to pacify Mabs a little. She deigned to walk more slowly so Bobby could walk at her side instead of behind her.

'Are *you* and Charlie walking out?' Bobby asked her.

'Aye,' Mabs said, puffing herself up with some pride. 'He'll say nay if you ask him, but that's only a lad's way. He dances three times with me what he dances wi' t' other lasses, and look.' Mabs put out a floury hand to show her a cheap paste ring that glittered with a greenish sort of sparkle on one of her fingers. 'He won this me at fair when it come to Settle. That's like being engaged, that is.'

Bobby felt rather sorry for the poor smitten girl. She was forward and confident but very green still; naive about the world, and about men. Her feelings for Charlie were little more than the passing fancy of a vigorous, healthy young person, Bobby hoped, but if Mabs had given him her heart... well, Bobby couldn't help feeling that Charlie Atherton was the last man who should be trusted with that particular organ.

'That was very sweet of him,' was all she could think of to say. 'He must think a great deal of you, Mabs.'

The girl beamed at her, all animosity put aside now she'd successfully staked her claim.

'Grandad's in t' parlour,' she said, jerking her head to a door on their right. 'You'll take a mug o' tea, Miss?'

'I'd love one, thank you. It's going to take me a long time to warm up after my walk.'

Mabs disappeared down the passage to the kitchen, and Bobby went into the parlour to seek out Andy Jessop.

Chapter 16

The old farmer was sitting in an easy chair in the inglenook smoking a clay pipe when Bobby came in, his slippered feet resting on the settle. His eyes were half closed as his head sagged back and an aged Old English Sheepdog snoozed at his feet, the pair of them looking a picture of rustic contentment. She felt almost guilty at having to disturb the happy scene. It would make a perfect painting for Mary Atherton.

She hung back, waiting for the old man to register her presence and wishing Mabs had stayed to make the introductions. Eventually, the man took a last wheeze on his pipe, sighed, and opened his eyes.

He looked taken aback when he saw Bobby. Clearly he'd been expecting a member of his family. She guessed Reg hadn't notified him of her coming, in that case.

'And who might thee be?' he demanded in that gruff, abrupt way that seemed to be part of the culture of the Dales. His accent was so thick it took Bobby a moment to 'get her ear in' so she could understand him. The old Dalesfolk who lived on these sorts of remote farms often sounded to Bobby as though their speech could barely have changed since their Norse ancestors first settled here.

Bobby rummaged in her handbag to take out her notepad and pencil, brandishing them like some sort of talisman. 'Reg Atherton sent me. From *The Tyke*. Bobby Bancroft.'

Andy stared at her. 'Tha's from t' paper?' He put all the emphasis on the 'tha', as if he couldn't comprehend how on earth this slip of a girl could be working for an actual, real-life publication.

'That's right.'

Andy continued to stare. Bobby wished he'd invite her to sit down. The sudden change in temperature from the icy cold of outside to the fireside warmth of Andy's parlour was making her feel a little dizzy. The fire was burning peat dug from the moor surrounding the farm, filling the air with a rich, earthy aroma that felt a little oppressive.

'What, and tha writes bits and all that?' Andy asked, still in that same tone of ringing disbelief.

'Yes. I'm the junior reporter.' That didn't seem like enough of an explanation, with Andy still staring at her in wonder, so Bobby added, 'Mr Atherton couldn't get a boy. Because of the war.'

'I suppose tha does recipes and knitting and all like that?'

'I do all sorts,' Bobby said. This wasn't strictly true yet, but she hoped it would be before too much more time passed now that she was looking at her first byline.

'And tha knows how to do good writing? Did well in thi schooling, hey?'

'I've been trained, yes,' Bobby said, although Andy's expression remained sceptical. 'May I sit down, Mr Jessop?'

'Aye, go on,' the man said with a magnanimous nod. 'Tha looks badly. Shouldn't be standing about.'

Gratefully Bobby pulled a cane chair with a fleece thrown over it to the fire so she could sit by him. The aged sheepdog lifted its head to look at her, then went straight back to sleep.

Usually when Yorkshire folk chose to use the familiar form of 'thee' and 'tha' with an adult stranger, it was seen as something of a snub. 'Don't thee tha them as they thas thee' was a comical phrase Bobby remembered her mam using to admonish them when they were children – a reminder that they must always use the more respectful 'you', however they were addressed by others. Bobby wasn't offended that Andy Jessop

139

chose to use the familiar form with her though. When you reached such a grand old age as he had, you were entitled to be familiar with everyone.

'Happen tha's fair nithered after thi walk, is tha?' Andy asked as he refilled his pipe with pungent black twist tobacco.

'I'm sorry?'

'I said I reckon tha mun be fair nithered.' He clocked her blank expression. 'Feeling t' cold, like.'

'Oh. Yes, very. I didn't realise it would be such a trek to get here. Not that it's a problem at all,' she added hastily. 'I enjoyed the scenery.'

'Troy give thee trouble?'

She smiled. 'Not nearly as much as a goose called Norman, although I did feel I could have done with a red cape to wave in case someone gave Troy the order to charge.'

It wasn't the world's greatest joke but Andy seemed to appreciate it, letting out a roar of laughter. When he was done, he regarded her with a more benevolent air.

'So Atherton's found hissen a lass to do his dirty work for him,' he observed jovially. 'God help him then.'

Bobby wasn't quite sure what to say to that. She decided it was probably best to change the subject.

'Your granddaughter was going to make a brew for us to drink while we chatted,' she said. 'We can wait until she brings it in before we start if you like.'

'Ah, she'll take her time fetching it. She's allus thrang, same as her mam.' He cackled. 'Thrang as Throp's wife.'

'Thrang?' Bobby was still struggling with much of the local terminology.

'Aye, thrang – busy, tha knows. A hundred and one more important things to do than tend to t' owd man.' Andy gave a throaty chuckle. 'Too busy to run round after me but never too busy to run after t' lads, that's our Mabs. Let her enjoy her youth, I say – it'll be gone afore she knows it. Tha'd best ask us what tha's got to ask us, lass, and tea mun come when it comes.'

Bobby was pleased to find him compliant. She had been worried, given his surprise about her sex, that he might send her away and demand to talk to someone male instead.

The problem was, she didn't actually know what she had to ask him. Reg had sprung the interview on her with no word of a warning, and she hadn't had a chance to prepare a list of questions before setting out. 'Ask about Christmas' was the only instruction Reg had given her. Bobby had been hoping Andy would be so grateful for a willing audience he'd happily ramble away for himself.

'I suppose you've lived in this farmhouse a long time?' she said after a moment, pencil poised.

'Aye, that I have.'

Bobby waited, but apparently that was all the answer she was going to get.

'How long?' she asked.

'Sin our mother delivered us, here in front o' this fire. That'll have been… 1859, I reckon. Happen on eighty-one year.' He fell silent a moment, staring into the flames. 'It mun have been a right special occasion, if they'd spared coal to light it. Can't remember it being lit much apart from Christmas Day when I were a lad.'

'What did you do at Christmas when you were a boy?' Bobby asked, seizing on the one question she had ready.

'Nowt much. It were just another day, really. The fire were lit, and that were a rare treat, and we went twice to chapel, and our mother gave us all a little cake o' sugared bread each. It were summat to look forrard to but not like they do it now, wi' trees and feasting and all like that.'

'So times were hard when you were young?'

'Aye, lass, they were that.' Andy's brow darkened. 'Nine bairns our mother delivered, and me the only one lived to see man's estate. Nine! I've eight brothers and sisters buried down in t' chapel yard.'

'Oh gosh, how awful,' Bobby said feelingly. 'I am sorry, Mr Jessop.'

'Now tha'd think that were a true tragedy if tha heared of it today, wouldn't tha?'

'Surely it would be a tragedy whenever it happened.'

Andy laughed grimly. 'Nay, not then it weren't. Not like now. Folk didn't give thee sympathy then, the way tha just gave it me. There were nowt o' that sort. They congratulated thee!'

'Surely not.'

'Well, happen not in so many words, but they wouldn't say sorry. They'd say, "ah well, Peg, it'll be one less mouth to feed come winter" or "she's wi' t' Good Lord now, waiting for thee". And Mother'd agree with 'em even while she were grieving for another bairn lost. And she grieved for 'em every one, our mother. She were a good sort.' Andy's watery eyes fixed again on the fire. 'I often think about our Meg,' he said softly, as if to himself. 'Nobbut nine year old when she went to sleep. We'd lost so much, yet I prayed we could've kept little Meggie. But… wasn't to be. He can be cruel, Him upstairs. I've many a time felt I'd like to ask Him what the heck he's thinking on. Happen I'll get my chance, soon enough.'

Bobby's pencil skittered over the paper, jotting this down in shorthand. The man's grief was raw, even after all these years; she could see it in his face, hear it in the crack of his voice. But she wrote with the uncomfortable feeling that these weren't the sort of happy, warm memories Reg had sent her here to collect for the Christmas number.

'There must have been some happy times when you were a child too,' she prompted Andy.

Andy snorted. 'Happy! Young lady, when I were a lad we were "happy", as tha puts it, if we survived one day to t' next. The Seventies were hell for them as made a living off land. We were eating what we could catch – rabbits, squirrels, moorhen, wild geese – and if we caught nowt, we et nowt. Bitter as gall is thi wild goose, but we were terrible glad to get it. "Happy" meant days we went to bed wi' summat in us bellies, and them were few and far between.'

'But… I mean, don't people usually talk about the good old days?'

'Aye, they talks about 'em, but they wouldn't want to gang back to 'em. They're good only because they're gone, to my mind. It's easy to be sentimental when tha's sitting by t' fire with thi belly filled and all thi bairns healthy and grown. Tha forgets the pain and the fear, that tomorrow Death might come to call.'

'Yes,' Bobby said slowly, thinking of the older folk she knew and their fixation on times gone by. 'I suppose that's true.'

'I'll tell thee what "good old days" were, Miss Bancroft,' Andy said darkly. 'They were rickets and typhoid and consumption and they were never, never enough. They were poison in t' watter and in t' air – poison that took bairns from their mothers. They were long days and a childhood that were ovver afore it began because we all on us had to graft – bairns an' all – if we wanted to live to see another day.' He scoffed bitterly. 'Nostalgia. Don't talk to me about nostalgia – aye, and that little paper o' thine the worst for it, wi' thy rosy spectacles looking out at past like it was nobbut sunshine and plenty. Our Mabs has read me bits out o' it; I know. Makes me sick to my stomach when folk my age get on about it. "Oh, we were poor, but we were happy." The devil! They've forgotten how many bodies are in churchyard with a cause of death of "good old days".'

Bobby stared at him, her hand still.

He frowned at her hovering pencil. 'Is tha not writing this? I thought Atherton wanted my memories for t' paper.'

'I think, um… I think he wanted something a little more…'

'Aye, I know. A little more "good old days",' Andy said with a wry smile. 'Well, tha can tell him from me that he can't have it. These are my memories, for better nor worse, and he can print 'em as they are or he can leave 'em in my head where they belong.'

Bobby thought this over.

Andy's memories were evidently not what Reg was expecting. Far from forming the basis of a heart-warming

Christmas piece about life in the Dales in decades gone by, they sounded like the very bleakest parts of the works of Dickens. Eight siblings lost to poverty, hunger, disease and hard work; a childhood of relentless graft and misery. Bobby wasn't going to earn her byline from this piece, no matter how hard she worked to write it, since there was no chance Reg was going to print it. Really she ought to terminate the interview and leave.

And yet... Andy was right. *The Tyke* did present a rose-tinted view of the past, in spite of Reg's ambition to be the chronicler of a dying age. The editor was too concerned with keeping up people's spirits as the war raged than with presenting things as they actually were. When they included articles about life in the Dales in years gone by, they were invariably accompanied by a drawing of a prosperous farmhouse kitchen, with rabbits and hams strung up from the rafters and a fat, lusty farmer's wife kneading dough with her sleeves rolled to the elbow. If hardship or want was ever mentioned in the pages of *The Tyke*, it was as an admonishment to the younger generations who 'didn't know they were born'; a self-aggrandising act by their elders.

But Andy's memories, as tragic as they were and as bitter as he sounded about the hand his life had dealt him, were as much a part of this place as anything else in the magazine – and what's more, they were real. He didn't build a martyrdom of them but spoke candidly and without sentimentality about his grief for the family he'd lost. Why should the old man be asked to misrepresent his own life to cheer up soldiers and city-dwellers he'd never met if that wasn't the truth of it?

'Keep going, Mr Jessop, please,' Bobby said firmly. 'I'll write down every word, exactly as you say it.'

'Ahh.' Andy looked satisfied by this. 'And tha'll print it faithfully? None o' this *nostalgia*?' He spat out the word as if it was a curse.

'I can't promise it will be printed at all. That's up to Mr Atherton, and you're right. I believe he was hoping for some-thing a little more... cheerful. But it's your life, Mr Jessop, and you shouldn't be forced to present it differently than it happened for the benefit of our readers. Whatever you choose to tell me, I'll write it just as you say.'

He smiled. 'Tha mun really be a reporter then, lass.'

Bobby smiled back. 'I hope you're right.'

Now that Bobby had gained his confidence, Andy Jessop really opened up about his eighty-one years here in this farmhouse. Although his memories were far from what Reg had been expecting, they weren't entirely bleak. Following a grim childhood marred by want and loss, the agricultural slump of the late 19th century did eventually end. Andy shared some warm memories from after this period when he was a young man, talking about his life on the farm raising his two daughters and one son with his much-missed wife Dot, who had passed away in the flu epidemic during the last war.

'She were a good sheep body, and tha can't ask for more in a wife than that,' Andy told Bobby, blinking on a tear. 'Never shirked graft, didn't our lass. Bonny too, in our courting days. But aye, she were a right grand sheep body.'

Bobby smiled as she noted this down. Evidently for Andy, being a hard worker and 'a good sheep body', whatever that meant, was the greatest compliment he could pay his partner in life. It wasn't the sort of romance you saw in the films Lilian adored, but it was love, all the same. The real kind that could keep weathering life's storms after the honeymoon roses had long faded.

Mabs came in with a pot of tea and some fresh-baked ginger parkin as their conversation was ending. Bobby, who had a keen appetite after her walk over the moors, eyed the parkin hungrily as Mabs put her tray down on a small table between them.

Her grandad reached for her hand and gave it a hard squeeze. 'Tha's a good lass, Mabs.'

'Ah, get away,' Mabs said, although she looked pleased at the mark of the old man's affection. 'What've you been saying for t' paper, Grandad?'

'Oh, load of old nonsense,' Andy said dismissively. 'But this young lady thinks some folk might want to read it.'

'Grandad, sithee how she writes it,' Mabs said, nodding to Bobby's pencil scribbling over the notepad. 'It's like a special language. She showed us at hop yesternight. It's right clever how she does it. Like one of them codes they use to send messages to spies in Germany and places.'

Andy frowned. 'Special language?'

'Show him, so's he knows you're not a spy,' Mabs said to Bobby. Smiling, Bobby presented Andy with the notepad. The old man took out a pair of wire half-moon spectacles, perched them on his nose and squinted at the symbols.

'Aye, this don't look like proper writing, right enough,' he said. 'Not that I can read it either way, mind.'

'Grandad never learned how to read,' Mabs told Bobby.

'Why was that, Mr Jessop?' Bobby asked.

'Never seemed much point,' Andy said with a shrug. 'Or enough time. We got a little schooling wi' t' parson, but it were mostly parroting scripture.'

'That's a shame.'

'It's life, that's all.' Andy glanced wistfully at a well-stocked bookshelf opposite the fire. 'Still, I regret it sometimes when I see t' bairns wi' their nose in one of them. It mun be nice to escape world for a spell.' He was silent for a moment, then his gaze returned with fascination to the page of shorthand. 'What's this for then, this special writing?'

'It's called shorthand,' Bobby said. Clearly, this skill was enough of a novelty out here in the Dales as to be quite a party trick. 'It lets me write a lot faster than the usual sort of writing – three times as fast. I learned it when I was training to be a... a reporter.'

'Aye, I saw thee writing like thi hand'd drop off while I were jawing just now.' Andy stared thoughtfully at the little squiggles that decorated the page. 'I reckon tha mun be bobbin-bright to learn that.'

'That's what I said,' Mabs chimed in. 'You should ask her to write your letters, Grandad. She knows better'n me how to pick the good words.'

'Tha means tha's got better things to do than court for any other body,' Andy said, laughing. 'Aye, I reckon I might ask her at that.' He patted her arm. 'Frame thissen then, lass. Better gang back to thy baking afore tha gets a clout from Mam.'

Mabs departed, leaving them alone again.

'Now then, young lady wi' t' clever brain,' Andy said to Bobby when Mabs was gone. 'How would tha like a little job extra?'

Bobby blinked. 'A job?'

'Aye, that's right. I'm after a… now what's the word I'm wanting? Sounds like "amen". Long word, means someone that writes things for thee. Like Mark did for Peter in Bible.'

Bobby thought about this.

'Amanuensis?' she hazarded.

'That's it. A body as writes stuff down for folk. I can't do it missen, not having my letters, and Mabs has no patience for it. She's embarrassed doing it, I reckon.'

Bobby frowned. 'Embarrassed?'

'Aye.' Andy looked a little embarrassed himself, his fingers playing with the stem of his pipe and a slight blush painting his papery cheeks. 'See, I've got a… a friend I likes to write to.'

'I see.'

He looked up at her. 'A lady friend, is what I mean.'

'Oh! I see.'

So the old farmer was courting, was he? Well, it was never too late for love, Bobby supposed. Why not the old as well as the young? She suppressed the smile that had risen on her lips, not wanting to offend the old man's pride.

'She's a widow lady, lives over the way on a farm in Smeltham,' Andy told her. 'We've an understanding, me and Ginny – least ways, I reckon so. She's a good, canny old lass and I'd like for us to spend our last days together if it was what she wanted. Only it's hard for me to plight my troth, so to speak, when I've not the words to make missen clear.' He met her eyes earnestly. 'But thee. Tha knows words, and I reckon a body clever enough to learn that special writing of thine mun know what makes a good letter.'

'You're asking me to write to your sweetheart for you?'

He laughed hoarsely. 'Sweetheart. What a word, at our time o' life. Aye, that's what I want all right. I'll pay thee, mind — won't have it no other way. I've a pal pays half a crown a go to have his letters written by some nob over Settle way, and I'll pay not a penny less to thee.'

'Oh, I couldn't accept—'

He raised a hand to silence her. 'Not a penny less. Matter o' pride. Now I like to write to Gin once a week, show her I'm thinking about her, like, and building up to popping the question. What does tha say, Miss Bancroft?'

Bobby hesitated. It was a strange sort of offer. On the one hand, she suspected Reg might not like it much, knowing she was working out of hours as a love-letter scribe for elderly illiterate farmers. On the other, she'd grown to like Andy Jessop over the past hour of learning about his life and character, and his love affair with the widow lady was really rather sweet. Not to mention that an additional two and six a week, small amount though it was, would still make quite a difference to her finances given her low wage. She could send it all home to Lilian, to help them get by until she was able to earn a little more. And if Reg didn't like it, well, he ought to consider giving her a pay rise so it wasn't necessary.

'All right,' she said when she'd thought it over. 'I'd be glad to write your letters for you, Mr Jessop.'

Chapter 17

'And I suppose I ought to ask Ginny how her old sow's getting on,' Andy said. 'She's had a spot of bother since she farrowed last wi' blocked teats, I heared from t' hired man there. What's a good way of putting it, does tha reckon, Miss Bancroft?'

Bobby's pencil hovered over her pad as she thought this over.

This was the second love letter she'd written for Andy since his unusual request, and actually, she rather enjoyed the challenge of how to approach them. Andy Jessop had been a farmer practically from the cradle, and he couldn't stop being one now simply because he happened to be in love. Bobby's job was to take his prosaic concerns about his lady friend's farming arrangements and turn them into something 'a bit lovey', as the old man put it. He was determined to make his proposal officially no later than the end of January, and he was insistent that Bobby make his intentions as clear as she could without actually popping the question for him.

'I think perhaps you ought to focus less on the pig's complaint and more on your concern for how your friend is coping with it,' Bobby said. 'That shows you care about the situation she's in, but for her sake more than the pig's.'

Andy nodded thoughtfully. 'Aye, there's wisdom in that, right enough. How will tha write it?'

Bobby was rather touched by the old farmer's faith in her skill. It made a pleasant change from the usual attitude to her career and ambitions that she encountered from men, especially those of the older generation.

'I think I'll put this,' she said. '"I hope you're managing well with your old sow's complaint and it's not giving you too many sleepless nights. I'd hate to think of it affecting your health or happiness. You must let me know if I can help you with her in any way."'

Andy took his clay pipe from his mouth and laughed hoarsely. 'What can I do all t' way ovver here? We aren't married yet, lass.'

'Exactly. This gives a hint that you'd like to be on hand to help her in a more personal capacity in the future. Besides, it's more about the sentiment than what you can actually do. It shows you're worrying about her, you see?'

'Ah well, tha knows best. Write it down then.'

Bobby did so.

'Any more news for this letter or shall I sign it off?' she asked.

'Aye, that'll do for this week.'

'I suppose this will be the last letter before Christmas. I'll wish her a merry Christmas from you to finish, shall I?'

'Right.' The farmer flushed slightly. 'Better put a few of them thear crosses on t' end, eh?'

Bobby smiled as she added three kisses below his name as requested.

'Shall I read it back?' she asked.

'Aye, go on.'

She did so, Andy nodding his approval each time she paused to draw breath.

When she was done, he took a long draw on his pipe, looking thoughtful.

'I reckon that's the stuff, right enough,' he said at last. 'Aye, I'm fair capped wi' that, lass. Sounds a right good letter. Here's thi wages.'

Bobby flushed with pleasure at the compliment as Andy fumbled in his pocket for a dirty half-crown piece and handed it to her.

'I'm going home for Christmas tomorrow, to spend it with my family back in Bradford,' she told him when she'd stashed the coin in her purse. 'If it's OK by you, I'll walk over the Sunday following New Year. I suppose you'll have had a reply from Ginny by then and we can write the next letter together. Only a couple more and I think it'll be time for you to ask her your big question.'

Bobby spoke lightly, but she hoped she'd still be here in Silverdale to write Andy's letters when 1941 arrived. Reg hadn't given her another piece to work on since he'd sent her to interview Andy. She'd handed her article about Andy's memories to him a fortnight ago, faithfully written to be true to the old farmer's account, but Reg hadn't spoken a word to her about it. In fact, he hadn't spoken to her about much at all. Bobby sensed he was angry about the angle she'd chosen to pursue, but it was frustrating to be given the silent treatment instead of having it out with her and telling her straight out that he wasn't going to use it. She had no idea if it had been included when the Christmas number had gone to print, and what was worse, she didn't know if Reg's coolness towards her indicated that he was considering sacking her in the near future. Would she be coming back to Silverdale after Christmas? She sincerely hoped she would.

–

When Bobby had popped Andy's letter into an envelope, she offered to take it down into the village and post it for him. It was a Sunday afternoon, so her time was her own until Mary expected her back at Moorside Farm for the Sunday dinner. This was usually when homesickness started to bite, and Bobby liked to keep herself busy to try to stave off the pangs. More often than ever now, she wished she had a friend in the village: someone young like her, who might want to accompany her to the pictures in Settle or join her on her now regular moortop rambles.

There was Charlie, of course. He was always free with his social invitations, but Bobby was sensitive to the fact that when a young, single man and woman spent significant amounts of time in each other's company, it was likely to give rise to gossip – especially when the young man in question was Charlie Atherton. She occasionally allowed him to persuade her to the pub for a drink and a chat, but the cinema felt like a step beyond that. Bobby remembered her mam saying that as far as she was concerned, if a lad and lass were seen at the pictures together on more than three occasions then they ought to be considered engaged. Bobby could only imagine Mabs Jessop's reaction to any rumours along those lines.

What Bobby really wanted, assuming she would be staying in Silverdale for at least a little while longer, was a friend of her own age and sex. But the only girl she knew around here was Mabs, who seemed to admire her, certainly, but who felt too young and giddy to be a good match for Bobby as a bosom companion.

The other village girls gave her a wide berth. Generally they regarded this interloper from the city with a wary suspicion, drawing husbands and sweethearts closer when she passed by in case she planned to use her sophisticated townie wiles to lead the local lads astray. Every day Bobby missed Lilian and her friends back at home.

When Bobby reached her old bike, which she'd propped against the wall of the post office, she crouched down to examine it.

She'd had a shock, after she'd trekked back over the moors following her first visit to Newby Top, when she'd sat on her bike and felt a sudden, sharp pain in her rear. Bobby's squeal had soon shed light on the culprits, as a gang of small boys who'd been watching from around the side of the blacksmith's ran away giggling in delight. An examination of the bike showed a drawing pin had been stuck to the saddle.

The second time she'd got back from visiting Andy, it was worse: strong glue had been smeared on the seat. Bobby hadn't noticed this until she'd arrived back at Moorside Farm and torn a big hole in the seat of her skirt, the fabric of which had remained behind on the saddle when the rest of her dismounted. While the elders of Silverdale showed their hostility to strangers with narrowed eyes and terse manners, the village youngsters had more practical means of making it clear she wasn't welcome here.

Bobby sometimes wondered why she was so keen to hang on to this job. She'd written precisely two pieces in the time she'd been here, neither of which she was certain were going to appear in the magazine with her byline. Other than that, mundane tasks like filling envelopes and typing Reg's letters still formed the bulk of her working day. There was nothing fun to do in her leisure time, and even if there had been, she had no one to do it with.

She was lonely, homesick, and hurt by the villagers who continued to be cold towards her. The two pieces she had written so far were hardly the sort of reporting she'd dreamed of as a girl, and the future was unlikely to yield anything better – assuming Reg ever gave her another piece to work on after the mess she'd made of the interview with Andy. Whereas home was familiar, full of people she knew and cared for, and there was always something in the city to do and a friend to do it with. Even if Bobby had been able to make friends here, there was precious little fun she could afford to have on her tiny salary. Even a cheap shilling seat on the balcony at the pictures on a Saturday night was an expense she could hardly justify with the folk at home relying on her, especially when she added to it the bus fare to Settle and back.

And yet… Bobby couldn't quite bring herself to give up on her job at *The Tyke*. It really had felt like fate, when Reg had appeared in the *Courier* offices that day with his advertisement. Although it felt like she'd experienced disappointment after disappointment since she'd come, Bobby still clung on to that sliver of hope.

An examination of her bike saddle soon revealed today's booby trap: a coating of black oil, the same colour as the saddle so it wasn't immediately obvious. Presumably, the gag was that she would mount the bike and immediately slip right off again, causing much hilarity to the watching boys as she fell on her bottom. Bobby took out her handkerchief to wipe the oil away, glad she had one she was happy to dispose of in addition to the 'lucky' hanky Charlie had given her.

'Very funny,' she announced to the village at large. She couldn't see anyone, but she knew there must be a gang of tittering boys lurking somewhere, waiting to see if they'd managed to catch her out again.

'What's very funny?'

She looked up from her bike saddle. Charlie had appeared behind her, looking rather smart for once in a charcoal-grey two-piece suit. He had his hands thrust into his pockets, however, in such a way that it gave him rather the air of a schoolboy dressed up against his will for the Sunday School treat.

Bobby beamed, pleased to see a friendly face after the latest evidence of the locals' dislike for her, then tried to arrange her features into a more modest expression of friendly welcome.

'Absolutely nothing is funny,' she said. 'Certainly not oil all over my bike saddle, holes in my skirt or drawing pins sticking in my – well, never you mind where it was sticking. Somewhere painful, that's all you need to know.'

Charlie laughed. 'The village lads have made a target of you, have they? You must be one of us then.'

'How so?'

'Oh, they never play pranks on someone unless they're starting to like them.'

'Really? I'd hate to think what they do when they don't like someone. It cost me my best skirt.'

Warm after her brisk walk, Bobby had taken her overcoat off and stuffed it into her bicycle basket. Charlie glanced approvingly at the walking costume she'd spent some of her scant salary on. She had been worried the loose slacks, knee-length woollen socks and sturdy shoes she'd purchased might make her look a little manly, so she'd paired them with a tight-fitting sweater that emphasised her figure. The effect of the costume as a whole was actually rather flattering.

'You look good today,' he said. 'Where've you been?'

'For a walk on the moors.' Bobby hadn't told anyone about her secret love letters on behalf of Andy Jessop. This was partly for the old man's sake, since it was, after all, his own personal business who he courted, and partly for her own, since she sensed Reg wouldn't be very happy about her working a second job on the Sabbath.

'What are you all dressed up for?' she asked Charlie, matching the light, teasing tone he always used with her. 'Has the father of some unfortunate girl whose reputation you've ruined caught up with you to march you to the altar?'

'Not me. I'm too fast for 'em,' he said breezily. 'If you must know, I've been to chapel with Reggie and Mary. They'll be here in a moment; we've been having an after-church saunter. I spotted you in the distance and scampered ahead so I could have you to myself for a little while.'

Bobby raised an eyebrow. '*You've* been to chapel?'

'Well, why not? I'm a God-fearing young lad, I am. His own harp and cloud reserved upstairs for when the day comes.' Charlie put one hand on his heart. 'I must say, I'm rather hurt you're so surprised by it.'

'Hmm. Let me apply my powers of deduction,' Bobby said, with the flicker of a smile. She enjoyed matching wits with Charlie when they bumped into each other, even though she tried not to be in his company too often. 'You're no more likely to spend the Sabbath on your knees than I am. If you were in church today, it means you must want something. Which begs the question, Charlie Atherton: who are you trying to make a good impression on, God or your brother?'

'You know, Bobby, you're wasting your talents on *The Tyke*. You could be Silverdale's own Lord Peter Wimsey.'

'Well?'

'A little of both,' Charlie admitted. 'I told you I was planning to join up after Christmas. That's what prompted today's visit to holy ground.'

'You're really going to go through with that?' Bobby wasn't sure why, but somehow she'd thought Charlie would think better of it. Since vets were a reserved occupation, he had the perfect reason to fight his war here on the Home Front. Farm animals were important in keeping the country fed, so no one could argue Charlie wasn't doing his bit for the war effort. The entire reason for the reserving of some occupations was to prevent what had happened in the last war, when some essential professions had found themselves dangerously short of men.

'The wheels are already in motion,' Charlie said. 'RAF, like I wanted. There's my medical to get through, then I'll be given a date to begin training. I'm hoping Reggie might help me make arrangements for someone else to take over my practice for the duration.' He glanced upwards. 'But I did feel a little talk with the man upstairs might do me good. It makes you stop and think about your life, going off to war.'

Bobby smiled. 'You've been getting philosophical? I don't believe it.'

But Charlie didn't smile. He looked uncharacteristically thoughtful, and rather far away.

'I suppose it will all be all right,' he said vaguely. 'Won't it?'

'You mean your practice?'

'The war. I mean, I suppose we'll win. I know it's looking sticky out there at the moment, but it would seem so unfair, wouldn't it? If the other side came out on top after all this.'

Bobby frowned. 'It's funny, but I've not really thought about it.'

'Neither had I until recently. I just assumed the bigwigs who arrange these things knew what they were doing and that... it'd all be sorted out somehow. That's a child's thinking though.' He glanced over his shoulder, where Reg was hobbling slowly towards them on his stick, arm in arm with Mary. The cold seemed to exacerbate the pain in his leg, but he would insist on taking his Sunday walk in spite of that.

Bobby hadn't seen Reg and Mary that morning. She'd told them she was planning an early walk on the moors and packed herself a breakfast of bread and butter the evening before to take with her. However, she only needed to take one look at Reg's face to see he was not in a good mood.

'So you're here, are you?' he grunted when they reached her.

'Good afternoon,' Bobby said, determined to be polite even if Reg didn't intend to be. 'Yes, I've finished my walk. I was about to bicycle back to the farm and see if Mary needed any help with the dinner.'

'That's very good of you, love,' Mary said. 'You work hard enough without helping me on your day off.'

'Huh,' Reg muttered. 'Hard work. Chance'd be a fine thing.'

Mary nudged him. 'Oh, pack it in, you grumpy old beggar. It's no good taking your bad mood out on young Bobby. She didn't ruin your precious prints, did she?'

Bobby frowned. 'What prints do you mean?'

'Cyril Johnson was supposed to be sending me some prints of his drawings of Malham for the February number,' Reg said. Cyril Johnson was a local artist of middling talent who worked in Indian ink, and whose work they often featured.

'And didn't he?' Bobby asked.

'No, he did. Problem is, they've turned up with the ink all smudged. Useless. He should've covered them over with art paper. It'll be too late for the February deadline by the time he's sent them again.'

'What will we put in the art supplement then? That's four pages to fill. Have we other prints we can use?'

'I don't know that there's any *we* about it,' Reg muttered sulkily. 'I'll find something, don't you worry. I've faced many a crisis bigger than this since I started this thing.'

An idea occurred to Bobby.

'But I know the perfect artist you could feature,' she said, beaming. 'She lives right here in Silverdale, so there'd be no need to wait for her to post prints. You could collect them from her directly.'

Reg laughed. '*You* know an artist, do you? After two months living here you know an artist in this village, when I, who was born here, thought I knew every man jack in the place?'

'Yes, I do.' Bobby glanced at Mary. 'Don't I?'

Mary shook her head. 'Now don't start with that daftness again.'

'Reg, your wife is a very talented woman,' Bobby said, ignoring her. 'Perhaps it's hard for you to see that, when you're used to taking her for granted, but she is.'

Reg raised an eyebrow. 'Taking her for granted?'

'I mean, you take her talent for granted. Mary's watercolours are worth ten of anything Cyril Johnson's ever done. If I were you, I'd be begging her to let you feature some of her work.'

Reg laughed. 'I can't believe I'm hearing this. To *let* me use her work? So she'd be doing me a favour, would she?'

'That's right, she would,' Bobby said staunchly, determined, if Reg was planning to sack her in the near future, that she wasn't going to back down over this. 'I'm sure Mary would get a lot of good offers from magazines if she chose to publicise her paintings.'

Mary laughed. 'Now there's a fine thought, Reg. I could make our fortune for us.'

'You leave that to me, our lass,' Reg said with a smile for her. 'Come on, let's go home and have no more of this foolishness. I'm famished.'

'I think Bobby's right, Reggie,' Charlie said, evidently deciding it was time to put in his two penn'orth. 'Why shouldn't you feature Mary's paintings, just because she has the ill fortune to be married to you? You know I've often said that I've rarely seen better work from an amateur.'

Reg frowned at him. 'And who asked you?'

Charlie shrugged. 'No one, as usual, but that rarely stops me having my say. You'll need to fill those supplementary pages with something, you know.'

'I can bring forward the March art and commission something else for that number,' Reg said. 'Conspiring against me with the womenfolk, are you, Charlie?'

'I'm giving you good advice. It'd do you no harm to take some from me for a change instead of dishing it out.' Charlie put an arm around his brother's shoulders. 'Now, don't sulk. Let's leave the girls to walk back together and you can come and have a beer with me while your dinner's cooking, see if it can chase away that bad mood. There's a matter I want to talk to you about anyhow.'

'Hmm. Not another loan, by any chance?'

'Not this time. A rather more noble endeavour. I'll tell you on the way.'

Reg sighed. 'All right. Mary, I'll see you back at the house.'

Bobby noticed how he pointedly left her out of the goodbye as he departed with Charlie.

Chapter 18

Mary tucked her arm into Bobby's. 'We'll take the scenic route, shall we?'

'I'd better not leave my bike here,' Bobby said. 'Not that I think anyone would bother to steal it, but I dread to think what mischief those little so-and-sos would do if I left it overnight. They've still got paint in their arsenal if they took a fancy to paint my bottom blue.'

Mary laughed. 'Oh, that's just bairns' devilment. They did the same thing to Charlie when he was first back from school.'

'Did they?'

'Well, likely it'll have been the big brothers of the current mischief-makers. They decided Charlie must've got too big for his boots, going off to get educated, and reckoned they'd bring him down a peg or two.'

'That makes me feel a little better,' Bobby said. 'I wonder he didn't tell me when we were talking about it earlier.'

'There's nowt more fragile than a man's pride,' Mary told her with a knowing nod.

Bobby wheeled the bike beside her as she followed Mary through the village, towards the Wesleyan chapel where the Athertons did their worshipping. It was a simpler building than the Anglican church, St Peter's, that sat a little further down the lane: small and unassuming, with only two tall, arched windows to indicate that this was a place of worship and not someone's home. It was surrounded by a little churchyard, dotted with marble stones and crosses dating from two hundred years ago to the present day.

'How did Charlie deal with the pranks?' Bobby asked.

'They stopped of their own accord in the end,' Mary told her. 'Lads soon grow bored when folk get wise to their tricks and stop falling for them. Besides, people around here like Charlie. He's got that way about him.'

Bobby smiled wryly. 'And I haven't. I know.'

'Oh now, that isn't what I meant,' Mary said, giving her arm a squeeze. 'Folk need to get used to you, that's all. It was different for Charlie, being born and reared up here. But they're warming to you, I can tell.'

'Can you? I can't.'

'Aye, well, you don't know the people here the way I do. It's not something they'd say right out to you. But you'll start to notice a change after Christmas, mark my words.'

Bobby sighed. 'If I come back after Christmas.'

Mary frowned. 'You aren't thinking of leaving us?'

'I don't want to. I won't deny I miss my family and my friends, but I don't want to give up on my work here. I only thought Reg might not want me back.'

'Did he say as much?'

'No, but he's been very cold since I did that interview for him. I knew while I was talking to Andy Jessop that it wasn't what Reg had wanted, but… well, it seemed to me that Andy had a right to tell his own story, as it really happened. And if that doesn't fit the picture Reg wants to paint, then…'

'Then what?' Mary said quietly.

'Then it isn't journalism, is it? It's storytelling – fiction,' Bobby said. 'When I came for my interview, Reg gave me this passionate speech about the changing ways of life here and how they ought to be preserved as a part of history. It really got me fired up. If Reg doesn't print the piece I wrote about Andy, after all his fine words—'

'—you'll have to leave,' Mary said, catching Bobby's meaning with her usual quickness. 'Aye, I suppose you will.'

'I'd rather stay than go. But I'm not doing what I believed I'd be doing here, and there are some things I can't compromise on, Mary. I won't lie to fit Reg's agenda, even if there is a war on and it's our job to keep up morale and all that. People like Andy Jessop deserve the right to be heard, and to have their memories preserved as they are and not as Reg thinks they ought to be. Yes, even if they were too poor for anyone to think it important enough to teach them to read and write so they could record their memories for themselves. And I was bloody proud of that piece, and it ought to be published.'

Mary was staring at her. Bobby flushed, the scowl that had settled on her face lifting. She realised she'd been talking rather too loud, and rather too warmly.

'Sorry for swearing,' she said in a quieter voice.

'Never mind about that. I married an old soldier. I've heard far worse.'

'I shouldn't be talking about this to you. Are you angry with me?'

'No,' Mary said. 'Actually, I'm impressed. You're quite right, Bobby. It's a matter of right and wrong, and I'm proud of you for knowing the difference so well.'

Bobby smiled. 'Thank you.'

'Do me a favour and don't give up on Reggie though. He's not used to being crossed – well, of course, he isn't. He's a man. Still, that doesn't mean it isn't good for him to be crossed every now and again. He knows his right from his wrong too, and though it sometimes takes him a while, he usually finds his way from one to the other if you give him time to work it out.'

'You don't think he's planning to sack me?'

'I couldn't say. He's not said a word to me on the subject. He knows I'd play merry heck if he suggested it, no doubt,' Mary said. 'But if I know Reggie like I think I do, he'll have found the right path in spite of his sulks. You'll likely find he's printed your article, and by the time you come back to us after Christmas, he'll have convinced himself the way it's written was all his own idea in the first place.'

Bobby sighed. 'I hope you're right.'

Mary looked at her. 'You do yourself no favours with him though, Bobby. Why on earth did you press him about my silly old paintings? He was in a foul enough mood from the pain in his leg.'

'Because I really believe they're good. Cyril Johnson couldn't produce anything near that quality. Reg is blind to it because he sees you as only his wife, and I want him to realise you've always been more than that. I thought I might as well press the point, since he's planning to sack me anyhow.'

'You don't know that.' Mary pressed her arm. 'Ah well, you're a sweet girl to think of me.'

'I'm sorry. I should really have asked if it was what you wanted before I got carried away with the idea. It just seems such a shame that the only people who can enjoy your paintings are Reg, Charlie and me, and no one else ever gets to see them.' A thought occurred to Bobby. 'And you know, if you were embarrassed about them being in your husband's magazine, you could always use a pen name. Lots of artists do.'

'It does make me feel funny, hearing myself called an artist,' Mary said with a smile. 'I must admit, there was a time when I was a lass that I'd dream of people seeing my paintings hanging in a gallery or at an exhibition. I'd daydream about them whispering among themselves, "who is that talented artist?" while I stood incognito on the edge of the crowd, like some silly character in a story for girls. But it's a long time since I grew out of that sort of daftness.'

Bobby smiled. 'I don't believe you did grow out of it. Not really.'

'Ah well, happen that's it. But I can't see my Reg changing his opinion, all the same.' Mary nodded to the old churchyard. 'We'll cut through here.'

Bobby followed Mary through the gap in the wall that surrounded the cemetery.

'Is this where Andy Jessop's family would be buried?' Bobby asked, glancing around the graves.

'Aye, they're here somewhere. That's the Jessop stone, I think.' Mary pointed out a simple flat slab near the wall, at the furthest distance from the chapel itself. 'One grave for mother, father and eight bairns. Poor souls, they all of them deserved better.'

Bobby went to read the list of names on the slab. Victor Jessop, who died at fifty-four. His wife Margaret, taken from the world aged forty-six. Eight children, none of whom had survived beyond their twelfth year. Only Andy had remained to experience adulthood.

It was such a hard, cold, cruel life. Bobby felt her anger rise to think of it. The suffering of all those poor children! Put to work almost as soon as they could stand upright, while in other parts of the country, children no better than they had lived pampered lives of ease and plenty. Bobby could well understand Andy's intention, when he reached the pearly gates, to demand to know what God had been thinking of.

'It doesn't seem fair, does it?' she said to Mary. But when she looked around, she discovered Mary wasn't at her side. She was standing in front of another grave by the church door, her head bowed.

Bobby left her bike leaning against the churchyard wall and went to join her.

'Oh, Mary,' she whispered when she read the inscription. She slipped her hand into the older woman's. 'I'm so sorry.'

'She'd be twenty-three if she were alive today,' Mary said quietly. 'Your age, Bobby. I like to think she'd be something like you.'

'I'm sure she'd be far better.'

Bobby read the inscription again.

In memory of Nancy, daughter of Reginald and
Mary Atherton
Who died 22 December 1919
Aged two years

'Spanish flu?' she asked Mary softly.

'No. There was something wrong from birth, my poor little babby. We knew we could lose her at any time. First there was the war, Reg's leg, then… then we lost Nancy the very next year.' Mary choked on a sob, and Bobby pressed her hand tightly. 'You can't tell me that's right. You can't.'

'It isn't right. It isn't fair.'

Bobby felt in her pocket for her handkerchief, then remembered it was covered with oil from her bicycle seat. Instead she fished out the one Charlie had given her, which she kept folded in her handbag, and handed it to Mary to dab her eyes.

'We couldn't have another,' Mary said. 'Doctors said it'd be the same over and over if we did. What killed Nancy would take them all from us. I felt so angry when they told us that. Angry at God, and at the world.' She sighed. 'Happen I should be grateful, when there's Peg Jessop buried not six yards away with eight of her bairns beside her. Plenty more families suffered the same. But losing a bairn… it's almost enough to make you give up on your faith. Except you don't, do you? Because that's when you need it most.'

'The day my mam died, I marched right into her bedroom and broke the big mirror in there,' Bobby said absently. 'There was this rage in me I couldn't get rid of, and I just had to *break* something. Mam hated that mirror at the end, standing opposite the bed, forcing her to watch her reflection getting sicker every day, but she wouldn't let us take it away.'

'Did breaking it make you feel better?'

Bobby gave a wet laugh. 'Not for very long. It didn't bring her back, did it? But I was glad it was gone.'

'You must miss your mother a great deal,' Mary said softly.

'Every day.'

'What was she like?'

'She was… better than the life she got. Intelligent, though she had little education – too intelligent to be wasted in the mills. She was tough on us bairns, making us work hard at our lessons, but only because she wanted better for us than she'd had herself. It was my mam who encouraged me when I said I wanted to write.' Bobby smiled. 'She said I could be anything I wanted to be if I only made the most of my brain. No one in my life has ever believed in me like she did.'

'She sounds a good woman.'

'She was. Cancer took her too young.' Bobby looked at the baby grave. 'There's always something, isn't there? All those awful diseases that killed Andy Jessop's brothers and sisters, things like consumption and rickets, and the hunger and the poverty. Then just when it feels like things are getting better for ordinary people, another war comes along and we're burying young men who never wanted much but to stay at home, marry their girls, raise bairns…'

'Charlie told you he's volunteered to join up, did he?' Mary said.

'Yes, he mentioned earlier.'

'Aye, he told me on the quiet too. Said he was breaking it to Reg this afternoon. Reg won't like it, but he'll be impressed he's done it. He's always complaining that his brother's too fond of an easy life. What are your thoughts?'

'The same, I suppose,' Bobby said. 'I admire him for doing it when he's perfectly entitled to stay here, but it's hard not to worry. I wish it didn't have to happen.'

'No more do I,' Mary said with a sigh. 'He's a good lad, in spite of his recklessness. The closest Reg and I ever had to a son. I always thought our Charlie was a better man than he likes people to believe he is.'

'I don't know about that, but he's an easy man to like.'

Mary smiled. 'The young ladies certainly seem to think so.'

'I meant strictly in a friendly way, I promise you,' Bobby said, laughing. 'I'm not interested in courting.'

'Neither is Charlie, I'm sure. I don't think you can call the way he acts with women "courting".'

Mary looked at the monogram on the handkerchief she was still holding, then regarded Bobby curiously for a moment.

'What is it?' Bobby said.

'Oh, nowt. A passing thought, that's all.' Mary squeezed her hand. 'I'm glad you found your way to us, Bobby. I never knew there was a hole in our lives until you came to fill it.'

Bobby smiled. 'Thank you. I wish Reg felt the same. I do want to stay.'

'Reg never knows how he feels until he's decided how he ought to feel.' Mary handed back the handkerchief. 'Think no more on it, Bobby. You go home and enjoy Christmas with your family, and leave Reg to me.'

–

Bobby never found out whether Charlie had broken the news to Reg that he'd volunteered to join up, or if, between them, they'd been able to make arrangements for Charlie's veterinary practice. She didn't see Charlie again before heading home the next day for a week's Christmas holiday, and Reg didn't volunteer any information. He was still giving her the silent treatment. Heeding Mary's advice to let him work out his thoughts by himself, Bobby decided not to confront him about her piece on Andy Jessop before she left to return home to Bradford. She did, however, have one final encounter with him when she went in to say goodbye.

She'd already said her farewells to Mary in the kitchen after they'd exchanged Christmas gifts: a rather tearful goodbye on both sides. In spite of her cool reception in the village and the disappointment of her daily work, there were some things in Silverdale Bobby was really going to miss. She'd miss Mary a lot – miss their evening conversations by the fire after Reg had gone to bed and the almost maternal bond that had started to build between them. She'd miss Gil at the post office, with his curling stamps and his surprisingly accurate weather forecasts. She'd miss the humane, earthy quiet of her talks with Andy

Jessop and helping him with his letters to his love, Ginny. She'd miss the unpredictability of life here, where you never knew when you might find yourself sharing a bus journey with a friendly lamb or have your way blocked by a gunslinging goose. She'd miss the now familiar sight of Mrs Hobbes's outrageous feathered hat as it waved in the wind while she pedalled home from the pub with Norman in her bicycle basket. And she'd miss Charlie, she supposed. Life was going to be very different without his schoolboy grin and genial conversation now that he was going off to war.

'You take care of yourself, and be sure to come back,' Mary said, tapping her arm a beat on the last five words to emphasise her point.

'If I'm wanted, I will.'

'You'll always be wanted here, Bobby – by me, at any rate. Now go say goodbye to Reg.' Mary lowered her voice. 'And be gentle, eh? It's a bad day for him.'

'Is his leg giving him pain again?'

'No. No, this is… summat else. You might find him in a bit of an odd mood.'

That sounded rather worrying. Warily, Bobby picked up her case and made her way to the parlour to find Reg.

He was at his desk, but he wasn't working. There was an almost empty glass in front of him, alongside a largish envelope. He was staring at his typewriter with his hands buried in his thinning hair, an odd look on his face. It wasn't angry or happy or… or anything at all really. It was only sort of… helpless. Bobby had never seen him look like that before.

'Reg, I'm going to go now.' She hoped he wouldn't offer her a lift to the bus stop. The look on his face, so un-Reg-like, was a little scary. She'd prefer not to be alone with it.

'Happen you might tell me summat first,' he muttered, not looking at her.

Bobby had a lot of experience of drunkenness in men. She'd seen it in her old workmates at the *Courier*, in the boys who sometimes made unwelcome advances to her and Lilian at the dance halls, and of course, frequently in her father. She knew it looked different in every man – Tony Scott became flirtatious, Don gregarious, and her father... well, her father just survived another night. In Reg Atherton, it was almost invisible: the only clue was a slight thickening of his voice. His accent had grown broader too, as it must've been when he was a lad before years of town living had softened it. Yet he was certainly drunk, although it was barely two p.m. What could have prompted that? Was it a regular occurrence? If it was, she hadn't noticed it before today.

Bobby wondered that Mary wasn't more annoyed. She had clearly known the state of affairs when she'd warned Bobby about Reg's 'odd' mood.

'What do you want to know, Reg?' she asked, trying to preserve her usual tone in the hope Reg wouldn't realise she'd noticed the state he was in.

'How long has tha been working on the side for Andy Jessop?' he asked, finally turning to face her.

Bobby flushed, although really she felt that there was no reason to feel ashamed of supplementing the meagre salary Reg paid her. 'I'm not working for him. He pays me a half-crown to write letters for him sometimes, that's all, him not being literate. I like doing it for him, and it's my own time.'

'Aye, well, when I hire someone, I expect their work to be kept for me.'

'I know. Sorry.' Bobby turned to go, then turned back again. 'I needed the money, you see.'

He laughed hoarsely. 'Half a crown? What're you going to do, put it on a horse?'

'I need it to help my family. It might not be much, but when I'm earning so little here, an extra two and six a week can make a lot of difference.'

Reg's expression softened slightly. 'Been sending money home, has tha?'

'Yes. My father… he…' Bobby swallowed. 'He drinks. I can't blame him for it – no one can. He's got shellshock, from what happened to him in the last war. It's the only thing that helps him, and it costs so much for whisky now. I send half my money and the half-crown from Andy home so my dad won't ever have to wake up screaming and find there's nothing in the house to help him.'

Reg was silent, scowling at his empty glass.

'I'm sorry,' Bobby said. 'If you want to give me my cards, I understand. But I'd really like to stay. I didn't mean to betray your trust.'

'That piece you wrote…'

'About Andy?'

'Aye, that one. What possessed you?'

'I thought it was important,' Bobby said quietly. 'Andy Jessop's been through a lot in his life. To take that away from him because it doesn't fit with the way we wish things had been in the past, because we prefer this fiction of "the good old days" to the bleak reality of what it meant to be poor back then… it's wrong, Reg. You don't have to print it, and I suppose you never will, but I had to write it. For Andy's sake.'

Reg fell silent again, the same glazed expression in his eyes that Bobby had seen too often in her father's. Assuming he had retreated now to a world of his own, she mumbled a 'goodbye' and headed for the door.

Reg roused himself. 'Wait.'

'What is it?'

He took a piece of paper from his desk, wrote something on it in pencil and slipped it into the envelope next to his glass, which he then sealed.

'Take this,' he said, holding it out to her.

Bobby frowned as she took it. 'What's in it?'

'Nowt to get too excited about. Call it a Christmas present.'

'Oh. Um, thank you.' She slipped it into her handbag, too busy wondering at Reg's strange mood to spare any time for the mysterious envelope.

It was only when she had her hand on the doorknob, about to leave the room, that a couple of loose connections in Bobby's brain came together to jog her memory. Charlie had said she could be Silverdale's answer to Peter Wimsey, but she'd been very slow to tumble the correct conclusion today.

Today was 22 December: three days before Christmas.

In memory of Nancy, daughter of Reginald and Mary Atherton, who died 22 December 1919.

So that was it. The empty glass, the helpless look…

'I am sorry, Reg,' she said softly, turning back to face him. 'About Nancy. I hadn't realised until now that today was the anniversary.'

He laughed bleakly, drinking the last drop of amber liquid from his glass. 'Tha's been talking to my missus.'

'She's been talking to me.' Bobby paused, wondering what else to say. 'I hope you and Mary have a happy Christmas. Look after yourself, Reg. I'll see you again soon, I hope.'

Chapter 19

'Well, don't leave me on tenterhooks,' Lilian said. 'What was in the envelope from Reg, Bobby?'

It was the following evening: the night before Christmas Eve. Bobby and Lilian's middle brother Raymond was on leave and had brought his wife and children over to spend the evening with their father, who was having one of his better days, so the girls had gone out together for an evening of fun. Lilian had insisted on it, stating confidently that she was sure Bobby hadn't had even a sniff of a good time since she'd moved to 'the back of beyond', as she described Silverdale. So they were having a drink in their favourite pub, the Rose and Crown, dressed up in their best frocks and with the prospect of meeting some friends for dancing afterwards. Bobby was rather excited. It felt like a long time since she'd been dancing, unless you counted the Smeltham hop, but that had really been work rather than play.

Of course, Bobby couldn't deny that good times hadn't exactly been the order of the day in Silverdale. There'd been the hop over in Smeltham, and the occasional drink in the pub with Charlie. Bobby mentioned these to Lilian in only the most cursory manner, knowing how her sister was prone to seizing on anything that sounded like it might develop into a romance – which to flirtatious Lilian meant any encounter with a single man, be it ever so innocent. Other than that, her leisure time had mostly been spent in reading or knitting, or, when the weather allowed, rambles over the fells.

Still, now that Bobby was home, she found she was missing her quiet life in Silverdale almost as much as she'd missed her life here while she'd been away. Her little talks with Mary as they knitted together in the evenings; passing the time of day with Gil on her daily visits to the post office; visiting with Andy Jessop and helping him woo his lady friend... these humble parts of her daily routine weren't exactly exciting, but they held a rustic charm that Bobby knew she would never be able to communicate to her vivacious, fun-loving twin no matter how she tried.

Although Bobby had promised to come home whenever she could, this was her first visit to Bradford since starting her new job. It felt difficult to justify the cost of the journey now her low salary meant that every penny counted. There was a lot Bobby had left out of her letters to her sister, not wanting her to know how disappointed she'd been in the work when she'd left home filled with such optimism, but it felt easier now they were together again to share what had been troubling her. Over their drinks, she had told Lilian what she'd learned of Reg and Mary's tragic loss, of her disappointment over Reg's rejection of her article about Andy Jessop, and of her confrontation with a drunken Reg when she'd bidden him goodbye the day before.

'I don't know what was in the envelope,' she said in answer to her sister's question. 'I haven't had the courage to open it yet. I slipped it into the top drawer of the sideboard at home.'

Lilian frowned. 'Really? I've never known you to run the other way when there's a mystery to be solved. I'd have expected you to tear it open as soon as you left Moorside.'

'I was afraid to,' Bobby admitted. 'I've been so worried Reg has been thinking about letting me go, after the way he reacted to the interview piece I wrote for him. What if it's a letter telling me I'm not welcome to go back after Christmas?'

'Surely he'd tell you something that important to your face. It'd be rather cowardly to do it in a letter.'

'I don't know. He's a hard man to get to know, Reg Atherton. I've really got no idea what he'd do.' Bobby sighed as she took a sip of her drink. 'I feel like I don't know anything about him, Lil, even after two months living in his house and working with him every day. Or at any rate, I don't understand anything about him.'

Lilian looked thoughtful. 'He's lame, isn't he? I suppose it must affect your mood, being in pain all the time.'

'I think it's grief as much as the pain in his leg. The little girl they lost – Nancy. I know a lot of people lost bairns in the old days, but it must've been a terrible thing, even if it was common. I can't imagine what it must feel like, can you?'

'No.'

They finished their drinks in pensive silence.

'When do you think you'll open it?' Lilian said after a while. 'The letter from Reg, I mean. You can't put it off forever.'

'I want to enjoy Christmas first. It's going to be our last one with all of us here for a little while, with you and Jake off to basic training and Ray about to ship out – last family Christmas for the duration maybe, however long that's likely to be.'

'Reg said what was in the envelope was a Christmas present, didn't he?' Lilian said, brightening. 'Maybe it's money. We could use some extra.'

'I think that's just his sense of humour. I doubt he can afford to pay me a Christmas bonus. He's nearly as skint as we are, living on the subscription postal orders as they come in. It's lucky Mary's got such a talent for economising.'

'You like her.'

Bobby nodded. 'She's kind and clever. She reminds me of Mam a bit, except she goes easier on me than Mam ever did on us. She's what I'd miss most if Reg really did let me go.'

'Not his brother – the young vet?' Lilian asked, lifting an eyebrow.

It was typical of Lilian to concoct a romance between her and Charlie, in spite of Bobby's attempts to mention him as little as she could in her letters.

'No,' Bobby said firmly.

'Are you sure?'

'I told you, Lil: Charlie's only a friend. He's not at all the sort I'd go for, if I was interested in going for any sort at all. I'd want a man who was steady. Charlie's too much of a thrill-seeker – more your type, in fact.'

'Is that so? I shall have to come for a visit.'

Bobby smiled. 'I wouldn't hurry. There seems to be a waiting list for Charlie Atherton among the girls in the village.'

'Do you think there can be any future for that magazine?' Lilian asked. 'If it's still struggling after a year...'

Bobby shrugged. 'I don't know. I hope so. There's something... special about that little mag. I don't know how to explain it but it's got a character all of its own – almost like a living thing. *The Tyke* deserves the opportunity to thrive. I think it'll be easier for us once the war ends and it's not such a struggle to get paper.'

Lilian laughed. 'A living thing? You get so sentimental about stuff.'

'Says the queen of romance,' Bobby said with a smile. 'Who's the current beau, Lil? Someone I know, or are you saving yourself for Ty Power?'

'Oh, I'd drop anyone for Ty.' Lilian grinned. 'But since he isn't immediately available to me, Jimmy Sloane doesn't make a bad substitute.'

'Jimmy Sloane from the chemist's?'

'That's right. We've been walking out for three weeks now.'

Bobby laughed. 'A new record. I'm impressed.'

'Ah well, I wouldn't start baking the wedding cake yet,' Lilian said, leaning back complacently as she examined her ringless wedding finger. 'I intend to do a lot of being young and fancy-free before I settle, our Bobby.'

'Of course you do. You're you.' Bobby lowered her voice. 'How's Dad been? He seems better.'

'He seems it, but... to be honest, I think that's just the effect of having us all at home. It makes him feel more secure when the family are around him.' Lilian sighed. 'He's been getting worse, Bobby. I thought I was imagining it, the decline, but there are definitely more bad days than good now. More nightmares.'

'Oh, Lil.' Bobby reached for her sister's hand. 'Why didn't you say? I'd have come home more often if I'd known you were struggling with him.'

'I know you would. That's why I didn't say. You need to save your brass.'

'How is he coping at work?' It was Bobby and Lilian's biggest worry that their dad's mental condition might one day deteriorate so much that even his routine job at the mill would be beyond him. Money was enough of a struggle as things stood.

'He can manage as long as he's sober,' Lilian said. 'I always hide his supply once he's in bed so there's no temptation to start drinking in the mornings. But he looks so tired, Bob.'

Bobby sighed. 'I never should've left. I should've stayed at the *Courier*. Nothing's worked out as I expected it to.'

'Don't say that. It's still early days for you. Better things might be on the horizon; you never know.'

'What better things?'

Lilian shrugged. 'Reg might give you a pay rise. You might be recruited by a better publication. Hitler might be overcome with festive spirit and send us his surrender as a Christmas present. The war can't last forever.'

'None of that would help us with Dad. We need to make plans for when you leave home in six weeks' time.' Bobby paused. 'Maybe Don would have something to suggest. I'm seeing him and the other boys from the *Courier* tomorrow night for a Christmas drink.'

'What could he possibly suggest that we haven't thought of ourselves?'

'I don't know. I just think he might be able to help. At any rate, I know that if he can, he will. He's been a good friend to me.'

'I really don't think we should discuss Dad outside the family, Bob. People might talk. Call him a drunkard – or worse.' Lilian lowered her voice. 'Folk can be funny about shellshock. They might say he's a coward, if they know about the nightmares.'

Bobby's brow knit. 'If they're going to say that, they'd better say it to my face.'

'They won't. They'll say it behind your back, and if Dad hears about it while he's working at Butterfield's then he'll be mortified we told anyone.'

'Don wouldn't say anything like that. He lost two brothers in the last war. He understands.'

'But he might talk to others who don't.'

'He wouldn't do that. We need help, Lil. Let me have a discreet word with him.'

Lilian still looked worried. 'You're sure he's trustworthy, this friend of yours? He's a newspaperman.'

Bobby laughed. 'So am I, aren't I?'

'Yes, but he's a real one. Being a reporter is like being a professional gossip. Who knows who he might tell?'

'He wouldn't let me down,' Bobby said, deciding to let Lilian's comment about 'real' newspapermen slide for now. 'Let me handle it, Lil, OK?'

–

Bobby had been looking forward to meeting her old colleagues from the *Courier* at the Swan for a Christmas Eve drink and a game of darts. Don had been a good correspondent but a letter wasn't quite the same as a face-to-face conversation, and she'd missed Jem and Tony too.

She met them at the *Courier* offices and they walked over to the pub together. A group of girls from one of the mills had already commandeered the dartboard and were having a competition to see which of the four of them could get the highest score. This was like a red rag to a bull for Tony, who immediately oiled up to them to suggest a match between the girls and the *Courier* team. He and Jem arranged the game while

Don went to the bar and Bobby claimed a table for them near the dartboard.

'Just like old times, eh?' Don said when he came back from the bar. He took a seat beside Bobby and slid a half-pint of beer over to her.

'Apart from that,' she said, nodding to the pencil moustache he'd grown since she'd moved away.

'Joanie suggested it. We saw *Gone With the Wind* last month and now she's fixed on making me look like Clark Gable.' He gave it a stroke. 'Well, does it suit me?'

'Not as well as it suits Clark Gable.' Bobby reached into her handbag and passed him a little packet wrapped in brown paper. 'Here. A Christmas present from the country, for Joan. And I suppose you can have some too. Don't let anyone see, will you?'

He opened it and quickly wrapped it up again before anyone noticed. 'Butter! Where did you get it?'

'Mary Atherton churns her own. I thought you might appreciate a little bit extra off the ration with your Christmas dinner.'

'Thanks, Bobby. The missus will be thrilled.'

'You're welcome.' She took a sip of her beer. 'Well? Any new gossip for me?'

Don nodded to Tony and Jem. Tony was chatting up one of the women on the opposing darts team, leaning against the wall while he tried all his usual lines on her. Jem was looking on in awe, perhaps hoping to pick up some tips.

'Flo gave Tony his marching orders,' Don said. 'I can't blame the girl, although it's a pity for Tony. She was a steadying influence on him, and he did care about her, as far as someone like Tony Scott can care about anyone besides himself.'

'That's a shame,' Bobby said. 'Why did she end it?'

'Too many reports of him flirting with other women all over town, I should think. She never gave him his ring back though.'

Bobby nodded approvingly. 'Clever girl. Any other news?'

'Jem got his call-up, so we're going to be a man down again soon. Clarky's been off work with a cough for a fortnight so it's been down to me to advertise for a replacement and keep everything ticking along smoothly in his absence. I've been running around the place like a clockwork soldier.'

'Is Jem old enough to be called up?'

Don nodded. 'Turned eighteen last month.'

Bobby looked at the cub reporter, flushing to the roots of his hair as Tony tried to interest him in one of his new girlfriend's pals. Jem was a shy boy, rather gormless, and very attached to his mother and two sisters. He seemed so young still – so very far from being a man, although of course he was one by law. Too young to go to war. He made Bobby think of Jake.

'I hope he'll be OK,' she said.

'He'll be fine. This business can't go on much longer. It'll probably be over before he finishes his training.' Don shuffled to face her. 'Well?'

'Well what?'

'Well, what's the news at your end? Are you coming back to us? With Jem going and your experience on Reg's mag, I might even be able to talk Clarky into considering a junior reporter role for you. Mind, you'd still have to make the tea. Jem's brews are like dishwater.'

Bobby flushed. 'To tell the truth, I haven't had much experience so far. I've only written a couple of pieces, and neither has been printed yet.'

'Only two? You've been gone for ages.'

'Yes, well, I think Reg wanted to ease me in gently.'

He took a sip of his pint. 'What were they about, these pieces?'

'Oh, country things. I wrote one about a dance in a barn and another about an old farmer's childhood memories.'

Don shook his head. 'You're better than that, Bobby.'

Bobby wasn't sure she agreed. She'd enjoyed writing both pieces, even if Reg hadn't seen fit to print them, and there had been something about them both that had felt… significant, she supposed. But it was hard to get that across to Don, who saw only that she'd been writing the sort of twee, frivolous stuff he despised. Don was an old-school newsman: he liked facts and action and eschewed anything approaching sentimentality.

'Perhaps,' Bobby said noncommittally. 'But it's all there is.'

Don glanced at the mill girl throwing her final dart while Jem tallied up her score on the blackboard and Tony continued to make love to her friend. 'Suppose I'd better step up and take my turn in this darts match. See if that poor lass needs saving from Tony.'

'Let Jem go next. I wanted to ask you about something.'

Don, who'd half risen from his seat, sat back down. 'What is it now? Last time I heard that tone in your voice, you wanted me to help you get a job out in the middle of nowhere so I'd be condemned to a life of brewing my own bloody tea.'

'I just wondered...' She paused, flushing, before blurting out what she wanted to ask. 'You don't know where I could buy cheap whisky, do you?'

He shot her a concerned look. 'For yourself?'

'Goodness, no! It's...' She hesitated again, grimacing. '...it's for my dad. It's so hard to get it now, and he needs it, Don. He sleeps so badly without it, when he dreams about... you know.'

'The war,' Don said quietly. 'He wouldn't be the only one. Is there nothing else you can give him?'

'He was in the trenches, Don. I don't think Horlicks is going to do the job.'

'All right, don't take it out on me. I was only asking.'

Bobby sighed, pressing her fingers to her temples. 'Sorry. He had a bad night, which meant I had a bad night. I could hear him pacing until nearly four.'

'I meant, have you tried everything medicinal?'

'Everything we can legally get. Sleeping powders don't seem to help much – not like the whisky does, at any rate. It's got to the point now that I don't know whether it's the nightmares he screams for or the booze. I only know it's the one thing that brings him relief.' She rubbed her temples. 'I feel so guilty, Don.

Leaving him here alone. My brother and sister are going off to war soon, and then he'll have no one with him.'

'It was bound to happen eventually. That's the way of things. Bairns grow up and leave home to start living their own lives.'

'I know, but to go so far away, never knowing how he's coping…' She looked at him. 'Do you know anywhere I could buy it cheap? Dad's buying it from a pal at the mill who gets it from the black market, and it's costing him a quid a bottle. It doesn't need to be good stuff, so long as it's strong.'

Don glanced behind him and lowered his voice. 'I might know a man who knows a man. It's not whisky, but it's as strong as. He distils it himself out of potato peel and all sorts of other stuff. Tastes like hell, but if it's oblivion your dad wants, it'll do the job. Eight bob a bottle, and this bloke's got plenty of it.'

Bobby smiled gratefully at him. 'Can you get a couple of bottles for me? I'll send the money out of what I've managed to save.'

'Don't worry about that. I'll make sure your old man's sorted out and keep an eye on him for you after your sister moves out, if you'll do us a favour in return.'

Bobby frowned. 'Me? What favours can I do?'

'I'm glad you said that to me and not Tony,' Don said, laughing. 'It's our Sal I'm worried about.'

'Worried? Why?'

He rubbed his forehead. 'I'm not right sure, to be honest. Joanie thinks I'm dreaming it, and when I spoke to Sal, she said it was nothing. But you're a reporter. You know how it is, when that sixth sense starts whispering to you.'

'I know,' Bobby said, feeling pleased at being described as a reporter by a journalist she admired. 'What is it you're worried about?'

'I'm sensing she's not completely happy at that place they've evacuated her to,' Don said. 'We weren't allowed to bring her home for Christmas but they had a parents' day at the school by way of festivities, and she seemed rather quiet. I might be imagining it, but when you get back to Silverdale, I'd be grateful if you could go over and see how she's getting on. You scratch my back and all that.'

'I'd be happy to, if I'm allowed.'

'They're a bit awkward about who they'll let in. Even parents are only allowed a certain number of visits per year, and they have to be scheduled well in advance. But you're press, which ought to carry weight with the woman in charge. See what you can do, eh?'

'I will. I wish you'd let me pay you properly for the booze though. I'd have checked on Sal anyhow if you'd asked.'

'You can pay me in instalments, starting with getting me another pint in while I go take my turn in this darts match.' Don rolled his eyes as Tony approached them, swaggering slightly as if hoping the eyes of the girls he'd been attempting to charm might be following him. 'Heyup, here's trouble.'

Bobby laughed. 'Don't worry. Since leaving town, I've been confronted by feral geese, bulls the size of houses and hordes of Dalesfolk who can't abide outsiders. I think I can handle one little Tony Scott.'

'You could when he had a girl. He's like a tomcat in heat since Flo dropped him. Quick, run off to the bar while I get rid of him.'

But it was too late. Tony had reached them and slid into the seat beside Bobby, his arm snaking instantly around her shoulders.

'Go on, Don, go up and take your turn,' he said. 'You're holding us all up. I've made a bet with Poppy that if we win she has to let me take her to The Majestic next week, so use your good arm, eh?'

Don glanced at Bobby. 'You all right here?'

'I'll be fine. You go ahead.'

'Well, have you heard the good news?' Tony said when Don had gone. 'I'm in the market for a wife again. Bobby, this could be your lucky day.'

Bobby smiled. 'You want to bet on a darts game for it? If you win, I'll meet you at the Registry Office first thing on Boxing Day in purest virginal white. If you lose, you get yourself neutered so the womenfolk of Bradford can walk the streets unmolested. How about it?'

Tony, who knew she was the superior player even though he always refused to admit it, dodged the question by withdrawing his arm from her shoulders, taking out his packet of Woodbines and lighting one.

'You look good, Bob,' he said through a mouthful of cigarette. 'Quite pretty and blooming. Is that rouge or country air?'

'A little of both.'

'How's that gorgeous sister of yours these days?'

'Still too good for you.'

'Do you think so? I heard she was walking out with that pasty-faced lad from the chemist.'

'None of your business.'

'You haven't got a young man yourself yet?' he asked, blowing smoke nonchalantly. 'I thought you might have better luck out in the country than here. They've probably never seen a lass without muck under her nails before.'

'I've been fighting them off with sticks, Tony,' Bobby said soberly. 'I can't throw myself away on any old farmer, can I? Not with prime examples of masculinity like you queueing up for my favours.'

Tony grinned. 'You know, Bob, I've missed you. You were the only one around here who never put up with any of my crap.'

Bobby grinned back. She couldn't help liking Tony, in spite of… well, in spite of the fact he was Tony.

'I've actually missed you a little bit too,' she said. 'Don't let it give you any ideas.'

Tony nodded to Don, who was taking his turn in the darts match. 'Has he given you all the news then?'

'About Jem being called up? Yes, he said.'

'Not that. Clarky.'

'I heard he's not so well.'

'Worse than that, if you ask me.' Tony lowered his voice. 'He's been getting weaker ever since you left. Something in his lungs, the doctors reckon.'

Bobby frowned. 'Clarky didn't tell you that, did he?'

'Course he didn't. No one told me, I went and found out for myself. I'm a reporter, aren't I?'

'That's a matter for debate,' Bobby said. 'How did you find it out?'

'Someone always knows, if you can figure out where to ask. Go to the right pub at the right time and you can find out anything, Bobby: that's my reporter's tip for you.' He gave her a knowing look. 'If you ask me, Clarky's not long for this world.'

'Don't be daft. He was fine when I left last month. He can't have declined that quickly.'

'I'm not joking. Don's been practically running the place for weeks now, since well before Clarky put himself to bed. Wouldn't surprise me if the old man never came back to work.' He nodded to Don. 'And if you want a bit of career advice, love, you could do a lot worse than toadying up to our Donald a bit. Because what you're looking at there, if my journalistic instincts don't deceive me, is the next editor of the *Bradford Courier*.'

Chapter 20

A loud yell pierced the air, jerking Bobby out of sleep. She fumbled for the lamp by the bedside and looked at her alarm clock. It was just after four a.m.

'Well, merry Christmas,' Lilian mumbled beside her. 'Shall I go or will you?'

'I'll go. Where's the whisky?'

'Usual place. Locked in the bottom of the kitchen dresser.'

Bobby got out of bed, pulled on her dressing gown and slipped her feet into her slippers, then went downstairs to retrieve her dad's bottle of Scotch from the kitchen. She poured a large measure, drank a fingerful herself for a bit of Dutch courage, then took it to her father's bedroom.

It was such a familiar routine now, she could do it almost without thinking. The unpredictable part of it was what she might find when she opened her father's bedroom door.

She discovered him kneeling at his bedside with his hands clasped, muttering frantically. Bobby supposed you might call it a prayer of sorts, although there was no more substance to it than the words 'good God, good God' muttered over and over while he whimpered and rocked back and forth.

'Dad,' she whispered, holding out the whisky like a lucky charm. She knew better than to touch him unexpectedly when he was in this state.

His head jerked towards her so sharply she was sure she heard his neck crack.

'Who sent you?' he whispered. 'Was it them?'

'It's me, Dad. It's Bobby,' she said gently. 'Your daughter Roberta – you remember.'

A faint haze of recognition appeared in his eyes. 'Roberta?'

'That's right. Mam named me after you. Do you know me?'

'I… there was a Roberta. And another one. Two bairns that came together.'

'Lilian.' She smiled. 'You used to tell us we were found in the cabbage patch. One baby in each half of a cabbage. I believed that for such a long time.'

Her father looked confused still, but he managed a tremulous smile. 'Aye. That was it.'

Bobby put the whisky on the table by his bed and knelt beside him.

'Are we praying?' she whispered.

'Nowt else now can save us. Only a miracle.' He glanced upwards to heaven. 'If you believe in miracles.'

'I'll believe if you will.' She took his hand. 'Shall we say a prayer together?'

For some reason, this seemed to give her father comfort. He nodded gratefully, as if relieved of the burden of remembering how praying was supposed to work.

Bobby started to recite the Lord's Prayer, and after a moment, her father joined in. By the time they'd finished he was calmer, although there was still a wild look in his eyes that suggested the nightmare hadn't entirely fled.

'Now get into bed and have your whisky,' Bobby said in a soothing, singsong voice, as if he were a child. Obediently he got under the eiderdown, and she handed him the glass. He sipped it as if it were warm milk.

'You're a good lass,' he murmured, the whisky quickly achieving the desired goal of stupefaction as he sagged back against the pillow. 'You've always been a good lass, Nell.'

Bobby flinched at hearing him call her by her mother's name.

'It's Bobby, Dad. Your daughter.'

'Bobby,' he echoed. 'Clever girl, Bobby. School prize for writing. We were right proud, Nell and me.'

Bobby smiled, pleased to think that this of all things he was able to remember through the fog: the primary school prize-giving when she was eleven, when she'd been called up on stage, quivering with nerves, to receive the prize of a book and a certificate for a story she'd written.

Her father's eyes were closed now. Bobby gave his hand a squeeze before tiptoeing out of the room, once again feeling that stab of guilt, knowing she would soon have to leave him to deal with his demons alone. At least there was the reassuring thought that Don would be here to look in on him from time to time.

It was nearly five, and there seemed little point returning to bed. She'd leave the rest of the household to sleep while she began the preparations for Christmas dinner. There would be eight of them for the meal, and even with rationing and shortages, there was still a lot of food to get ready. It would be wise to get an early start.

Bobby made herself a cup of tea, stirred up the embers of the fire in the living room, turned on the Christmas lights and took a seat next to the tree, where their modest gifts lay wrapped in old newspaper. She leaned back with her eyes closed as she sipped the hot liquid.

Something about the strange little scene with her father had left her feeling… not sad exactly. Wistful. The day of the school prize-giving, when her name had been called out of everyone in the school and her writing praised above all of her peers, had felt like the crowning achievement of Bobby's life at the time. Her mam had been so thrilled, talking enthusiastically about the life that lay ahead of her, and her dad had given her a shilling and told her she was a canny lass, and he was proud of her. It had never occurred to her, then, how much life could change in a few short years.

It had been just three years later that her mam had started getting ill. From that point on, Bobby and her siblings had had to live with the daily pain of watching someone they loved, someone who had been the linchpin of their family life, getting frailer and frailer with each passing day. The boys had been young still: Raymond just twelve, and Jake not much more than ten. Bobby and Lilian had found themselves suddenly adults at fourteen, watching their father's mental health decline even as their mother suffered in body. They hadn't realised, until Mam was no longer able to be the main caregiver in the household, just how much of their father's illness she'd kept hidden from them.

And then, two years later… they'd lost her. That had really been the point of no return for Dad. He'd never been fully with them since that day.

Bobby glanced at the presents under the tree. Christmas had never seemed right since they'd lost their mam. It felt a little like putting on a show these days. They tried to do everything right, as it ought to be – gifts, food, the tree with its shining glass ornaments. But it would never be the same as it had been.

Bobby's thoughts drifted to Andy Jessop and the bleak Christmases of his childhood. No treats apart from a fire, a little sugar cake and extra church. And every year, fewer siblings to share it with. This made her think of Reg and Mary and their little girl Nancy, who had died days before her third Christmas, and her gaze drifted to the sideboard where she'd stored the letter Reg had given her.

Well, she might as well open it now, while she was feeling pensive. It couldn't make her mood any glummer, and if she was going to be sacked, she should probably know about it sooner rather than later. Bobby put her tea down on the table and went to fetch it.

It was quite a fat envelope. If it was a letter, it must be a long one. Perhaps Reg had abandoned his customary taciturn style in order to go over in exact detail exactly why she wasn't cut out for the job of reporter, including everything she'd failed in from the day she'd started. Or perhaps it was a wad of money, as Lilian surmised, and in fact Reg valued her services so highly that he'd stuffed an envelope full of five-pound notes for her as a Christmas gift. Bobby couldn't help laughing at the idea. She knew Reg no more had a secret stash of five-pound notes than she did.

When Bobby drew out the envelope's contents, she discovered it was neither a letter nor a gift of money, but a copy of *The Tyke*'s Christmas edition. Despite it being on sale for a fortnight, she'd managed to avoid it, turning her face away every time she'd seen it on the newsstands. She couldn't bear the unpleasant reminder of her last scene with Reg and her worries about her job.

There was a card bookmark inserted between two pages. Bobby opened the magazine where it was marked and tossed the bookmark on to the coffee table.

She stared at the article. Blinked. Stared at it again. She wasn't quite sure whether to believe her eyes.

Bobby looked up when a hand appeared on her shoulder. Her sister had materialised behind her in her nightgown.

'So here you are,' she said. 'I wondered what had happened to you when you didn't come back to bed.'

'Lil, look!' Bobby showed her the double-page spread in the magazine, complete with a pen-and-ink drawing of a moorland farmhouse in similar bleak surroundings to Newby Top.

'"Memories of a Yorkshire Farmer",' Lilian read. 'Well?'

'It's my piece! The one I wrote about Andy Jessop.' Bobby's eyes skimmed the pages. 'Oh my goodness! Lil, he's not changed a word. He's printed it exactly as I wrote it.'

'Reg?'

Bobby nodded. 'I was so sure he'd thrown it away or... I know he was angry with me about it. What could have changed his mind? He knew he'd included it in this number and he never said a word to me about it.'

'Perhaps he was too proud. Men don't like admitting that they were wrong about something.' Lilian picked up the book-mark from the table, frowning. 'Bobby, have you looked at this?'

'Hmm?' Bobby's eyes were still fixed on the article. She couldn't wait to see Andy's face when she showed it to him, although, of course, he wouldn't be able to read it. She could read it to him and watch his expression as she did so.

'This.' Lilian dropped the bookmark on top of the magazine spread, forcing Bobby to look at it.

Bobby picked it up. 'Oh my gosh!'

On the card was a photograph of her, the one Reg had asked for from her 'for the file' when she'd started work. Her name was printed on it and above that, in big capital letters, was the word *PRESS*.

'The person to whom this card is issued and whose photograph is attached hereto is… is a member of the National Union of Journalists!' she read out loud.

Lilian laughed. 'That's you, Bobby.'

'It's… me.' She felt like she was in a dream. But it was her. There was her name and her photograph, a space for her signature, and that beautiful, glorious word in imposing capitals: *PRESS*. 'It's me. Lil, I'm… I'm press!'

'Just like in the films,' Lilian said gleefully, throwing her arms around Bobby's neck for a hug. 'Oh, I'm going to get you a hat. A real reporter's fedora.'

'I can't believe I'm actually a reporter. I mean, officially and everything!' Bobby stared again at the card. She couldn't stop staring at it. It was the most beautiful thing she'd ever seen.

'Is there anything else in the envelope?' Lilian said, releasing her from the hug. 'A note or anything?'

'Yes there is. I saw him write it, right before he gave me the envelope.' Bobby slid her hand inside it, feeling for the note.

'What does it say?' asked Lilian when Bobby had drawn it out. Less familiar with the editor's scrawl, she couldn't make it out as her sister could.

'"That'll do, lass. Quid a week, take it or leave it",' Bobby read.

Lilian frowned. 'I don't understand.'

'You have to know how to speak Reg. In as few words as he can get away with, he's saying well done and giving me a pay rise to twenty bob a week.'

'Where does he say well done?'

Bobby laughed. 'That's the "that'll do, lass". It's what a farmer says to his dog to call it back after a good day's work.'

'Are you telling me you're Reg's sheepdog?' Lilian asked, smiling.

'I suppose I am. I do the running so he doesn't have to.' Bobby beamed at Reg's note. 'A pound a week, Lil!'

'That's still ten bob less than you got at the paper.'

'Yes, but it's a big improvement on twelve and six.' She looked up. 'And my press card and my first byline. I'm actually a reporter now! How about that for a Christmas present?'

Chapter 21

Time sped by after opening her gift from Reg – and from Mary too, Bobby supposed, in addition to the knitted gloves her landlady had given her the day they'd said goodbye. While the editor's wife almost certainly hadn't known about either the article, the press card or the pay increase, her quiet, steady influence over her husband always felt instrumental in anything good that happened for Bobby.

Her week's holiday seemed to flash by in a moment, and yet at the same time, it felt like it dragged on forever. Bobby couldn't wait to get back to work, now she felt like she was finally a real reporter, and she was looking forward to seeing the people she'd left behind in Silverdale – not only Mary and Charlie and Reg but the villagers too. There was her friend Andy Jessop, of course; cheery Gil at the post office; eccentric Mrs Hobbes and her beloved Norman… Bobby even found herself missing the telltale titters of the cheeky boys who played pranks on her and her bicycle whenever she left it unattended.

And the countryside. Yes, she missed the landscape of her new home rather keenly. So frightening to her once, now Bobby dreamed of the high fells, the barren moors, the rolling fields dotted with sheep and crisscrossed with silver drystone walls. Bobby had never felt as closed in by the huddled buildings of her home town as she did now.

It was going to be a bittersweet goodbye when she left Southampton Street this time; the end of an era as the family home emptied and the younger generation of Bancrofts all went their separate ways. It was the last time Bobby would see Lilian and Jake before they departed for their wartime positions with navy and army respectively. Her brother Raymond was about to be shipped overseas to join the fighting, which, of course, brought its own worries.

And her father... well, he'd have Sarah, Raymond's wife, coming over every day to cook his meals, and Alice, the widow lady who lived next door, had promised to sit with him in the evenings whenever she could. Don would visit as he'd promised, of course. But Bobby still felt guilty, worrying about what would happen when Dad awoke in the night with no one in the house to comfort him. It wasn't going to be easy to ration his alcohol intake, making sure, as they had done for years, that he had enough to banish the fog of his terror but not so much that he was in danger of hurting himself. She'd reminded Lilian to write out strict instructions for Sarah before she left as to how much whisky – or whatever the potato peel spirit Don had brought around on Boxing Day was called – should be measured out and left for him overnight, but it was a tricky calculation when some nights were worse than others. On no account, though, must he be given unrestricted access to the whole bottle. Without his family, there would be no restraint.

When the day dawned for her to return to Silverdale, Bobby sprang out of bed and was busy packing her case before the clock had struck six a.m.

Lilian yawned as she pushed herself up in bed. 'Up already? Anyone would think you couldn't wait to get away from us.'

'Don't be daft. I'm just champing at the bit, raring to get back to work,' Bobby said. 'You can't pretend you're not looking forward to starting training.'

Lilian smiled at the navy-blue Wren's uniform now hanging on their wardrobe door. It had arrived two days after Christmas, and she'd immediately dashed upstairs to try it on. Of course, it flattered her enormously, but most clothes did.

'I can't wait until I'm allowed to turn male heads wearing that beauty around town,' Lilian said. 'It's my favourite of the women's services uniforms – so much nicer than those ugly khaki ATS suits.'

'You mean you joined the Wrens for the uniform?' Bobby shook her head. 'And I thought you were being so patriotic, joining up.'

'No you didn't.'

'You're right, I didn't. I thought you fancied yourself in the uniform.'

Bobby frowned as a knock sounded at the front door.

'Who can that be, calling so early?' she asked.

'You'd better go see since you're dressed already,' Lilian said. 'I don't want to go down in my nighty.'

Bobby closed her case and went downstairs to answer the door. A young lad in motorcycle leathers was standing on the step.

'Is there a Miss Roberta Bancroft here?' he asked.

'That's me.'

'Telegram for you, Miss.' He handed it to her. 'Not bad news, I hope.'

'Oh.' Bobby stared at it. 'Um, no, I shouldn't think so. Thank you.'

When the boy had mounted his motorcycle and ridden off, she wandered back upstairs with the telegram.

There were plenty of people who lived in fear of telegrams these days – and with good cause – but Bobby had no need of doing so. No one close to her was in immediate danger – not yet, at least. But she couldn't for the life of her think who might want to send her a telegram. Could it be from Reg? Something urgent he needed to tell her about the world of Silverdale? She felt a stab of worry, wondering if Mary and Charlie were all right.

'Who was it?' Lilian asked when she got back to their bedroom.

'Messenger boy.' Bobby held up the telegram.

'Who's that for?'

'Me. Lord knows who sent it.'

'Well, read it and find out.'

Bobby opened the envelope and squinted at the telegram in the dim light, the lightbulb casting only a faint glow through the dark card of the blackout shade.

'"Bull, two. No to Bert. New vehicle. Can't wait. Love CA",' she read.

'What does that mean?'

Bobby pondered a moment as she deciphered it. Charlie Atherton's style of writing a telegram was not dissimilar to how his brother wrote all the time, although in his case, she suspected it was more to do with saving himself pennies than any innate terseness.

'It's Charlie. He's telling me to wait by the Bull and Heifer when my bus drops me off there at two,' she said. '"No to Bert" – Bert's the local coal man. He gives people a lift down on his wagon for an eightpence fee. Charlie's telling me to say no if he asks because he's going to pick me up in his new car.'

'A new car! He must be doing well for himself.'

'I've no idea. He never mentioned anything to me about intending to buy a new car. I wonder anyone's buying them at the moment, when it's so hard to get petrol to run them.'

Lilian raised an eyebrow. 'What did the last bit of his message say? "Can't wait to see you"?'

'It just says "can't wait",' Bobby said, showing her the telegram. 'To show off his new car, I should think he means.'

'Bobby, don't be so coy. He paid an extra penny to add "love". That must mean he's an admirer. I tell you all about my boyfriends, don't I?'

Bobby laughed. 'More than I could possibly want to know, Lil.'

'Well? Is he a beau, this vet? He sounds like he wants to be, if he isn't already.'

'You wouldn't say that if you knew him. He flirts with everything in a skirt; I'm not special. I don't think he knows how *not* to flirt.'

'But you like him though, don't you?'

'Very much, but he's the last man I'd ever consider becoming romantically involved with,' Bobby said firmly. 'Charlie's like an overgrown schoolboy, always up to some mischief. That sort of man wouldn't suit me.'

Lilian raised a suggestive eyebrow. 'I don't know. A man who can convince you to stop working so hard and have some fun sounds like he could suit you very well.'

'That's up to me. And I am decidedly not interested in Charlie Atherton as anything other than a friend.'

Lilian smiled. 'He sent you your first ever telegram though. That ought to get him into your good books. Do you remember when we were bairns, how you always said the thing you wanted most was for someone to send you a telegram?'

'I remember. And now, just the word "telegram" is enough to make people shiver. It goes to show, it isn't always good to get what you wish for.' Bobby read the telegram from Charlie again, lingering over the words. 'I wonder what his new car is like?'

Bobby found out the answer to her question that afternoon when Charlie came driving up the road from Silverdale to pick her up. Quite literally 'driving', as he drew to a halt beside her in an old-fashioned pony and trap.

It was a small carriage, little more than a seat balanced between two large wheels, with enough space for two people to ride comfortably side by side. Charlie sat in the middle of it, holding the reins of a smart-looking white pony and grinning all over his face.

'What on earth, Charlie Atherton?' Bobby demanded with mock indignation.

'Now, Bobby, don't get all sentimental on me. You know how I hate a scene. I missed you too, all right?'

She nodded to the trap. 'When you said you had a new vehicle, I assumed you meant one with a motor.'

'Boxer's better than any motor, aren't you, boy?' Charlie said, slapping the horse's rump. It let out an appreciative whinny. 'And I'll tell you why. He doesn't run on petrol, which means I now have unlimited use of my own transport when every other lad around here is bewailing the fact he can no longer take his girl to the pictures on a Saturday night because he can't spare the coupons. Go ahead, congratulate me on my cleverness.'

'Oh, the cleverness of you,' Bobby said dryly.

He shuffled over on the seat. 'Climb in then. I brought a cushion for your delicate lady's bottom.'

'As touching as your consideration for my bottom is, Charlie, I've made few enough friends in Silverdale without riding back into town in state in a carriage.'

'It's a two-man trap, Bobby, not the Gold State Coach.'

'Still, I think I'd better walk, thank you.'

'Come on, don't be so stuffy. It wasn't so long ago that practically everyone around here used to ride around in these. No one will look twice at you.' He turned a tragic look on her. 'And poor Boxer will be so disappointed not to get to know you after he's come all this way. Besides, you've got your case to carry.'

Bobby didn't mention her other concern: what the villagers were likely to think when they saw her and Charlie Atherton riding along side by side, with only a pony for a chaperone. But it was hard to say no to Charlie when he made that face, and she had missed his conversation. Giving in, she sighed and climbed up beside him. Charlie grinned at her before making a clicking sound to Boxer, who obediently trotted off.

'There's going to be a delicious scandal, isn't there?' Charlie said, as if he'd read her thoughts. 'You. Me. A cosy little carriage for two. Do cuddle up if you're chilly.'

'You enjoy being gossiped about, don't you?'

'Of course I do. It makes me feel all warm and relevant. I believe Oscar Wilde expressed similar views on the subject. Why, don't you?'

'It's all very well for you,' Bobby said, hugging her case against her to shield her body from the rush of chill wind. 'I've got my reputation to think about. My name's already mud around here without it getting around that I'm a fallen woman who's been seen buggy riding without her petticoats with the village cad.'

He smiled. 'I missed you, Bobby. It's been boring as hell since you went. Did you have a nice Christmas?'

'I suppose so,' Bobby said. 'I was a little worried when I left that I might not be coming back, but... did you see the Christmas magazine?'

'I read it cover to cover,' Charlie said, putting his hand on his heart. 'Well, no, that's a lie: I never read them cover to cover. I did read your article though.'

Bobby was dying to know what he thought. Daft as a brush he may be, but Charlie Atherton was still an intelligent man, and she respected his opinion. One reason she enjoyed Charlie's company was that he always demonstrated a respect for and interest in her career ambitions that none of her other male acquaintances – with the exception perhaps of Don Sykes – had ever displayed. But she didn't want to seem too keen for his approval, so she only said, 'I'm glad your brother decided to print it. I know it wasn't what he wanted.'

'It was a good piece. The sort of thing Reggie ought to print more of. Andy Jessop's absolutely right: people prefer to remember the past as they wished it had been rather than how it was, and that stops them appreciating everything they have in the present.'

Bobby smiled. 'You really did read it. I thought you might just be trying to impress me.'

'I am. That was why I read it.' He glanced at her. 'It was good writing though. A little long – I'd have left out some of the farming details myself. Those that know farming know them already, and those that don't, don't care.'

She cocked an eyebrow. 'Are you an expert on writing now?'

'No. Only on people.' He steered Boxer to the right to take them across the old bridge into the village. 'Other than that, I was impressed. A very moving piece. You managed to stay away from sentimentality and still make me blub.'

Bobby wondered if she knew another man who'd so happily admit to crying without worrying it would make him seem 'pansy'. Charlie was an odd being – one of a kind. What must it be like to live in his world for a day? She'd give anything to find out.

'Thank you,' she said, with genuine gratitude. 'I appreciate that.'

She was rather enjoying her ride. It was bumpy, yes, and in open countryside the January wind went right through you, but it was still far more comfortable than either the coal wagon or her old bike. The landscape today was crusted with a sugary frost, sparkling invitingly under the bright winter sunlight.

'Hullo, here's fun,' Charlie said, nodding to a colourful display wobbling in the distance. 'I'd recognise those feathers anywhere. It looks like Mrs Hobbes is out for a stroll, looking for winter greenery to steal. You know, she's the most dreadful gossip. We'll have everyone in Silverdale talking about us by teatime.' He sounded thrilled at the prospect.

'Who is Mrs Hobbes, Charlie?' Bobby asked. 'Do you know much about her?'

'Why do you ask?'

'I don't know. Something in my gut tells me there's a story there. The way she tries to speak one way, but her voice keeps pulling back towards Scotland. That hat, Norman, her daily dinnertime pint… she interests me. Eccentrics always do.'

'No one really knows who she is,' Charlie said. 'There was never a Mr Hobbes – not while she was here. She just appeared one day when she came to work as nanny for Topsy Sumner-Walsh at the manor house. Now Topsy's all grown up, Mrs

Hobbes stays on as a sort of companion to her. I go up there sometimes when Norman's ailing – well, he's never really ailing. He's as strong as an ox, that goose. But she frets about him, so I give her some coloured sugar water for him and tell her to keep me informed of his progress. She thinks I'm a veterinary genius.'

'That makes two of you then,' Bobby said, lowering her voice now Mrs Hobbes was in earshot. The old lady wasn't on her bike today but was walking Norman on a lead as if he were a dog. She seemed to be attempting to introduce him to one of the female geese who frequented the beck, the ones who had been turning up their beaks at his attempts to impress them the day Bobby had first met him. Charlie slowed to a halt so he could pass the time of day with her.

'Now Norman, you must be a little more charming than that,' Mrs Hobbes was admonishing her pet. 'Let's try again.'

She took some crumbs of bread from her pocket and threw them to the other goose. Norman immediately hissed at his potential mate before stealing the bread for himself.

'Oh, you are hopeless, you really are,' Mrs Hobbes said, tutting.

'Having some trouble, Mrs Hobbes?' Charlie asked jovially.

'It's him,' she said, pointing accusingly at Norman. 'High time he found himself a wife, but you can't teach him a thing. He's far too greedy to court properly.'

'Have you tried some romantic music to help the mood?' Charlie enquired, keeping his face as earnest as possible. 'Perhaps you might sing a little Nat King Cole or Bing Crosby for them. Girls always swoon for that crooner stuff.'

Mrs Hobbes looked thoughtful. Bobby, who was struggling to keep a straight face, took out her handkerchief and pretended to blow her nose.

'I suppose it's worth a try,' Mrs Hobbes said. 'Yes, I'll do that. Thank you, young man.'

'It's my pleasure as always, Mrs Hobbes.' Charlie doffed his hat to her, and Bobby caught a snatch of 'Only Forever' before they drove on their way.

'What are you smirking about?' Charlie said. 'That was perfectly good advice.'

She shook her head. 'I wasn't smiling about that. Well, I was, but I was thinking… it's good to be back.'

Chapter 22

'Right, lass,' Reg said to Bobby over breakfast the next morning. 'Good to have you back. Now it's time to go to work.'

Mary shook her head. 'Oh, Reg, not today. It's New Year's Eve.'

'What of it? Working day like any other. She's just had a week's holiday, hasn't she?'

'But she shouldn't work the whole day when everyone else is celebrating. Let her finish early so she can go into the village to enjoy the festivities with the other young people.'

'That's exactly where I want her to go, and take her notebook with her,' Reg said. 'Charlie's doing the first footing around the village tonight. Should make a nice little piece, but damned if I'm hobbling round with him. I don't keep a dog to bark myself.'

Mary rolled her eyes at Bobby. 'He'll work you to death now he's paying you more, this husband of mine. Anything to get his money's worth.'

'It's all right, Mary,' Bobby said. 'I've been dying to get back to work. I'd be happy to go along and report on the New Year celebrations.' Little did her employer and his wife know that since she'd received her precious press card, it had lived in her pocket or handbag, nestled against Charlie's lucky handkerchief.

'Come into the parlour when you've eaten and I'll tell you about the first footing,' Reg said. 'I take it you don't know the custom?'

'No, not really.'

After breakfast, Bobby joined Reg in the parlour. Her desk was as she'd left it, with the black leather case of her Remington typewriter shining in the centre – Mary had clearly been keeping it polished in her absence. The machine had been a gift from Bobby's parents to celebrate her being accepted to Pitman's College and was much treasured still. She had toyed with the idea of taking it home for Christmas in case she wouldn't be coming back, but decided this would be tempting fate and left it in its place. Next to it was a little pile of letters.

'Did you want me to type these for you?' she asked Reg.

'Do as you please with them. They're your letters.'

Bobby frowned. 'Mine?'

'Your name on 'em.'

She picked one up and looked at the address.

Roberta Bancroft, c/o The Tyke magazine…

'Who'd be sending me letters?' she asked Reg.

He shrugged. 'No use asking me. Open one and find out.'

Bobby took a seat at her desk and opened the top letter.

Dear Miss Bancroft,

I wanted to write to tell you with what pleasure I read your article about the old farmer, Andrew Jessop. His younger sister Margaret and I attended the Sunday School at Silverdale Chapel together, and she was my very good friend until we so sadly lost her young. Although I am now an old lady of seventy-seven with grandchildren and great-grandchildren, it brought a tear to my eye to be reminded of that little girl I loved so dearly and to know through your magazine that Meggie's short life has not been entirely forgotten. Please pass on my regards to Mr Jessop and remember me to him.

Yours,

Caroline Adams, née Metcalfe (Mrs)

'It's about the article I wrote,' Bobby murmured.

'Aye, I thought it might be,' Reg said, with the hint of a smile.

Bobby tore open the next envelope. This, too, was from a reader with whom her article on Andy Jessop had resonated. In total there were five letters, all praising her article for its honesty, compassion and absence of maudlin sentimentality.

'People like it.' She beamed at Reg. 'They really like it! I was worried it would be too bleak for our readers.'

'Bleak or not, it's real. Genuine. Owt that's honest like that will always touch folk.'

'But you asked me to write—'

'I know what I asked you to write. And in future, I'll thank you to follow your instructions.' He paused. 'But happen… you were right to stand by this one like you did.'

This, Bobby suspected, was as close as Reg had ever come in his life to admitting he was wrong about something. She nodded an acknowledgement, judging it best not to make a fuss.

'What made you change your mind about printing it?' she asked. 'I was sure you wouldn't put it in.'

'It's good writing. Like I said, it's honest, and readers like owt that's honest.'

'But Andy's childhood was so tragic.'

'So were lots of folk's round here. It's no good pretending different because we don't like the truth. That's part of what we're trying to do with the mag too, make sure those stories aren't forgotten – or it should be.'

'I agree,' Bobby said quietly. 'Thanks, Reg. For giving me another chance, and for giving me a pay rise, and for… I suppose, for letting Andy have his voice.'

'Aye, well, don't start talking soft about it,' he muttered.

'Can I keep these?' Bobby said, nodding to the letters. 'I'd like to read them to Andy. I think he'll be pleased to know his story has touched people.'

'They're your letters. Do as you please with them.'

Bobby tucked them into her handbag.

'Now then,' Reg said. 'First footing. You say you've not heard of it.'

'Well, vaguely. Isn't it a Hogmanay tradition in Scotland?'

'Not only over the border. Most Dales villages observe the first foot, although the blackout's a bit of a bugger when it comes to keeping it up. Still, we managed it last year, even in the dark. Supposed to bring luck for the coming year, and we need all we can get of that at the moment.'

'What happens during the first footing?'

Reg dug out a book from the untidy mess of papers on his desk, opened it at a particular page and held it out to her. A woodcut image showed a young man with a lantern, holding a plate bearing a coin, some bread and a piece of coal.

'It's supposed to let in the new year,' Reg said. 'The village chooses a tall, dark man – that'll be our Charlie this year – to make the rounds of the houses from the stroke of midnight on. He's to be the first across your threshold, with a silver coin to bring wealth, bread to bring food, salt to bring flavour and a lump of coal to bring warmth through the coming year. When the first foot's visited every house in the village that wants him, folk gather in the church hall for a dance.'

'What do you want me to do?'

'I've asked Charlie to fetch you at eleven tonight. You'll need your writing things with you – and mind, it'll be pitch dark, so you'll not find it easy to make notes.'

Bobby remembered that not so long ago, Reg had forbidden his brother from fraternising with her. Perhaps this fraternisation was acceptable, since it was in the name of duty. Or perhaps he'd given it up as a lost cause, since forbidding Charlie from doing something was only likely to make him more determined to do it.

Bobby experienced a rather treacherous shiver of excitement at the thought of spending an entire evening with Charlie. She generally tried to keep him at arm's length – partly because she didn't want him to assume any romantic interest from her, partly because he was such a universal flirt that she couldn't take his attentions to her seriously, but also, she was forced to confess to herself, because she found his casual, teasing flirtation rather more appealing than she wanted it to be. She'd been in denial about it for some time now, but it was necessary to admit that Charlie Atherton could be dangerous to her – and to her career. She liked him a little too much, and now here she was, getting excited about being given a licence to spend the evening with him under the guise of 'work'. Bobby knew she needed to nip her feelings in the bud if she wanted to succeed in her role here, and quickly at that.

–

Charlie knocked at the front door a little after eleven. Bobby slipped out to join him, wrapped up in her scarf, hat and the gloves Mary had made for her as a Christmas gift. It was a cold night. With a combination of the blackout, the thick woollen gloves and the beginnings of numbness in her fingers, Bobby wasn't sure how she was going to make any notes – she was sure she could barely hold a pen, let alone write with it. Hopefully, she'd be able to remember the most important details.

'It's nice to know I've got my brother's approval to take you out for once,' Charlie said, offering her his arm.

'It's strictly business, as well you know.' Bobby hesitated, then tucked her arm in his. Lord knew what people would think when they saw them going about arm in arm, but if she was making her way to the village in the dark, the alternative was likely to be falling in the beck.

'Ah, you always say that,' Charlie said cheerfully. 'I know you don't mean it.'

In his other hand, Charlie held a blacked-out bicycle lamp, which provided a tiny sliver of faint light. Panels around the lamp stopped too much light escaping, and the top half of the glass had been painted black. It was so dim that they might as well have had no light at all, but the lighting restrictions were very strict. They could be looking at a twenty-bob fine each if they were found to be breaching them.

'It's not ideal, is it?' Charlie said. 'In the old days, I'd have had a lantern on a stick to first foot by. That's war for you.'

'What makes you so lucky?' Bobby asked.

'I've no idea. Apparently, we tall, dark men bring good luck so long as we're not doctors or undertakers. Short, red-haired men, on the other hand, bring absolutely terrible luck. Poor Gil Capstick's devastated that he'll never get a turn at being first foot.'

'What about women?'

'Oh, women bring appalling luck. Mind you, that's true all the year round,' he said with a grin.

'Isn't a vet a kind of doctor?'

'I suppose he is. It's only the human-tending kind who are bad luck though. It probably goes back to Plague times or something.'

'What happens when you've done your first footing?' Bobby asked.

'Then the household inhabitants are free to go about their business again, knowing the new year has been let in and their threshold crossed with luck.' He guided her to one side to prevent her stepping into an icy puddle. 'Although first they have to pay me for my services, of course.'

'What's your fee?'

'A glass of something warming usually, but I'll accept a kiss from a lady of the house in lieu.'

'That doesn't surprise me in the least,' Bobby said, laughing.

He shrugged. 'I didn't make the rules, you know. Ancient traditions aren't to be fiddled with.'

'Have you done it before?'

Charlie shook his head. 'It's my first year. Marmaduke Graham was last year's first foot. Duke's an amateur boxer, and not a very good one either. Tall, dark and the physique of a Greek wrestler, but with a face only a mother could love. He's usually got either a fat lip or a couple of black eyes, and his nose has been broken so often that it's about three inches wide across his face. Needless to say, folk were keen to pay him in drinks rather than kisses.' He laughed. 'Despite the size of the man, by the time he reached the last house he was as drunk as a lord. It was more a first stagger than a first footing. He just managed to slur out "blessings be upon this house and all who sail in her" before he went down. Face first on Mrs Armitage's hall carpet.'

Bobby couldn't help laughing. 'Was she angry?'

'Not at all. She'd got her good luck, that was all she cared about. And Duke had got himself another fat lip. He still said it was the best night of his life.' Charlie glanced at her. 'I'm glad I've got you to help me though. I haven't got the physique of a Duke Graham to carry that amount of spirit. Are you a whisky drinker?'

Bobby thought of the sips she occasionally took of her dad's drinks before she took them to him, steeling herself for what she might find when she entered his room. She turned her face slightly, in case Charlie should see her guilty expression by the dim light of the bicycle lamp.

'I don't think you need to worry about that,' she said, trying to keep up her usual light tone. 'I'm sure the women of Silver-dale will be happy to pay you in kisses.'

He smiled. 'I hope you're including yourself in that.'

Bobby ignored that comment.

'Where are we starting?' she asked.

'The church hall. Some local bigwig usually gives a speech. I think Topsy is doing it this year.'

'You mean Lady Sumner-Walsh?'

'That's right,' Charlie said. 'Then at about quarter to midnight, everyone scampers back to their homes and waits until the first foot has crossed the threshold. That's when I start my work.'

'How many houses are in Silverdale? Thirty or so?'

'In the village itself, yes, around that. The farms up in the hills have to make their own first footing arrangements. Damned if I'm fell walking in the dark.'

Bobby raised an eyebrow. 'Thirty drinks? No wonder this boxer was falling down by the end.'

'Oh, they don't all go in for the old superstition. Some folk think it's ungodly; others just think it's nonsense. I know which houses won't want me. There'll probably be about twenty calls to make tonight.' He nodded to St Peter's Church. It was dark, of course, the stained glass windows all blacked out, but Bobby could hear a hum of conversation coming from inside. 'Let's go in, shall we? I'm quite interested to hear what Topsy has to say. I can't imagine her making a speech.'

Bobby blinked as they entered the church hall, her eyeballs throbbing for a moment as they adjusted to the light. There were about a hundred villagers in there, dressed in their warmest clothes and chatting excitedly. A large pot with something spiced and steaming in it stood in the middle of a table, where a woman Bobby recognised as Till from the dance at Smeltham ladled it into mugs for people. Bowls of pork pies and mushy peas were lined up for folk to help themselves.

'Mulled wine to help you warm up?' Charlie said, nodding to the pot.

'No, thank you. Not if I'm going to have to help you with your whisky.'

'Well, here's Topsy. Looks like we got here just in time.'

Bobby watched as Lady Honoria Sumner-Walsh appeared at the lectern, beaming at everyone.

She'd heard the name several times since she'd arrived in Silverdale, although she'd never seen the woman herself. Lady Honoria was the owner of Sumner House, a stately home set within extensive grounds on the outskirts of the village – the same stately home, in fact, as Don's little daughter Sal was currently stationed at. Its public-spirited owner had volunteered it as a school for evacuees at the start of the war and moved herself into a small cottage in the grounds for the duration.

Bobby had built up a picture in her mind of this Lady Honoria, expecting someone staid and middle-aged, most likely in a tweed twinset and sensible shoes. She'd revised this when she'd learnt of the nickname 'Topsy', which Charlie, who seemed to be on familiar terms with the woman just as he was with everyone, always used. Bobby's new picture had been of someone rather more jolly, like a ruddy-cheeked and enthusiastic games mistress at a girls' school, but still decidedly plain and middle-aged.

The real Lady Honoria, however, was neither of these things. Not only was she young – perhaps little older than Bobby herself – but she also looked like a film star. Not beautiful exactly, but with a charm and glamour that carried you away before you could notice that. It was obvious that Charlie was very happy to let himself be carried away by it. He was staring at Lady Honoria with a smitten look that Bobby found supremely irritating.

Why? She wasn't jealous, surely? Charlie flirted with every woman he met. But this time, that look in his eyes… it felt different. Bobby felt something she didn't like rearing its ugly head inside her.

'Isn't she something?' Charlie breathed. 'When she comes into a room, it always reminds me of when I saw *The Wizard of Oz*. You know, when Dorothy opens the door in Oz and her world is suddenly in colour for the very first time. Topsy's the most Technicolor person I've ever seen.'

Honestly. He could at least make an effort to hide it, if he must be in love with other women right in front of her.

'She's very pretty,' Bobby said, trying not to sound too grudging. 'If you know her, you could do me a favour and get me an introduction. I want to speak to someone about arranging a visit to the manor house. My friend's little girl is one of the evacuees, and I'd like to go and see her.'

'If you like.' He lowered his voice. 'Hush now. She's going to speak.'

Lady Honoria's voice matched her appearance. It was slightly breathless and husky, in a way that made Bobby think of smoked honeycomb. Anyhow, the men in the room seemed to like it, staring at the woman with the same sort of enraptured expression as Charlie. Bobby spotted Mabs on the other side of the room, arms folded as she glared at Honoria, and felt a surge of fellow feeling for the girl.

The speech itself was nothing special: the usual clichés about getting rid of the old and ringing in the new, seeing in the new year with hope for a world at peace and all that sort of thing. But Charlie hung on every word as if it was the very deepest philosophy, like the devoted worshipper he clearly was.

'Incredible,' he muttered when the speech was over.

'Are you able to introduce me now?' Bobby asked. The room was starting to empty as people hurried back to their homes to await the lucky visit from Charlie.

'Hmm?' Charlie forced himself down from his cloud to rejoin the land of the living. 'Oh. All right.'

He took her arm and pulled her unceremoniously to the lectern where Lady Honoria was folding the notes from her speech. Not for Bobby the rapturous gaze and smitten sigh, as if she were a goddess fallen to earth. Charlie handled her like she was a sow he needed to examine.

'Hello, Topsy,' he said, beaming at the girl. 'Excellent speech. Very inspiring.'

'Thanks, old thing, that's wonderful of you to say. I thought it was a lot of rot myself, but then speechifying was never my forte.' Honoria had been bending to put her notes away in a bag on the floor. Now her head popped up above the lectern. 'Oh! You brought me someone.'

She sounded thrilled about it, and Charlie laughed.

'This is Bobby Bancroft,' he said. 'She works for my brother. I'm to be her top story in a future edition of *The Tyke*. She's going to write about the first footing.'

Honoria looked awed. 'Oh, but you don't really work for that magazine? Darling, you're only a child! However did you manage it?'

Bobby felt a little dazed. This Lady Honoria was so far removed from what she'd expected her to be that it was making her dizzy.

'Um, I'm not sure I did,' she said. 'There weren't enough boys who wanted the job so Reg had to give it to me.'

Honoria regarded her sternly. 'Now, I won't stand for that, Miss Bobby Bancroft. You'll have plenty of men in your life trying to bring you down. Don't do the job for them. If you're a reporter, then I have no doubt that you deserve to be one.'

'She does,' Charlie said, with a fond glance at Bobby. 'I'll bring you some of her work, Topsy. She's quite a writer.'

'I do admire that,' Honoria said earnestly. 'I've always been such a dunce at anything of that kind – you could probably tell from that ghastly speech I wrote. I'm ever so jealous of anyone who has a gift for it.'

Bobby almost laughed at the idea of Lady Honoria Sumner-Walsh – wealthy, charming, and with the entire male population of Silverdale under her spell – being jealous of her.

'I actually wanted to ask for a favour, um… your ladyship,' Bobby said, grimacing as she wondered if that was the right way to address someone of Honoria's rank.

'Oh gosh, don't,' Lady Honoria said, looking horrified. 'It's Topsy, please. All my friends call me Topsy.'

'Oh. Thank you. Um, I wanted to ask if it was possible to arrange to visit one of the children at the evacuees' boarding school. I thought perhaps you might be able to organise it, since it's your house. She's the daughter of a friend of mine from town and I promised to drop in to see how she was.'

'I can't see why not,' Topsy said. 'I have little to do with the running of the place now the government have their hands on it, but I do still own it and foot most of the bills. I'll speak to the head woman there for you.'

Bobby smiled gratefully. She was discovering that, like Charlie, Topsy Sumner-Walsh was a hard person to dislike even if you really wanted to. 'Thank you, that's awfully kind.'

'And you must pay me a visit in my humble little cottage too, when you come. Bring me some of your writing so I can fall at your feet and worship you for your talent.' Topsy pressed her arm, beaming. 'I would so like a girlfriend from the village. One who won't talk to me about blasted sheep! Now I'm not a snob – I can't abide those toffee-nosed sorts – but I can't listen to talk of farms, farms, farms all the livelong day. It's all anyone in this village seems to think about. You'll come, won't you, and talk to me about jolly things that don't involve a single, solitary sheep?'

'I'd be glad to,' Bobby said, and was surprised to find that she meant it.

'Yes, do! We'll have tea and all civilised things, and you can meet Maimie and Norman too. Maimie is sort of my... well, I don't know what she is now. She used to be my nanny, and now she's really just my Maimie. I found I couldn't get by without her, even if I was grown up.'

Bobby glanced at Charlie. 'Maimie... Hobbes?' He nodded.

Topsy looked delighted. 'You know her already?'

'Not quite as well as I know Norman,' Bobby said, laughing. 'We had what you might call an altercation the day we met.'

'Oh, he's a cantankerous old thing. I shall be sure to box his ears thoroughly on your behalf.'

'Don't worry. We're firm friends now.'

Charlie nudged her. 'Bobby, we ought to go. It's nearly midnight, and they'll be expecting me at the first house.'

Of course there was to be no peal of bells to signal the arrival of the new year. The church bells had been silenced back in June, to be used only in the event of a German invasion.

'Yes, all right,' Bobby said.

He took Topsy's hand and kissed it – very different from the way he said hello or goodbye to her, Bobby noted. The best she

213

could expect was a cheeky joke about her bottom and the offer of a drink at the pub. She much preferred that sort of thing to hand-kissing, but at the same time, she felt a certain resentment that Charlie didn't see her as the sort of girl to offer such a gesture to.

'Always a pleasure to see you, Topsy,' he said in his gentlest tone. 'I mean that sincerely.'

'I don't expect you to come all the way to the cottage to be our first foot,' Topsy said, smiling. 'Still, Charlie, you ought to have your payment. It is good luck to welcome the new year with a kiss, after all. Here.'

She stood on tiptoes to kiss his cheek. For the first time since she'd known him, Bobby was sure she saw Charlie blush.

Chapter 23

'She's impressive, isn't she?' Charlie said as they made their way to the first house by the faint light of his bicycle lamp. 'I've never known anyone quite like Topsy.'

'She's certainly... a force of nature,' Bobby said.

'There'll be no escaping her now she's decided to make a project of you, you know.'

Bobby frowned. 'Project?'

He nodded. 'Topsy doesn't have friends so much as projects. Or playthings might be a better word. She'll soon be dressing you up in her clothes, changing the way you do your hair and trying to introduce you to men she thinks are suitable for you.'

'Not if I have anything to do with it, she won't,' Bobby said decisively. 'Does she do that with you?'

'She does it with everyone she's fond of. Topsy's sweet, but she's far too used to having her own way. I thought I'd warn you in advance before she adopted you as her particular friend.' He shone his lamp on a small cottage with a wreath made from pine leaves and dried orange slices decorating the door. 'Wilfred and Louisa Clough. They're bound to want some luck bringing. Here, you hold the light.'

Charlie handed her the bicycle lamp. He was carrying a sack over one shoulder, which he opened now. From it, he took a small plate, a lump of coal, a morsel of bread, a salt cellar and a sixpence piece. He arranged the bread, coal and coin on the plate, sprinkled a little salt beside them and put the cellar away again. Bobby, meanwhile, tucked the bicycle lamp under her arm, took out her notepad and attempted to make some notes with her fumbling gloved fingers.

Charlie balanced the plate on one hand and knocked on the door with the other. It opened on to a dark hallway. Of course, the inhabitants of the cottage would have to turn out their lights before opening up for Charlie, to avoid the light spilling out of the doorframe and a rap on the knuckles from Amos, the village's over-enthusiastic ARP warden. Bobby could make out a tall, bony woman she recognised as Louisa Clough, the village postmistress.

'A happy New Year and good tidings to all who dwell in this house,' Charlie said jovially, striding over the threshold and handing her the plate.

'Charlie Atherton,' Mrs Clough said, beaming at him. People always seemed to beam when they saw Charlie, even those who disapproved of him. 'Tha don't allus bring good luck when tha crosses a threshold, I'm told by t' mothers of pretty lasses.'

It felt good to hear the local accent again after her trip home, Bobby reflected. It was deeper and less nasal than the accent of her home town; a soft, gentle burr.

'It's good luck for the pretty lasses,' Charlie said, smiling back. 'At any rate, they always seem pleased to see me. How will you be paying me, Louisa? With a drink or with a kiss?'

'I reckon tha'd better have a drink to warm thee, and let thy young lady here warm thee wi' kisses,' Louisa said, nodding to Bobby.

'Oh no, I'm not…' Bobby fished in her pocket for her press card and waved it in front of her like a lucky charm, although it was too dark for Louisa to read it. 'I'm here from *The Tyke*, making notes for an article.'

'Ah. The lass from t' paper,' Louisa said, smiling at her. 'I couldn't see your face in the dark, Miss. Will you take a drink too? It'll warm you up.'

Bobby blinked, rather surprised. She'd encountered Mrs Clough in the village many times before – it was she who served her at the post office on the days when Gil wasn't behind the counter, and like a lot of the villagers, she'd always regarded Bobby with that wary suspicion they reserved for 'off-comed 'uns'. Yet now she was all smiles. Perhaps it was the festival atmosphere that had put her into a benevolent mood.

'She can share mine,' Charlie said. 'Save yours to toast the new year, Louisa. There'll be dancing at the church hall once I've set the rest of the village free.'

Mrs Clough transferred the gifts to a plate of her own on the sideboard before returning Charlie's plate to him. Her husband Wilfred then appeared with a glass of something in his hand, which he gave to Charlie.

'Bristol sherry,' he said. 'Been saving it since afore t' war. Ought to warm the cockles, lad.'

Charlie drank half, then handed the glass to Bobby. She hesitated before drinking it down. It did warm the cockles, sending a warm glow spreading from her throat right down into her toes.

'Which house will we go to now?' she asked Charlie when they'd left Louisa and Wilfred to enjoy their new year celebrations.

'I think the Ackroyds are next.'

'I didn't realise the bread and things you have to carry were given as gifts.'

'Oh yes. Otherwise, you're taking the luck away with you again. The coal's to be burnt on the first fire of the year.'

'But if there are twenty houses to do at a tanner a visit, you're going to be down ten bob by the time you're done.'

'The sixpences don't come from my private purse. The church and chapel have a little fund for the first foot gifts. Strange really, when it always feels like such a pagan sort of thing, but it's a harmless enough tradition, I suppose.' He glanced at her. 'Louisa Clough was very friendly towards you tonight. Did you notice?'

'I know, isn't it strange? She hardly gives me the time of day usually.'

'I suppose you must have passed then,' he said with a smile.

'Passed?'

'Passed the Silverdale test. Your third month here with hardly a kind word for you so far and you're still hanging on. If there's one thing these people admire, it's tenacity.' Charlie stopped at another house and started taking the next lot of first foot gifts from his sack. 'Not that you're quite one of us – yet – but they're definitely starting to accept you. I noticed it a little before Christmas.'

'Mary said that too. I didn't notice anything though.'

'You don't know what to look for. I do.' He knocked on the door. It opened a moment later, and Charlie once again boomed 'a happy New Year and good tidings to all who dwell in this house' as he strode over the threshold.

Bobby had expected this routine to become rather dull after the first few houses, but actually, it was interesting to observe how each household received their bringer of luck. Some seemed anxious to hurry Charlie away – husbands with young, attractive wives especially, Bobby noticed. Others would have detained the two of them for most of the evening were it not for Charlie's commitment to getting the job done. Of course, the villagers still awaiting his visit were trapped inside, unable to join the dancing at the church until they'd received their first foot.

All ensured he was adequately paid – this seemed to be an important part of the ritual, without which the luck Charlie had brought would evaporate. Households with single daughters favoured a kiss as payment, while others offered a glass of something 'warming' – spirits, beer or strong homemade wine. Charlie offered to share all these with Bobby, so that by the time they were approaching the final house, she not only felt nicely warmed but also rather tipsy. Other than the occasional fortifying sip of her dad's whisky, she wasn't a drinker of spirits and had discovered that they tended to go to her head when taken in sufficient quantities. Charlie, too, seemed rather merry and had even become so bold as to slip his arm around her waist as they walked from house to house. Bobby remained sensible enough to detach herself from this over-familiarity, however. Charlie didn't object when she moved away from him, or even seem to notice much. He merely smiled at her.

'Mrs Armitage, last of all,' he said. 'You'll give me a dance afterwards, won't you? They'll be celebrating at the church until the small hours.'

'I think I ought to go home to bed,' Bobby said, focusing on the house a little woozily. 'I'm not used to drinking this much.'

'But the night is young.' He cocked his head to listen to the muffled music now emanating from the church hall, where a pianist had struck up 'Roll Out the Barrel'. 'It's 1941, Bobby! This is going to be quite a year, I can feel it. It's going to be the year we win the war.'

'War…' Bobby's sluggish brain stirred. 'You're going to war. Aren't you?'

'Yes.' He sounded quieter suddenly; more serious. 'Very soon, I should think. I passed my medical, at any rate. Fighting fit and ready for action, if you please. Now I'm just waiting to find out when I start training.'

'I hope…'

'What?'

'I hope…' She shook her head to free it of the warm, pleasant fog that was likely to have her saying something she might regret if she wasn't careful. 'Nothing. Only… take care of yourself out there, won't you, Charlie? I'd hate for anything to happen to you.'

'I never knew you cared, Bobby.' Charlie turned to smile at her. 'I do wish you'd let me take you out properly sometime.'

'Where would you take me if I did?'

'Wherever you wanted to go. Boxer would be thrilled to oblige, I'm sure. We could go to the pictures if you like, and do naughty things in the back row in the dark. There's a new Cary Grant on that ought to be just your thing – about a lady reporter. Or we could go dancing if that's more to your taste.'

'I can't,' Bobby said, somewhat wistfully. 'I don't go out with boys – not on dates.'

'Why not? You're young. You ought to be out enjoying yourself.'

'Because if I go out on dates, I might catch feelings for someone.' The alcohol in Bobby's system seemed to be making her more honest than she was wont to be on the subject of romance. 'And if that happens, then before you know it, I'm trapped at home washing some man's smalls while the bairns are roaring in the nursery and everything I ever wanted to do in my life has gone up in smoke, all because I let myself fall into someone's deep brown eyes for a little too long at a dance.'

'Does he have brown eyes then, this man?'

'Brown, green, blue – whatever colour they are, I don't intend to let myself fall into them to find out.'

Charlie smiled. 'It's funny, but I can't picture you washing my smalls.'

'I wasn't talking about you. I meant the male of the species in general is something I have to be wary of.' She looked askance at him. 'Besides, something tells me you aren't the marrying kind.'

'How so? I'd make a terrific husband.'

She laughed. 'To four or five different wives, no doubt.'

'You know, I'm really not this caddish despoiler of maidens you like to paint me as.' He nudged her. 'How about we make each other a promise? I won't fall for you if you don't fall for me. Then we can just have some fun. Admit it. You like spending time with me.'

That was the problem. She was afraid of liking it a little too much.

'Let's do the last house, then we can go home,' she said, judging it to be time she changed the subject.

'All right. But I still think you should come for at least one dance before bed. It's good luck, probably. Everything is good luck at New Year.'

'Well… I'll think about it.'

He started arranging the last of his first footing gifts on the plate.

'Is this where the boxer bloke fell down last year?' Bobby asked, nodding to the cottage before them.

'That's right. But I think that thanks to you sharing my fees, I can still manage to stay upright.'

'You mean thanks to all those girls who wanted to pay you in kisses rather than drinks.'

'I know, I felt so vulnerable. Hands like octopuses, some of the farmers' daughters around here.'

'Yes, I noticed how manfully you tried to fight them off,' Bobby said soberly.

He grinned at her before knocking on the door.

It opened a moment later, and Charlie launched into his speech. But he barely got further than 'A happy New Year to—' before he was yanked into the house.

Chapter 24

'Oh, Charlie, thank God you've come,' the woman who'd pulled him inside said fervently. 'You're needed sore in here, lad. I was about to send our Tess out to find you.'

He beckoned Bobby to come in after him. 'What's wrong, Mrs Armitage?'

'It's our dog, Maid,' Mrs Armitage said, closing the door behind him. She barely seemed to register Bobby's presence, casting her a single fretful look before turning her attention back to Charlie. 'She's been badly all night, and now she's refusing to eat or move off her bed. Can you take a look at her?'

'I'm rather... well, I've visited a lot of houses tonight. I'd prefer to see her in the morning, when I've had a chance to sleep it off.'

'And what if she don't last while morning?' Mrs Armitage said, wringing her hands. 'She's suffering, Charlie.'

He frowned. 'Suffering?'

'Aye, bad, I think. You must do summat for her. You must.'

'I'll do what I can,' he said quietly. 'Take me to her.'

Mrs Armitage flashed him a smile of gratitude and relief. 'You're a good lad. I don't care what some folk round here say.'

'What shall I do?' Bobby whispered to Charlie as they followed Mrs Armitage down the hall. 'Do you want me to leave?'

'No, I might need you.' Bobby had never heard the brisk, commanding tone Charlie now adopted as he took off his overcoat and jacket and rolled up his sleeves, ready for work. 'Just do whatever I ask. Worst comes to worst, you might need to help me get her back to my surgery. I don't much like the idea of carrying a sick dog two miles in the blackout when I'm tiddly – it's not going to help her to be jolted around if there's something wrong inside. Still, if it's the only way...'

Bobby nodded. 'Whatever you need, Charlie.'

Mrs Armitage led them to the back of the house and into the kitchen. In front of a roaring fire was Charlie's patient: a young border collie bitch. She was lying curled in an old vegetable crate that had been lined with blankets, her eyes glassy and her breath coming in ragged pants.

'I brung her in from the barn where she usually sleeps with the other dogs and made her a bed here by the fire,' Mrs Armitage said. 'I hope that was right.'

'Yes, you did well.' Charlie scanned the prostrate dog with a look of concern. 'Poor lass. She's not looking happy.'

'She's dying, isn't she?' Mrs Armitage whispered. 'Oh, God! Tess is going to be heartbroken.'

'I can't say what's ailing her until I've examined her.' Charlie fell to his knees beside the dog. There was no trace now of the lopsided grin and slightly thick speech that the spirits he'd drunk had elicited in him earlier. Now he was entirely the steady, professional vet, frowning with earnest concentration as he ran his hands over the dog's flank. It was a side of him Bobby had never seen before – an entirely different Charlie.

'You must put her to sleep if... if it comes to it,' Mrs Armitage said. 'I won't have her suffer. Oh, but our Tess. She's reared Maid from a pup, trained her an' all – the first of our sheepdogs that was all her own. Ken gave the pup to her not long before he died. I don't know how I'll break it to her.'

'Let's not go running away with ideas like that,' Charlie said firmly. 'We'll see what I can do for her before we make any life or death decisions, shall we?'

'Aye,' Mrs Armitage said with a weak smile. 'You know best then.'

'Now, perhaps you can help me,' Charlie said, looking up to flash her a reassuring smile. 'If you have any old, clean towels that I can use, I'd be greatly obliged.'

Mrs Armitage nodded, looking grateful she was able to help. 'I'll fetch them for you directly.'

She bustled out, leaving them alone.

'Why do you need towels?' Bobby asked.

'I don't. Mrs Armitage needs to feel like she's helping, and she needs to keep busy and out of my way so I can find out what's upsetting poor little Maid here.' Charlie started feeling under the dog's belly, and she let out a tiny yelp. 'Ah. Something bothering her there, it seems. Help me get her over, can you? She might bite if she's in pain. I'll hold her jaw if you can ease her on to her side.'

Bobby nodded and crouched down to help.

Maid gave them little trouble, however. She seemed too miserable and too exhausted to put up much of a fight and made only the slightest attempt at a snap as they turned her over.

'The Armitages are devoted to their dogs,' Charlie told Bobby as he pressed gently on different parts of the animal's stomach. 'Old Ken Armitage used to breed and train them, before he passed away. Sold them all over the country. His boy Cap fetched a record price at Skipton Market in '32. Now his young daughter's after following in his footsteps. She's only ten, poor wee mite. It'll devastate her to lose her first dog, especially since Maid was a last gift from her dad.'

'Have you got any idea what could be wrong?'

'Her belly's swollen, but I can't feel any foreign body. Mammary glands enlarged and sore, some discharge – that could be what made her yelp.' He looked up as Mrs Armitage entered with the towels. 'Ah. Here we are.'

'Take these,' she said, passing them to him. 'They're the only ones I have, but don't you worry about that. If they can help Maid, that's the most important thing.'

'Thank you.' For appearances' sake, Charlie used one to cushion the dog's head.

A little girl had come in with her mother and was lurking shyly behind her skirts – this, Bobby presumed, was Tess, the child who had trained Maid.

'Will she be all right, Mr Atherton?' the child whispered.

'I'll do everything I can to make sure she will,' Charlie said, smiling warmly. 'Now, Tess, can I talk to you about Maid for a moment? I suppose it's you who has spent the most time with her.'

Tess nodded, and Mrs Armitage drew her daughter forward.

'How long has Maid been like this?' Charlie asked gently.

'Well, it was nobbut two days ago she were running about same as ever. Mr Dixon lets me take her to practise wi' his yows. Then yesterday...' The girl let out a little sob. 'She were being ever so funny, Mr Atherton. Stealing the blankets from our bed and dragging them in front of the fire, and she took our Joyce's little dolly and put it in wi' t' blankets.'

'I understand,' Charlie said evenly. 'What happened next, Tess?'

'Then... then last night she stopped eating, and acted right tired, like she could hardly move. I couldn't get her to come out wi' me, not even for a little bit, though normally she never stops laiking. Wouldn't eat even a bit o' chicken off my hand, and that's her favourite. And she bit Mam! When she tried to take Joycey's dolly back, Maid give her a nip on the hand. She never done that before.' Tess gave him a pleading look. 'She in't a bad dog, Mr Atherton. Probably it were because she were badly, otherwise she never would've. You won't put her down, will you?'

'I'd only do that if she was in terrible pain. I know Maid isn't a dangerous dog.' Charlie paused. 'Now I need to ask... have you noticed Maid having lots of new dog friends recently? When she goes on her walks?'

The child frowned thoughtfully.

'Aye, I reckon she did have some,' she said. 'A fortnight sin there were lots of dogs hanging about, but I kept her away from them. Mam told me to.'

'And before that, did you notice she was swollen and bleeding a little at her back end?'

'She was,' Mrs Armitage said. 'I noticed spots of it when I washed her bedding. I guessed that meant she'd be coming into heat and told Tess to watch that she was kept right away from the lads, so we didn't end up with a litter. She's nobbut a year – it'd be fair dangerous for her to whelp at that young age.' She frowned. 'She can't be in the family way, can she? Tess said she were right careful.'

'I don't think she's pregnant, no. I've felt her stomach carefully. My diagnosis based on what you've told me is that she's suffering a phantom pregnancy, although I'd like you to bring her to my surgery tomorrow so I can confirm it for sure.'

Mrs Armitage glanced at Tess. 'Phantom pregnancy?'

'That's right,' Charlie said. 'The swollen stomach, the instinct to nest, the attachment to your little girl's doll, the fact she was so recently fertile – that all points to the same thing.'

'Is it dangerous?'

Charlie gave Maid a stroke and got to his feet. 'It's not very comfortable for her, and she may feel lethargic and depressed for a little while, but it isn't life-threatening.'

'Can you give her medicine then?' Tess asked, looking hopeful. 'To make her like she were before?'

'Time is the only medicine she needs – time, patience and kindly treatment. But if she's still off her food tomorrow, I'll give her an appetite stimulant when you bring her in. For tonight, keep her hydrated and try to get her to eat if you can.' He bent down to give the dog a tickle between the ears, and she gave the stone flags of the kitchen floor a few limp thumps with her tail. 'You'll soon be right again, old girl. Just try to keep your strength up, eh?'

Tess ran forward and threw herself at him for a hug. Charlie, taken aback, patted her head in a bewildered sort of way.

'Thank you, Mr Atherton,' she said. 'I was so scared she'd die. I'm glad you come tonight.'

'Oh, well, that's my job, you know,' Charlie said, looking rather pleased.

Mrs Armitage smiled at the girl. 'Well, I think it must be off to sleep with you now we've had good news, Teresa Armitage. It's long past bedtime. Go and check on Joycey before you get into your nightgown.'

The girl nodded happily and ran off upstairs, looking like the weight of the world had been lifted from her little shoulders.

'Thank you, Charlie,' Mrs Armitage said when Tess had gone. She nodded to Bobby. 'And thanks to you, Miss. I don't suppose this was what you were expecting when your young man took you out tonight.'

Bobby flushed. 'Oh, he's not... well, it doesn't matter. I didn't really do anything.'

'Nonsense,' Charlie said, smiling at her. 'I'd have likely got a nip or two if you hadn't been here to help me turn her. I'll have a veterinary nurse position for you whenever you decide to give up on that magazine of my brother's, Bobby.'

'Oh Lord, your brother.' She stifled a yawn. 'I'd better go home. He'll still expect me to be up for breakfast at the same time tomorrow, even if I have been out all night.'

'Sorry I made rather a mess of your first footing,' Charlie said to Mrs Armitage as she showed them out. 'I hope it won't affect your luck this year.'

She smiled. 'Seems you've brought some with you already. I were fair flayed we'd lose that pup of ours tonight. How much do I owe you?'

'Don't be daft. I'll not take a fee for that.'

'Nay, you must. You've your living to make, same as we all have.'

'I barely did anything. Besides, I was here anyway. Call it a favour.'

'You're a good lad,' she said feelingly. 'Will you both take a drink instead, then?'

Charlie put a hand to his head. 'I think I can feel the rest of my first foot payments catching up with me, thank you all the same. One more and I'll likely be spread out on your floor as a fetching rug, in the style of Mr Marmaduke Graham.'

The woman laughed. 'Well, I'll keep it for when you're in better fettle. Goodnight, Charlie. Goodnight, Miss. And a happy New Year to you both.'

When they were outside, Charlie took out his handkerchief so he could yawn behind it.

'I don't think I can face any dancing after that,' he said to Bobby. 'I'd better walk you home.' He wobbled slightly and steadied himself on Mrs Armitage's garden wall. 'On the other hand, perhaps you'd better walk me home. I'm feeling a little... odd.'

Bobby laughed and took his arm.

'That was very impressive, you know,' she said as they wandered in the direction of Moorside Farm.

'I didn't do anything. Nothing wrong with the dog that time and care wouldn't cure. Phantom pregnancies in bitches aren't uncommon, as Ken Armitage would certainly have been able to tell his wife and daughter had he still been with us.'

'You reassured that scared little girl, and you were calm and professional despite having probably a few gallons of wine, beer, whisky and goodness knows what else sloshing around inside you. Why didn't you charge her?'

'Charge her? For telling her there's nothing to worry about at two in the morning when I'm half-cut? She's struggling as it is since her husband died.'

'That was good of you.'

Charlie was silent, staring thoughtfully into the darkness as they walked somewhat unsteadily towards home.

'Poor old Maid,' he said after a while. 'I wish there was more I could've done for her. She looked so unhappy, didn't she? It must be a miserable business, waiting for bairns that'll never come.'

'You're thinking about your brother,' Bobby said softly.

'I suppose I am. I was a child myself when they lost Nancy so I don't remember much, but I know Mary was desperate to have more. I think she'd have happily filled the house with little ones – she was made to be a mother. She was devastated when the doctors told her there couldn't be any others. I suppose they both were, although Reggie rarely talks about it.'

'I can't imagine how it must feel to lose a child.'

'I can imagine it. I just try not to.'

Bobby sighed. 'I can't help thinking about Andy Jessop and all those siblings who died in infancy. His poor mother.'

'Yes. All too common in those days, but I don't suppose it was any less heartbreaking for that.' Charlie stopped walking and turned her around to face him. 'Bobby...'

'What?'

'Look, I know you think I'm a flirt and a scoundrel and a cad and all sorts of other unspeakable things you no doubt whisper about me under your breath when I'm not paying attention. Perhaps you're right. I don't think I'm a wicked man, but I suppose I've lived a pretty worthless sort of a life up to now.' He pressed a hand to his head. 'This might be the drink talking – I doubt I'd have the nerve to say it sober. But I'm not... that is, I would like you to think...'

'What would you like me to think?'

He put his hands on her shoulders to draw her closer to him. Bobby knew that wasn't allowed. She ought to push him away, oughtn't she? But the alcohol she was unaccustomed to drinking, and seeing him so calm and firm as he'd tended to the sick dog in a way that was quite unlike his usual devil-may-care self, seemed to have broken down her resistance. Instead, she sighed and closed her eyes for a moment.

'You shouldn't do that,' she murmured, but Charlie ignored her.

'I suppose I'd like you to think better of me,' he whispered. 'I know you think I flirt with every pretty girl I meet—'

'You do flirt with every pretty girl you meet, Charlie.'

'All right, I do, but only in the way of common chivalry and good manners. Ladies like to be flirted with, and I'm a sociable sort of being who likes to be liked. With you though… it's not the same as it is with everyone else.'

Bobby smiled. '"Oh darling, you're not like the other girls". I've heard that one before.'

'I mean it. You're different, Bobby. I feel differently about you than I do about the others.' He took a deep breath. 'And I'll probably regret this tomorrow, but I'll kick myself if I don't do it now while I'm still full of Dutch courage.'

Before she knew what was happening, Bobby found herself being swung into Charlie's arms. The next moment his lips were on hers.

For a moment, Bobby gave in and relaxed against him, relishing the feeling of his strong arms around her body and the earthy, masculine scent of tobacco and dogs and whisky that hung around him. The pleasant fog of earlier had returned to make her feel she was in a romantic dream, almost like a film of her life, where handsome men who were fun to be with and kind to children and animals kissed her with tender passion. But somewhere inside her, the voice of a more sober, sensible Bobby was screaming.

'Mmm… No!' She pushed Charlie away.

He frowned. 'Bobby? What's wrong?'

She shook her head, laughing. 'Oh, you almost had me there. Was this your idea tonight? Did you suggest it to Reg?'

He blinked. 'Did I suggest what?'

'This. The first footing. Me reporting on it so you could get me all to yourself for an evening. All those drinks you so generously shared with me, hopeful I might lower my guard. All those girls who paid you with a kiss, hoping you might make me jealous enough to want a turn myself. The dog and the little lass and…' She pushed hard against his chest, making him stagger slightly. 'You… you bloody… man!'

Charlie looked thoroughly confused now. 'What am I supposed to have done? I mean, sorry if I misjudged the situation – there were quite a lot of drinks – but I thought you liked me. At any rate, I can tell when a woman's enjoying being kissed, and you quite definitely were.'

'I told you I didn't want to get entangled with any man!' Bobby snapped. 'I told you I needed to focus on my career. But you just couldn't respect that, could you? Even though you know you're not really interested in romance with me – that you're only out for a good time with the last girl around here you haven't already had one with.'

'Bobby, I promise that isn't—'

'Even though you know you're in love with someone else,' Bobby snapped, ignoring him. 'What am I to you? Someone to use and toss aside, like the others? Good God, Charlie! I mean, I had at least believed you respected me – that we were friends.'

'In love with someone else? Look, if you're talking about that kid Mabs—'

'Oh, don't be absurd. You know exactly who I'm talking about.' She jabbed his chest. 'Listen, Charlie Atherton, just stay away from me, all right? I'm not interested in kissing you, I don't want to go on any dates with you, and I don't want to be friends with you – not after this. I want to be left alone. The sooner you can get that into your head, the happier we'll both be.' She fished the lucky handkerchief he'd given her the day they met from her pocket and threw it at him. 'And you can take this back as well. I don't believe it's brought me an ounce of luck, except the bad kind.'

Bobby turned on her heel – as best she could after all the drinks – and marched off in the direction of Moorside Farm, humming 'The Ride of the Valkyries' to herself. A confused Charlie stared after her, clutching the handkerchief.

Chapter 25

The following Sunday, Bobby was stomping across the moors for an appointment with Andy Jessop.

It was now five days since her encounter with Charlie, and she hadn't been able to get their kiss out of her mind. It had been affecting her work, which she knew couldn't be allowed to continue. As she strode towards Newby Top – the route now so familiar she could do it almost without thinking – she tried to make some sense of her feelings on the matter.

Bobby had been kissed by boys before, when she'd been young and still harboured dreams of romance. She'd been nothing but a green little girl then; too foolish to know that she couldn't have her cake and eat it when it came to husbands and careers. She might even have imagined herself in love on one or two occasions, when she'd been a child barely out of school. Yet, in spite of that, the kiss with Charlie had still felt like her first one.

Mostly thinking about it made her angry – partly with Charlie, for kissing her when she'd made her views on romance quite clear to him, but mainly with herself. She ought to know better now than to think she could have it all – romance and a career too. Bobby liked to think she was pretty savvy after her time working at the *Courier*, listening to the talk of the men there, and she'd grown up with two brothers. She knew what men were, what they wanted, and how they talked about women in their own spaces. And yet... she had enjoyed kissing Charlie. She'd given in to it, far too easily, and the first foot drinks they'd shared were no excuse for that. She had drunk too much on occasions in the past, usually under Lilian's bad influence, but she'd never lowered her guard like that with a man before.

It was Maid's fault really, she decided. There had been something compelling about seeing Charlie at work, tending to the sick dog. Until that point, Bobby had thought of Charlie Atherton as a fun yet frivolous jack-the-lad who thought little about anything but his own pleasure – really only one step up from her old friend Tony Scott. Seeing him with the dog and the little girl had shown her a new side to him; a side that was humane, gentle and caring in a way it surprised her he was able to be. And that… that was far more dangerous to Bobby than either his good looks or his charm. Her only option was to avoid him as much as she could – which was no easy task given she worked for his brother and they lived on the same land, but she could try.

And yet… she couldn't stop thinking about him. About the kiss they'd shared, and the way he'd tended to Maid, and the pleasure she got from his lively company and clever conversation.

Every night before sleep, she listed the reasons Charlie Atherton couldn't and shouldn't be a part of her life. He was a flirt and a gadabout, fun to be with for a little while but hardly husband material. Even if he was husband material, which Bobby was convinced he could never be, she didn't want a husband. She had work to do, and men were a distraction she didn't need. Besides which, Charlie certainly didn't see her in the role of future wife, although he might be happy to toy with her for a while until the real object of his affections became aware of his feelings. Bobby was convinced that it was Topsy Sumner-Walsh who Charlie loved. That look of enslaved idolatry in his eyes as he'd watched Topsy give her speech had made it quite clear.

Logically, everything pointed to Charlie not being the man for her. Heartbreak would surely follow if Bobby let her feelings progress. So then, why couldn't she get him out of her mind?

Reg was annoyed with her too. Constantly dwelling on the kiss with Charlie was affecting her sleep, her focus and her work. Her editor had thrown the piece she'd written on the first footing back at her when she'd handed it to him on Friday.

'And what do you call this?' he'd demanded.

'What's wrong with it?'

'What's wrong with it? It's riddled with mistakes, both typing errors and facts, and it's about four hundred words too long. What have I told you about subbing your copy before you hand it to me? You're wasting my time and your own if you don't.'

She'd sighed. 'Sorry, Reg. It was so dark while we were going round that I couldn't make many notes. I had to write it mostly from memory.'

'I'm not surprised you can't remember owt. I heard you and my brother were on a spree that night. Don't say I didn't warn you about him.' He'd given her a piercing look. 'You and our Charlie walking out officially now, are you?'

'No,' she'd said firmly. 'It was a job, that was all. I won't be seeing him again.'

'Glad to hear it.' He'd regarded her curiously for a moment before tapping the piece she'd written on the first footing with the tip of one inky index finger. 'Cut the word count and fix those errors. There's *Traditions and Folklore of the Yorkshire Dales* on the shelf if you need to check your facts. And in future, try to keep your mind off my brother and on the job you've been given.'

'I will.'

But would she? Bobby had tried to banish Charlie from her life, ignoring multiple attempts to get her alone so he could talk to her, but she couldn't seem to banish him from her brain. Or her heart.

She reached the five-bar gate that opened on to the track down to Newby Top Farm and hoisted herself over it.

Today was an important day. Today was the day Andy had decided it was time to ask his friend Ginny a most important question.

Bobby was shown into the house by Mabs, where she discovered the old farmer in his parlour, staring gloomily into the fire.

'Is anything wrong, Mr Jessop?' she asked as she helped herself to a seat.

'Nay, nowt much. Just fretting. Daft really.' He roused himself and handed her a letter. 'What does tha make of this? I had our Mabs read it to me. Come this morning.'

Bobby skimmed it quickly. It was a letter from Ginny, full of domestic news, much as her letters always were. She talked of developments on the farm, her eldest granddaughter's pregnancy, the trials and tribulations of her two youngest grandchildren at the village school. It was all rather sweet and cosy, if somewhat restrained. Bobby found it very hard to tell from Ginny's letters what answer a proposal was likely to elicit. Both Ginny and Andy were of the generation where the open expression of affection, particularly in writing, didn't come naturally to them.

'She sounds well and happy,' Bobby said when she'd finished. 'And she must have written and posted this the day she received your last letter if it came with today's post. That must surely be a good sign.'

'Aye. Maybe.' Andy nodded to the letter. 'What does tha make of that bit halfway through about her new heifer?'

Bobby read it again.

> We have had some little excitement this week when my Annie calved more than a month ahead of time. We had the veterinary out but all was well, however. Annie is now nursing prettily — a tiny heifer who my grandsons have christened Rocky, after their favourite talkie cowboy. They are a comical pair! Mr Shaw from nearby Snap End Farm kindly brought some blankets for our new arrival and sat up with me that first night, as there was

a worry we might lose young Rocky, him being so small.
However, as I said, all was well.

'It sounds like good news,' Bobby said, wondering what there was in the tale to make the farmer look so glum. 'The calf isn't in danger now, it seems.'

Andy propped his chin on his fist. 'Harry Shaw is Ginny's age: full ten year younger than me and all his own teeth still. Widower. Drives a motor car too.'

Bobby glanced at the letter. 'Oh. I see.'

'Says she sat up all night wi' him.'

'I don't think that means she thinks of him in any romantic way. It sounds like he was doing her a good turn, as any neighbour would.'

'Aye, that's how it starts.' Andy sighed. 'I hope I'm not going to look a silly old fool at the end o' this, Miss Bancroft.'

'I'm sure that won't happen,' Bobby said soothingly. 'Ginny is fond of you, I'm convinced of it.'

'She don't say so, does she? She's pally enough wi' me, but she don't say owt about fond.'

'No, but nor do you. She writes back as quickly as she gets your letters though, and there's always a kiss on the end.'

'That's just women. Always free wi' their kisses, when all they've to do is write 'em down.' He roused himself. 'What's up wi' thee then?'

Bobby blinked. 'Me?'

'Aye, tha looks tired. Atherton working thee too hard, is he?'

'Oh. No. I've... been sleeping badly, that's all.'

He laughed hoarsely. 'When I were young, they'd tease thee and say tha were in love for watching all night. Trouble wi' t' lads, is it?'

'No,' Bobby said, flushing.

He laughed again. 'Thy cheeks are pink enough to show a lie where there is one. We're a pretty pair, eh?'

236

Bobby smiled. 'I suppose we are. Come on. Let's write this letter, then at least one of us has a chance at being wed and happy.'

'What about Harry Shaw? If he's been pressing attentions on Gin—'

'Then you want to get your proposal in before he does, don't you?' Bobby said, taking out her notebook and pencil.

Andy laughed. 'I knew I liked thee for a reason, lass. What will I say then?'

Bobby sucked the end of her pencil.

'I think for this letter, straight to the point is best,' she said after thinking it over. 'A proposal shouldn't feel like an afterthought or postscript; it should be the main event. The only event, in fact.'

'It'll be short then, won't it?'

'Quality over quantity, Mr Jessop.'

'How does tha make a start on summat o' that kind?'

'Well I'm far from an expert, never having done it myself, but in books the gentleman usually expresses his deep admiration for the lady, tells her he'll be miserable without her, she's the only one he cares for and all that sort of thing. Then if she accepts, he goes to speak to her father.'

Andy laughed. 'Her favver's been in t' churchyard these fifty year.'

'All right, perhaps we can skip over that part,' Bobby said. 'How did you propose to the first Mrs Jessop?'

Andy's eyes were far away as he summoned up the memory.

'Well, she'd inherited a little farm of her old man's along with a couple o' fine lonk tups,' he told Bobby. 'I were rearing swadis then, but I'd a fancy to cross 'em, and I said to her, "Dotty, if I were to put one of thy lonk tups on to my Swadi yows, I reckon the lambs'd be summat to see, like." And she said, "Aye, I could loan thee one, and I wouldn't charge thee neither, sin tha's an old friend o' t' family's". So I said, "Nay, I'll pay my way. Tha can have my farm as fee if tha wants it. Only thing is, tha has to take me along wi' it. Will tha have me, lass?" And she blushed right prettily and said she would. Is that how they do it in books?'

Bobby smiled. 'Not exactly. But it's rather sweet, all the same.'

Andy rubbed his neck, looking embarrassed. 'Don't know about that, but it worked for us. We're realists in this part o' t' world, Miss Bancroft – we don't hold much wi' fancy. Still, I loved my Dot and that's the honest truth. That never altered over all them year until the Lord wanted her.'

'I know,' Bobby said quietly.

'Can't propose that way to Ginny though, can I? She hasn't got no tups.'

'All right, how about…' Bobby considered for a moment, thinking back to the proposals she'd read in novels. 'Something like "Dearest Ginny, I hope this missive finds you well. In my letters, I've endeavoured to convey my ardent respect and admiration for you. I am now writing to confess that this goes beyond the ordinary measure of friendship, and I hope I won't offend you by asking you to consider a formal proposal of marriage."'

Andy squinted. 'Don't know about all that. Sounds a bit funny to me. She'll think I've gone strange if I start talking nobby all of a sudden.'

'What would you say if she was here in front of you then?' Bobby asked, pencil poised. 'In your own words.'

'Well, I…' His eyes glazed and his lips moved for a moment as he tried to find the right mode of expression. 'I suppose I'd say, "Gin, tha's a trim, canny lass for thi years, and what's more, tha's got a good heart. I aren't much to write home about these days, I know, but I'm good for a few year yet. If tha'll have me, then I'll do what I can to make thee happy." Can tha make that sound a bit more like what tha'd read in a letter?'

'I think so.' Bobby scribbled in shorthand for a moment, then read him back what she'd written. '"Ginny, I want you to know that I've come to care for you a great deal. You're kind and sensible, and in my eyes, you're truly beautiful. I haven't much to offer, but if you were to agree to be my wife, I'd be a good companion to you for the rest of my days and do what I could to make you happy." How does that sound?'

'Aye, that's good. That's what I meant, all right.' He gave her an impressed nod. 'We'll hear great things of thee one day, young lady. Never knew one like thee for words.'

She smiled. 'I don't know about that, but I'd be very happy if you were right.'

'I only hope I live to see it.' He peered through his spectacles at the bags under her eyes. 'Keep up with thi words, lass, and don't let lads distract thee. Talent like thine comes from on high. It oughtn't to be wasted.'

Bobby tore off the top page of her notepad so she could copy out his finished message to Ginny in longhand on a fresh sheet, ready for posting.

'Don't worry, Mr Jessop,' she said firmly. 'I've got no intention of letting myself get distracted, by lads or anything else.'

Chapter 26

'Bobby! Hey, Bobby!'

She ignored the deep voice calling her name, took her bike from where it was leaning against the wall of the farmhouse and pointedly mounted, throwing the satchel full of magazines for posting into the basket.

'Bobby, please.' Charlie approached from the tree he'd been leaning against while he waited for her and put his hand on the handlebars to prevent her riding off.

'Kindly let go of my bicycle, Mr Atherton,' Bobby said coldly. 'I'm at work, as you well know.'

'Come on. You're not going to keep this up forever, are you?'

'I don't know what you mean. I've told you on several occasions that I have no interest in discussing anything privately with you, or being alone with you under any circumstances. I think that's only prudent in an unmarried woman when a man of your reputation is on the loose, don't you?'

'But I'm not a man of my reputation. I mean, I am, but...' He sighed. 'Look, I'm sorry, all right? I'd had too much to drink, so had you, and I was... ungentlemanly to do what I did. Rest assured it didn't mean anything.'

Bobby glared at him. Did Charlie really think that having insulted her with an uninvited kiss, he could now appease her by suggesting the whole thing had been an error of judgement and the encounter entirely meaningless? How like a man! Not for him the worry and sleepless nights that had been a feature of her life since New Year – unless Charlie's sleepless nights were for Topsy Sumner-Walsh, perhaps.

'Have you quite finished, Mr Atherton?' she asked with icy politeness.

'You're really not going to talk to me like a human being? You look like a spinster librarian when you purse your lips like that.'

'How chivalrous of you to notice,' she said with a dry smile. 'I can talk like myself if it'll make you feel more at ease. Drop dead, Charlie.'

He met her gaze with a look of helpless pleading, and Bobby steeled herself against those deep brown eyes that looked into hers so soulfully. He certainly knew how to use them to his best advantage. Bobby was reminded forcefully of Mary's painting: the stag on the bridge at daybreak.

'Nothing I can do to get you to forgive me?' Charlie asked.

'Yes. You can stay out of my way and let me do my job.'

'You know, I distinctly remember that you kissed me as much as I kissed you.'

'Exactly the sort of thing I'd expect an incurable cad to say. You might also remember that you'd spent the night plying me with drinks to make me lower my guard.'

Bobby pushed down on a pedal with her foot, hoping to propel the bicycle out of his grip, but he held it with a firm hand.

'Hang on a moment,' he said. 'I wasn't waiting out here for you just to try to get you to listen to me, although it goes without saying that I wish you bloody would.' He fished in his pocket for an envelope. 'I was waiting to give you this.'

Bobby shook her head. 'I'm not reading notes from you either.'

'It's not from me. I bumped into Mabs in the village and she asked me to give it to you when I saw you.'

'Oh. Well, I suppose that's all right.' She took it from him.

Too curious to wait until Charlie had gone, Bobby tore the envelope open. It contained a note of only three words. It was written in a neat, feminine hand that she guessed belonged to Mabs, writing under direction from her grandfather.

She said yes.

'Good news?' Charlie said, noting Bobby's smile as she read it.

'A friend's engagement – not that it's any of your business.'

'Andy Jessop?'

'It could be. Can you let go of my handlebars please?'

'All right.' Grudgingly he let them go. 'Will you meet me for a drink at the Hart after you've posted your magazines?'

'No.'

'Please, Bobby, just to talk. There's no danger in the pub, is there? No quiet, secluded corners where I can get you alone to press my oh-so-disgusting attentions on to you.'

'I couldn't even if I wanted to, which I don't,' Bobby told him shortly. 'I'm going to visit Lady Sumner-Walsh. She sent me a note this morning inviting me to her cottage.'

'You're going to see Topsy?'

Huh. That had made his ears prick up. Of course it had.

'Yes, she's asked me to tea and then we're going to visit my friend's daughter at the evacuees' home.'

'Would you like me to keep you company? I warned you Topsy can be... a little much sometimes. She gets over-excited by new people.' He smiled fondly. 'She can be such a child.'

'I think I'm quite capable of holding my own with her, thank you very much,' Bobby said coolly. 'Goodbye, Mr Atherton.'

She pedalled away, leaving him staring unhappily after her.

–

Bobby hadn't quite believed Charlie when he'd told her on New Year's Eve that the villagers must be starting to accept her. There had certainly been more smiles and bonhomie from the Silverdalians than she was wont to see from them as they'd travelled from door to door carrying out the first footing, but Bobby had ascribed that to the fact it was a festive occasion – and, of course, Charlie had been with her. However, in the two weeks since then she had noticed a palpable change in people's workaday attitudes.

The Dalesfolk smiled now when they saw her bicycling through the village with her basket full of magazines to post. Men touched their caps to her, women nodded in greeting, and some even stopped to pass the time of day with her.

There was a lot of pride locally in 'our paper', Bobby had discovered. Once a month, she made the trip into Settle to drop off the magazine copy with their printers there for galley proofs to be made up, and she always popped into the newsagent's to pick up Reg's copy of the *Bradford Courier* while she was in town. On one occasion, she had spotted someone from the village in there with a friend and heard him observe to his companion, 'that's our little paper, that' with some pride as he'd pointed out the latest number of *The Tyke*. This seemed to be typical of local people's attitude towards the magazine.

This, Bobby supposed, was the reason she now began to find herself more accepted by the good folk of Silverdale. She wasn't one of them, but off-comed 'un or not, she was still part of 'our paper'. The pranks of the village boys seemed to have stopped too. Slowly but surely, and without her even noticing, Bobby had become part of the fabric of the village. She couldn't help wondering if this had been Reg's plan all along, when he'd made posting the magazines a part of her routine.

It was mid-January now and snowdrops had started to appear on the banks of the beck, like heralds of new life and better days to come. Bobby smiled as she bicycled through the village to the post office, and every person she encountered had a smile for her in return. She hadn't felt much like smiling lately, after her falling out with Charlie, but afternoon trips into the village were a highlight of her working days.

Reg had allowed her to finish early today in order to pay her visit, so that she could make the most of the limited hours of daylight. After dropping off her stack of magazines with Louisa Clough, the postmistress, Bobby mounted her bike again to cycle in the direction of Sumner House. It was a ride of some three miles when you took into account the mansion's extensive grounds, but Bobby didn't mind. Now she had grown used to the countryside, she enjoyed her walks and rides, especially since the happy signs of spring had started to appear. Early calves huddled with their mothers in the fields, birds chattered and snowdrops dotted the grassy banks. Bobby found that she was looking forward to the long days of sunshine that spring and summer would bring to her new home.

She had been pleased to receive Topsy's note that morning, inviting her to tea. In spite of a little jealousy she had been doing her best to repress over Charlie – as well as worry about what it might mean to become one of Topsy's 'projects' – Bobby hadn't been able to help liking the woman when they'd met at New Year. She'd been craving friendship with young people her own age since coming to Silverdale – young people who weren't Charlie Atherton, with all the danger his friendship entailed – and Topsy seemed equally anxious to make a friend out of her. The lively, attractive heiress couldn't be short of hangers-on of both sexes, so the fact she'd chosen Bobby as a recipient of her friendship felt rather gratifying. Today's visit also meant that Bobby would be able to pay her debt to Don by checking on the welfare of his daughter Sal, since her friend had been as good as his word in his promise to keep an eye on her father.

She had had a letter from him yesterday. This had followed one from Lilian two days earlier to tell her that Jake had left for basic training, with a cursory goodbye for his family and a long and tearful farewell with his Triumph motorcycle. Lil informed her that Raymond would be shipping out in one week's time to North Africa – although, of course, her sister had been unable to name the location in her letter for fear of 'careless talk'. There had been enough said over Christmas for Bobby to work out where her brother was being posted, however. Lil herself was full of excitement about her own imminent move to Greenwich in mid-February, where she would begin training as a Wren. It had made Bobby rather sad, thinking of the family nest emptying as her siblings left home, and filled her with worry for her father. Lilian was always sparse in her descriptions of life at home, which made Bobby suspect there was more going on than her sister was prepared to say. It would be typical of her twin to conceal information she believed would worry her.

But the letter from Don had reassured Bobby to an extent. He had visited her dad the week before, taking with him fresh supplies of whatever the liquor was that his friend made from potato peelings. Her dad, who craved only oblivion and the ability to forget his memories in sleep, hadn't commented on the decline in the quality of his spirits – he cared merely that it was strong. Don reported that he had found the old man in fine fettle, inhabiting the real world for once as he boasted of his two soldier sons and filled with friendly camaraderie for the man who Bobby knew reminded him of his lost brother.

Don wrote conservatively and without sentimentality, according to his style, but nevertheless, his words were infused with a great deal of compassion. The men who had suffered in the last war were, Bobby knew, always guaranteed to elicit care and sympathy from her pragmatic but secretly tender-hearted friend. Apparently he had taken her dad to a local pub, where the two men had chatted over a pint. Bobby had felt a hundred times better after reading Don's report and vowed to write that evening with her effusive thanks, but now she had Topsy's invitation, she could go one better and repay him in a more practical way by looking in on Sal.

Don had sent other news too. Tony's hunch, it turned out, had been correct. Mr Clarke wasn't quite at death's door, as Tony had hinted to Bobby over Christmas, but he had found himself in hospital when his cough had progressed to pneumonia. Under orders from his doctors to rest as much as he could if he wanted to enjoy many more years on the planet, old Clarky had made the decision to retire from the *Courier* and

– just as Tony had predicted – the proprietors had promptly appointed Don to the editorship in his place. All of this he reported modestly, as if it was of only minor importance, but Bobby could sense he was justifiably proud. It felt right to her, too. Clarky had been a vague and frightening presence in his office upstairs when she'd worked for the *Courier*, but it had always felt like Don's newspaper at heart.

Chapter 27

Bobby had heard a lot about Sumner House, but although she'd seen it from a distance during her rambles, this was the first time she'd viewed it up close. It was a grand and imposing sandstone building with a large lake at the front where geese and ducks cruised sedately. There was a sort of turret on the left of the building, giving it the air of a fairy-tale castle, and an ornate rose window above the arched front door.

There was no sign of the house's current residents, the young evacuees, although Bobby supposed they would have finished lessons for the day. What a wonderful place for them to live though! All would have come from the cities, from tiny terraces or slum housing, and this would be their first taste of country life. Bobby could imagine them running around the grounds playing their childhood games, fishing in the lake perhaps, enjoying all that fresh air and open space.

It occurred to her what a magnanimous gesture it had been on Topsy's part to offer her beautiful home up for the war effort. Sal must surely be happy here, although no doubt she missed her parents and her old friends back in Bradford. Somewhat reassured, Bobby located the little path Topsy had referred to in her note of invitation and followed it to the cottage in the grounds that Topsy and Mrs Hobbes were occupying for as long as the big house was needed.

She had no need to knock at the door. When she arrived it was already open, Mrs Hobbes emerging from the house with two geese on leads. Bobby recognised one as Norman, who was flashing resentful looks at the second goose as it walked staidly at Mrs Hobbes's other side.

'Oh. It's you,' Mrs Hobbes said with a vague smile. She called over her shoulder. 'Topsy! Visitor for you.'

Topsy appeared almost immediately, running out of the house like a schoolgirl at half past three on the last day of term. She beamed when she saw Bobby, and immediately grabbed her for a hug.

'Um. Hello,' Bobby said, rather windswept at the warmth and energy of her welcome.

'Darling, I'm so pleased you could come,' Topsy said. 'Oh, did you bring me some of your writing? I did tell you to come prepared for me to worship you.'

Bobby blushed. 'I do have a December edition in my bag if you really want to read it. That has my article on Mr Jessop, the old farmer at Newby Top. It's the only thing I've had printed so far.'

She took it from her handbag and handed it to Topsy.

'Thank you. I can't wait to read it.' Topsy cast it a cursory glance before her attention was claimed by something else. She giggled and nodded to Mrs Hobbes with her two geese. 'Look at Maimie. Isn't it foolish? She's brought one of the geese from the stream in the village to have a date with Norman.'

'I don't see what's foolish about it,' Mrs Hobbes said stiffly. 'Certainly it's no more ridiculous than one of your madcap schemes, young lady. Geese mate for life. Why should my poor Norman be the only one without a wife? He's four now, and all the goslings from his clutch paired but him.'

'That's because he's such a grumpy little waterfowl, no one will have him.' Topsy smiled at Mrs Hobbes's frown and went to put an arm around her. 'Oh, now don't be cross, old thing. I think it's very sweet, the way you matchmake for him.'

Mrs Hobbes consented to smile. 'If you'd let me do it for you instead, perhaps I wouldn't need to spend so much time on my Norman.'

'When I want a husband, you'll be my first port of call,' Topsy said, putting one hand on her heart. 'Only let me have a little fun first, do.'

'Hmm.' Mrs Hobbes looked at Bobby. 'When Topsy talks about "having fun", it's really another way of saying "getting into trouble". I hope you came forewarned and forearmed, Miss Bancroft.'

Bobby smiled. 'I did, thank you.'

'Come on then, you pair,' Mrs Hobbes said to the geese. 'We'll take a romantic walk to the lake and then I shall chaperone while the two of you have a swim. Norman, I expect gentlemanly manners and your best behaviour.'

They walked off up the path: a comical sight, with Mrs Hobbes's iconic feather hat bobbing between the two waddling tailfeathers.

'She's a darling, but she's rather mad,' Topsy said, slipping her arm into Bobby's. 'I don't doubt that if I asked her to find me a husband, as she so often begs me to do, she'd have me on a lead swimming around the lake with him as well. Who warned you about me? Charlie, I suppose?'

Bobby had thought that Charlie Atherton was the master when it came to moving from one conversation subject to another with the speed of a train, but Topsy could certainly set him a pretty pace.

'Um, yes,' she said. Something made her add, 'But not in a mean way. I think he was worried I might not be able to keep up with you.'

'He's a love but he really ought to mind his own business,' Topsy said as she led Bobby into the cottage. 'I never interfere with his little romances. I don't know why he has to interfere in mine.'

'You sound like you've known him a long time,' Bobby said as Topsy half-guided and half-pushed her into a large easy chair by the fire.

'Oh, yes, forever. At least, well, no, I should say about three years. Isn't he just the most awful flirt?'

Bobby might have laughed at that comment before New Year's Eve. Now, for some reason, it made her feel unutterably sad. However, she forced a smile.

'He's terrible,' she agreed.

'Isn't he? You know, he has about half the women in the village in love with him, even some of the married ones. I think Maimie might be a bit in love with him too – well, he's always so kind to Norman that she can't help it.'

Tea had been laid out on the table. Topsy threw herself into an armchair, frowned at it for a moment, then jumped up and started pouring them both a cup. She seemed to do everything with ten times the energy of an ordinary human being.

'Not that I mean to insult him,' she said as she stirred the tea. 'Dear old Charlie. I'm abnormally fond of him. It's just that he's all talk and no action, you know?'

'Is he? Um, thank you.' Bobby accepted the cup of tea that had been thrust in her direction.

'Well I mean, I do expect when a man flirts with me that he ought to follow it through one way or another, don't you? He should at least try to fall_in love with me, or be dastardly enough to press unwanted attentions on me, or something of the kind. Charlie makes love to everyone, but he never seems to *do* anything.'

Bobby wondered what Topsy would make of the kiss she and Charlie had shared on New Year's Eve if this was really what she believed. He'd certainly had plenty of action to go with his words on that night.

'I think he likes having people fall in love with him, then he gets bored,' Topsy went on. 'I've introduced him to heaps of wonderful girls and he flirts and flirts, but nothing ever seems to come of it. I think that's quite shocking in a man, don't you?'

'Um, yes. Very.' Bobby sipped her tea, sensing there was little she needed to do in any conversation with Topsy Sumner-Walsh except nod occasionally.

'I suppose you're in love with him too, aren't you?'

Bobby felt her treacherous cheeks heating in a blush. Topsy's eyes widened.

'Oh, you are!' she said, her little white hands flying to her mouth. 'Darling, I'm so sorry! I was only teasing. I had no idea you were one of Charlie's conquests.'

'I'm not... that is, we're just friends. We *were* friends,' Bobby corrected herself. 'You're right. He's a terrible flirt. I've got no time for men like that.'

'No more have I, although he's a dear sweet thing to me, of course. I wish he'd settle down with someone nice. It isn't fair having so many girls in love with him at once. My other boyfriends complain about him to me all the time. There simply aren't enough women to go round.' She examined her nails airily. 'I sometimes think I ought to marry him myself, just to put a stop to him.'

'But... I mean, don't you have to marry a lord or something?'

Topsy laughed heartily. 'Oh Bobby, darling, you really are too adorable. No one cares a fig about that sort of thing nowadays.' She tossed down a finger sandwich. 'Well, no, that isn't quite true. There are a lot of old friends of my father's who care a great deal about it. But I'm over twenty-one, so yah-boo to them, I say.'

Bobby couldn't stop herself from asking.

'Then why don't you marry Charlie?'

'Oh, I don't think I could be a vet's wife,' Topsy said, wrinkling her perfect nose. 'It's so... sort of provincial, isn't it? I just know I'd end up fat and plain, and the house would smell horribly of dogs and things, and there'd be no fun in it at all. Besides, we'd be the worst sort of influence on one another, you know. We're both far too prone to disgracing ourselves. Charlie needs a wife who's intelligent and steady and... well, sensible, I suppose. I only hope for my sake she isn't too dull, for I shall have to befriend her, of course.'

Bobby smiled. 'Of course.'

Topsy seemed to be bored of the topic of Charlie now. She cocked her head to one side, like a curious bird, and gave Bobby a thorough examination. She peered at her hair and her clothes, not even trying to hide her approval or disapproval of the various parts of her figure and attire.

'Do you always do your hair in that horrid severe way?' she asked when she was done.

Bobby patted her bun. 'I do when I'm working. I like it to be out of my way.'

Topsy clapped her hands. 'I say, you must let me style it for you sometime. I've a real talent for it, you know. I wish I'd been born ordinary, and worked as a ladies' hairdresser, and lived somewhere normal and dull as I suppose you did.' She helped herself to another sandwich from a tray and ate it at the speed of light before letting out a tiny burp behind her fingers. 'I know absolutely pots of eligible men,' she told Bobby, once again moving to another conversation topic with dizzying speed. 'Of course, the only problem is that the handsome ones are as poor as mice, and the rich ones either ugly or as old as Methuselah, but I know I can find one you'll like. You will come to a party here the next time I throw one, won't you? I can't wait to introduce you to my little set.'

Bobby was starting to realise why Charlie had warned her about Topsy 'adopting' her. She had been quite firm in her statement that she would refuse to be made a project of, but the problem was that Topsy was rather hard to resist. She worked so quickly, and with such charisma and energy, Bobby could see how easy it would be to find yourself a Topsy project without even realising it.

'If I'm available,' she answered cautiously, half wishing she was still on speaking terms with Charlie so she could ask what any party of Topsy's was likely to entail. Although he'd probably be in attendance at the party himself, wouldn't he, as a friend of the hostess? The last thing Bobby wanted was to find herself at a party with Charlie Atherton, where there'd probably be dancing and soft music and champagne and other dangerous things. The idea that he might spend the whole night ignoring her while he gazed in besotted fascination at Topsy was even more depressing.

Topsy bolted another sandwich and tossed down the rest of her tea, acting in every respect like a woman who had no time to waste in life.

'Well, shall we go to the house?' she asked Bobby. 'I've arranged your visit with the headmistress there. She was ever so stuffy and cross about it. She's a horrible ugly thing, and I know she doesn't like me. I should think all the children hate her – I know I do. But she couldn't really object, since it is my house, so she agreed in the end. I'm to take you up at four when the children are having a study hour.'

Bobby, who couldn't eat and drink at the speed Topsy seemed to be able to, still had half a cup of tea and the best part of a cucumber sandwich left. However, she was keen to see Sal as soon as possible and was finding Topsy's company and conversation at least as exhausting as it was entertaining. She put down her teacup and saucer and nodded.

Chapter 28

Bobby had been hoping that after escorting her to the house and making her introduction to the headmistress there, Topsy would leave her alone to visit Sal, but her enthusiastic new friend seemed to have no intention of letting her out of her sight.

The headmistress, Miss Newbould, was a solid, ruddy-cheeked, no-nonsense individual built on roughly the same scale as a Valkyrie, with muscles like a man. She reminded Bobby rather of her games mistress at school. She hadn't liked her games mistress. Bobby had never suffered under her, but the woman had nevertheless been free with her hands, picking on the weaker children who couldn't excel in sports. She hoped Miss Newbould wasn't the same sort.

'Miss Newbould, this is the person I spoke to you about – Miss Bancroft.' Topsy spoke in a tone rather more prim and proper than the one Bobby had heard her use so far, which was no doubt a way of expressing her dislike. 'She's the young lady from the magazine who wishes to visit her friend's daughter.'

Miss Newbould gave Bobby a wary look.

'As long as a visit is all it is,' she said. 'We don't need prying journalists upsetting the apple cart here, Miss Bancroft. Not that we've anything to hide, you understand, but it would worry the parents to think their children weren't safe from press intrusion.'

'I'm here to visit my friend's daughter at his request,' Bobby said. 'Nothing more than that, I assure you.'

'I would rather like to see how my property is being used while we're here, however,' Topsy said, smiling sweetly. 'I wonder if we could request a little tour, Miss Newbould?'

Miss Newbould looked like this was the last thing she felt like giving, but since it was Topsy's house, she had little choice in the matter.

'Of course,' she said, forcing a tight smile. 'Follow me.'

She led them through endless wood-panelled corridors to a large room, the walls lined with books, where several long tables had been set out.

'The library,' Topsy said. 'You're using it as a dining room, I presume.'

Miss Newbould nodded. 'In fact, it's used for both mealtimes and lessons, as it's the second largest room. The main hall, of course, we use as the dormitory.'

'What do the children eat?' Bobby asked. 'If you don't mind me enquiring.'

'Good, hearty fare for growing bodies,' the headmistress informed her rather pompously. 'Porridge and a spoonful of cod liver oil for breakfast, bread and cheese for lunch, and in the evenings, meat and potatoes or a stew of some variety.'

She turned to lead them to another room, and Topsy nudged Bobby.

'If I were a pupil, I'd revolt until they brought me a dessert,' she whispered. 'Honestly, isn't she the most awful bore?'

Bobby pretended she hadn't heard, although she couldn't help smiling.

The next room, which Topsy informed Bobby had previously been the ballroom, contained a range of equipment: vaulting horses, climbing poles and other things you might expect to find in a school gymnasium.

'This is the games room,' Miss Newbould told them. 'The children have access to this whenever they wish, in their free time as well as during lessons, to encourage healthy play. We must look after the bodies as well as the minds, mustn't we?'

'Of course,' Bobby said. 'Not all children will be strong enough for a lot of physical exercise though, will they?'

'They soon bloom under our care,' Miss Newbould said, her voice suffused with pride. 'Once they're away from unhealthy cities and poor diets, they quickly grow sturdy and strong. Often parents tell me they hardly recognise their offspring when they visit. That is the best thing about having a school in a place such as this, with all that wonderful fresh air blowing over the hills.'

Bobby thought of Sal, who she remembered as a small, quiet child, underdeveloped for her age and rather studious, with huge eyes set in a pale, thoughtful face. She was her parents' pride and joy, the only child they'd been able to have, and had often been sickly in her early childhood. Bobby knew what a wrench it had been for Don and Joan to decide on evacuation after the raid on Bradford the previous summer, when over a hundred bombs had fallen on the city. Could this be behind Sal's unhappiness? She was far too slight and weak to ever be a sporty child, despite Miss Newbould's views on the transformative powers of diet and exercise.

'Still, there must be some who can't manage a lot of exertion – those who've been ill, for example, or who have conditions such as asthma,' Bobby said. 'Are they able to use the library instead if they choose?'

Topsy nodded. 'I told Miss Newbould my library was at the school's disposal, with the exception of a few valuable volumes I took away with me. I'd rather see it used than gathering dust.'

'We do not allow access to the library outside of school hours,' Miss Newbould told her stiffly.

Topsy looked appalled by this. 'But why on earth not, when there are so many wonderful books in there?'

'The children spend enough time reading in their lessons and the evening study hour. They mustn't damage their eyes. In their free time, we like to encourage healthy exercise in the games room and around the grounds.' She beckoned them to follow her once again. 'Let me show you to the girls' dormitory.

The children are having a study hour, after which they may have an hour of free time before their evening meal. Miss Bancroft, I have given Sally permission to finish study half an hour early and make the time up in the play hour so that you might talk with her.'

Very generous, Bobby thought wryly. Surely the child could be granted half an hour of holiday rather than having to 'make the time up' when she ought to be playing with her friends.

The dormitories were in the great hall, the largest room – the girls in the lower hall on the ground floor and the boys in the upper hall above. Rows of beds had been arranged in there, each with a chair beside it for its owner's possessions. On the beds sat girls aged from seven to eleven, all with a textbook of some kind on their laps. It was rather spartan, Bobby thought, like an army camp. The children didn't look poorly treated or unhappy though. Many of the girls looked up to smile at her as she passed their beds. Most seemed blooming and healthy on their diet of solid, starchy food and extra games.

She was rather shocked at the change in Sal's appearance when they reached her bed, however. The child had always been pale, but now she was almost white. She looked exhausted as she pored over her textbook, blinking hard as if her eyes were struggling to take in the words. Bobby was sure she'd lost weight too.

'Sally, I believe you know this young lady,' Miss Newbould said to the girl in unduly stern tones, as if knowing Bobby was somehow a matter for discipline.

Sal looked up and smiled vaguely. 'Yes. Hello, Miss Bancroft. Dad said you'd come.'

Miss Newbould looked at her wristwatch. 'There is half an hour until the end of study time. You may use that period to talk with Miss Bancroft and make up the time in your play hour later. I hope I can trust you to be conscientious about the additional time.'

'Yes, Miss Newbould,' Sal said obediently, looking up at the headmistress with her big eyes.

Bobby noticed a look in Miss Newbould's eyes that the woman didn't seem able to conceal. She recognised it at once. Contempt. Her games mistress had looked exactly that way when considering a vulnerable child she had decided to make a target. Topsy seemed to notice it too. She was frowning at Miss Newbould with evident dislike.

'Shall we go into the grounds and have a little walk?' Bobby asked Sal. The child nodded gratefully and stood to put on her coat and outdoor shoes.

Bobby led Sal out to the lake as the sun began to sink below the ridge of the fells. Mrs Hobbes's hat was visible across the water, blowing gaily in the breeze. On the lake, Bobby could see Norman and his lady friend trying their best to avoid one another as they circled around.

'That's Norman, look,' she said to Sal, pointing him out. 'He's on a date.'

Sal's earnest, anxious expression lifted briefly as she broke into a smile.

'With that other goose?'

'Yes. His owner wants to find him a goose wife, but he's too grumpy. It's silly, isn't it?'

Sal laughed. 'It sounds like Beatrix Potter.'

'Yes, it does, rather.' Bobby smiled. 'Perhaps Norman's girl-friend is Jemima. Do you remember?'

'Yes, Jemima Puddle-Duck. That was one of my favourite stories when I was little.'

'It was one of mine too.'

Bobby hadn't spent much time around children – at least, not since her brothers had been small – but she had always found Sal easy to talk to. The earnest little girl, looking so much younger than her ten years, loved to read and to write just as much as Bobby had at her age. She felt like a kindred spirit, and Bobby enjoyed recommending books to Don that his daughter might like or helping him choose presents for her. He deferred to her judgement, assuming that as a woman she had a natural and instinctive understanding of children, but it was really as a lover of words and stories that Bobby found herself relating to Sal.

'Shall we sit on that little seat and have a talk?' Bobby said, nodding to a bench that overlooked the lake. 'We don't have very long.'

'All right.'

Sal followed her to the bench and they sat down, watching the geese on the lake.

Bobby wondered how to begin. They hadn't much time, and she could certainly see why Don had been concerned about his daughter. Sal had always been a quiet soul, too earnest and sickly to laugh and skip as the other children did, with her nose always stuck in a book. But now she seemed tired too, and Bobby didn't much like how pale she'd become since the last time they'd seen one another.

'Your dad wanted me to visit,' she said. 'He asked me to make sure that you're happy here. Are you? Your headmistress seems very strict.'

'She is,' Sal said in a faraway sort of voice. 'Much stricter than Miss Barker at my old school.'

'Does she punish you often? Hit you?'

Sal shook her head. 'Not much. She says she doesn't think it's right to hit young ladies. The boys get the slipper if they do something wrong, but the girls mostly only get lines to write.'

'Oh.'

Bobby fell silent as she thought about what to ask next.

'You must miss your parents a lot,' she said.

Sal shrugged. 'I did, when I was here first, but I got used to being by myself after a while. I wish I could go home though.'

'Why? Are you unhappy?'

The girl flushed and shook her head. Bobby patted her hand.

'It's OK,' she said softly. 'You can tell me. If Miss Newbould—'

She stopped, frowning, as she noticed something on Sal's wrist. The girl followed her gaze and whipped her arm away, putting it behind her back.

'Sal, how did you get that bruise?' Bobby asked in a low voice.

'Please don't tell my mam and dad,' the girl said, looking up at her with wide eyes. 'They'll be worried. I hate it when they're worried about me.'

'Did one of your teachers do that to you?'

'No. I... I did it in games. I fell.'

'Show me.'

Reluctantly Sal withdrew her arm and presented it to Bobby to examine, and she rolled up the girl's sleeve to take a closer look.

No fall had caused this – Bobby could see that immediately. There were the distinct marks of fingertips where someone had squeezed hard and without mercy on the tender flesh.

'Who did this, Sal?' she asked gently. 'You won't get into trouble if you tell me. Was it a grown-up?'

'No,' the girl said, flushing. 'You promise you won't tell my mam and dad, Miss Bancroft?'

'I can't make that promise; I'm sorry. But I won't do anything that will make things worse for you.'

'It was... it was that Mavis Addaway,' Sal blurted out, closing her eyes as if it hurt her to say the name.

'This is another girl here?'

Sal nodded, her eyes still closed. 'She... she hates me. I don't know why. Because I'm not good at games, maybe – she's the best in our class, and she laughs at me because I can't do it like she can. She takes my reading books and my tuck shop money, and if no one looks, she takes my dinner too. I try to hide at playtime so she won't find me but she always does, and she hurts me where she thinks no teachers will see the mark. She tells the other girls she'll hurt them too if they ever let me play with them. They're all afraid of her.' Sal let out a little sob. 'I thought she might get bored and stop, but she won't, Miss. She won't ever leave me alone unless the war stops and we get sent home.'

'Oh, my love.' Bobby put her arm around her and gave her a squeeze. 'What a nasty little bully. Why didn't you tell anyone?'

Sal sniffed. 'I told Miss Newbould. She said I should do more games if I wanted to get big and strong. Then I could fight back.'

'She didn't do anything to stop it? Punish the girl, or talk to her parents?'

'No. She said I had to toughen up and learn to stand up for myself.' The little girl snuggled into Bobby's arm as if it made her feel safe to be there. 'I've been ever so scared since she came to school, Miss Bancroft. I'm not so scared of bombs or Germans or anything as I am of Mavis. I can't sleep from worrying about it.'

'How long has this been going on?'

'Since October, when she came here from London.' Sal looked up at her. 'Can you make it stop?'

'I can,' Bobby said firmly. 'I promise you, Sal.'

'I have to go back. I'll be in trouble if I don't finish my work.'

'Yes, let's get you back.' Bobby's brow knit into a determined frown. 'And then I need to have a word with your Miss Newbould.'

Bobby marched back inside, a woman on a mission. When she'd escorted Sal back to her bed, she went in search of Miss Newbould. It didn't take her long to find her. She could hear raised voices coming from a room at the end of the corridor outside the dorm, one of which belonged to Miss Newbould. The other belonged to Topsy Sumner-Walsh. Bobby threw open the door and marched in without knocking.

'—I'm sure we're all very grateful for your generosity in giving us your home for the duration, Miss Sumner-Walsh—' Miss Newbould was saying.

'Lady Sumner-Walsh,' Topsy said, lifting her chin.

'Lady Sumner-Walsh,' Miss Newbould repeated through gritted teeth. 'But the fact you own this house does not give you the right to dictate to me how I run my educational establishment. My methods are producing a generation of happy, healthy children here who will be the future of this country one day, and I'm afraid I don't care if you feel that they are wrong.'

'Not all of them are happy and healthy,' Bobby said. Two sets of eyes turned to her.

Miss Newbould raised an eyebrow. 'I'm sorry?'

'Are you aware that for four months, one of the children in this school has been tormenting another to the point of ill health?' Bobby demanded. 'You don't need to answer that because I already know the truth. Sal told me.'

Topsy frowned. 'What happened, Bobby?'

'I'll tell you what happened. I discovered a quiet, sensitive little girl who's being starved to malnourishment and exhausted into illness by a bigger child – not to mention the bruises I discovered all over her arms. And when she complained of this to an adult – one responsible for her care and welfare in the absence of her parents – she was given no help except to be told to do extra games.'

Topsy shook her head. 'The poor little thing. That's appalling.' She glared at Miss Newbould. 'Well, do you have anything to say for yourself?'

The headmistress drew herself up. 'My methods are my methods, Miss Bancroft. I am preparing these children for life, and there'll be no one to coddle them in the real world. The little girl needs to toughen up, or she'll forever be targeted by those who see her as weak.'

'You mean people like you,' Bobby snapped. 'That child is sick! She had problems with her health all through her childhood, and now you're turning a blind eye while she's being beaten and starved? I've never heard anything so inhuman in my life.'

'It's for her own good, I assure you. One more term here and I'm sure she would—'

'One more term! I doubt her parents will let her stay here one more day when they hear about how she's been treated. Rest assured I'll be speaking to them about your attitude.'

'And I'll be speaking to the board of governors,' Topsy said, folding her arms. 'The chairman is an old friend of my father's, and my godfather. I can't imagine he'd approve of this sort of thing.'

'The governors have already stated that they support my methods completely,' Miss Newbould informed them haughtily.

'I wonder if they'd feel the same way if those methods and their consequences were laid bare to the public.' Bobby fished for her press card, which she always kept close, and held it up. 'What do you think, Miss Newbould? Should I tell them?'

For the first time the woman sagged a little, looking nervous.

'I stand by everything I've done here,' she said, but there was a little tremor in her voice.

'We'll see how that works out for you, shall we?' Topsy said with a deceptively sweet smile. 'Come on, Bobby. Let's leave Miss Newbould here with her "methods".'

Bobby was still seething when they got outside.

'That poor child!' she said to Topsy. 'She looked terrified when she told me what had been going on, and I had the devil of a time getting it out of her too. Another month and she'd be in hospital, I'm sure of it.'

'I had no idea that was the way Miss Newbould was running the place or I'd have stepped in sooner,' Topsy said, looking nearly as angry as Bobby felt. 'I don't doubt the capable children are thriving, but those who are ill or weak are being left to rot under her regime. It's a disgrace.'

'I had a teacher like her,' Bobby muttered darkly. 'Worse in a way, because she seemed to enjoy beating the children she saw as weak. Miss Newbould's more misguided than sadistic, I should think – at least, she really seems to believe these methods of hers are what's best for the children. But something has to be done. I'd take Sal away myself right this moment if it was allowed.'

'What will you do? Will you write about the school in your magazine?'

Bobby laughed. 'In *The Tyke*? We publish articles about rope-making and sheep and drystone wallers, Topsy. Investigations into school mismanagement aren't really our area. No, the press card was to scare her more than anything really.'

'Well, do we have a plan?'

'I think your suggestion was best. Since you know the chair of governors, you ought to be able to arrange an interview with him. But I have to do something about Sal right away, before any more damage is done. She'll be safer in Bradford than at that school if they're not going to protect her from this bully. Do you have a telephone?'

'Yes, but the dial is broken,' Topsy said. 'We can receive calls, but we can't make them at the moment. The big house has one that I use if I need to phone anyone.'

'I can't call from there with Miss Newbould spying on me. I'd better bicycle back to Moorside and ask Reg if I can make an urgent call on the magazine's phone.'

Bobby usually made any personal calls she needed to from the public telephone box in Settle, since Reg was reluctant to allow her the use of the phone at Moorside Farm. He'd had it installed at some expense when he'd started his magazine, and insisted it was strictly for business purposes, not to be clogged up with frivolous calls. However, she was certain he'd allow her the use of it in an emergency, which this most certainly was. As soon as she arrived back at the farmhouse, she jumped off her bicycle and dashed inside.

When she reached the parlour, she found Reg on the phone already.

'Hold on, don't hang up yet. She's just come in.' He covered the mouthpiece. 'Bobby. I was about to come out and look for you, lass.'

'Reg, please may I use the phone?' she asked breathlessly. 'It's an emergency. I need to telephone Donald Sykes right away.'

'Don?'

'Yes, please. I'll pay you for the call, or you can take it from my wages. It really is urgent.'

'I've got Don on the line now. He telephoned to talk to you.'

'Oh. Did he? That's convenient. Thanks.'

Reg looked concerned, but Bobby barely registered this as she took the receiver from him.

'Don, listen,' she said, still out of breath from her ride. 'I want you and Joan to come and take Sal home, as soon as you can. She'll be better off with you than here until you can find somewhere else. That school… they're not mistreating the children exactly, but I really don't like how they manage the place, and she's very unhappy.'

'Bobby, can you be quiet and listen to me a moment?' Don sounded worried, but Bobby was too focused on her concerns about Sal to pay much attention.

'There's a bigger child making her life miserable, and the teachers refuse to do anything except tell her to "toughen up". I know you want her to be safe, but there's only been one raid on Bradford and there must be other places she can—'

'Bobby!'

She stopped talking, noting the urgency in his voice. 'What is it?'

'We'll fetch Sal tomorrow if you really think it's for the best, but I didn't call to talk to you about that,' he said. 'Your sister asked me to call – she's too upset to do it herself. You need to come home right away. This evening, if you can.'

'Don? What's happened?'

'It's your father. He's in hospital.'

Chapter 29

Of course, Reg gave her a leave of absence as soon as she told him what had happened, and Bobby hurried back to Bradford as quickly as buses, trains and her own two feet could take her there.

It was a horrific journey. Don hadn't told her what had happened to put her father in the hospital or what his chances of survival were — he'd only said it was bad, and that, as the details were delicate, he'd prefer not to discuss them over the telephone.

All through her long journey, nightmare scenarios ran through Bobby's head. Had he got so drunk he'd fallen into the path of a passing tram? Or set fire to the house? Would he still be alive when she got to the hospital or was there no hope? Perhaps it was worse, even, than death. Perhaps he would lose the use of his legs and be condemned to a life where he could do nothing but sit in a chair haunted by horrific memories. As harsh as it sounded, she would wish for death for him rather than that.

It was late evening and pitch dark when Bobby arrived back in Bradford. Luckily she knew those cobbled streets almost as well as she knew her own body, and she easily found her way on to the tram that went past St Luke's Hospital. When she arrived, she was shown by a kindly nurse to a waiting room. There Lilian sat, pale and drawn, blank eyes fixed on the door.

'Hello, Bobby,' she said in a toneless voice.

'Lil, what happened? Tell me quick, please. I'm going mad.'

'Don't worry. He's going to be all right, the doctors say. They pumped his stomach and got most of it out. He's awake now – Don's in with him. I let him go in first, so I could get myself under control before Dad saw me.'

'Oh, thank God he's safe,' Bobby said, letting out a sigh of relief. Then she frowned as Lilian's words registered in her brain. 'They pumped his stomach? Why?'

Lilian was still staring at the door as if only half present. 'It was an accident. That's what we'll tell people.'

'You don't mean...'

Lilian seemed to rouse herself, turning to Bobby finally. 'They laid him off from work today, Bob. He's been concealing extra spirits around the house, for weeks now. I thought they were all locked up, but there was a bottle of whisky or whatever the stuff is he's been drinking under his bed, and another in the airing cupboard. Don found them when he searched the place, after... when the ambulance came.'

Bobby sank into the chair by her sister. 'The mill laid him off?'

She nodded. 'He's been drinking in the morning, and at work too – from his private supply. It was only a matter of time until they found out he was drunk on the job.' She let out a strangled sob. 'He never said a word about being sacked or I wouldn't have gone. I swear I wouldn't, Bobby.'

'Gone where?'

'To the Palais with Jimmy. Dad seemed all right – at least, no worse than usual – and Don was due to visit later on. I thought I could leave Dad for a couple of hours, but... getting laid off must've hit him hard. I didn't know until I bumped into one of the girls from Butterfield's at the dance hall and she asked me how he was coping. Of course I rushed straight home, but... it was too late.'

Bobby felt a surge of foreboding. 'What was too late?'

'I was. So was Don. He was there when I got back, with Dad, waiting for the ambulance he'd gone out to telephone for. It's lucky I'd left the door unlocked, or it would have been another hour until I got home to find him.' She let out another sob. 'It's all my fault, Bob. You should've seen him, lying there so white and lifeless. I honestly thought he was dead.'

'Lil, you still haven't told me what happened. Did he drink himself into a stupor or... or what?'

'He took all the sleeping powder we had in the house and washed it down with an entire bottle of booze,' Lilian said simply.

'What? He could've killed himself!'

'I think that was the idea, Bobby.'

'You mean... he did it on purpose? Suicide?'

'We'll tell people it was an accident,' Lilian said quietly. 'No one needs to know any different.'

Bobby's head was spinning. She just couldn't wrap her brain around what had happened. Her dad...

'But *we* know,' she said at last.

'Yes.' Lilian turned to her. 'Bobby, I'm going to contact Greenwich tomorrow and tell them I need to resign my commission on compassionate grounds. I can't join the Wrens. Not now.'

'What? No! You can't do that.'

'I have to, don't I? We can't let him live alone after this. It isn't safe.'

'Surely... surely there's another way.'

'Don't you think I've tried to think of one? There isn't, Bobby. If he's left alone and he tries again... Even if he survives, next time everyone will know the truth. They'll take Dad away from us – put him in one of those institutions for mental defectives.' She sighed. 'He's a proud man, even now. That'll be worse than death to him.'

Bobby was silent. She knew too well how true her sister's words were.

'Do you think losing his job was the final straw for him?' she asked at last.

Lilian nodded. 'It was the only thing that made him still feel like a man, you know? That despite the nightmares and the drinking and the times he got lost inside his own head, he could at least support his family and keep a roof over our heads. I suppose all of us leaving home so close together didn't help either.'

'No. It mustn't have.' Bobby fell into a thoughtful silence. 'I feel just awful, Lil. This is all my fault. I put myself and my career ahead of the family, and now... now this has happened. It's a judgement on me.'

'You couldn't have predicted this.'

'Couldn't I?' Bobby thrust her fingers into her hair. 'I knew when I left that he was struggling. I knew he'd been getting worse since then; you told me so over Christmas. And of course it was going to affect him, all of us moving away, no matter how we tried to make sure he was provided for. I ought never to have gone.'

'I was no better, going ahead with my plan to be a Wren regardless. I thought there was a way we could make it all work somehow. I wanted to think that.' Lilian sighed. 'It seems so unfair, having to put our dreams to one side. But I suppose sacrifice goes along with being an adult. With being a woman especially.'

'Yes. I suppose it does.'

The door opened and Don appeared.

'Bobby.' He smiled with relief. 'Thank God you're here.'

Lilian stood up. 'How is he, Don?'

'He's already forgotten what happened. If I were you, I wouldn't remind him of it. He'll only feel humiliated.' He glanced from Lilian to Bobby. 'Which one of you wants to go in? One visitor at a time. They say we've got an hour before they close the doors to us.'

Lilian wiped her eyes with the back of her hand. 'I'll go. I'm ready now. I need to tell him... tell him I'm sorry.'

She marched steadfastly out of the room as if going into battle. Don took her place next to Bobby.

'Thanks,' Bobby whispered.

'For what?'

'Looking after my dad.'

'Huh.' Don propped his chin on one fist. 'If I was a better caretaker, I'd have made sure I knew damn well where all those bottles I brought went to. I'm surprised you'll still talk to me.'

'It wasn't your fault, or Lilian's either. No one could have known he'd do that.' She glanced at him. 'Has he really forgotten what he did?'

'I don't know. It suits him to say so, and it suits me to go along with it.'

'He'd be so humiliated if people knew... that it wasn't an accident.'

'Only four people know that, and there's no reason they can't forget it again just as well.' Don gave her hand a pat. 'Don't worry, love. His secret's safe with me.'

'Don, I feel so guilty. I should never have left him.'

'I know you're bound to feel like that, but you've got your own life too, Bobby. Besides, if you'd been here, I doubt you could have prevented it.'

'Why do you say that?'

'There's only so far you can keep watch over someone if they've made up their mind to self-destruction. Perhaps you might have held it at bay a little longer, but in the end, it would be inevitable. It's not what's outside – it's what's in your dad's head that's the problem.'

'It's still my responsibility. Dad's my responsibility.' Bobby lapsed into a pensive silence.

'Thanks for going to visit Sal, by the way,' Don said after a little time had passed. 'We'll go get her tomorrow if that's really what you think is best.'

Bobby stirred herself. 'Yes. The sooner, the better, I think.'

'You say the school aren't cruel to the children?'

'They're not cruel or neglectful exactly, but it seems to me that they're shirking their responsibility to care for them adequately. The headmistress has this ethos – she's obsessed with making sure the children are physically fit and tough enough to face the adult world. In principle it sounds like a healthy attitude and the majority of the children I saw there seem to be thriving, which I suppose is why the governors don't intervene, but it's not an environment where anyone sickly or sensitive is going to be happy.' She scowled. 'There's a horrid little bully who's been making Sal miserable, and the headmistress refuses to do anything about it except to tell her to "toughen up". She's losing weight, Don, and she looks exhausted. She told me she couldn't sleep for worrying. That she'd rather face the bombs than this girl Mavis who's been making life hell for her.'

'As bad as that?'

'Worse. The child beats her as well. I saw the bruises.'

'The devil she does! I'll have Sal out of there tomorrow morning.' He shook his head. 'She never said a word to us, the poor mite. When we visited for Christmas, she promised us she was as happy as a sandboy at the place.'

'She didn't want you to worry about her. She was quite upset when I wouldn't promise not to tell you, but I knew I had to do something. It's making her ill.'

'I'll have that headmistress's head on a spike for this,' Don muttered.

'Get Sal out of there first. She's better off here, at least until you can find a more suitable home for her. Then you can figure out what to do about Miss Newbould.'

'Aye, I'll not have her there another minute. I don't care what the law says about taking her out of school. They can lock me up for it if they like, but I shan't leave my little girl there to be mistreated.' He nodded to the door, where Lilian had appeared with one of the nurses. 'Here's your sister. It's your turn to go in, Bobby.'

'Yes. All right.' She took a deep breath and got to her feet.

Bobby left Lilian with Don and followed the nurse to the ward where her father was being treated, feeling rather nervous.

She had no idea what she was going to say to him. Suicide was one of those things that happened to other people, never within your own family. It was a subject too shameful for most people to feel comfortable talking about.

Could her dad really not remember that he'd attempted to take his own life? Would he try again if his family weren't there to watch him constantly? It was hard to imagine what the future might hold now that this had happened. It changed everything.

She found herself thinking of Charlie; remembering how calm and firm he'd been the night he'd treated Maid. 'Dependable' wasn't a word Bobby imagined anyone who knew him would use to describe Charlie Atherton, but underneath his flirting and fun, Bobby sensed there was another Charlie – one she could rely on in a time of crisis. There was something reassuring about his presence. She wished he was there with her.

Bobby found her father sitting up in bed. She had been preparing herself to be shocked by his appearance, and he was certainly pale and gaunt with a sickly tinge spread over his flesh, but actually, he didn't look nearly as bad as she'd expected after his ordeal. He had a copy of the *Bradford Courier* spread across his lap, which Bobby guessed Don had brought for him, and was peering at it, frowning.

'Hard work without my glasses, this,' was the first thing he said to her. 'Can't see a bloody thing.'

Bobby took a seat by his bed quietly, although she longed to give him a hug and sob on his neck; let all her feelings out. She knew her father hated any over-the-top display of affection.

'I'll bring them for you,' she said.

'No need. I'll be home tomorrow.' He lifted his gaze from the paper to look at her. 'So you've come back again.'

'I came to see you. Don called and told me you… weren't so well.'

'Load of fuss over nothing,' he muttered, closing the news-paper. 'Never felt better in my life.'

Bobby sighed. 'Dad…'

'Aye?'

'Why didn't you tell anyone the mill had laid you off?'

His eyes glazed, then he scowled. 'They'll be sorry. I'm only fifty. I'll get another job yet.'

'You won't if they catch you drinking at work.'

He shot her a sharp look. 'Who's been telling you lies like that? Never touch a drop but to wash down a meal.'

She reached for his hand. 'I just want you to be safe, Dad,' she said softly. 'I hate to think of you… that is, if you're struggling with things, I really wish you'd talk to us so we can help you.'

'Lot of nonsense. Nowt wrong with me. I'm as fit as a man half my age.'

Bobby lowered her eyes. It was clear that denial was the only way her father could cope with what had happened today, and there seemed to be no way of breaking through that.

'You know we all love you,' she said. 'We want to help you stay safe and happy. All right?'

'That's women's talk.' But he summoned a shaky smile for her. 'Soft lass.'

She smiled too. 'You'll let the women look after you for a while then? Just until you're better.'

'Nowt wrong with me, I keep telling you.' He pressed the hand in his firmly. 'But if it's going to stop you and your sister pecking like hens at me all day and night, you can make a fuss for a little while.'

A nurse had appeared and was lurking around the bed with raised eyebrows, clearly signalling to Bobby that the visiting hour was over. Bobby took the hint and stood up.

'That's all I wanted to hear.' She bent to kiss her father's forehead. 'Take care of yourself, Dad. For me, eh?'

He was silent for a moment, his head lowered.

'I must be a terrible burden to you,' he said quietly.

This, Bobby knew, was as close as he was likely to come to discussing what had really put him in a hospital bed.

273

She looked earnestly into his eyes. 'You mustn't ever think that. You're no such thing, Dad.'

'Aye, well. No point crying about it.' He looked up at her, and when he spoke again, there was an unfamiliar softness in his voice that Bobby hadn't heard there since she was a child. 'I'm right glad you've come home again, Bobby. Right glad.'

Chapter 30

Bobby was in the kitchen of the little house on Southampton Street, cooking a stew for tea, when the door opened. Her father had come down in his dressing gown and slippers and was leaning heavily on the doorframe to support himself.

'Dad,' she said, beaming at him. 'Are you sure you're well enough to be up?'

'I'm as well as I ever was, as I keep telling you,' he said. 'What's more, I'm as hungry as a hunter. What's that you're making, lass? I could smell it from upstairs.'

'Beef stew. Well, it's more gravy stew, but there's at least some meat in it, and I baked bread to mop it up with. You need something heartier than bread and butter for your tea while you're recovering. I'll serve up as soon as Lil gets home from work.' She left the pot bubbling to kiss his cheek. 'You sit down and I'll bring you a cup of tea. There's an ENSA show on the Forces Programme, I think.'

When he'd gone next door to settle into his easy chair by the wireless, Bobby leaned over her pot for a moment, closing her eyes.

She had now been at home a week, and her father's recovery had progressed rapidly. In fact, he was practically thriving after his recent brush with death. Giving himself up fully to rest, freed from the tedium and long hours of the mill and with his daughters attending to his every need, Bobby couldn't remember when she'd seen her father so jolly – or so lucid. The doctors had advised that he refrain from alcohol to give his liver time to heal after what had happened, which the girls had worried was

275

going to be a problem, but other than a few medicinal drafts in the middle of the night to counteract the effect of a nightmare, he'd coped very well. He hadn't asked for it either, which Bobby felt was a good sign. Already he looked healthier, and his daughters were cautiously optimistic that his hospitalisation marked a turning point in their father's battle with his demons.

The only problem was, when he'd told Bobby that day in the hospital that he was glad to have her back, he seemed to believe that was to be a permanent state of affairs. Bobby didn't dare to disabuse him, when he was still fragile and in need of care, but she was starting to wonder what she was going to do about it. Reg had been more than generous in granting her compassionate leave from work, telling her to take as much time as she needed and on full pay too, but she needed to make a decision soon about what she was going to do.

And that wasn't her only worry. There was also Lilian. Bobby had persuaded her twin not to resign her commission in the Wrens just yet, knowing how much it meant to her, and instead Lil had requested deferment for an additional week for compassionate reasons. This, Bobby hoped, would buy them some time while they tried to come up with a solution. But no solution had presented itself, and Lil was due to leave in a month. It was painfully obvious to Bobby now that their father couldn't be allowed to live alone. And yet, why should Lil have to give up on her dreams? It seemed so very unfair.

Finally, there was the question of money. Bobby was earning a paltry pound a week, and although she was sure her siblings would contribute to the household income, things were going to be very tight indeed without her dad's salary from the mill. It was evident that he was no longer in a state of health, either physically or mentally, where he could work long hours without it causing him depression of spirits, and he wasn't a young man either. Bobby had racked her brains, but she just couldn't think of a solution to their problems. Everything seemed… hopeless.

She peeked through the door into the living room, where her father was laughing heartily at a comic song on the wireless.

It made her smile to see him happy, but she felt a little sad too. How long could it last if the status quo at home were to change for him again?

There was a knock at the front door. Bobby wiped her hands on her pinny and went to answer it.

'Knock knock,' Don said when she found him on the doorstep. 'Is Rob laiking out?'

Bobby smiled. 'If you're asking if he's up to the pub then I think it's a little early in his recovery, but I'm sure he'll be thrilled to see you. Come in, Don.'

He followed her into the living room. Her dad got slowly to his feet to clap the younger man on the back.

'I thought I'd stop by while the girls are at the pictures,' Don said, shaking his hand. 'They're gone to see some tripe from Walt Disney – *Pinocchio*, I think it is. I was glad to have an excuse to leave them to it.'

'Pull up a chair and fill your pipe, lad,' Bobby's dad said, gesturing to the seat by the fire.

'Actually, Rob, could you spare your daughter for a moment before I get too comfortable? There was something I wanted to discuss with her privately.'

It was a mark of her dad's trust in Don that he agreed to this without hesitation. He was always cautious about his daughters spending time alone with men, even if they were married.

'You can come into the kitchen, Don,' Bobby said. 'I've a stew you can keep an eye on for me while I brew the pair of you some tea.'

Don followed her in and closed the door behind him. When they were alone, he took a piece of paper covered in type from his pocket and unfolded it.

'You sent this in to the paper,' he said, holding it out to her.

Bobby flushed. 'Oh. Yes.'

It was a report she'd written on what she'd witnessed at the evacuees' boarding school, including all the details of Miss

Newbould's damaging 'methods' and their effect on the children who weren't strong enough for prolonged physical exertion. With it, Bobby had included a letter explaining that this was to be Don's security if the board of governors refused to act on his complaint about Sal's treatment. She could have given it to him directly, of course – he'd visited her father twice since he'd been released from hospital – but somehow sending it to the *Courier*, and to Don in his official position as editor, had felt more proper.

'Like I said in my letter, I don't want a byline or anything like that,' she told him. 'I just want the school to be exposed if the governors won't act on what you've told them. The parents of the children there have a right to know how Miss Newbould is running the place. You can publish it anonymously, or put your name to it if you want. Reg wouldn't like me writing for another publication while I'm employed by *The Tyke*.'

'Bobby, you do know this is an excellent piece of journalism, don't you?'

Bobby frowned. 'Is it?'

Don pulled out a couple of chairs from under the little dining table. 'Here, sit down.'

'Wait a minute. Stew. And tea.'

She turned the stew down and left it to simmer, filled the kettle and put it on the hob to boil, then took a seat. As usual, Don got straight to the point.

'I'm here to offer you a job,' he said.

'But I've got a job.'

'I'm here to offer you a better job. A job that's worthy of your talents – not just women's interest stuff but the real meat. Who's that lady journalist from the last war you were always bending my ear about when you worked for the *Courier*?'

'Dorothy Lawrence,' Bobby murmured.

He waved her report at her. 'This would be the sort of thing she'd do, wouldn't it? Exposing cruelty and mistreatment in a school and knowing what to look for to find it out – someone who can do that is someone I want on my staff, Bobby. Tony wouldn't have been able to write this in a hundred years, and the new cub we hired hardly knows his arse from his elbow. I'm lacking a right-hand man, and I want him to be you.'

'But… what about *The Tyke*?'

Don sighed and put the piece she'd written down on the table between them. '*The Tyke* is a nice enough little magazine for what it is. But as I've told you time and again, you're better than that. Is this really what you imagined for yourself when you said you wanted to be a reporter? Writing pieces about country dances and Thirsk Cricket Club and… I don't know, the mating habits of wood pigeons, for twelve and six a week?'

'A quid a week. Reg gave me a pay rise after Christmas.'

'Did he indeed?' Don leaned back and folded his arms. 'I'll treble it.'

She frowned. 'What?'

'You'll be on the same wage as Tony: three pounds a week, plus your expenses. Not that you aren't worth two of Tony Scott, but that's a good salary for a woman. I've got big plans for the *Courier*, Bobby, and I'd like you to be a part of them – as a fully fledged reporter, not a junior.'

'But—'

'I should think that would be enough to support your dad, if he can't find another job, and it means you can stay here to take care of him – I know it's been on your mind, worrying what's going to happen to him. Not to mention that you'll finally be doing the job you always told me you were desperate for. What do you say?'

'It's… a very generous offer,' she said quietly.

'I bloody know it is. One that can solve all your problems. So?'

Bobby stood up to stir her stew, as much for something to do as anything. She felt dazed.

Don was absolutely right: if she took his job, it would be a solution to everything she'd been worrying about over the past week. Lilian could join the Wrens as planned, knowing their father wouldn't be left to live alone. With a salary of sixty bob a week, money would no longer be such a worry. And Bobby would finally be a reporter – a real, fully fledged reporter on a respected weekly newspaper with a circulation of 60,000. Her job at *The Tyke* had only ever been intended as the first step on the ladder, and now here was Don offering her the chance to jump up several rungs at once.

So why was something holding her back?

'Sorry, Don. I know I ought to jump at the chance, and I'm honestly so thrilled and… and proud you think I'm worth it,' she said with an apologetic smile for her friend. 'But would you mind if I took tonight to sleep on it and talk it over with my sister?'

Don raised an eyebrow. 'Really? I thought you'd be biting my hand off. Are you holding out for a deputy editor position or something?'

'Don't be daft. It's just… it's a big decision. I was really starting to make a life for myself out in the Dales.'

'Are you joking? Sod the Dales, Bobby.'

'I'd miss it, that's all. Miss the people.'

'I swear you must be allergic to success.' Don laughed. 'Or is it a specific person who's holding you back? You haven't got yourself besotted by some country swain out there, have you? Shoulders like oak trees and stinks of cow muck? Bobby, I'd never have believed it of you.'

'It isn't that,' Bobby said, although she couldn't help blushing slightly. 'I'd just grown fond of the place. I've made friends there.'

'I'm offering you everything you ever wanted here, love. You're not seriously going to turn that down for a life tramping through manure in a village so insignificant that it isn't even included on most maps?'

'I'm not turning it down. I'm asking for twenty-four hours to… get my affairs in order.'

'It's a job, Bobby, not death by firing squad.' Don stood up. 'But if that's what you want, so be it. You know where to find me.'

She smiled gratefully. 'Thank you.'

He looked again at the report she'd written on the school at Sumner House. 'You mention a Lady Sumner-Walsh as the owner of this place. Know her, do you?'

'Yes, a little. She was with me when I went to see Sal.'

'Reckon she'd give us a quote to use with this? Always adds credibility if you can say you've got a nob on your side.'

'I think she might. She was ever so angry after she saw what her house was being used for.'

'Right, then I'll let you get in touch with her. Doesn't matter what she says really, so long as she's backing up your version of events. If the governors refuse to cooperate, I'll run this in next week's issue.' He nodded to her. 'And I'll hear from you tomorrow on the other thing, eh?'

–

Lilian was late home – Bobby guessed she'd gone out with one of her boyfriends after work, which she couldn't begrudge her. Her sister needed some relaxation time after what had been a difficult week, and it didn't take both of them to look after Dad. Still, she felt anxious waiting for her twin to come back. She was desperate to discuss Don's job offer with her and know her thoughts on the matter.

Of course, she guessed Lil was going to be all for it. She never had understood what *The Tyke* was all about, and the salary was a big consideration – not to mention the fact that she could then follow her dream of being a Wren after all. Still, Bobby needed to share her thoughts with someone. They were only confusing her, whirling around her head with nowhere to go.

Don couldn't be persuaded to share their tea, but he did stay to spend some time with her father while Bobby washed up afterwards. When she was done, she took off her pinny and went into the living room, where the pair of them were playing Whist.

'I have to go out and make a telephone call,' she said. 'I won't be long.'

She'd decided she may as well kill some time speaking to Topsy Sumner-Walsh as staying at home fretting, and then Don could have his quote before he left.

There was a call box around the corner. Bobby grabbed her coat and handbag from the hall and went out.

It was Mrs Hobbes who answered the phone. There was rather a lot of noise in the background. It sounded like Topsy was having some sort of a gathering.

'Is Lady Sumner-Walsh available to talk briefly?' Bobby asked. 'It's Miss Bancroft.'

'I'll fetch her for you,' Mrs Hobbes said, and a moment later, Topsy herself was on the line.

'Darling!' she said in her usual gushing tone. She sounded a little tipsy. 'Where on earth are you? I thought you'd surely have come back to us by now. It's really quite cruel to stay away when I've got so much jolly company I'm dying to introduce you to.'

'Sorry,' Bobby said. 'I've had to take a leave of absence to come home for a little while. My father's been unwell.'

'Yes, I heard about that. Well, no, actually I thought I heard that he was dead. I'm very glad for your sake that he isn't,' Topsy said earnestly. 'When will you come to see me again? I told Seb Abercrombie all about you and now he's desperate to meet you.'

Bobby felt herself once again being sucked into the whirl-wind world of Topsy Sumner-Walsh and tried to get the conversation back on track.

'I'm not sure when I'll be coming back to Silverdale,' she said. 'My father's still recovering. Listen, I was wondering: did you speak to your godfather? The chair of the school governors?'

'Oh yes, that,' Topsy said in a vague sort of voice. It was clear her attention had moved on to other things since their visit to the school. 'Yes, I rang him directly the next day. He didn't sound at all concerned. A good, healthy way to run a school, he said when I told him about that rotter Miss Newbould – although of course he went to Eton, where they go in for all that sort of thing. And do you know, apparently I can't just have my house back if I don't like it! There's a new law or something that says they can use it for the war effort as long as they like and I can't do a thing about it. Isn't it appalling?'

'Um, yes,' Bobby said. 'My friend sent a complaint too, when he found out the way they'd treated his daughter, but the governors didn't reply. He's the editor of the *Bradford Courier*. Anyhow, he's planning to include a piece I wrote about conditions at the school, since the governors won't take action.'

'Good,' Topsy said with some satisfaction. 'I can't wait to see the look on Miss Newbould's face. She looked frightened to death of that little card you showed her.'

'I was wondering, would you be willing to be quoted? Just to say how shocked you were to find out how your house was being used, or something like that?' Bobby paused. 'Then the children's parents will understand you didn't know anything about it, when it all comes out.' This, she thought, might carry some weight with Topsy.

'Of course, darling, if it will help those poor little children. You make something up and put my name on it.'

'I'd prefer it to come from you.'

'Oh, all right,' Topsy said. 'Then you can quote me as saying… I never liked that ugly, beastly Miss Newbould, and I wasn't surprised at all that she turned out to be a wrong 'un. And I think it's a crime that the government can take people's houses off of them and do whatever it likes with them without the owner's permission, especially when they've been so public-spirited as to offer the use of them. There.'

Bobby ran through this in her head, her lips moving as she tried to formulate it into something that sounded a bit more like a newspaper quote and a bit less like Topsy Sumner-Walsh.

'So what you're saying is, you're shocked at the use to which your house has been put and the treatment of some of the children there, and you hope that those responsible are dealt with accordingly?' Bobby suggested diplomatically.

'Yes, that will be all right, I suppose.'

Bobby fumbled in her bag for her notebook and scribbled this down in shorthand before she forgot it.

'Oh, but darling, I haven't told you my news,' Topsy said gleefully while Bobby wrote, the telephone receiver tucked between her ear and shoulder.

'Hmm?' Bobby's attention was only half on what Topsy was saying as she wrote down her quote.

'Well, it was really all thanks to you that I decided to do it,' Topsy said. 'That little talk we had in the cottage. He really can't be allowed to continue breaking hearts all over the place, and he's such a dear old thing, and so handsome. He'll be even more dangerous when he gets his RAF uniform, I'm sure. It's a public service, really, to take him off the market. And perhaps it shan't be so bad, being a vet's wife. Besides, he can give all that up if he marries me. I've got pots of money I'm not using.'

Bobby frowned. 'I'm not following you.'

'I'm talking about Charlie, darling. I've decided I will have him after all.'

'You've decided…'

'Bobby, don't you understand what I'm telling you? Charlie and I… we're engaged to be married.'

Chapter 31

'You're quiet tonight,' Lilian observed as she and Bobby had a drink together in the Rose and Crown, the pub near their home. Or near Bobby's home. Lilian, who was proudly wearing her WRNS uniform as she savoured the glances of admiring men, would be leaving in the morning for Greenwich.

As it was their last night together, Sarah, their brother's wife, had come over to sit with their father and Bobby had treated her twin to a night on the town: first the pictures to see Lilian's favourite film, *Rebecca*, for the sixth or seventh time, then the pub, and finally dancing. Although dancing was the last thing Bobby was in the mood for tonight.

She had been back in Bradford for one month, only leaving the city for a single short trip to Silverdale to collect her few possessions before starting her new job at the *Courier*. Reg and Mary had been kind to her – so kind that Bobby couldn't help feeling guilty, although she knew she'd done the right thing in resigning from *The Tyke*. What choice did she have, after all? Her father needed her, and the job Don had offered her was too good to turn down. It was exactly the sort of journalism she'd dreamed of all her life.

Reg had been understanding about her father's predicament, although, of course, she hadn't shared the full truth of what had happened that night. Instead, she'd told her employer that her father had taken an accidental overdose of his sleeping powder after losing his glasses. Reg had waived her notice period at the magazine, told her she was a grand little worker and he was proud of her, then shaken her hand vigorously and wished her well. Mary had hugged her tightly, promised not to forget her and to write regularly, and said that Bobby must visit her 'country mother' as often as she could. Bobby had paid a visit to Andy Jessop too, who'd thanked her for everything she'd done for him and expressed his hope that she'd return for his wedding to Ginny in March, and to Topsy Sumner-Walsh, who had pouted prodigiously when she'd discovered she wasn't going to be able to talk her new friend out of leaving.

Charlie she hadn't seen. In fact, she'd avoided going anywhere she might encounter him, staying away from his little barn-cottage-surgery, the pub and his other haunts. If she saw him, she'd have to congratulate him on his upcoming wedding to Topsy, and Bobby knew the words would stick in her throat.

She didn't know why, really. Of course, she'd known he was in love with Topsy from the moment she'd seen them together. There was no betrayal in the case. Charlie was a free agent, and there'd never been any sort of understanding between him and Bobby. In fact she'd actively pushed him away, romantically speaking, knowing that out of every man she'd known, Charlie Atherton was the only one who could prove a real threat to everything she had planned for her career. And yet she knew, as soon as Topsy had told her she was to be Charlie's wife, that she could no longer live and work in Silverdale.

But this too must pass, Bobby told herself. She'd soon settle into her new routine back home, and then Charlie, Topsy, *The Tyke*, Silverdale... it would all be a distant memory. It was better that way. Soon, she was sure, she'd even stop dreaming about the place.

'Penny for your thoughts then?' Lilian said when her sister remained silent.

'Last night I dreamt I went to Silverdale again.' Bobby laughed softly and took a sip of her half-pint.

'You've lost me, love.'

'Oh, I'm being daft. I had a dream last night that I was back in the Dales. Only it was... different. It was all different. You know at the start of the picture, when Joan Fontaine's looking through the mist and overgrown trees, she sees Manderley and it's become a ruin?'

'You didn't dream that, did you?' Lilian shook her head. 'We've seen that film too many times.'

'It wasn't like that. It was Silverdale, just as it was when I lived there.' Bobby sighed. 'But everyone had forgotten me. It was just the same as when I first arrived there in the autumn. All those people I'd come to know well, looking at me with dislike and suspicion. Even Mary, who was always so kind to me. Even… even Charlie.'

'You think about him a lot,' Lilian said softly.

Bobby didn't have the energy to lie; not any more.

'Yes,' she said quietly. 'I didn't realise how much I felt for him until he was gone.'

'If you have feelings for him, why don't you tell him?'

'What good will that do? He's engaged to someone else, Lil. Someone wealthy and lively and attractive, who I could never hope to compete with. Someone I know he's in love with – I've seen it with my own eyes.'

'But he kissed you, didn't he?'

Bobby grimaced. 'I wish I'd never told you about that.'

'Well, didn't he?'

'Charlie kisses a lot of people, I should imagine. If I try to convince myself he's got feelings for me simply because he flirts with me, I'm going to have to join a long queue of other women with the same idea.' She finished her drink. 'Anyhow, things have worked out for the best. It was fate, really, Topsy stepping in when she did. I can tell exactly what would have happened if I'd allowed my feelings to go any further down that road.'

'What?'

'Nine chances out of ten, I'd have had my heart broken. Charlie isn't the settling kind – not with anyone who isn't Topsy Sumner-Walsh, at any rate – and he's never taken any pains to hide that from me.'

'You don't know that,' Lilian said. 'From what you've told me, he does sound fond of you. I thought as much from the moment he sent you that telegram.'

'Perhaps he is fond of me, but he's in love with Topsy. And if he settles for me because he can't have Topsy, where does that leave me? Trapped in a home with a husband whose affections are lukewarm at best, with everything I ever wanted to achieve in life snatched away from me.'

'I suppose when you put it like that…'

'It's for the best, Lil. The logical part of my brain knows that, and it knows how lucky I am to have been spared. My heart's going to take a little time to catch up, that's all.'

'Will you go to the old man's wedding?' Lilian asked. An invitation from Andy and Ginny had arrived with the post that morning. 'I suppose your friend Charlie will be there.'

'The whole village will be. Silverdale doesn't do weddings by halves.' Bobby lapsed into silence, sipping her beer. 'I don't know. I'm not a part of the place any more. I can't help thinking it would be like my dream, everyone giving me the cold shoulder and acting as if they barely know me.'

'But it was all your doing. You helped him with his wooing.'

'I know. I'd like to go and give my congratulations to Andy, but… we shall see.' Bobby slid her glass to Lilian. 'Let's have another, and talk about something more cheerful. I can't go dancing in this mood, and I want to be able to say I saw you off properly.'

'All right.' Lilian hesitated, and reached for her sister's hand. 'Bob, you are happy, aren't you? I'd have resigned my commission like a shot if I'd thought this wasn't what you wanted, but the job at the *Courier* sounded like what you've been hoping for your entire life.'

'It is.' Bobby summoned a smile. 'It's just taking me a little time to adjust to the sudden change in my life, that's all. I am happy, Lil. You're right, I've got everything I always wanted, and I don't need to feel guilty any more about not being here for Dad. When you're home on leave I'll be dancing a jig and waving my stockings in the air for sheer joy, I promise you.'

–

'Your assignment for today,' Don said when Bobby got to work the next morning. He chucked a file of papers on to her desk. 'I want you to sift through this lot. It's some cuttings and background information on a case going to trial at the assizes this afternoon that I want you to report on. Nasty business.'

'What is it?' Bobby asked as she sat down.

'Sex crime. Rape and murder of a nineteen-year-old girl from over Clayton way who was walking home from a dance in the blackout. The man responsible was a respected parish councillor and father of two, apparently. I don't trust Tony with stories like this. He's too prone to collecting salacious details at the expense of the key facts.'

Bobby shuddered. 'That poor girl. I hope they hang the bastard.'

Don sat down at his desk to pore over some proofs. 'Don't let your heart rule your head, Bobby. Be a journalist first and a woman second if you want to make it in this game. You don't need an opinion. You need a story.'

'Yes. All right.'

Bobby started working her way through the information in the file Don had given her, making notes on anything that seemed relevant.

The case was horrific, and Bobby was forced to go through every detail as she made her notes ready for the trial. The information in the file included a coroner's report, among other things, and a photograph of the body. The girl, Pauline Barwick, had been strangled with one of her own stockings. She looked so young…

By dinnertime, Bobby was feeling rather queasy.

'I'll go out for some pies, shall I?' she said to Don.

'You don't have to do that any more,' he said without looking up from his work. 'Your time's too valuable to waste on errands. The kid can get the pies when he gets back.'

'Right.'

Tony arrived with Len, the new sixteen-year-old junior reporter.

'Oh, nice,' Tony said when he'd approached Bobby's desk to see what she was working on. He picked up the photograph of the murdered girl. 'How come you're getting all the juicy stories these days, Bobby? Editor's pet.'

'You'd have been welcome to this one,' Bobby said, wrinkling her nose. 'This poor girl went through hell before she was killed. It's traumatic even reading about it.'

'Front page for that one, then. Nothing sells papers like sex and death, especially if you can get the two together.' He glanced at Don. 'Why is she getting this sort of thing to report on while I'm out covering peeping toms at ATS barracks and disputes about errant husbands not paying their wives maintenance? I'm the more experienced journalist.'

'Because she's a better writer than you,' Don told him shortly. 'Not to mention that I trust her to actually go where she's sent and not to the nearest pub.'

Tony grinned, unperturbed at this summary of his professional skills.

'Are we playing darts tonight?' he asked.

Bobby shook her head. 'I can't. My sister left this morning for Greenwich. My dad'll be waiting for me to make his tea.'

'Oh, come on. Leave the old man to open a tin of corned beef or something. We never win when you're not there.'

'I can't, Tony.' She stood up and grabbed her handbag. 'I'm going out to get the pies. I need some fresh air.'

–

When Bobby arrived home after work, she went through her usual routine: checking that the kitchen cupboard where she stored her dad's alcohol was still locked, looking to see that no glasses were by the sink with the smell of booze on them. When she'd satisfied herself that all was as it should be, she called up the stairs to her father.

'Dad?'

He appeared at the top of the stairs in his vest, his face covered in shaving foam.

'Where the devil have you put my razor blades?' he demanded. 'I've looked a right daft bugger this last half hour, covered in foam with nowt to get it off.'

Bobby couldn't help laughing, and her dad gave a reluctant smile too.

'You know I keep them locked away,' she said. His razor blades were sealed in the same cupboard as his whisky, along with the bread knife and carving knife.

'Damn fool thing to do, when you know I need to shave,' he muttered. 'Don't see why you can't leave them by the sink, same as usual.'

'I want to keep an eye on how many are left. We need to make things like that last, Dad. You know, shortages and everything.'

That was the explanation she and Lilian had decided to give him, and he seemed to accept it – or at least he pretended to.

'I'll fetch you one.' She went to get it, then followed him upstairs and pretended to be doing something in her own room so she could watch him shave.

'You go downstairs,' she said when he'd finished. 'I'm going to make some bread and cheese for tea, then if you like we can have a game of cards and listen to the evening play together.'

'When's your sister coming home?'

'She's gone, Dad. Do you remember? Lilian left this morning to go to her war work down south. It's just us now.'

'Oh aye,' her dad said vaguely. 'That's right. I'd forgotten.'

As soon as he'd gone downstairs, Bobby took the blade from his razor, rinsed it and slipped it into her pocket to go back in the cupboard. Then she went to brew the tea and prepare their food.

While she made the cheese on toast, Bobby reflected on how the same food tasted different here to how it did in the countryside. Perhaps it was because the cheese in Silverdale was made by dairy farmers from their own herds. Bobby couldn't say where Mary Atherton got her flour from, but wherever it was, the bread it made was a darn sight tastier than the gritty brown loaves they lived on here in the city.

What would her friends in Silverdale be doing now, Bobby wondered? The carriage clock in the living room had chimed six. Mary and Reg would be having their own tea now, she supposed. She thought wistfully of bacon and scones. Perhaps Charlie would have joined them, as he sometimes did of an evening – Mary insisted that he couldn't live every night on 'bachelor fare' and must have a proper hot meal inside him now and again. Or perhaps he was at the cottage in the grounds of Sumner House, bathing in the smiles of his betrothed. Bobby speared a slice of bread rather too violently with her toasting fork and held it up to the flames of the kitchen fire to brown.

And then… what usually happened next? Bobby would stay in the kitchen to help Mary clean up after the meal while the men went into the parlour to discuss the war, the state of the government, and generally put the world to rights over pipes and cigarettes. Bobby and Mary would join them, everyone would settle where they liked best, and they'd spend a pleasant evening listening to the wireless or gramophone records while the men smoked and the women knitted or sewed, a wolfhound occasionally laying its huge grey head in your lap.

'Damn!' Bobby dropped the slice of flaming toast and sucked her fingers. She'd been too lost in her daydream of days gone by to notice the flames licking around it. Cursing, she tossed it into the fire and went to cut another slice.

That wouldn't do. Food was scarce enough without her Silverdale nostalgia costing them bread.

Nostalgia. The word made her think of Andy Jessop; how he'd spat the word to her the day she'd gone to interview him. He'd been absolutely right, of course: the past always looked better when you didn't have to live in it. Bobby thought with affection now of her quiet evenings with Reg and Mary, a picture of domestic bliss, but at the time she had missed her life at home terribly – missed the excitement of the city, with its dance halls and cinemas where the young people who had been her friends were enjoying themselves. And now she was back at home, it was Silverdale that haunted her thoughts. It seemed she was destined never to be satisfied, even while she had everything she'd always said she wanted. She carried through the tea on a tray, silently berating herself for her ingratitude.

'Where've you been all day?' her dad asked as she put the tea down on the coffee table and poured them each a cup.

'At work. It's Tuesday, Dad.'

'Aye, that's right,' he said vaguely. He roused himself. 'What work have you been doing?'

'I was reporting on a criminal case. I spent all morning making notes, then this afternoon I went to watch the trial.'

'What was the trial for?'

She suppressed a shudder. Making notes on the case had been traumatic enough, but the trial had been even worse. As well as quite horrific levels of detail about the rape and murder of poor Pauline Barwick, there had been tearful statements from her parents and fiancé that had made it very hard for Bobby to remember Don's advice that she shouldn't let her heart rule her head. Her instinct had been to stand up and scream at the judge that if he didn't hang the man then he was a fool, and the defending counsel ought to be bloody ashamed of himself for sticking up for him. However, she had managed to keep her temper and avoid a charge of contempt of court.

'Murder,' she told her dad. 'A girl of nineteen. She'd been… interfered with. Interfered with and then strangled.'

Her dad frowned. 'I don't like you knowing about such things, Bobby.'

'It's my job, Dad. I don't have any choice. Besides, I'd rather know about them as not. Otherwise, I wouldn't know the dangers that are out there for women.'

'Will they hang him, this man?'

'Yes, there was a unanimous guilty verdict. I'm glad. That means he won't be able to hurt anyone else.'

Still, she had pitied the man's wife as he'd been escorted from the dock. The wife had been pale and stern, staring straight ahead as he'd been marched away and refusing to meet his eye. It was she who would have to explain what had happened to their two young daughters. The man had ruined so many other lives when he'd chosen to take just one.

Bobby found it hard to understand how her colleagues were able to deal so calmly with cases such as this. She'd seen them sift through folders of information like the one she'd been given today a dozen times when she was still a humble typist. Don was entirely impartial, emotionless and professional when he wrote reports on murders and sex crimes: the consummate newspaperman. Tony, as Don had observed, seemed to relish the most gruesome and salacious facts about such cases, writing reports on them that read like something from a penny dreadful. Bobby could tell when he'd stumbled over something 'juicy', as he described it, because he always let out a long, low whistle before scribbling it down in his notebook.

Was it because she was a woman that she found herself filled with anger when she covered these stories, as Don had suggested? Was that why the details turned her stomach? Or was it because she was still new to the newspaper game? Perhaps Bobby, too, would one day be able to look at a photograph of a murdered girl with nothing but a low whistle, taking pleasure in the fact that her story would make a compelling item on the front page.

Bobby didn't much relish the thought of becoming hardened to those sorts of cases. It felt right that they should be shocking to her, and worrying that she could ever find them otherwise.

And yet this was important, wasn't it? It was real journalism, informing the public that a crime had been committed, that justice had been done, and warning them about the dangers that might await them outside their front doors. If Dorothy Lawrence could serve in the trenches, witnessing first-hand all those horrors that Bobby knew about only through her father's nightmares, then she could surely cope with reporting on the occasional murder. She needed to learn to be pragmatic and detached, that's all, as Don was.

There was a knock at the door, and Bobby pulled herself from her reverie.

'I suppose that must be Sarah with the bairns,' she said to her father as she stood up. 'She said she might come over tonight to sit with us. I imagine she thinks we'll be missing Lil.'

She went to answer the door, but it wasn't her sister-in-law and nieces who stood on the step outside.

It was Charlie.

Chapter 32

'Charlie.' She blinked a few times, reassuring herself it was actually him and not a vision conjured by her overheated brain.

'I'm sorry to turn up out of the blue like this. I had to come and talk to you. It was an emergency,' he said, an anxious look on his face. 'Can I come inside?'

Bobby hesitated, her heart thumping as her head spun. It felt strange seeing him here. He looked wrong in Bradford, somehow, like a mirage. Like a dream of Manderley.

'Why are you here?' she asked, still blocking the doorway.

He caught the expression on her face. 'Don't worry, I haven't come to try and kiss you or anything like that. It's about Reg, not me. He's too proud to admit... Well, I'd rather tell you inside. It's chilly out here.'

'We can't talk inside. My father's there. He doesn't like me consorting with strange men.'

For the first time, Charlie's worried expression lifted into a smile. 'I've missed you calling me a strange man, Bobby.'

She almost smiled back but managed to restrain herself.

'Hold on,' she said. 'I'll make sure everything's locked up that ought to be locked up, then we can go to the pub around the corner while he has his tea.'

After she'd made her excuses to her father and left him to his toasted cheese, Bobby led Charlie to the Rose and Crown.

'What did you have to lock up?' Charlie asked as he followed her down the dark streets.

'Just valuables and things,' Bobby said, grimacing slightly at the lie. 'Not that we have many, but there are my mother's pearls.'

'You never said goodbye, you know,' he said quietly. 'Before you left.'

'I felt that was best.'

'Yes. I suppose I can see why you'd feel that.' He was silent for a moment. 'This is where you're from, is it?'

She nodded. 'I was born here.'

'It's very... small.'

'Bradford? No it isn't.'

'I mean the spaces are small. I can't imagine living somewhere as a kid where you couldn't run and run when you wanted to.'

'Well, we didn't all have your privilege,' Bobby told him shortly. 'We're born where the universe decides to drop us. It isn't a matter of choice.'

When they reached the Rose and Crown, she ushered him inside and allowed him to buy her a drink, since she was too tired to argue about it.

'Where's Boxer?' she asked when they were seated in the snug.

'I thought I'd better come on the train. It's a long journey for a little horse, especially pulling a great heavy lump like me.' He took out a cigarette and lit it. 'Bobby... there's no easy way to put this. I need your help.'

She frowned. 'You do?'

'Not only me. I'm here partly as an emissary from Mary. There's a crisis occurring at Moorside, and you're the only one who can help us out of it.'

'Is everyone all right?'

He shook his head. 'Reggie isn't. He's had the flu for a week now, and if he keeps on as he is doing, he's going to end up with pneumonia or something worse. Mary's worried to death about him. He's been running a temperature of a hundred and five, and he just won't do as she and the doctor tell him and stay in bed.'

'I'm very sorry to hear that,' Bobby said. 'But I don't understand how I can—'

'Here.' He fished in his pocket and handed her an envelope. 'I brought a letter from Mary. She was going to post it to you, but I thought it might help if I delivered it by hand. It explains everything.'

She frowned as she read it.

Dearest Bobby,

I hate to be a nuisance. I know you must be very busy with your new job and caring for your father, but I'm honestly at my wit's end with Reg, and I've been left with no choice but to beg for a favour.

The copy for the next edition of that blasted magazine is supposed to go to the printer Tuesday next, and Reggie is far too ill to be out of bed. But he won't be told! Twice this week I've found him barefoot at his desk, tapping on that infernal machine of his. Goodness knows what nonsense he was writing, when you could practically burn your hand on his forehead. And this morning, the final straw when I found him sprawled on the parlour floor on top of a pile of papers. He had a dizzy spell, collapsed to the ground, and his stick rolled out of his reach so he couldn't get himself right again. He was there two hours before I woke and heard him calling for me from downstairs. Men are such children when they are ill, don't you find?

He refuses to delay the magazine's deadline, and so, dearest Bobby, your country mother finds she is forced to ask for your help. I've got it out of Reg that this March magazine is almost complete, but there is the Editor's Journal section still to write, as well as some miscellaneous items of copy to finish and all the articles to be read, *corrected and typed clean before they are sent for galley proofs to be made up. It can't be more than a single day's work, I believe, or perhaps two at the most. No one else knows the magazine as Reg does: only you. Of course, you would be paid for your time at the same rate as in your new job, and if you wanted to bring your father along and stay overnight, Charlie has said his cottage is yours for as long as you need it. Please do let me know by return of post if you would be able to help your old friends in Silverdale one last time.*

 All my best love,
 Mary

'Is Reg going to be all right?' Bobby asked when she had finished reading.

'If he stays in bed and does as the doctor orders, he'll be as right as ninepence in a fortnight. If he doesn't, he's going to put himself in hospital. I'm amazed he didn't catch his death last night, on the floor for two hours in his pyjamas and bare feet.' Charlie put out the last of his cigarette and regarded her earnestly. 'Will you come? It's only you and Reggie who know what's needed, and he's in a state of delirium half the time with the fever. My brother's too proud to ask you to come himself, but he wishes he had your help: I heard him say as much in a lucid moment. As Mary says, you can stay in my cottage. I'm preparing to move out anyhow.'

Of course. He would be getting ready to move in with Topsy after the wedding, wouldn't he? That meant it must be soon. And one day, after the war, Charlie would be living with her in the big house: lord of the manor, if you please, like Maxim de Winter in *Rebecca*. That definitely didn't suit him. Charlie was very much of the irresponsible younger son persuasion; not at all the stuff country squires were made of.

Would he be an actual lord, since Topsy was a lady? Perhaps he would. Very odd to consider it. Or would Topsy lose her title for marrying a commoner, the way people did in books? Bobby wasn't quite sure how these things worked in modern times.

'If I came, I'd have to bring my father,' she said.

'That's all right. There's room in the cottage for you both. I'll stay in the farmhouse.'

Bobby hesitated.

Did she really want to go back to Silverdale? She'd been trying so hard to banish the place and its occupants from her mind, and now here it was again, back to haunt her. Charlie Atherton, too – the part of Silverdale she'd been trying to banish harder than all the rest. And now he was sitting right in front of her, looking at her with those hard-to-resist brown eyes.

'It sounds like there's a lot of work still to do,' she said. 'Are you sure it could be done in two days, if I were to work on it over Saturday and Sunday this week?'

Charlie flashed her a grateful smile. 'I knew you'd help us.'

'For Reg's sake, and Mary's,' she said, in case he should think it was him she was keen to do favours for. 'But you didn't answer my question. Will there be enough time this weekend?'

'Reggie says it can be finished in no more than a couple of days, if you're happy to work on the Sabbath. I'll help you however I can and use Boxer to take it to Settle to drop off with the printer on Monday.'

'I'm surprised you'll have the time.' She took a sip of her beer, which had gone largely untasted so far. 'Aren't you busy making arrangements for the wedding?'

He laughed. 'The wedding? I'd say I'd done my part by agreeing to be involved in the thing. No, Bobby, I'm all yours.'

So that was it, was it? The only reference to his upcoming nuptials she was going to get from him. The last time she'd seen Charlie, he'd been anxious to explain his presumption in kissing her on New Year's Eve – a kiss that had all been a drunken mistake apparently; that had meant nothing at all to him. The next she'd heard, he was engaged to Topsy Sumner-Walsh. Bobby felt she was owed at least an apology for his ungentlemanly behaviour, if not an explanation. She had deliberately mentioned the wedding to raise the subject and give him that opportunity. But apparently, Charlie felt he'd acted perfectly properly in playing with the feelings of two women at once – not to mention who knew how many more.

But she wasn't going to hold Charlie's behaviour against Reg and Mary. The Athertons had both been kind to her in their different ways. They'd given her a start in the world of journalism and welcomed her into their home like a member of the family. Bobby owed them everything, and now they needed her.

'I'll come straight after work on Friday,' she told Charlie.

–

'Where are we going?' Bobby's dad grumbled as she helped him board the train at Forster Square Station.

'I told you, Dad. We're going for a weekend away in the country.'

'What for? We were fine at home.'

'Because I promised to do a favour for some friends there. Besides, the fresh air will do you good.'

'Huh.' But he consented to take a seat in the compartment while Bobby loaded their small cases into the overhead racks.

She was hoping he might cheer up when they boarded the Pennine bus to Silverdale. It had been a long time since she had visited the countryside with her father, but she did remember their family trips to Baildon Moor on the Whitsuntide holiday when she and her siblings had been bairns: how he'd breathed the moorland air deeply and exhorted them to games of Chase and Hide and Seek, waxing lyrical about the health benefits of fresh air. However, it was already dark when they got to Skipton, and in the blackout none of the countryside was visible.

Charlie met them at the Bull and Heifer with his pony and trap. The trap was built for two and it was a tight squeeze to get them all in, but they managed it. Bobby found herself pressed far more closely against Charlie than she was comfortable with, her suitcase on her lap. She tried not to dwell on the feeling of his warm body against hers, reminding herself that she had even more reason now to be wary of him, since he was engaged to another woman. But it was only one weekend, and then, hopefully, they wouldn't have to see one another again.

She shivered, and told herself it was the cold.

When they reached the little barn-home that Charlie called Cow House Cottage, he left the trap next to Reg's old car at the bottom of the track and led Boxer to the stable. Then he showed them both inside.

'It's a bachelor establishment so I can't offer you any great luxuries,' he said as he showed them around. 'As I told Bobby, Mr Bancroft, I'm in the middle of moving out at the moment, but all the important furniture is still in place. There is electricity and a telephone – I had one installed when I put part of the building to use as a veterinary surgery.' He opened a door. 'My surgery's in here. I wouldn't go in there, unless you particularly enjoy the smell of ether and examining bull emasculators.'

'Did you find someone to take on your practice?' Bobby asked.

'The vet at Smeltham has an assistant he's minded to make a partner. He's planning to hire another junior so he can take on my work here too.'

'So Cow House Cottage is going to be empty.' Of course when he returned from the war, it would be Topsy's home Charlie would be going to, not his own.

'Yes.' He cast a wistful look at the examination table in his surgery. 'I'd be lying if I said I wouldn't miss the work, and this place. I've lived here since I graduated from college and it's been a cosy little home to me. But England expects that every man will do his duty, as the old saying goes.'

Bobby's father had maintained a frosty silence since Charlie had picked them up. She could sense he was suspicious of this young man who was all smiles and bonhomie with his daughter. But he broke his silence now.

'Off to war, are you?' he asked in his usual gruff way.

'Yes, the RAF,' Charlie said. 'I'm going this summer, once I've made arrangements to hand over my practice.'

'I read in the paper as vets were reserved.'

'That's right. I volunteered.'

'Volunteered, did you?' Bobby's dad looked at him keenly. 'Which are you then, lad? Brave or stupid?'

'Possibly both. I don't suppose I'll find out until I get up there.'

Her father seemed to approve of this answer, and he treated Charlie to a rare smile.

Charlie showed them around the rest of the cottage, which consisted of two bedrooms, a parlour and a kitchen, all on the same level, with an outhouse it shared with the main farmhouse. It was an odd sort of place, Bobby felt, with a character all of its own. Clearly it had never been intended as a home, unless it was for residents of the four-legged variety, but some enterprising Atherton ancestor had managed to turn it into one. There were two windows, one at each end of the barn, with a ladder needed to reach them, and numerous small slits in the walls that had been plugged up with plaster to ensure no light spilled out during the blackout. The bedrooms were more like stalls, with partition walls to separate them from the parlour but no ceiling. Apart from the surgery, which was in an attached side building, all the rooms were divided in the same way: separated by a stone partition wall from the neighbouring rooms but sharing the same high-beamed ceiling. It made Bobby feel a little like she was in a dolls' house.

'Have you both eaten?' Charlie asked when he'd finished giving them the tour. 'Mary said you must go up to the house for a supper if you hadn't had anything.'

'That's all right. I brought a packet of sandwiches for us to have on the train,' Bobby said. 'It's after nine and I don't want to disturb Reg, since he's supposed to be resting. I'll see them both in the morning.'

'All right. I'm sleeping in the old nursery tonight so I'll see you at breakfast, ready to do whatever journalistic task you think my big stupid brain can manage.'

Bobby glanced at her father, who was examining a shelf of books in Charlie's parlour.

'Could you, um, show me where the privy is again, please?' she asked Charlie.

He frowned. 'I'd have thought you'd remember that. You lived here for months.'

'Yes, but... I'd like a reminder. Please.'

'All right.'

She followed Charlie outside and closed the door behind them.

'Ah,' he said. 'You don't want to know where the privy is.'

'No. I want to ask you to do something for me.'

He put one hand on his heart. 'Anything, fair lady.'

'Firstly, I want you to cut that out. I didn't come back to be flirted with. Secondly, if you're not busy tomorrow and you really want to help me, would you do something with my dad? Go for a walk on the moors or something?'

'I thought you needed help with the magazine.'

'All I need is a word with Reg, if he's well enough, and access to his typewriter. After that, I think I'll be better off being left alone to get the job done. Civilians will only slow me down.'

He laughed. 'Is this the same girl I met in October, who worried she didn't have what it took to make it as a junior reporter? Now you're all set for a temporary editorship.'

'Well, will you do it?'

'If it's really going to be more use to you than being an extra pair of hands on the magazine. I'm sure your father can take care of himself though, can't he? I got the sense he didn't like me much. He's barely spoken a word to me all the way here.'

'He's warming to you, I think,' Bobby said, smiling. 'Anyhow, I'd feel more secure knowing you were with him.'

'Why's that?'

'Because… he doesn't know the area. He might get lost or be headbutted by Troy or savaged by a rampant Norman. I'd feel better knowing he was with someone who knew their way around. He enjoys country walking – at least, he used to.'

'All right, if that's what's going to be the most help to you.' Before she could register what was going on, Charlie had leaned forward and planted a single kiss on her cheek. 'It's good to have you back where you belong, Bobby Bancroft.'

Chapter 33

Breakfast was always served promptly at half past seven at Moorside Farm, weekends no exception. Bobby woke her father early, and, having persuaded him to dress and wash himself at the small basin in Charlie's surgery, she took him to the farmhouse. Mary was in the kitchen frying bacon, with Charlie seated at the table waiting hungrily for his grub.

'Good morning,' he said, smiling at them. 'Did you both sleep well?'

'Aye, not bad,' Bobby's dad muttered.

'Mary, this is my father, Robert Bancroft,' Bobby said. 'Dad, this is Mrs Mary Atherton. She was very kind to me when I was working here.'

Mary wiped her hand on her apron and held it out. 'Welcome to our home, Mr Bancroft. It's our pleasure to have you here. I must apologise that my husband can't be here to greet you, but he's rather unwell, I'm afraid.'

Bobby's dad, whose default state of curmudgeonliness had been exacerbated by finding himself in an unfamiliar place, softened rather in the face of Mary's warm welcome. He consented to smile. Everyone always did smile for Mary.

'Thank you,' he said, shaking her hand.

'You must be very proud of this daughter of yours. We loved having her here with us. Such a well-brought-up young lady.'

Bobby's dad glanced at her. 'Aye. I am that.'

Bobby patted his arm, touched.

'Take a seat, please,' Mary said. 'I hope you're both hungry. I've cooked enough to feed the five thousand this morning, not knowing what appetite you were likely to have.'

Bobby laughed. 'I think we can manage to do it justice, can't we, Dad?'

'I don't think I'll struggle,' he said, almost jovial now Mary had put him at his ease.

Bobby examined Mary, who looked tired. There was a fretful look in her eyes she was trying to hide, but Bobby couldn't help noticing it.

'How's the patient, Mary?' she asked.

'Oh, he's as stubborn as a mule and as sullen as a schoolboy,' Mary said, giving the bacon in her pan an exasperated poke. 'Thank goodness you've come, Bobby. You're the only one who'll know how to deal with him. He won't trust anyone but you with his precious magazine and he won't postpone the deadline. He's determined to finish it for Tuesday, even if he kills himself in the process.'

'Is he no better?'

She sighed. 'A little. The fever's dropped this morning, but he complains his head is aching and his chest feels like sandpaper and of a hundred other things. You know, I never appreciate the hard work done by nurses until my Reg is ill.'

Mary put a plate of bacon and eggs on the table, and the men started helping themselves.

'My Nell used to say I were worse than the bairns when I were badly,' Bobby's dad observed. 'I think women like to make a fuss about their men making a fuss.' He glanced at Mary. 'But they're good to us. Better than we deserve.'

Bobby shot him a surprised look. It wasn't like her father to contribute such a long speech to the conversation unprompted, especially with strangers. For a moment he'd almost sounded like his old self, as he had when her mother was alive. He didn't seem to notice her looking at him, tucking happily into his bacon and eggs.

Mary laughed. 'I can't deny it gives the village house-wives summat to gossip about, comparing menfolk,' she said. 'Everyone likes to think theirs is worse. We wouldn't swap you though.' She rapped Charlie's knuckles with her wooden spoon as he reached for more bacon. 'Although happen any wife of yours will say different, Charlie Atherton. I swear you'll eat me out of house and harbour before I get you safely wed. Leave some of that bacon for the guests.'

Charlie thrust his hands into his pockets in a comical manner, like Billy Bunter caught with his fingers in the biscuit jar. 'Sorry, Mam.'

Mary glanced at Bobby. 'Not eating, love?'

'I will in a minute,' she said. 'But if Reg is awake, do you mind if I see him first? I don't feel right eating without seeing how he is.'

'Aye, you'd do well to go in now while he's not feverish. I don't want to wake him once he's nodded off again.'

'Does he know I'm here?'

'Not yet. He'd have been tumbling down the stairs in the middle of the night to talk to you about the magazine if I'd told him when you'd arrived. You go up, and I'll try to keep Charlie's fingers off the bacon for you.'

–

Bobby left them to their breakfast and made her way upstairs, past the nursery that had been her old room to the bedroom Reg shared with Mary. She knocked on the door, and a moment later, a hoarse voice bade her come in.

Reg was propped up in bed on a stack of pillows, looking hollow-eyed and his flesh a little yellow. A bottle of evil-smelling medicine sat on the bedside table beside him, and there was a piece of paper poking out from under one pillow where it had been inexpertly concealed.

Bobby frowned at him. 'What's that under your pillow, Reg?'

'Nowt.'

'It's some copy, isn't it? Have you been subbing in bed while Mary wasn't looking?'

He managed something like his old grin. 'Aye, well, what my missus don't know won't hurt her.'

She held out her hand, looking stern. 'Give it to me.'

Reluctantly he handed it over, with the air of a naughty schoolboy.

'So you're back, are you?' he grunted.

'I am. Pleased to see me?'

'Huh. Wouldn't know about that. But since you're here, you might as well sit down.'

Bobby sat in Mary's chair by the bed, suppressing a smile.

Men, honestly. However such a ridiculous species had come to rule the world she had no idea. Her father was exactly the same: incapable of properly expressing joy or happiness, or melancholy or hurt, no matter how deeply felt it was, because his pride wouldn't let him. Were these emotions really so unmanly, when every human being had them? It wasn't every day that Bobby felt glad to belong to 'the gentler sex' – a term she felt sure had been coined by someone who had never met Miss Newbould – but just now, she was glad that she had society's permission to show how she felt without being expected to conceal it.

It was evident that Reg was pleased to see her in spite of his words. His eyes, watery from his recent bout of illness, had crinkled at the corners when she'd come in, and he'd shuffled up eagerly on the pillows. She knew he wanted her here; Charlie had said so. But he was a man, of course, and it was a matter of pride with him to pretend he could cope even after days of fever and delirium. He had to act as though it was only with the greatest reluctance he now tolerated her help, and for the sake of his manly pride, Bobby would have to go along with it.

Thankfully, having grown up with a father and two brothers and after working in the almost exclusively male environment of the *Courier*, Bobby knew how to handle men. What she had to do now was make Reg think that letting her take over the mag for a day or two was all his idea.

'What brings you here then?' he asked, reaching for the medicine bottle and taking a swig of what was in it. It smelt foul, and judging by the face he made, it tasted even worse.

'I brought my dad for the weekend, to show him where I used to live,' she said airily. 'I thought it would do him good now he's suitably recovered from his illness. Mary mentioned in her last letter that you weren't so well, so I thought I'd drop in and see how you were bearing up.'

'*Courier* treating you well? Getting lots of big stories?'

She smiled. 'Come on, Reg, I know you've read them.'

'Happen I might've seen a couple of your bylines,' he admitted grudgingly. 'Not bad, lass.'

'How are things with *The Tyke*? I suppose you must be going to print with the March edition soon,' she said, as nonchalantly as she could.

'Aye, Tuesday.' He broke into a fit of coughing. 'If I could only shake this damned foolishness, I could have it finished by Monday. Mary keeps hiding it all from me. I tell her the fever's gone, but she's got me sealed in here like a bloody prisoner of war.'

'I'm sorry to hear that. Can no one help you finish it off? Charlie?'

'That hulking idiot? It's a magazine, not a colicky horse.' He coughed again. 'No one knows the mag but me. No one knows what it's all about – its tone, its humour, what needs to be done before it's ready.'

'Well, that's not really true.' Bobby paused for a short moment to give more impact to her words. 'I mean, I know those things, don't I?'

'Huh. What good is that to me, when Don Sykes has filched you off me?'

'Don doesn't own my free time, and I'm here now. If you want me to help, Reg, I will.'

He looked at her. 'I thought you were on your holidays.'

'Well, we really came so my dad could visit an old comrade in Smeltham,' Bobby said, deciding a little white lie for the sake of Reg's health must be permissible. 'I'd only be the third wheel once they got together and started talking army days. It sounds like it'd be more helpful for me to stay here while he pays his visit.'

'Hmm.'

She met his eyes earnestly. 'Reg, look. You and Mary were very kind to me when I worked here, and if it wasn't for you taking a chance on me, I'd never have got my position on the *Courier*. It seems to me I owe you both a favour, so if I can help her to stop worrying and you to get well by taking on the rest of the work for the March number, I'd like to do it. I feel guilty as it is for leaving you both, especially when Mary said in her last letter that you still hadn't been able to recruit a new junior reporter.'

He narrowed his eyes at her. 'This isn't something you and my wife have cooked up between you, is it?'

'Absolutely not,' Bobby said firmly. That was technically true, since in fact it had been Mary and Charlie who had cooked it up between them.

'Well, then I suppose… just a few bits of copy. I'll be right tomorrow to finish it.'

Bobby smiled at him. 'Where do I start?'

'Take that down to the parlour,' he said, nodding to the confiscated sheet of copy on her lap. 'It's a poem someone sent in. Needs correcting and typing fresh. On my desk you'll find some other bits and bobs for subbing, and there's *Traditions and Folklore of the Yorkshire Dales* on the bookshelf to finish a piece I started on mythical Yorkshire creatures. Letters from readers need sorting, and there's the Editor's Journal pages – there's a folder of bits I've been saving up you can use for them. There's your article on the Smeltham hop to go in too. Been saving it to have something merry for the beginning of spring. Go through that lot and report back on how you get on.'

'I won't let you down, Reg.'

Bobby had to give it to the man. After a week and a half of illness, to be able to recall everything that needed doing off the top of his head like that was rather impressive. He seemed as sharp as a tack, despite the fever.

She went into the kitchen to have her breakfast, then sent her father off for the day with Charlie while she went to work. Her dad seemed quite cheery after his hearty meal. He'd warmed easily to Mary, who was only a few years younger than him, and when Bobby had re-entered the kitchen, she'd found them sharing some memories of the music hall stars of their youth. Charlie offered to take him to a local beauty spot – Byles Crag, an impressive limestone structure some four miles' walk away – and he agreed almost affably.

After they'd departed – accompanied by the Athertons' two huge hounds, Barney and Winnie – Bobby went into the parlour to sift through the untidy mass of Reg's papers. Mary followed.

'Oh Lord,' Bobby said, clutching her head when she saw the state of the editor's desk. 'Did he get even untidier since I went away?'

'He's made a right mess trying to work while he's ill,' Mary said. 'I hope you can find everything you need.'

'I suppose I shall have to.'

'Do you want some tea while you work?'

'No, thank you. I think you had better just close the door and leave me here for a little while so I can impose some sort of order.'

Mary smiled. 'Well, good luck.'

Chapter 34

One of Bobby's major frustrations while working at *The Tyke* had been that the magazine's proposed contents, like most other things, tended to live not on paper but in the untamed jungle of Reg's brain. When she reached the parlour, she discovered nothing had changed in that respect. Various folders and files on his desk were home to newspaper cuttings, scribbled pen portraits, items from church newsletters he'd jotted down; anything he felt was interesting enough to form the basis of an article, or perhaps an item in the Editor's Journal section of the magazine. This was a little like an extended editorial, featuring bits and pieces of Reg's thoughts and anything else noteworthy he felt ought to be included. The rest of the mess on the desk consisted of readers' letters, articles sent in by hopeful amateur writers, poems in Yorkshire dialect, and profiles of Dales characters living and dead written by either Reg or the little gaggle of freelance writers who contributed to the magazine. There was no order to anything and no indication of which item might feature in which number, but Reg always seemed to know where to find everything he needed. Bobby would just have to make out as best she could.

The only items that were kept neatly filed were the woodcuts, engravings, cartoons, photographs and drawings that were included on the magazine's glossy supplementary pages. Many of these were originals, the only copies, and needed to be kept safe until they had been reproduced by the printer, at which point they could be returned to their creators. These were carefully stored in labelled card folders in the filing cabinet drawer in Reg's desk. Feeling that this was as good a place to start as any while she tried to whip the next edition into some sort of order, Bobby opened the drawer.

She took out the card folder for March 1941 and opened it.

'Well, well, well,' she said softly to herself, smiling at the top image. It wasn't an original but a photograph of the real painting, sadly in black and white, although the beauty of the stag's eyes somehow still came across. It was very familiar, an old friend now – Mary's watercolour of the bridge over Silverdale Beck that had hung in Bobby's old room. So Reg had decided to include some of his wife's art in *The Tyke* after all.

Bobby found a spare scrap of paper and started creating a contents page for the magazine, noting first that four pages of pictures for the centre of the mag had been provided. That still left twenty-four pages to fill, however.

Hunting around, she discovered a page plan detailing advertisements for this edition and their size, which accounted for another five pages. Then there was the poem Reg had given her to correct – 'Daffodils, the golden heralds of springtime', sent in by some aspiring Wordsworth. An article on spinning in Craven; directions for a walk through Upper Nidderdale; a word sketch of an old Dales chimney sweep, with pencil drawing, and Bobby's article on the Smeltham hop all appeared to be for this number. All were written by freelance journalists aside from her dance article and the spinning piece, which had been written by Reg. Some of these had accompanying line drawings attached to them with a pin, and Bobby hunted among the papers on the desk to see if any other drawings might have gone astray. This, she estimated, would account for another ten pages of the magazine, including the pictures.

Bobby glanced down her contents. That filled nineteen of the twenty-eight pages, and then the contents would take up one, and the readers' letters usually spanned another two. The letters were all stored in a folder, with no suggestions as to which number they ought to be included with, but she could pick out those that felt most appropriate to the season. Then the remaining six pages would be filled by the article Reg had asked her to finish on mythological creatures from Dales folklore, and the Editor's Journal.

It was rather an honour to be trusted with this particular section of the magazine. As the name suggested, it was Reg's own particular bit, written in the first person and consisting of his observations on day-to-day life in the Dales – the changing pace of life there, the impact of the war and new technology, and his memories of times gone by. Despite the big and important stories Bobby had been assigned since her return to the *Courier*, many of which had taken up a significant number of column inches on the front page, somehow the Editor's Journal section of *The Tyke* felt… overwhelming. Bobby decided she had better save that until last and instead eased herself in gently by working through some of the already written pieces that needed correcting.

She soon found herself smiling as she read through the piece on the Dales chimney sweep, finding her old job settling around her like a well-worn glove despite more than a month away. The sweep was long dead, described in the article by an old man in his seventies who remembered this colourful local character from when he was a boy, but there was still something about the way the sweep spoke that reminded her of the thick dialect of Andy Jessop. She wondered how her old friend was getting along and whether he was nervous as his wedding to Ginny approached in a month's time.

The sweep had been a notorious practical joker, Bobby discovered, including, one dark night, dressing up in the hide and horns of a slaughtered bull to frighten villagers into believing he was the devil. She could imagine Charlie playing a similar prank.

When she'd finished correcting the copy, she completed the article on mythological Yorkshire creatures. That didn't take too long, since all the information she needed was to be found in Reg's old volume of folklore. That was rather dry in its style, however, and she tried to give the words a more engaging slant as she wrote, infusing them with the sort of dry, deadpan humour she knew their readers liked.

The creatures were rather interesting. There was the giant spectral black dog known as the gytrash that roamed Baildon Moor – Bobby was glad she hadn't known of that legend as a child, when she and her family had gone for Whit walks around the place. Then there were the mysterious lights known as peg-o-lanterns that appeared on the moors or hovering over bogs, said to be the torches of fairies or evil spirits. Could any of it be true, Bobby wondered? Or was the gytrash simply another mischievous dalesman dressed up in an old fur to scare his neighbours? She rather liked the thrilling shiver you got down your spine when you imagined there might be truth in the tales – as long as she was indoors in front of a warm fire and not roaming the moors by night.

–

Finally, all her copy was laid in neat piles and she came to tackle the Editor's Journal, the section she'd been dreading more than all the rest. Bobby sucked her pencil, as she always did while she was thinking, and tried to work out how best to tackle it.

Reg always wrote in the first person, beginning with an introduction suffused with humour and his own distinctly Dales voice. He would often follow this with some observations on local life here in Silverdale. The Dalesfolk loved it when they were mentioned in Reg's journal, with Gil Capstick at the post office practically swooning when he discovered the editor had made a reference to his unique way of predicting the weather – although he'd made it clear to Reg that any sharing of his specific methods would be met with dire wrath. Bobby felt rather curious to see the cheery little sub-postmaster's dire wrath. After that, Reg might muse on the season, discuss what was taking place on local farms and outline any snippets of news he'd come across that he felt might interest the readers. It was a hotchpotch of everything and nothing, but it was Bobby's favourite part of the magazine to read.

But she wasn't Reg. She was Bobby, and she could only write as herself.

That was it. She should write as herself. When she had first arrived here in Silverdale to start work at *The Tyke*, she had hoped the stern Dalesfolk whose brows knit with suspicion whenever she ventured abroad would someday accept her as one of their own. But they hadn't. When they had started to accept her, it had been for what she was: a townie and an outsider who lived and worked among them. They hadn't accepted her as a fellow daleswoman but as 'the lass from t' paper'. Our paper, as it was so often known.

Bobby took her pencil out of her mouth and started to write.

> *I must begin this number with both an explanation and an apology, for it is not a Tyke who writes to you this month but a Tyke-ess. Our intrepid editor Mr Atherton has, very sadly for his acolytes here in the Dales, been called away on a most important expedition. He has gone to explore the wilds of Northumberland first mapped by Dr Livingstone in 1857, which, we are told, have recently been invaded by a ferocious and feral pack of Cheviot hoggs from Upper Nidderdale. So it is not Reginald Atherton who writes to you today but Roberta Bancroft, formerly of this parish, who takes over the Editor's Journal for this number only.*
>
> *And thus I must add the apology to follow my explanation, for since you last heard from me, I have committed a most foul act of treason in leaving these Dales for a life in the city. I can only say in my defence that I miss these rolling fells and wind-scorched moors almost as much as I miss the stubborn, forthright, warm and wonderful Dales people. I miss them as often as I*

dream of them, and I dream of them every night. I was pleased to discover on my return, however, that the Dales seem to be getting on capitally without me — almost as if I were never here. I am rather hurt that they can bear the loss so well, but such is my punishment for abandoning them.

I notice since my absence that there appears to have been an outbreak of spring in the region, with the strangest little blooms bursting out all over. Of course, being a city dweller I do not know their names, but I believe my favourites must be those little yellow blighters with the trumpet-like noses that adorn the roadsides and riverbanks...

Bobby continued in this tongue-in-cheek style for several more paragraphs, writing as a sort of parody foreign correspondent, slightly pompous and entirely clueless about the countryside — as clueless as she herself had been when she first arrived in Silverdale, in fact, although exaggerated for comic effect. She remained lost in her words until a knock sounded at the door, and Mary appeared.

'Gosh,' Bobby said, blinking at the change in light as she looked up. 'When did it start to get dark?'

Mary smiled. 'Some time ago. Reg is asking for you.'

'I thought he'd have summoned me every hour on the hour demanding a report,' Bobby said, laughing.

'He would, if he'd been awake. Fortunately, Morpheus paid a visit shortly after you left him this morning. A convenient side effect of his medicine is that it will tend to make him drowsy. He needs the sleep, and it keeps him out of trouble.' Mary came over to the desk and glanced over her shoulder. 'Do you mind me seeing what you've been working on?'

Bobby flushed. 'It's the Editor's Journal section. I don't know if Reg is going to like it much, but it felt too dishonest to write as him. I tried to write it in the style I know the readers like but still keep my own voice.'

Bobby handed her the piece, and Mary was soon laughing as she read it through.

'I believe you're wrong,' Mary said. 'I think Reg will like it very much. A lovely blend of humour and emotion. He appreciates that.' She put it down on the desk. 'What made you think to write it that way?'

'I suppose… I wanted it to be mine, if I was writing it,' Bobby said. 'In my old job at the *Courier*, when I was the typist there, I used to write items for another journalist and they'd appear under his byline. At the time I was just glad to write, but I couldn't stomach my words being put into someone else's mouth now. Not after all I've done in the past few months.'

'This makes it sound like you miss the Dales,' Mary said quietly, her gaze drifting to Bobby's journal.

'I do. I've always thought of myself as a complete townie, but it gets under your skin, this place. Not only the landscape. The people too.'

'You know Reg would love to have you back, if that was what you wanted.'

Bobby sighed. 'I can't. I've got my dad to think about, and my job at the *Courier*. I don't mean to sound mercenary, Mary, but it's three pounds a week. I need it now I'm supporting two of us – I doubt my dad's going to be able to find work again, with his… his health problems. And I'm doing something important there. The stories I work on at the *Courier*, exposing school mismanagement, reporting on murder trials… that matters. It was what I always dreamed of when I made up my mind to be a journalist.'

'I like to think that what Reg is doing is important too,' Mary said. 'For all that I blast that magazine to hell a hundred times a day or more, he's right.' She gestured to the pile of papers for the March edition. 'This is history, just as much as your "important" murders and things. Perhaps even more so, for who would know what our lives were like in this forgotten part of the world a hundred years from now if Reg hadn't made it his mission to preserve it?'

'I know. I'm sorry. I didn't mean that to sound dismissive.' Bobby smiled. 'Here, let me show you something.'

She opened the filing drawer and drew out the photographs of Mary's paintings.

Mary regarded them with surprise. 'Well, where on earth did these come from?'

'I suppose Reg arranged for them to be taken. Didn't he tell you?'

'No he didn't.' She smiled, shaking her head. 'The old fool. What does he want with these then?'

'They're to go in the March edition. I imagine he intended to surprise you with them.'

'The old fool,' she said again, but she looked as pleased as anything. 'You'd better go up to him, or he'll be fretting. I'll come with you.'

Bobby gathered together the papers she'd collected from Reg's desk and took them upstairs with her.

'All right, Reg, here's your report,' she began briskly as soon as she reached his sickbed. She laid down the contents page. 'This is a list of everything that's to go in the March number, with predicted page count. I suspect a couple of pieces might overrun so there could be cuts to make on the proof. I think the only things that need to be typed are the piece I wrote on the mythological creatures and—' she flushed slightly '—and the Editor's Journal section. I've marked the corrections on the finished copy, but there were only a few literals so I think they can go to the printer as they are and they can fix it when they set the type. I'll type those two items tonight then it's done and dusted.'

Reg looked over the papers she'd spread out in front of him, but he didn't speak.

'Show me the Editor's Journal,' he said at last.

Bobby had been hoping he wouldn't ask to see that. She suspected Reg would have preferred her to write as him, in his style. But she couldn't be Reg; she could only be Bobby.

'Here you are,' she said, fishing it out of the pile.

He read it in silence, stony-faced, both Bobby and Mary watching him anxiously. Finally, he delivered his verdict.

'Aye, not bad,' he said, handing it to her. 'That bit about hearing the nightingale singing in the fells will need changing. Too early for 'em. Change it to song thrush.'

'And… that's all?'

'Rest of it'll pass.' He looked up at her. 'That'll do, lass.'

She beamed. 'Thanks, Reg.'

'And what's all this about my paintings then, you daft old man?' Mary asked, putting her hands on her hips.

Reg rubbed his neck. 'Aye, well. Happen if you look at them with the eye of someone lucky enough not to be married to you… they're a good job. Doesn't seem right to keep them to myself.'

'I knew you'd learn to appreciate me one of these days,' Mary said with a smile. 'Come here.' She leaned over the bed to give him a kiss, and Bobby, smiling, turned to look out of the window to give them a moment's privacy.

It was twilight but it wasn't pitch dark, and the blackout curtains not yet drawn. In the large field beside the house, Bobby could make out four figures, two of which looked distinctly gytrash-like. But when she looked more closely, she realised they were only Reg's dogs having a game of Fetch with Charlie and her father.

'They're back,' she told Mary.

'Ah, good. Just in time for tea. Let's go down. Reg, I'll bring you something up on a tray.'

–

As the two women walked downstairs, Mary seemed to have something on her mind.

'Will you go home tonight, if the magazine is ready to go for setting?' she asked.

'I want to type those last two items first. I'll see how long it takes me. We'll have to go in the morning if it gets too late. The last bus is at nine.'

'You're certainly welcome to stay as long as you like, Bobby. It's a pleasure having you back.'

She seemed about to say more, but just then the front door opened and in came the excited dogs, followed by the two men. Barney jumped up at Bobby and Winnie at Mary, absolutely thrilled to see these humans they'd met a thousand times before.

Mary laughed. 'Get down, you daft hound, before you knock me over. Charlie, whyever do you let them get so excited?'

'Oh, let them enjoy themselves, Mother,' Charlie said.

Bobby smiled at her father. He looked quite happy, his cheeks rosy from his walk and the game with the dogs. He approached her to give her a squeeze, which was the most affection she could remember him showing her in a long time.

'Now then, lass,' he said in a voice practically jolly. 'Did you finish your work?'

'Nearly. I need to type a couple of things, then it's all done. We can go home tonight if I finish before the last bus, or tomorrow morning if you'd rather wait until it's light.'

'There's no need to rush back, is there?' Charlie said. 'You'd planned to stay for two days. Why not take one as a holiday, and show your dad some more of the sights? He hasn't seen the waterfall, or the gill. I'll keep you company if you like.'

'He's seen the inside of the pub though, I don't doubt,' Mary said, pursing her lips.

Charlie shrugged. 'We had one pint, that's all.'

'The last bus will be at two tomorrow,' Bobby said. 'It's Sunday, don't forget.'

'That's all right. I'm sure Boxer would be happy to take you both as far as Skipton Station, if you don't mind cuddling up. Perhaps I might even convince Reg to loan me the Wolseley and some of his precious petrol, after the favour you did him today.'

'I suppose we could stay a little longer.' Bobby glanced at her father. 'If you'd like to.'

'Aye, I reckon I could bear a bit more of this place,' he said. 'It's amazing what a dose of fresh air and good eating can do for you. I feel like a man twenty years younger. You ought to go out there and get a lungful yourself, Bobby.'

She smiled. 'I'll do that. Tomorrow, when I've finished with this magazine.'

She went to the parlour with her papers. Charlie followed her, closing the door behind them.

'You know you'll never really be finished with this magazine, don't you?' he said.

'What does that mean?'

'Only that you need it. Or it needs you. You've got the same look in your eye about it that my brother gets. Sort of hungry.'

Bobby glanced at the closed door. Charlie followed her gaze.

'Oh, don't worry, I'm not going to kiss you again,' he said. 'I know how it upsets you. I wanted to have a word in private, that's all.'

'What about? The wedding?'

'Not about the wedding. Why are you so convinced everything's about the damn wedding?' he said impatiently. 'It's about my cottage.'

'What about your cottage?' Bobby couldn't imagine what that could have to do with her.

'It's going to be empty soon, like I told you. It isn't me who owns it, you know.'

'Isn't it?'

'No. My brother owns the farmhouse, the grounds and everything in them – Dad left everything to him when he died. There's a story behind that, which I'll save for another day. Anyway, Reggie lets me live here rent-free, where he can keep an eye on me.' He looked at her. 'He'd like you back, Bobby. Back at *The Tyke*. And I think that in your heart, you'd like to come back.'

'I can't come back. I work for the *Courier* now, writing the news. Real news, Charlie.'

'Just because it's real, that doesn't make it more important.'

She looked away, staring into the fire. 'It isn't only that. There's my father.'

'That's what I'm trying to tell you.' Charlie came closer and rested one hand on her shoulder. 'If you were to come back, there'd be Cow House Cottage available to you. I don't mind moving out a little early and staying here with Reg and Mary until I leave, if I can still make use of the surgery during the day. I feel sure Reg would be happy with that arrangement.'

She frowned. 'You mean...'

'I mean you could move your father here, to Silverdale, to live with you in the cottage. He seemed happy today, Bobby. And from what I've read in your face and your voice, that isn't something he often is.' He gave her shoulder a squeeze. 'We'd like you to come back. All of us. I'd like you to.'

'Would you?'

'Very much indeed. Nothing's been the same here since you left. Think about it, all right? Oh, and here.' He took the handkerchief he'd once given her from his pocket and handed it to her. 'Take this back. I've a feeling it might have brought you more luck than you know.'

Chapter 35

Three weeks passed, and Bobby did think about it. She thought about it every morning when she awoke, and when she lay in her bed at night. She thought about it when she walked past a newsstand and saw the March edition of *The Tyke*, which she'd worked so hard to bring out on time. She thought about it whenever she got a letter from Mary in the post, telling her about the goings-on in the village.

Her short trip to Silverdale and the work she'd done on the magazine hadn't exorcised the place from her mind as Bobby had hoped it might. If anything, it had made it worse. She still dreamt of the place; still missed the people she'd met there. Missed Charlie.

And that was exactly the reason she couldn't go back, wasn't it? To go back to Silverdale, to live in the place alongside Charlie once he was married to Topsy and settled at Sumner House… she couldn't bear it. Bobby had spent a long time trying to deny her feelings for Charlie Atherton, but seeing him again that weekend, pressing up close against him on the trap, the scene when he'd returned her lucky handkerchief and looked so deeply into her eyes… she just couldn't do it any more. She wished Lilian was here to listen to her cry and talk about him and cry some more, but she wasn't. All Bobby could do was cry in the night, silently sobbing into her pillow in the bed she now occupied alone.

Charlie was the main consideration, but he wasn't the only one. There was her salary, which would drop suddenly from sixty shillings a week to twenty if she returned to Silverdale – a sum on which she had both herself and her father to support. And there was her job at the *Courier*. Bobby knew what *The Tyke* was doing was important in its own way, but it wasn't news, and her ambition had always been to be a newspaperman. Now she had achieved that, and Don had even hinted there could be a deputy editor position in her future if she continued to work hard and well – a feat few women reporters could dream of achieving. Perhaps she might even work her way on to one of the national newspapers eventually, as she'd always wanted to. Don was right: she did have a talent for it, as she'd proven to him when she'd written about the school. Such had been the success of that story that several parents had revolted to put pressure on the governors. Eventually, Miss Newbould had been let go in favour of a caregiver with a more balanced view of how to keep her charges well and healthy. Bobby's words had achieved that. Could any amount of articles about spinning in Craven and long-dead chimney sweeps compare?

'Good morning,' she said to her dad when she rose one Friday for work. It was the day before Andy and Ginny's wedding, and Bobby could see the invitation peeking out from behind the carriage clock on the mantelpiece. She still hadn't made up her mind whether she ought to go or not. She wanted to, to wish her old friend well, but another trip to Silverdale... she wasn't sure she could bear to leave the place again if she returned.

'Mmm,' her dad said, not looking up from the situations vacant section of his newspaper. He went through it diligently every morning, circling jobs of interest to him with a pencil, but as far as Bobby knew, he hadn't actually applied for any. It was as though losing his place at Butterfield's had cost him his nerve, and now he never got any further than circling. He'd asked her for a drink with his tea yesterday evening, for the first time in a long time. She hoped this didn't mark the beginning of another decline.

'I'm going to work now,' she said. 'Sarah's going to come over and take you to her house for breakfast. I think she's got some kidneys in. That'll be a treat, eh?'

'Mmm.'

Realising she wasn't going to get much more out of him this morning, Bobby gave up and left the house.

When she arrived at work, Tony was the only other one there. He was at his desk with his feet up, sucking on the barley sugar sticks he ate perpetually whenever he was trying to cut back on cigarettes. And, he was reading the March edition of *The Tyke*.

'What on earth are you doing with that?' Bobby asked him.

He removed the barley sugar. 'I saw it on the newsstand and thought I'd see what sort of work our editor's pet used to do. Jesus Christ, Bobby. Did you really used to write this stuff? There's an article about spinning wool that I could use instead of sleeping pills.'

'I didn't write that, but yes, I wrote some of it.' He was trying to rile her, and she was determined not to rise to it.

'And this is what Don thought was worthy of elevating you to the upper echelons of the *Courier* with the real journalists, is it? He must be in love with you or something.'

'Actually, it was the report I wrote on his daughter's school,' Bobby said shortly, taking a seat at her desk. 'Can you shut up, Tony? I need to finish writing this piece about the Gregson Case.'

The Gregson Case was another particularly gruesome story Don had assigned to her – worse than some of the others she'd had to write because the victim was a child. The poor thing had been locked in an attic room, where he was beaten and neglected by his parents until he was one day found dead by a neighbour concerned about the smell. As important as it was to inform the public of the facts, it made Bobby sick to her stomach to work on it. She was half inclined to ask Don to assign her some lighter items, like the 'girl stuff' pieces on WI cake sales and things that Tony used to make her write for him, except that she worried Don would stop taking her seriously if he felt her sex made her incapable of doing her job.

Don himself appeared and sat down at his desk.

'Morning, fellow reprobates. Bobby, is that Gregson piece done yet?'

'No it's not done yet. I've only been here five minutes. I'm working on it, all right, Don?'

He blinked. 'All right, there's no need to snap. Women's problems or something?'

Bobby put a hand to her head. 'Sorry. I think it's this piece making me irritable. It's just... horrible. If I met these parents, I'd... I don't know what I'd do, but it'd still be less than they deserved. Any chance of something a bit less grim next, Don?'

He shook his head. 'Got to learn, Bobby. Got to toughen up. You grow a skin to help you cope with it after a while. It's what you need if you're going to make it as a newspaperman.'

'Yes, but not all at once, surely. Not so you become hardened to the inhumanity of it.' She looked at her notes and curled her lip at the description of the poor murdered child's suffering. '"Toughen up." You sound like Miss Newbould, Don.'

He leaned back in his chair and started filling his pipe. Bobby wrinkled her nose at the strong smell of his Tom Long tobacco. Reg had rarely smoked during working hours, and she couldn't quite seem to get used to the smell again since coming back.

'For your own good,' he said calmly. 'We all had to go through it, Bobby. If you're going to make it as a newspaperman—'

'But I'm not a newspaperman, am I?' Bobby snapped, throwing down her pencil so that it clattered on the desk. 'I'm not a man at all. I'm a woman, as you two keep pointing out to me. And if that means having compassion and... and feelings, and being angry and sickened when some poor kid or a defenceless girl is killed, then what the hell is wrong with that? It doesn't make me a bad journalist. What it makes me is a bloody human being. Maybe the rest of you could try it once in a while.'

'Definitely women's problems,' Tony muttered under his breath.

Don paused with his pinch of tobacco halfway to his pipe, looking taken aback.

'I didn't say you shouldn't care, did I?' he said. 'I said you can't let your feelings get in the way of a story. You need to use your head, not your heart.'

'Yes, well, I disagree.'

Don laughed. 'Do you indeed? You disagree with me, do you, with your oh-so-many years of newspaper experience? I was a cub reporter when you were in your pram, Bobby.'

'I still disagree, and I think I'm right to,' she said firmly. 'It's head and heart, isn't it? Using both is what makes a good writer – what makes an engaging story. Like the interview I did with Andy Jessop. Your head knows how to sort through the facts and what order it needs to present them in, but it's your heart that knows how to engage the readers' emotions. You have to combine the two. Reg said we got more letters about that piece on Andy than anything he'd ever printed.'

'That nothing-nowhere mag,' Don said dismissively. 'Are you still talking about that?'

'Because she's been working for it on the side.' Tony approached Don's desk and tossed his copy of *The Tyke* on to it. 'This is this month's edition and her name's all over it.'

Bobby glared at him. After all the times she'd covered for Tony over the pieces he'd got her to write, the mornings he'd played truant from work and the money-making schemes he was always running on the side, he'd tell tales on her to Don just like that. He'd been riddled with jealousy ever since she'd come back to work on the paper as his equal.

Don looked at the magazine, then up at her. 'What's this, Bobby?'

She flushed. 'Can we talk about it in private?'

'We can talk about it here.'

'It was a favour to Reg, that was all. He had the flu. It was in my own time. No one else could help him put it to bed and he was making himself ill trying to do it, so Mary asked me for help.'

Don glanced at Tony. 'Go out and get us something to eat, will you?'

'Now? It's first thing in the morning.'

'Yes, and I'm hungry. Fetch some butties or something.'

'Send Len when he gets here,' Tony said, folding his arms. 'I'm not the office errand boy.'

'Tony, bugger off for fifteen minutes, can you?'

'Oh, I see. It's like that, is it?' He cast a suspicious glance at Bobby. 'All right, fine. But don't think I don't know what's going on here.'

When Tony had gone, Don picked up the copy of *The Tyke* and leafed through the pages.

'You know, I should've realised you weren't cut out for this job the moment you told me you needed time to think about it,' he said quietly.

Bobby bowed her head. 'I'm sorry, Don. I've let you down. After all you did for me, and for Dad.'

'You haven't let me down. I just wish you'd been honest with me.' He stopped at the Editor's Journal section and smiled. 'This is funny.'

'Thank you.'

'Clever idea, writing it like a foreign correspondent who's stranded in some unfamiliar land. I suppose the readers like that sort of thing.'

'Yes.'

He put the magazine down. 'Bobby... I'm going to have to let you go.'

'Because of this?' Bobby said. 'I told you, Don, it was only while Reg—'

'Not because of this.'

330

'You're unhappy with my work?'

'I'm very happy with your work. I've said it before and I'll say it again: you're a natural writer, and you're worth ten of Tony Scott even on one of his good days.' He looked again at Tony's copy of *The Tyke*. 'You believe in fate, don't you? You talk about it enough.'

'In a way. At least, I believe some things are meant to happen.'

'Well then, wouldn't you say that's what this is? Reg gets the flu and you have to put his magazine to bed – that sounds like destiny or whatever you like to call it to me.' He sighed. 'It's got its fingers on you, that place, Bobby, and I can tell you now that you aren't going to be happy anywhere that isn't Silverdale. That's why I'm letting you go. But if you want to tell me I'm wrong, I'll be glad to change my mind. Am I?'

Bobby remained silent.

'Aye, I thought as much.' Don nodded to the magazine. 'It's this ridiculous thing, with its nonsense about gytrashes and chimney sweeps. It's under your skin, for some reason I don't think I'll ever understand. You are a reporter, Bobby, but you belong to something like *The Tyke*. Where you can use your head and your heart, and your writing will be all the better for it.'

Bobby was quiet for a moment. Her gaze fell on the page of notes she'd made about the Gregson Case, then on the copy of *The Tyke*. Finally, she looked up to smile at him.

'Thanks, Don.'

'Not that I won't miss you. You're the only person around here who talks like a sensible human being. Not to mention being the sole person on my staff who can actually write.' He pressed her arm. 'Take care of yourself, Bobby. Don't be a stranger.'

'You'll say goodbye to Tony and Len for me? I don't want to explain it to them.'

'I'll do whatever needs to be done. Just go. Go and be happy. I'll watch your future career with interest.'

She smiled. 'Likewise. Goodbye, Don.'

Chapter 36

Bobby didn't allow herself to worry about Charlie, or about how she was going to live on her small salary, or about anything else as she walked home. All she thought about was that Don was right: Silverdale was where she belonged. *The Tyke* was where she belonged. She should have realised that when she'd worked on the March issue, so lost in the work that she hadn't even noticed the sun go down. *The Tyke* was where she could use her heart, and her head, and everything else that made her the reporter and the individual she was. As for her feelings for Charlie… well, he'd be gone soon, off to basic training with the RAF. Out of sight and, hopefully, out of mind. Once he was gone, she could focus on her work and try to get over him before he came home to his bride.

She paid a quick visit to her sister-in-law on the way home to ask if she'd be able to cook for her dad tomorrow, as she had an urgent journey to make. Sarah had sounded rather irritated at the unexpected change to her routine, but she agreed. Then Bobby went home to talk to her father.

'You're home early,' he said when she came in.

'Um, we were given a half day's holiday. It's the King's birthday or something.'

'Oh.'

'Dad, can I ask you something?'

'If you must,' he said as he circled another job in the situations vacant column of his paper.

'I wanted to ask – can you put your pencil down a moment?' She went to perch on the arm of his chair. 'Do you remember that place we went to for a holiday – Silverdale? You know, the place where I worked for a little while?'

'Aye.' His eyes glazed as he thought of it, and Bobby was sure she noticed a little colour come into his cheeks.

'You liked it there, didn't you?'

'It were all right.'

'You said the air there made you feel twenty years younger. That you could've explored for a year and a day and still not have seen half of what it had to offer.'

'Reckon I did,' he said quietly. 'It were summat special, that bit of country. Well?'

'I just wondered… if I was to be offered my old job back, and there was a place for both of us to live, how would you feel about that?'

'Have they offered?'

'Not exactly. Well, perhaps. At any rate, they've not replaced me yet – Mary told me in her last letter that they still hadn't managed to recruit a new junior reporter. I'll have to go and talk to my old boss there. Before I do, though, just tell me: could you live there? I don't want to go without you.'

Her dad put down his paper, looking thoughtful.

'Aye,' he said at last. 'It's a good, clean, healthy place. Reckon I could live there all right.'

Bobby beamed at him. 'I hoped you might say that.'

The next morning she dressed in a hurry and dashed out to catch the early tram. The wedding began at eleven at the Wesleyan chapel, so she ought to be in time to see the happy couple leave, even though she would miss the service.

There was no coal man waiting for her at the Bull and Heifer, and in any case Bobby didn't want to get her best suit dirty, so she walked into the village. A couple of old friends were waiting outside the chapel. There was Boxer the horse, his trap bedecked with garlands of spring flowers and his white mane and tail in braids for the occasion. On the trap sat Charlie, looking very formal in a morning suit and top hat.

'Bobby!' He jumped down from the trap, looking delighted to see her, and before she could protest, he was swinging her around in his arms just as she had once seen him do to Mabs Jessop. Bobby couldn't even pretend not to be pleased to see him, laughing as the world whirled around her.

'Oh my word, you're a sight for sore eyes,' he said when he'd put her down. 'What are you doing here? I had no idea you were coming.'

'Well I am the architect of this particular match. I couldn't miss it, could I?' She nodded to the trap. 'I could ask you the same question. I didn't expect to find you and Boxer here in all your finery.'

'Didn't you? I thought you knew all about it.'

'No, how would I?'

'I don't know. I could have sworn you mentioned it to me. I supposed Mary had told you in one of her letters.' He patted Boxer's flank. 'We're to be chauffeurs for Mister and Missus. Rather a promotion, I think you'll agree. I believe we only narrowly beat Bert and his coal wagon to the job.'

Bobby longed to tell him she was back to stay, or that she wanted to be. She longed for him to swing her around in his arms again, and to melt on to his lips as she had that New Year's Eve. But that wasn't allowed, and if they were to co-exist here together as two civilised adult people who absolutely were not in love with each other in any way, she needed to begin as she meant to go on.

'Um, I'm not sure I ever properly congratulated you,' she said, flushing slightly.

'Oh. Thank you.' He frowned. 'On what?'

'On your engagement to Topsy, of course. She's a wonderful girl, Charlie. I hope you'll both be happy.'

'My...'

They were interrupted by the doors of the chapel flying open, and the happy couple emerged with smiles all over their faces. It warmed Bobby's heart to think that after an early life filled with so much pain and grief, Andy was now able to share this moment with the person he loved. Well-wishers threw rice and hot pennies, which were then eagerly gathered up by the village children – a Silverdale tradition, apparently. Ginny tossed her bouquet into the crowd, where it was caught by a delighted Mabs.

'Oh dear. You might need to go into hiding,' Bobby muttered to Charlie. But he had a faraway look in his eyes and didn't seem to be paying attention.

Andy had spotted her now and came forward to pump her hand heartily.

'Now then, here's one face I'm right glad to see here today,' he said.

She smiled. 'I wouldn't have missed it for the world, Mr Jessop.'

Andy nudged his bride. 'This is the lass I told thee of. There'd be no wedding without her. I told thee, Gin, no one like her for words. I was cackling like a bairn when young Mabs read me her bit in our paper this month.'

Now it was Ginny's turn to shake Bobby's hand, with a grip so firm Bobby was almost rattling. Ginny was a sturdy, healthy-looking woman of her age, with a wide, warm smile.

'It sounds like we owe you a lot,' she said. 'But I'm afraid all we've got to offer is ham sandwiches and a little piece of fruitcake at the pub. Shall we see you there?'

'Of course.'

'We're to ride in state,' Andy told her with a faux pomposity that was highly comical. 'Ginny, my love. May I hand you up?'

Ginny smiled and gave him her hand to be helped into the trap. Charlie climbed up next, with Andy squeezing in on his other side.

'I'll see you at the Hart,' Bobby said as Charlie clicked to Boxer to carry them off.

When they'd gone, Bobby went in search of Reg and Mary, who she knew would be somewhere in the crowd of well-wishers outside the chapel. It seemed like the entire village had gathered, Wesleyans and Anglicans alike, to see off the happy couple.

She soon discovered them in the now dispersing crowd, Reg leaning on his stick with his other arm through Mary's. They both looked sort of far away, as if thinking back to their own wedding day.

Mary blinked. 'Bobby? Oh my goodness! We had no idea you were coming today, child.'

'So you're back, are you?' Reg said, greeting her as he always did with the taciturn air of the dalesman who never gave anything away.

Bobby smiled. 'Aye. I'm back.'

'Ah. Now you're talking like one of us.'

'I hope so. I hope I am one of you. Because...' She took a deep breath. 'I lost my job at the *Courier* yesterday, Reg.'

'Oh dear,' Mary said, her brow knitting into a concerned frown. 'Whatever for? We've been reading all your pieces. You seemed to be doing so well.'

'Don felt that I didn't really have my heart in the job. And now I've thought it over, I quite agree with him.'

Reg frowned. 'And you think I'll have you back, do you? Just because you've got no better offer?'

'You don't understand.' Bobby glanced at Mary, who seemed to know what she meant and nodded encouragement. 'Don didn't sack me, exactly. He... I suppose you could say he freed me. He knew this was the only place I could be happy: here, working for you. He said *The Tyke* was where I needed to be.'

Mary smiled. 'I'm sure I remember saying summat of the kind myself.'

'You did, but I was too foolish to realise how right you were. It was really only yesterday, in the office, that I managed to make sense of it all.' Bobby looked at Reg. 'Would you still have a job for me? I don't mind if it's a junior reporter position. I don't even mind if you only want to pay me twelve and six, although Lord knows how I'll support myself and my father on that.'

'I suppose he still needs care?' Mary asked.

'Yes. I couldn't move back here without him.' Bobby flushed. 'But I did wonder... that is, Charlie said his cottage might be available. After he goes to war, I mean, and he said he could move out sooner if I needed him to and stay in my old room in the farmhouse. There'd be room for me and my dad in his cottage.'

'I suppose there would.' Mary looked at Reg. 'You'll have thought of that, won't you?'

'Aye. In passing.'

'I might've thought of it myself. In passing.'

Bobby laughed, and Reg finally deigned to smile at her. 'All right, lass, I'll have you back. Twenty-five bob a week is the most I can offer you, mind, and that'll be a stretch. You'll need to cook for yourself and your old man on that as well.'

Bobby couldn't help herself. She threw herself at him for a hug.

'Thank you,' she whispered. 'You won't regret it.'

'Huh. You told me the same when I hired you, and look where that landed me.'

'Oh, give over, you grumpy sod.' Mary smiled at her. 'I'm glad you're coming back to us. It wasn't right here without you. Let's go raise a toast to your new old job in the pub, eh?'

'I'd like that very much.'

—

But Bobby had no sooner walked through the door of the Hart when she was pulled unceremoniously back outside again by Charlie, who guided her down the side path leading to Troy's field.

'I need a word with you.' Charlie's expression was like none Bobby had ever seen on his face before. 'Do you or do you not believe I am currently engaged to Topsy Sumner-Walsh?'

'Well, yes.'

'And where did you receive this information, perchance?'

'From her, of course. She told me over the telephone. She said she'd decided that being a vet's wife wouldn't be so bad and she'd made up her mind to...' Bobby trailed off. 'You're telling me you *aren't* engaged?'

'That's exactly what I'm telling you. I'm not engaged now. I've never been engaged in the past. I am not engaged.'

'But why would she say...'

Charlie put his hand on his forehead. 'Because she's Topsy, of course. She thinks anything she wants is hers, men included. Me included. That all she has to do is let me know she's deigned to give me her hand and I'll jump to it. Lord knows when she was going to inform me of this one-sided engagement. On the morning of the wedding she'd organised, probably – although knowing Topsy, she's already forgotten all about it. These fancies of hers rarely last more than a week.' He laughed. 'Topsy Sumner-Walsh, a vet's wife! Can't you just picture it? She'd as soon marry a fisherman and spend her days gutting haddock as she would helping me with sick beasts. Mark my words: for all her egalitarian talk she'll marry some moneyed sort one of these days, and he'll just suit her.'

'But... you told me you were engaged,' Bobby said, feeling dazed. 'When you came to Bradford. I asked if you'd been busy making arrangements for the wedding, and you laughed and said you'd done your part by agreeing to it.'

'I thought you meant this wedding! I meant that I'd agreed to act as chauffeur and lend the pony and trap. I had no idea my participation was expected as groom.'

Bobby tried to rally a little. 'You can't tell me you aren't in love with her. Topsy. The way you gaze at her—'

'Of course I gaze at her,' he said impatiently. 'Topsy's a person who you can't help but gaze at. I suspect you've gazed at her a bit yourself.'

Bobby thought back to New Year's Eve, wondering if she had indeed had the same fascinated look in her eyes as Charlie. It's true that there was something compelling about the young heiress. Her enthusiasm, her charm, her whole personality: they commanded attention.

'The thing about Topsy is that she's like a butterfly,' Charlie said. 'She flutters here and she flutters there, bringing all that energy and colour, and people can't help but stop and look at her. I'm fond of her, I won't deny that. There are many ways in which I admire her very much. But as for being in love with her... She's a child, Bobby – spoilt, wilful and giddy. I couldn't love someone like that, not in any romantic fashion. I'm disappointed you could believe it of me.'

'So when you, um—'

'When I kissed you?' He took her hand and pressed it to his lips, as she'd once enviously watched him do to Topsy. 'That wasn't play. It wasn't flirting. It was real. Take it from a man who'll soon be fighting for his life in the skies, I don't kiss girls like that lightly. Only when it matters.'

'You said it didn't mean anything.'

'Yes, well, that was a lie. I thought it was what you wanted to hear. Actually it meant a hell of a lot, just like this one's going to.'

He drew her into his arms, and this time when she found his lips on hers, Bobby didn't try to resist. Why should she? There was no reason to reject his kisses now. No Topsy between them, no soaring ambition to make it on a national newspaper forcing her to keep him at bay. There was only the two of them.

'When do you go?' she whispered when he pulled back.

'July.'

'We don't have long.'

'Then we'll make every moment count.' He kissed her once more. 'Unless you're going to run away from me again?'

339

'No. I'm staying right here; I arranged it with Reg and Mary. I'm going to move into Cow House Cottage with Dad, if that's all right with you, and go back to work for *The Tyke*.'

He nodded his approval. 'It's where you should be. You suit it. It suits you.'

Bobby smiled as a couple of children in their wedding clothes ran past them, laughing as they threw handfuls of rice at one another.

'Yes. I've rather got used to being the lass from the paper.'

A letter from Betty

Hello to all my readers! I'm very grateful that you have chosen to read *A New Home in the Dales*, the first of the Made in Yorkshire series, and join Bobby and friends for the first part of their journey. This story has been inspired primarily by the founding of a Yorkshire institution, *The Dalesman* magazine, which published its first number in 1939 and is still going strong today. However, a large part of the inspiration must also be the beautiful countryside and indomitable people of the Yorkshire Dales. As *The Tyke* editor Reg Athelson points out, the Dales of the Second World War years was a world on the cusp of a new era.

Mechanisation sounded the death knell for traditional farming methods that had been in use for a century or more, while radio and cinema exposed the isolated communities to a world outside their own for the first time. It is this changing world that I've endeavoured to bring to life, as the backdrop against which my heroine Bobby attempts to pursue her personal dream of making a name for herself in the male-dominated world of journalism.

I'd absolutely love to hear your thoughts on this book in a review. These are invaluable not only for letting authors know how their story affected you but also for helping other readers to choose their next read and discover new writers. Just a few words can make a big difference.

If you would like to find out more about me and my books, you can do so via my website or social media pages, which can be found under my other pen name, Mary Jayne Baker:

Facebook: /MaryJayneWrites
Twitter: @MaryJayneBaker
Instagram: @MaryJayneBaker
Web: www.maryjaynebaker.co.uk

Thank you again for choosing *A New Home in the Dales*.
Best wishes,
Betty

Acknowledgements

My first thanks must go to my former agent, Laura Longrigg, for all her hard work and support over the years we have worked together. This was the last book we worked on as a team before her retirement, and I'm very grateful for her help in developing the concept and story.

Huge thanks also to my editor at Hera, Keshini Naidoo, for her work on this book – the first under a new pen name but the fifth title we've worked on together.

I'm also very grateful to my former colleague at *The Dalesman*, Adrian Braddy, who first suggested to me the idea of a story inspired by the founding of the magazine and has been invaluable in pointing me to a wealth of research resources. Monica Dickens' *My Turn to Make the Tea* was particularly useful for getting the perspective of a woman reporter in the 1940s.

The story also owes a lot to the writing of the legendary Bill Mitchell, who worked for *The Dalesman* first as a reporter and then as its editor over a period of nearly forty years (and continued to write for the magazine until his death in 2015). His memories of the magazine's early days, in addition to his interviews with Dalesfolk of the period, have proven invaluable. I also owe a debt to Settle Stories for their work in archiving and transcribing many of Bill's interviews.

Finally, I'd like to thank *The Dalesman* itself, the Yorkshire institution where I worked for several years and on which *The Tyke* is based: still going strong after nearly eighty-five years in print. Long may it continue!